Dead Man
Docking

Dead Man Docking

A Bed-and-Breakfast Mystery

MARY DAHEIM

WILLIAM MORROW
An Imprint of HarperCollins*Publishers*

This book is a work of fiction. The characters, incidents, and dialogue are drawn from the author's imagination and are not to be construed as real. Any resemblance to actual events or persons, living or dead, is entirely coincidental.

HarperCollins books may be purchased for educational, business, or sales promotional use. For information please write: Special Markets Department, HarperCollins Publishers, 10 East 53rd Street, New York, NY 10022.

FIRST EDITION

Designed by Nicola Ferguson

Printed on acid-free paper

Library of Congress Cataloging-in-Publication Data

Daheim, Mary.
    Dead man docking : a bed-and-breakfast mystery / Mary Daheim.—1st ed.
        p. cm.
    ISBN 0-06-056648-5
        1. Flynn, Judith McMonigle (Fictitious character)—Fiction.
    2. Shipowners—Crimes against—Fiction. 3. San Francisco
    (Calif.)—Fiction. 4. Women travelers—Fiction. 5. Cruise ships—
    Fiction. I. Title.

PS3554.A264D43 2005
813'.54—dc22

                                                              2004061365

---

05 06 07 08 09 JTC/RRD 10 9 8 7 6 5 4 3 2 1

To Lyssa—wife, mom, and editor.
You do it all,
and oh, so well.

Cast of Cruising Characters

Magglio Cruz—Self-made man, successful shipowner, and a gracious host who should stay away from pianos.

Consuela Cruz—Magglio's wife, an heiress who has a right to be embarrassed by a leftover scandal.

Erma Giddon—A rich San Francisco matron whose plus-size figure puts the "big" in bigotry.

Anemone Giddon—Erma's sheltered daughter, who has everything except what she really wants.

Jim Brooks—An aspiring doctor who needs more practice and is a less-than-perfect suitor for Anemone.

Ambrose Everhart—Erma's private secretary, whose public causes embrace more than endangered redwoods.

Horace Pankhurst—The Giddon family's financial adviser deals in cork futures and beautiful blondes, past and present.

Beulah—Erma's "colored" maid, who's a lot more colorful than she pretends.

CeeCee Orr—A blond bombshell who figures her figure can add up to big bucks.

Paul Tanaka—Cruz's second in command and first in charge of a widow's needs.

Émile Grenier—The ship's purser, whose superior French air is as noticeable as his mysterious limp.

May Belle (Dixie) Beales—A Southern belle who rings once too often.

Randolph J. Swafford—Ship captain and bluff English sea dog who may or may not be bluffing.

Blackie—A Mystery Man who may or may not be "Blackie."

Rick St. George—Debonair man-about-murder who takes sleuthing as seriously as drinking.

Rhoda St. George—Rick's slightly more sober better half, with beauty, brains, and a big, big bank account.

Dead Man
Docking

Chapter One

Judith McMonigle Flynn winced, flinched, and grimaced as she held the phone as far as possible from her ear. Cousin Renie was screaming obscenities at the other end and throwing in an occasional death threat. Unable to listen any longer, Judith severed the connection.

A minute later, she was swallowing two aspirin when the phone rang again. Reluctantly, Judith answered.

"What happened?" Renie asked in a more normal voice. "We got cut off."

"I hung up," Judith replied. "Your ranting gave me a headache."

"*You* have a headache?" Renie shot back, her words climbing several decibels. "How about *me*? I've never been fired before in my life."

"Cruz Cruises didn't exactly fire you," Judith pointed out.

"Moving their corporate offices to San Francisco means you can't have your usual hands-on control of their design work. You've still got plenty of clients. And," she warned, "if you start yelling again I'll hang up again."

Renie, known to the professional world as Serena Jones of CaJones Graphic Design, snarled into the phone. "Okay, okay. But they were a big source of my income with all those cruise magazines and hefty brochures and other promos that require artwork. I'm calling Bill's brother Bub and telling him to sue the pants off of Cruz Cruises. It won't cost me a dime, because Bub's such a good guy when it comes to family. If Magglio Cruz looks him up in Martindale-Gobble or whatever the ABA reference book is called, he'll see Bub has really impressive credentials."

Judith was aware that Bub Jones—whose real name was Millard—had had a very successful career as the senior partner in a large local law firm. Bub was also a man of integrity, despite his one eccentricity, which was wearing wigs to cover his baldness. Bub owned an office wig, a golf wig, a party wig, a trial wig, and a picnic wig. At home, he wore a baseball cap Renie had given him as a Christmas present many years earlier. The cap bore the words WISH YOU WERE HAIR.

"Good luck," Judith said to Renie.

Setting the phone down on the kitchen counter, Judith gazed out through the window above the sink. It was raining, typical Pacific Northwest March weather. It had been raining since November with only an occasional glimpse of sun and one brief January snowfall to break the monotony. Even a native like Judith yearned for a clear day.

Her dark eyes roamed to the reservation book she kept next to the computer. Only two of Hillside Manor B&B's six rooms would be occupied on this Wednesday night. There were three reservations for Thursday, but all of the rooms were booked through the weekend, thanks to St. Patrick's Day falling on Monday. The rest of next week looked thin. Maybe she could take time out to get her hair dyed.

Joe Flynn wandered into the kitchen, seeking a coffee refill.

Judith ran her fingers though her silver-streaked tresses. "I'm thinking about having some blond highlights put in at Chez Steve's Salon. Would you like that?"

"As opposed to this last dye job that makes you look like a skunk?" Joe nodded. "Yes, you'd look terrific with a touch of shimmering gold." He kissed her forehead. "What gave you that idea?"

"It worked wonders for Kristin," she said, referring to their daughter-in-law, who had somehow resolved a personal crisis the previous June by changing her hair color. "Maybe," Judith went on, "it'll pep me up. I'm running on fumes these days."

Judith had started to turn gray in her late teens, just as her mother had done. She'd dyed her hair for years, but after her first husband, Dan McMonigle, died, she'd let the black grow out, and had been silver-haired since her forties. Years passed before Renie finally convinced Judith that she'd look much better with at least some of her original color. Never one to make changes easily, Judith allowed almost another decade to pass before she heeded her cousin's advice. But now she was ready for an even more drastic transformation.

"Why don't you lighten up all your hair?" Joe suggested. "Maybe go brunette, close to your natural color."

Judith knew what Joe really meant. He was right—gold and raven hair might look harsh in middle age. Not wanting to give herself the chance to change her mind, Judith dialed the salon's number and made an appointment for nine o'clock the following Tuesday.

As the days passed by—still raining, and with occasional

gusty winds—Judith began to get excited about her new look. A few more reservations trickled in. She kept busy, and it was Saturday afternoon before she realized she hadn't heard from Renie. They usually spoke to each other at least once a day. They were both only children, and had grown up more like sisters than cousins.

Just before preparing the appetizers for the guests' social hour, Judith dialed Renie's number. The voice that answered on the other end was almost unrecognizable.

"Is that you, coz?" she asked, knowing it couldn't be Bill since he hated the telephone as much as Judith's mother did.

"I'm pouting," Renie replied. "I've been pouting since Wednesday."

"You can really pout," Judith said, "but you usually don't do it for more than a day. What's wrong now?"

"The same thing that was wrong when I last talked to you," Renie retorted. "That damned cruise line. I haven't heard back since I threatened them with Bub."

"It's only been two full working days," Judith pointed out. "They have to check with their Suits in response to your Suit."

"My Wig, you mean," Renie corrected. "I always refer to Bub as my Wig, not my Suit."

"Poor Bub," Judith murmured.

"What?" Renie spoke sharply.

"Never mind. By the way, I'm getting my hair colored Tuesday."

"Colored what?" Renie asked, her voice showing mild interest.

"Some kind of brown," Judith replied. "I'll let Ginger advise me."

"She's good," Renie conceded. "So's her husband, Steve. I sort of take turns between them."

"But you don't have to color your hair," Judith declared. "You inherited your mother's hair, which still hardly has any gray in it."

"It's not my fault," Renie said. "I'm just a freak of nature."

"True," Judith agreed, not without a touch of sarcasm. "Hey, I've got to go make crab-and-pork wontons for the guests. See you in church."

Judith and Joe did in fact see Renie and Bill at Our Lady, Star of the Sea's ten o'clock Mass. But Bill was lectoring at the service and had to sit in one of the side pews reserved for readers. Renie was in the row behind him, while the Flynns occupied their usual place in the middle of the church. At the Sign of Peace, instead of offering the person next to her a warm handshake and prayerful words, Renie clenched her fists and seemed to snarl. Clearly, she was still in a bad mood.

Later, when Judith and Joe pulled into the driveway, they discovered Gertrude trying to negotiate her motorized wheelchair up the back-porch ramp that had been added during Hillside Manor's renovation three years earlier. The old lady seemed to be stuck.

"Mother!" Judith cried as she tried to get out of Joe's beloved MG without damaging her artificial hip. "What's wrong?"

"It's that horrible cat," Gertrude asserted in her raspy voice. "Where'd he go now?"

Judith looked around the backyard, where daffodils, hyacinths, and other early spring bulbs bloomed. "I don't see Sweetums anywhere," she said, trying to budge the wheelchair. "How did the cat make you get stuck? I can't move this thing. Here comes Joe."

Gertrude heaved a sigh. "Not Knucklehead," she grumbled. "Call the medics. Call the cops. Call anybody but *him*."

"Now, now," Joe said. "Is my darling mother-in-law annoyed with me? How can that be?"

"It's easy," Gertrude snapped. "I'd stopped being annoyed if you disappeared."

Judith tried to ignore the ongoing feud between her husband and her mother. Gertrude had never approved of Joe—or Dan McMonigle. In fact, the old lady resided in the converted tool shed because she refused to live under the same roof with Judith's second husband.

Joe, however, wasn't having any luck with the wheelchair. "Is this thing turned on?" he asked.

"You bet," Gertrude replied. "Come on, push. You don't look like any ninety-pound weakling to me. Your big fat head weighs that much."

"Mother—" Judith began but stopped when she glimpsed Sweetums' large orange-and-white body creeping through Carl and Arlene Rankers's vast laurel hedge.

Joe's ruddy complexion was getting even redder. "Did you set the brake?" he inquired of Gertrude.

" 'Course I did," the old lady snapped. "How else could I keep from running over that cat? He wouldn't move. Should I have totaled him?"

"Why don't you two have an ornery-off?" Joe muttered. "The loser gets sent to the Home. So does the winner."

Gertrude cupped her right ear. "What? I can't hear you. I'm getting deaf, you know."

Joe released the brake. The wheelchair sailed up the ramp and onto the porch.

"About time," Gertrude said to Joe.

Judith opened the back door. "Why were you coming into the house?" she asked.

"To get a magnifying glass," Gertrude replied, proceeding down the narrow hallway and into the kitchen. "Mine's lost. I know you've got one, because you're always doing some kind of stupid sleuthing. Did I ask for a daughter who thinks she's Sherlock Holmes?"

"I don't use a magnifying glass to do it," Judith huffed. "Furthermore, you know perfectly well that I'm not a real sleuth. I've just had a run of bad luck getting involved in . . . unpleasant situations."

Joe was looking askance. "It's a hobby you should give up. How many times have I told you it's damned dangerous?"

Her husband's recurrent nagging about her involvement in crime and her mother's constant verbal abuse of Joe irritated Judith. "Skip it," she said stiffly. "It's been almost a year since I had a . . . problem."

"At least," Joe remarked, "when I was a homicide detective, I got paid for solving cases."

"Joe!" Judith glared at her husband. "Drop it!"

Joe, whose temper was usually more easily triggered than his wife's, knew when it was unwise to push her too far. "Okay." He nodded in the direction of the dining room. "We have some guests still eating breakfast. I'll see how they're doing."

"Thanks." Judith's tone was terse.

"I can't find it," Gertrude declared. "When's lunch?"

Judith pointed to the old schoolhouse clock on the wall. "It's not even eleven-thirty. Can you wait an hour?"

"Noon. You know I like my lunch at noon."

"I have to clear up from breakfast first," Judith said, still sounding cross. "The magnifying glass is in the junk drawer, next to the stapler."

"I already looked," Gertrude said. "There's so much junk, I couldn't find it."

Judith let out an impatient sigh. "That's why it's a drunk jawer. I mean, *junk drawer.* Honestly," she complained, "between you and Joe, I get so rattled, it's a wonder I can find the kitchen." She rummaged through the assortment of rubber bands, meat skewers, Band-Aids, batteries, Scotch tape, mailing tape, strap-

ping tape, and tape measures. "Here," she said, handing the magnifying glass to Gertrude. "It was under the take-out menus.
Why do you need it?"

Gertrude examined the glass as if it were a mirror. "It's my
movie script," she said. "They've made so many changes—revisions, they call them—that I can't read the handwriting in the
margins. And I sure don't like the new title, *Dirty Gertie Does Düsseldorf*. Granted, as the Greatest Generation, we didn't have all
these fancy appliances, but I wasn't ever dirty. We washed our
clothes, ran them through the wringer, and hung them on the
clothesline. Then we put them in the mangle for ironing. And
starch. We had starch in those days, boiled outside and stirred
with a wooden ladle. How could I be dirty after all that?"

Judith hadn't heard much of what her mother had said beyond the movie's title. "When did you learn that they weren't
going to call the film *Gertrude the Great?*"

"Friday," her mother replied. "I got one of those FedEx or
UPS or whatever packages. Your crazy cleaning woman, Phyliss
Rackley, brought it to me. She talked my ear off—as usual—
about being saved. Saved from what? I told her to save her
breath. She stayed so long I forgot she'd brought the package.
'Course, half the time, I don't open those things. Ever since they
decided to make my life into a moving picture they send all this
stuff on a truck. But I decided to open this one. Those packages
are piling up, in case you haven't noticed."

Judith had seen at least a half-dozen overnight parcels in the
toolshed. She'd even mentioned their presence a couple of times
to her mother, but Gertrude had ignored her.

"Isn't the movie coming out in a few months?" Judith asked.

Gertrude nodded. "June, I think. Or is it July?" She shrugged.
"As long as they pay me, they can show it anytime they want. But
I don't get this new title. I've never been to Düsseldorf. Or have

I?" Gertrude frowned. She was frequently forgetful—or pretended to be.

"Maybe I should take a look at those packages," Judith suggested. There was no annoyance in her voice now. She was too concerned about the detour that her mother's life story might have taken.

"I already got a big chunk of my money up front when they optioned my story," Gertrude said. "They call it a step deal. I don't know why, they know I can't go up steps. Anyways, later on I get a couple more checks, but I forget when. Still, I keep wondering why *Photoplay* and *Modern Screen* don't come around to interview me."

Judith didn't mention that she thought both magazines had long ceased publication. "Today's magazines are all about celebrities I've never heard of," she remarked.

"Then how come they're celebrities and I'm not?" Gertrude demanded. "Nobody's ever heard of me, either." She tapped the corner of *The Inquisitor,* one of her favorite tabloids. "You mean I'd have to pose in my girdle like these women who run around in their underwear?"

"Well . . ." Judith paused, listening to what was going on in the dining room. Joe was chatting with the couple from Los Angeles who had lingered over breakfast. They'd been on several African safaris and were bragging about their trophies. Judith wished Joe would suggest taking their coffee into the living room so she could clear the table.

"Let's go out to your apartment," Judith said, "so I can help you look through those parcels."

"You can toss 'em in the Dumpster for all I care," Gertrude responded.

"Maybe I will," Judith fibbed. But first she'd like to see what was inside the overnight envelopes.

"You could make my lunch," Gertrude said. "It's going on noon."

"So I could." It'd save Judith a trip to the toolshed.

She had started making a BLT for her mother when Joe finally managed to lure the L.A. couple out of the dining room. While the bacon was frying, Judith began clearing the solid oak table that had belonged to her grandparents.

"Blowhards," Joe murmured, standing in the doorway to the entry hall. "Do I care how they stuffed their dik-diks?"

"Probably not," Judith whispered. "What are your plans for the rest of the day?"

"Doing my homework on that arson trial," he replied. "It looks as if I'll have to testify."

"That's a pain," Judith said. "When does it start?"

Joe was moving into the entry hall, headed for the front stairs. Apparently, he was avoiding his mother-in-law by not taking his usual backstairs route. "Monday, the twenty-fourth. I don't have much time to prepare. I've got that high-profile divorce surveillance gig this week."

"Good luck," Judith said as Joe started up the carpeted steps. Sometimes it seemed that her husband was busier as a private detective than he had been while he was on the police force. But usually he enjoyed his work, and it paid well. Considering the current dearth of B&B reservations, the Flynns could use the money.

"Bacon's burning," Gertrude announced as Judith returned to the kitchen.

"Oh, dear!" Judith pulled the frying pan off the burner.

"I like it that way," her mother asserted. "You know that. And I like my toast burned, too. It makes my hair curly."

"A permanent makes your hair curly," Judith said, turning on the exhaust fan to clear the smoke. "You used to tell me those old wives' tales when I was a kid."

"So?" Gertrude shrugged. "Plenty of mayo, remember?"

"And butter," Judith added. Her mother's cholesterol was off the charts, but it didn't seem to affect the old girl's health.

Five minutes later, they were in the toolshed. Sweetums had joined them, curling up on Gertrude's small couch. Judith settled her mother into the armchair and put her meal on the cluttered card table.

Four express packages were in a pile behind the chair. The contents of the latest, however, were spread out on the card table. Gertrude set her BLT on top of the revised script and adjusted her dentures.

Cautiously, Judith bent down to collect the unopened parcels. "I'll leave the one you're reading here and take the rest," she said, noting that they were all about the same size and felt like the previous scripts she'd seen. "Here's your magnifying glass. It was under the packages."

"Oh. Then you can have yours back." Gertrude picked up half of the sandwich, ignoring the mayo, butter, grease, and tomato stains she'd left on the script. Sweetums jumped off the couch, yawned, and leaped onto the card table, staring at the BLT with covetous yellow eyes. "Better feed him before you go," the old lady said. "Otherwise, that cat and I'll end up in a scratching match."

"He has food in his dish here, food inside the house, and food on the back porch," Judith said, retrieving her magnifying glass and heading for the door.

"He likes bacon," Gertrude declared.

Judith didn't argue. She had laundry to do and beds to make and carpets to vacuum. Phyliss didn't work weekends. The previous summer, Judith had hired college students to help out in the cleaning woman's absence, but once school started in the fall, they headed back to campus. Always fearful of dislocating her artificial hip, Judith was at a point where she needed year-round Saturday and Sunday help. Maybe it was time to place an ad in the neighborhood weekly.

When she finished her chores around three-thirty, Judith was too tired to look over the packages from the movie studio. In fact, she fell asleep on one of the two matching sofas in the living room and didn't wake up until almost five. It was time to prepare the guests' appetizers. The scripts could wait. It was Sunday, after all, a day of rest.

Judith could use it.

'm tired," Judith announced to Joe over breakfast the next morning. "We haven't gone on a real vacation in ages. If I can get Carl and Arlene Rankers to take over the B&B for a week, why don't we go somewhere next month?"

Joe's round face grew pensive. "I suppose we could, once this trial is over. Where do you want to go?"

"Cancún. Hawaii. Miami. I've never been to any of those places."

The gold flecks in Joe's green eyes danced. "How about staying with Vivian in her condo on the Gulf?"

Judith bridled. "Don't even think about it. The best part about winter is that your ex-wife's there from October to June instead of living three houses down the street from us the rest of the time."

"You know I'm kidding," Joe replied. "Not after all those years with Vivian, watching her decide who her companion of the day would be. It was either Jack Daniel's or Jim Beam. I came in a distant third."

"How well I understand," Judith said softly. "With Dan, it was how much blackberry brandy he could down before starting his serious vodka drinking at eleven in the morning."

Joe grew serious. "Why didn't they marry each other?"

"You know why," Judith said softly, reaching across the table to caress her husband's hand. "Because we both made terrible mistakes."

For a few moments, Judith and Joe were lost in thought, recalling the unfortunate series of events that had led to each of them marrying the wrong person.

It was Judith who changed the subject back to a possible vacation. "I think we can afford a getaway. You decide where."

"The Caribbean appeals to me," he replied. "Jamaica, maybe. When I get a free minute, I'll do some research."

Judith nodded. But she had to put aside travel thoughts and tend to her guests, who were assembling in the dining room. It was only after they'd all checked out by eleven that she began to daydream again.

She was picturing herself lying next to a swimming pool with a mai tai when the phone rang.

"Ya-*ha*!" Renie shouted into her cousin's ear. "Bub did it again! I just heard from Magglio Cruz's Suits. They're going to keep me on a retainer as a consultant and send Bill and me on a free cruise!"

"You should take Bub," Judith said. "But hey, that's wonderful news. You've stopped pouting."

"You bet. But I don't have any cruise clothes. I must shop *now*. Want to come?"

Judy hesitated. "I can't," she finally said. "I've got a lot to do, including restocking the larder. Frankly, I'm worn out. In fact, Joe and I were talking about taking a break next month."

"Gee," Renie said, "it's too bad I couldn't have gotten a free cruise for you guys, too. I wonder if Bub—"

"Don't pester your poor brother-in-law again," Judith broke in. "When do you leave?"

"The cruise sails Friday," Renie replied, "so we have to fly down to San Francisco Thursday morning. That's the part I don't like. You know me—I think flying should be left to our feathered friends."

"You'll be fine," Judith assured her cousin. "I hear my fax machine ringing. Maybe it's a reservation. I could use some this time of year. Enjoy your shopping."

The fax was actually a cancellation for the coming weekend. Judith swore under her breath. The week was starting badly—at least for Judith. As she drove up to Falstaff's Grocery, she began to feel envious of Renie. Why did she get a free trip? Why could she take off almost anytime she wanted to? Judith felt as if she were chained to the B&B. She felt like a drudge, a tired drudge. She could sulk, too.

That night, she actually dreamed of sitting next to a pool. Except that it wasn't a pool—it was an endless body of water. She wasn't wearing a swimsuit, but a ragged coat that made her look like a bum. The mai tai was beside her, but it had been poured into a human skull. In the background, music played loudly—and louder and louder—until Judith awoke in a cold sweat.

But it was only a dream, Judith told herself, and eventually went back to sleep. By morning, she was still sulking when her cousin called to describe the cruise wear she'd purchased.

"The only problem is," Renie explained, "that the theme of the cruise is the thirties. We have to wear outfits from that era for dinner. I got the basics at Nordquist's, but today I'll have to check out some vintage shops to see what I can find."

"Poor you." Judith tried to keep the sarcasm out of her voice.

If Renie noticed, it didn't stop her from nattering on about the five-star San Francisco hotel they'd spend a night in or the VIP cocktail party or their suite of rooms aboard the ship. In fact, Judith managed to tune out the rest of her cousin's gush. She was wandering around the main floor with the cordless phone, noting that the Persian rug in the entry hall was wearing out, the bells-of-Ireland bouquet was wilting, and the St. Patrick's Day decorations would have to be taken down for storage in the basement.

At last, Renie rang off. Judith dragged herself through the rest of the day and slept like a rock that night. She didn't wake up when Joe got home around 2 A.M. after a long surveillance on the philandering husband in the high-profile divorce case.

"You look like a wraith," Joe declared when he came down for breakfast shortly after eight. "You're getting too thin."

"I know," Judith admitted. It was ironic. All her life she'd battled a weight problem, but since her hip replacement, she'd tried extra hard to lose pounds. "It's easier on the artificial hip, especially when I have to run up and down three flights of stairs in this house."

"You don't take time to eat properly," Joe accused his wife. "Have you had breakfast yet?"

"No," she confessed. "I've been preparing the meal for the guests and trying to get things done around here before I go to Chez Steve's Salon. I'll grab a bagel on top of the hill."

Joe, whose own weight was a few more pounds than it should have been, scowled. "Eat here. I'll make my special scrambled eggs."

"Don't bother," Judith began as the phone rang. "I have to feed Mother. I'm already late." She picked the receiver off of the cradle. To her astonishment, it was Renie.

"What's wrong?" Judith asked in an anxious voice. "Why are you up so early?"

"It's Bill," a frazzled Renie replied. "He's got a patient on a ledge."

Bill Jones was a retired professor of psychology from the University who still saw a few of his longtime patients. "What's he doing about it?" Judith asked.

"He's trying to talk the guy off," Renie answered. "The problem is, the nutcase is on the roof of a twenty-story building downtown, and you know Bill's terrified of heights. He won't go near this guy and has to use a megaphone to make him hear. I told Bill to let him jump, but you know my husband—he's conscientious."

It wasn't, of course, the first time Bill had had a suicidal patient. It puzzled Judith that Renie had called her about the situation, especially so early in the morning.

"Well," Judith said, as much for Joe's benefit as for Renie's, "Bill can't let this man jump. So why are you telling me this?"

"Because," Renie said with a big sigh, "if Bill can stop him, he'll have to do some serious counseling, which means he can't go with me on the cruise. That's why I advised Bill to let him take a dive."

"That's callous," Judith declared.

"He's getting tired of yelling through that megaphone," Renie retorted. She uttered an audible sigh. "I know, you're right. But I thought I'd tell you now, because if Bill can't go on the cruise with me, how about taking his place?"

Judith made a face. "You know that isn't going to happen."

"Probably not," Renie acknowledged, "but this guy won't talk to anybody but Bill. He never has. Bill's managed to dissuade him from suicide several times. The toughest one was when this patient put weights on his legs and tried to jump into the deep end of the swimming pool at the downtown YMCA. He actually injured himself on that one."

"How?"

"He was so agitated that he didn't notice the pool had been drained. Just in case, be prepared to come along with me."

I should be so lucky, Judith thought to herself after she'd hung up.

Or, as events unfolded, *unlucky.*

Chapter Two

Judith stared in the mirror at her new hair color and grimaced. "Did I say I wanted to be a redhead?"

Ginger added a few finishing touches to her client's coiffure. "It's not red, Judith. It's a very deep auburn with gold highlights. I think you look fabulous. The perm will loosen up in a few days, giving you just the right amount of wave. And I think cutting your hair just below your ears does wonders for your face."

Judith knew what Ginger meant: A long face, especially with a weight loss, made her look older.

"Really," Ginger said, gazing at Judith's image in the mirror, "your skin tone changes over time. Even if you'd kept your natural color like your cousin Serena has, it wouldn't suit your complexion. Besides, the lighting in here isn't natural. Color is exaggerated. I'm not kidding when I say you look at least five years younger. See what Joe thinks. I'll bet you a free eyebrow waxing that he's going to love it."

Judith was dubious. When she got home around two, Joe was gone. Phyliss Rackley dropped her mop when she saw Judith come in the back door.

"Jezebel!" she cried. "You've turned into a shameless hussy!"

For Judith, that was a positive reaction. "You think so, Phyliss?"

Phyliss waved a hand in front of her face, as if she could make Judith disappear. "Have you become a temptress? Poor Mr. Flynn!"

Judith's self-confidence was growing by the second. "Really?"

Phyliss nodded so hard that her gray curls bobbed up and down. "He won't let you out of the house, mark my words."

"Hmm." Judith forced herself not to smile. Ginger must be right.

For the rest of the afternoon, Judith felt her spirits lift. She was further cheered when a late reservation came in from a couple whose flight to Hong Kong had been canceled. By the time Joe got home around six, she couldn't wait for his reaction.

But there was none. Joe came in the back door, shouted at his wife, who was taking the guests' canapés out of the oven, and announced he had to change and leave immediately for a second shift on his stakeout. He raced up the back stairs without seeing Judith. He left the same way while she was chatting with the couple that hadn't been able to leave for Hong Kong. Her spirits began to slide again.

Renie phoned just as the guests left for their evening rounds. "I tried to call you earlier," she said, "but you weren't around, and I didn't leave a message. I wanted to let you know that Bill's making progress. He'd talked his patient down to the sixteenth floor. A few minutes ago, Bill got him down to twelve."

"Super," Judith said without much enthusiasm. "Is that good news or bad news?"

"Good," Renie replied, sounding puzzled. "The guy's still alive, and Bill doesn't have to stand on the roof and yell through the megaphone anymore. It was windy and cold up there."

"Bill must be exhausted," Judith noted. "Isn't he used to taking an afternoon nap with Oscar?"

"I drove Oscar downtown this afternoon," Renie replied, referring to the Jones's stuffed dwarf ape that had been a fixture on the family sofa for over a quarter of a century. "Bill and Oscar took a break while the emergency people kept an eye on Lorenzo."

"Lorenzo?" Judith echoed. "Is that the patient's name?"

"No," Renie answered. "Even to me, Bill never discloses his patients' names. But that's what we call him. I forget why."

As the doorbell rang, Judith excused herself and hung up. Two embarrassed old ladies from Springfield, Illinois, had forgotten their keys.

"We're going clubbing after dinner," the one with the very blue hair said, "so we won't get back until after you lock up at ten."

Judith went upstairs and found their keys on the Bombay chest in Room One. "Have fun," she said to her guests.

"We be cool," the other elderly lady said as they headed back to their waiting taxi.

Just after Judith delivered her mother's "supper"—as Gertrude preferred to call it—Renie phoned again.

"Down to seven," she announced. "Oops! Got a call on the other line. It may be one of the kids."

Renie and Bill's three children had all gotten married on the same day almost two years earlier. The newlyweds' careers had taken them to distant places around the globe. After constant griping because their thirtysomething offspring hadn't moved out of the house, the senior Joneses now complained because they saw their children only once or twice a year. Judith and Joe, meanwhile, were thankful that Mike and his family lived at a ranger station only an hour away.

At last, Judith had some free time to go through the unopened parcels from the toolshed. She started in chronological order, dating back to September. Scanning the script revisions, she saw that less fact and more fiction had been put into the script. Judith wasn't surprised. She—and Gertrude, for that matter—knew that the protagonist had become more of a symbol for the Greatest Generation than the real life Gertrude Hoffman Grover. But her first name was the same.

In the movie, Gertrude was a deeply committed women's rights advocate, speaking at rallies and shouting from a soapbox in New York's Times Square. Well, Judith thought, her mother was certainly one for equality, even if she'd never been farther east than Montana. The job as an ambulance driver in France during World War I was a stretch—Gertrude had never left town. She had joined the local Red Cross auxiliary, knitting items for the Doughboys and buying a couple of Liberty bonds. But her involvement in supporting Prohibition and busting up bottles of booze was going too far. Gertrude had never been a serious drinker, but she had been a flapper, rolling her stockings, dancing the black bottom, and drinking bathtub gin.

That, however, was included in the next few scenes covering the twenties. Judith had reached the part about Gertrude meeting Al Capone when the phone rang.

"Lorenzo's down to the third floor," she said. "Even if he jumps, he'll probably just bounce around and get banged up. You'd better check with the Rankerses to see if they can take over for you at the B&B."

Hanging up, Judith wondered if she might, in fact, be joining Renie on the cruise. It still seemed like an outside shot, however. She kept going through the script, marveling at the fantasies the writers had concocted for Gertrude's life.

The final scenes involved the doughty heroine in her advanced years, using a high-tech telescope to scan the heavens and wishing she could land on Mars. There were days, Judith thought wryly, when she wished the same for her mother.

But what startled her most was the separate envelope that had gotten stuck to the last page. It was addressed to Gertrude and marked URGENT.

Carefully, Judith opened the sealed envelope. Her dark eyes widened when she found a check made out to her mother. The amount was twenty thousand dollars. A brief note was attached stating that the sum was due to Gertrude on the first day of principal photography, September 10. Quickly, Judith opened the other envelopes. They contained more script revisions, but no checks. She hurried to the toolshed.

"Mother!" she exclaimed. "The producers sent you more money!"

Gertrude snorted. "About time." She reached to take the check and note from her daughter's outstretched hand. "Hunh. What does it say? Twenty bucks?"

"Use your magnifier," Judith urged in an excited voice.

Gertrude moved her empty plate and silverware, the jumble puzzle she'd been solving, and a deck of cards. "Ah. Here it is," she said, taking the magnifying glass out of her still-full soup bowl. "It's kind of messed up. Did you make that soup or did it just grow under the sink?"

"Very funny, Mother," Judith snapped. "It's from a leftover roast."

"You should have left it over at Rankers's house," Gertrude grumbled. "Are you going to clean that magnifier or not?"

Annoyed, Judith went into her mother's kitchenette and washed the glass. "Here," she said, "now read the damned thing."

Gertrude's expression slowly changed from testy to pleased. "Well, well! Isn't that nice. Maybe I can buy new corn plasters."

"Why not?" Judith was searching the card table, trying to see if there had been a check included with the most recent version of the script. "Are you sure there wasn't a separate envelope with this latest batch of revisions?"

Gertrude nodded several times. " 'Course I'm sure. I don't get the last check until the moving picture gets shown."

That made sense to Judith. "Why don't you let me put that check in the bank for you tomorrow?"

Gertrude, however, shook her head. "I'd like to look at it for a while. Besides, I'm not sure I trust you." She narrowed her eyes at her daughter. "In fact, with that floozy hairdo, I'm not sure I recognize you. You could be an impostor."

Frowning, Judith ignored the barb. "Don't you dare mislay that check," she admonished. "It's already several months old. The bank may not even honor it. Then you'll have to ask for a replacement."

"Don't fuss," Gertrude said airily, holding the check up close to her face. "What's today? Tuesday? You can take it in on Friday. Isn't that when you usually go to the bank?"

"Usually," Judith admitted. "Okay, a couple of days won't hurt, I suppose. But don't you dare—"

"I know, I know," Gertrude interrupted. "I'll watch it like a hawk."

Although she didn't say so, Judith still had misgivings.

Approaching the back porch, she could hear the phone ringing inside. Judith snatched up the receiver just before the call switched over to Voice Messaging.

"Good news!" Renie cried, then lowered her voice. "Except for poor Bill."

"What happened?" Judith asked, confused by her cousin's pronouncement.

"Bill convinced Lorenzo that he shouldn't commit suicide again," Renie began.

"I didn't know you could do it more than once," Judith put in.

"You know what I mean," Renie said. "I told you, this guy's tried it at least a half-dozen times before. Anyway, after Lorenzo got down to the third floor and saw Oscar, he asked why Bill had a stuffed monkey. Bill informed him that Oscar wasn't a monkey, he was a dwarf ape. Monkeys have tails, and Oscar doesn't, as I'm sure you've noticed."

"I haven't, really," Judith said, sometimes wondering if her cousin and her husband were crazier than some of Bill's patients.

"So Bill and this guy got into a real argument," Renie went on. "Lorenzo was convinced Bill was wrong because at one time he'd worked at the zoo. Lorenzo, I mean, not Bill."

"Define *zoo*," Judith murmured.

"What?"

"Nothing, coz. I coughed."

"In fact, when Lorenzo was working there," Renie continued, "he tried to kill himself by jumping into the lion pit. Unfortunately—or not—it was just after feeding time. Anyway, that was years ago, before they put all the natural habitats in at the zoo."

Judith picked an apple out of the fruit basket on the kitchen counter and began to munch. "Um."

"So Lorenzo told Bill that he had a primate book in his apartment, and he could prove that Oscar wasn't an ape. You can imagine how Oscar felt about all this. He was really getting irritated."

Judith kept munching. "Um-um."

"Then Lorenzo suddenly got off the ledge—he was sitting on

it, facing Bill and Oscar at this point—and came to the office doorway where Bill was standing. Even being three stories off the ground bothers Bill."

Judith was tempted to ask if it bothered Oscar, but kept quiet and wished her cousin would get to the point. "So what's the bottom line?"

"Well—Bill was tempted to go to Lorenzo's apartment to prove he was right about Oscar, but he realized that wouldn't be proper protocol," Renie explained. "So he let the medics take over, and now Bill's gone up to Bayview Hospital's psychiatric ward. I imagine Bill and Oscar will go to the cafeteria for something to eat while the MDs check out Lorenzo. The problem is," she went on, sounding worried, "Oscar hates hospitals. It's too bad I didn't take Archie to Bill, too."

Judith didn't want Renie to get started on Archie, the small cheerful doll. She had had to put up with that bit of fantasy when the cousins were both in the hospital for separate surgeries. Archie had a tiny suitcase that accompanied him when he stayed with any member of the Jones family who was hospitalized. The worst of it was that the three Jones children all believed in Oscar, Archie, and another small doll named Cleo who was a foulmouthed Oakland Raiders fan. Judith felt that the entire family had too much imagination—or they really were nuts.

"There must be a reason you're telling me all this," Judith said.

"Of course!" Renie sounded irked. "I already mentioned I had good news for you. There's no way Bill can leave town with Lorenzo in such a precarious emotional state." She paused and sneezed a couple of times. "Sorry—it's March, and my allergies are bothering me."

"Mine, too," Judith said impatiently. "Are you trying to tell me that I'm supposed to fill in for Bill?"

"Yes! Aren't you excited?"

Judith wasn't. Not yet. It seemed too good to be true. Indeed, panic began to engulf her. "Aren't you—we—scheduled to leave the day after tomorrow?"

"That's right," Renie agreed. "I told you to be prepared. Have you checked with Carl and Arlene?"

"No," Judith admitted. "I haven't mentioned the possibility to Joe, and he's not here." She felt frazzled. The cruise was like a mirage, appearing and disappearing.

"Then get hopping," Renie commanded. "You'll have to shop, too, and buy some vintage clothes for the thirties theme."

"Really . . . I don't know . . . Oh, dear . . ." Judith never liked making decisions, especially on the spot. "Can I sleep on it?"

Renie sneezed again before she replied. "No. If you tell me tomorrow you're not going, then I'm in a pickle. I couldn't ask anybody else because they'd have less than twenty-four hours' notice." She paused. "Okay, let's do it this way. You're worn out, you look like bird doo, and you're coming with me."

"You haven't seen my hair," Judith countered in a feeble voice.

"I expect to see it on the way to the airport. I'm hanging up now."

"No! Wait!" Renie was right. Judith desperately needed a break. "At least give me time to tell Joe."

"Good. Now get organized."

"I will. I'll call Joe and the Rankerses. I think I've got enough of what might pass for cruise wear. In fact, there's a trunk in the basement with old clothes Mother refuses to let me throw out." She hesitated, calculating what else needed to be done. "If Carl and Arlene can't take over for me, I'll ask the state B&B association. They have temporary innkeepers on call. And . . . by the way, where is the cruise going?"

"Atiu."

"Gesundheit." Judith repeated the question. "Where are we going?"

"I told you—Atiu, Pukapuka, Rarotonga, several stops in the Cook Islands. Read a map."

"I'll have to," Judith said. "I've never heard of any of them—except for the Cook Islands themselves, of course."

"They're due south of Hawaii," Renie said. "I wish they were closer to Guam. Then I could rendezvous with Tom and Cathleen."

The Joneses' elder son and his wife had moved to Guam after their wedding. Cathleen worked as an optician in a Catholic medical clinic and Tom taught European history at the university. Once again, Judith thanked her lucky stars that Mike and his family were so close.

Happily, Arlene and Carl agreed to take over Hillside Manor's operation for the two weeks that Judith would be gone. Not so happily, Joe pitched a fit.

"I thought you and I were going on vacation next month," he said, raising his usually mellow voice.

"We still can," Judith insisted. "We could go in May or June. April really isn't such a good time, with Easter being late this year."

"Is May any better?" Joe shot back. "There's Mother's Day, Memorial Day, and school's out early in the month for some college students. As for June—forget it. Now you're into the B&B's busiest time of year."

Joe was right. The last week of April, after Easter, would be the best time for them to go together. Judith frowned into the phone. "I don't know what to do. Renie insists I go with her."

"Renie should cancel. Bill can't go," Joe argued. "Why doesn't she tell those cruise bigwigs that she prefers another time?"

"She probably figures they'll renege," Judith replied, "maybe even on the retainer offer. She had to threaten suing them."

Joe snorted. "And once her mind's made up, hell can't hold her."

"Well . . . there's that, too."

"Got to go," Joe said abruptly. "Rich Mr. Zipper has just pulled into his inamorata's driveway."

Judith didn't dare broach the subject to her mother, at least not so late at night. Nor did she want to relay Joe's reaction to Renie. Reeling around in her quandary, she decided to go to bed.

But Judith couldn't sleep. She'd drop off for a few minutes, but weird dreams kept waking her up. A man wearing a slouch hat was playing the piano; when he removed the hat, he had no head. A large white bird in a satin evening gown and long strands of pearls had blood dripping from its claws. Two men in uniforms opened a bank vault to reveal a pile of handguns covered in caviar.

Mother was right, Judith thought to herself. *It must've been the soup.* She tossed and turned until Joe got home just before two o'clock.

"What's the matter?" Joe asked in an annoyingly innocent voice. "You've got the blankets all messed up."

"No kidding." Judith rolled over again, turning her back on Joe.

"Is it your hip?" he inquired.

"It's always my hip," Judith grumbled. "But that's only part of it. The rest of me doesn't feel so great, either."

"You mean because you aren't going on the cruise?"

"I haven't told Renie," Judith said, sounding crankier by the second. "In fact," she went on, sitting up and looking at her husband, "*you* tell her. Call her first thing in the morning."

Joe recognized the trap. Waking Renie before 10 A.M. was hazardous duty. Telling her that Judith couldn't go on the cruise was tantamount to setting off a ton of TNT.

"Renie's *your* cousin," Joe declared. "It's up to you to tell her."

"No." Judith pulled the sheet over her head.

"Sheesh." Partly undressed, Joe stood in the middle of the bedroom. He'd confronted hardened criminals, accompanied SWAT teams in hostage situations, and gone one-on-one with drug-crazed killers wielding assault weapons. He wasn't afraid of a little squirt like Renie. "Fine," he said, and finished getting ready for bed.

The next morning, Joe called Renie at ten-fifteen. "I'm afraid," he began in formal tones, "that Judith can't go with you on the cruise."

"Really?" Renie sounded mildly surprised. "That's a shame."

Joe was momentarily nonplussed by Renie's reaction. "You see," he said, compelled to explain further, "the two of us are planning a vacation next month."

"Yes, she mentioned that." Renie paused. "I hope it's not too late."

"Too late for what?" Joe asked.

"For her health," Renie replied in a concerned voice. "I assume you've made sure she's seeing a doctor."

"About what?"

Renie made an exasperated noise. "About the fact that she could have a stroke at any minute. For God's sake, Joe, have you *looked* at her lately? She's thin as a rail, she's pale, she's haggard, she's a train wreck waiting to happen. I can't imagine that her new hairdo helps much."

"What hairdo?"

"Touché," Renie murmured. "What's up with you, Joe? You're usually the noticing kind."

"I haven't seen much of my wife this morning," Joe said, sounding defensive. "She's been . . . avoiding me."

"No wonder."

Joe expected Renie to say more, but she didn't, which made him feel even worse. "Do you really think she's completely worn out?"

"Yes," Renie said, "I do. You two should have gone on vacation in January. After the holidays, she started to really go downhill. In fact, it wouldn't hurt her to take two vacations, one with me and one with you. I still can't believe you haven't seen how tired and frazzled she is lately."

"I know she's tired," Joe said, conscious of the serious note in Renie's words. "But I've been so damned busy, what with the case I'm on right now and the trial coming up next week. Yeah, it sounds lame, but there it is. I'm not as young as I used to be, either."

"Who is?" Renie sounded sympathetic. "Think about poor Bill, stuck with that nutcase up at Bayview Hospital. I almost canceled when he told me he couldn't go, but I was afraid I'd lose the Cruz account. I'm sorry you don't want her to go. The decision is yours."

Guilt. "You learned this from your mother, didn't you?"

"What?" Renie sounded puzzled.

"The guilt-trip thing. Aunt Deb invented it, didn't she? Or if not, honed it to a fine art."

"You bet," Renie retorted. "And think of all the crap I'm going to put up with because I'll be gone for two weeks. It's almost not worth it. But," she went on, "that's a separate issue. I firmly believe that your wife's health is precarious."

Joe was silent for a few moments. He'd been caught off guard by Renie's solemn attitude. She'd managed to scare him about Judith's health. And, he grudgingly admitted to himself, the decision was his wife's, not his. "Okay, she can go."

"Good," said Renie. "I'll return her in a much improved condition." She hung up.

Judith returned to the kitchen as Joe placed the phone back in its cradle. "Were you talking to Renie?" she asked in a despondent voice.

"Wow!" Joe cried. "Your hair looks terrific! This is the first chance I've had to see it in the light. By the time I got up, you were already scurrying around the house."

Judith was skeptical. "Thanks." She started loading the dishwasher with the tableware she'd brought in from the dining room.

"Let me do that," Joe said, nudging her out of the way. "In fact, let me take over for the day. You could use some time to yourself."

Judith wasn't just skeptical, she was suspicious. Maybe this was Joe's way of making up for vetoing the cruise. "How come?" she asked.

Joe put the last of the teaspoons in the silverware compartment. "Because," he said, putting his hands on Judith's sagging shoulders, "you have to pack. May I be the first to wish you bon voyage?"

Chapter Three

Judith spent the rest of Wednesday in a frenzy of sorting clothes, going through the old trunk and some other boxes in the basement, and filling her suitcases. In the basement, nostalgia had overcome her. Four generations of Grovers had stored items there: Grandma and Grandpa's first string of Christmas tree lights; Uncle Cliff's fishing-tackle box; her father's business-skills teaching texts; Auntie Vance's movie posters, including *King Kong, The Thin Man,* and *The Wizard of Oz;* photos of Uncle Al taken in the winner's circle at various West Coast and Florida racetracks; Uncle Corky's World War II army cap with its twin silver bars denoting his captain's rank; Aunt Ellen's high school yearbooks; Mike's handprint in plaster from his kindergarten days; the white-and-gold sari Judith had worn for her first wedding. She'd been sorry, all right, for nineteen years.

Judith also exchanged a half-dozen phone calls with Renie, checking on details and schedules. She not only wasn't tired, she couldn't remember when she'd been so excited. Even breaking the news to Gertrude went better than she'd expected.

"You *have* been looking peaked lately," her mother allowed. "Though I don't know why you need to go off on a boat to a bunch of islands where they probably have cannibals who'll make you into a stew. Not that you've got much meat on your bones."

"I've looked up the Cook Islands," Judith replied. "They're in the heart of Polynesia and belong to New Zealand. The islands sound lovely—and safe."

"If you say so," Gertrude said, then brightened. "With Arlene and Carl taking over, we'll play pinochle and I'll get to eat food I really like."

The Rankerses were fond of the old girl and indulged her every whim. Besides, Judith knew that Arlene and Carl would keep Gertrude from bedeviling Joe while he tried to focus on the upcoming trial.

That night Judith went to bed right after locking up the B&B at ten. The airport shuttle was due to pick up the cousins at 4 A.M. for their six-twenty flight to San Francisco. Renie had chosen the early time because she reasoned that she wouldn't be awake until after their arrival, and thus wouldn't be so terrified of flying. A couple of stiff shots of Wild Turkey would also help calm her nerves.

In fact, when Judith got into the shuttle after bidding her husband and her mother farewell, she realized that Renie was drunk as a skunk.

"Hiya, coz!" Renie said in a cheerful voice. "Whazzup?"

"Oh, good grief!" Judith exclaimed under her breath. Swiftly, she scanned the three other passengers: a young couple holding hands in the row behind the cousins and a silver-haired woman sitting ramrod straight next to the driver. They were all avoiding any glances at Renie.

Judith fastened her seat belt. "Just keep your mouth shut," she whispered to Renie. "And don't pass out. I can't carry you."

"S'a fine," Renie said, keeping her voice down. "S'a dark."

"Of course it's dark," Judith replied, again whispering. "It's March, it's four in the morning."

"Ni-ni," Renie said, and put her head on Judith's shoulder.

Judith didn't know whether she should kick Renie—or herself. Bill had told horror stories about air travel with his inebriated wife, including a flight from Vegas during which she'd spotted a former Olympic decathlon champion and jumped in his lap. It was hard to tell who was more embarrassed—Bill or the decathlete. It certainly hadn't bothered Renie.

The trip to the airport took less than twenty minutes in such light traffic. When the shuttle stopped, Renie jumped up like a jack-in-the-box, hitting her head on the vehicle's roof.

"Ouch!" she cried. " 'S building's na' verra tall."

"Holy Mother." Somehow—artificial hip and all—Judith managed to haul her cousin out of the van. "Take deep breaths," she ordered Renie. "Try to stand up straight while we check our luggage."

Judith had one suitcase and a carry-on bag. Renie had three suitcases, including a fold-over, and a train case. She communicated with the baggage attendant by nodding or shaking her head.

Security was the next hurdle. Judith was thankful that the line hadn't yet grown to the long, snaking proportions that it would later in the day. There was no problem for either cousin. Renie marched through like an automaton. Judith suspected that airport employees were used to the frightened flyers who drank, took tranquilizers, and even used self-hypnosis to survive their ordeal. Indeed, Judith wasn't fond of airplanes, either.

The cousins had more than an hour to wait until their flight boarded. Renie seemed steadier on her feet, and was leading the way to the correct terminal. But halfway there, she stopped.

"Where's the bar?" she inquired, gazing all around her.

"They aren't open this early," Judith replied.

"Yes," Renie said in a certain voice. "At least one bar should be open. Passengers who've just flown in from Singapore or Barcelona don't care what time it is here."

"Why don't we sit so you can go back to sleep?" Judith suggested.

"I need another hit," Renie declared.

"No, you don't," Judith shot back as she grabbed Renie's arm. "Slow down. I can't keep up with you."

"You're as bad as Bill," Renie grumbled. "Okay, we'll sit. But first, let's get some Moonbeam's coffee. There's a kiosk right over there."

That sounded harmless to Judith, especially since she could use a caffeine jolt. It should also sober up Renie—except that might not be a good idea.

Renie, however, chose a decaf blend. After stopping at a news shop to pick up a couple of magazines, the cousins proceeded to their designated waiting area. As usual, Judith found the people who were gathering around them more interesting than the magazine articles: a mother coping with twins who were just beginning to walk; a Greek Orthodox priest with a beard as fine as angel hair; an unhappy teenage couple who apparently were going to go separate ways; and a burly man who looked like a lumberjack but was reading *Bon Appétit*.

It wasn't until almost half an hour had passed that Judith noticed Renie humming to herself and sliding around in her chair.

"You haven't finished your coffee," Judith pointed out as Renie took another sip.

"Sure have," Renie replied happily.

Judith peered into the paper cup and sniffed. "That's booze!" she snarled at her wayward cousin. "You put booze in your coffee!"

Renie tapped the train case at her side. "Backup," she murmured. "For spoilsports like you and Bill. Hmm-mm-hmm . . ."

Judith surrendered. "You'll be sorry. You'll be sick on the flight."

"So? I won't care," Renie replied.

"It's illegal to bring liquor aboard a plane," Judith pointed out.

"I'll finish it before we board," Renie countered. "Then I'll buy more when the beverage cart comes by."

"No, you won't." Judith reached down and snatched Renie's wallet out of her big black purse.

"Hey!" Renie cried. "Put that back!"

"No." Judith put the wallet in her own handbag and zipped it shut. "If you don't stop being a jackass, I'm going to turn in my ticket and go home. I mean it. This is no way to start a vacation."

Renie focused her eyes and stared at her cousin. "You're serious."

"Yes."

Renie continued staring at Judith. Finally she sighed. "Okay. I'll be good. But I'll be terrified."

"So will I," Judith said.

"I wonder how Bill and Joe will like being widowers."

"Shut up."

"Maybe we should take out that insurance they sell to passengers."

"Shut up."

"Maybe I should buy more gum. My ears really pop, especially on landing. *If* we land."

"Shut up."

At last, Renie did. She didn't say another word until the boarding call was announced. It was Judith who broke the silence after they got on the plane and were searching for their seats.

"You have the one by the window," Judith said. "Do you want me to sit there so you don't have to look out?"

"I like to," Renie replied. "Then I know where I'm crashing."

"Fine."

Renie sat down and immediately delved into her purse. *Not more booze,* Judith thought in dread. But her cousin pulled out her rosary and began to murmur prayers. She'd finished the last bead by the time they reached cruising altitude. For the rest of the flight, Renie gazed out the window in silence. She didn't speak again until they landed on the tarmac at San Francisco.

"We made it!" she exclaimed in an awed voice.

"No kidding," Judith replied.

"Maybe we can take the train back," Renie suggested.

Judith, who felt like a nervous wreck, said nothing. It wasn't the worst idea she'd ever heard. Whatever good the cruise might do her, it could be undone by another airline flight with Renie.

The rest of the itinerary went smoothly. A limo sent courtesy of Magglio Cruz transported them from the airport to the St. Francis Hotel on Union Square. Judith immediately felt the thrill of the city by the bay. She and Renie and Cousin Sue had visited San Francisco for the first time over forty years earlier. From the Barbary Coast to the Top of the Mark, they'd sensed history, mystery, sin, and sophistication. They had hills at home, but not like San Francisco's, with handsome old houses built side by side, or views of the Golden Gate Bridge and the bay with Alcatraz Prison as its centerpiece. It was the beatnik era of Jack Kerouac and the City Lights bookstore; the Purple Onion and the Hungry i; Lenny Bruce and Mort Sahl; the Kingston Trio and North

Beach; Vesuvio's and Lefty O'Doul's. The three cousins had lapped it up like so much spiked cream.

Now, after having visited San Francisco in the intervening years, Judith realized that she and the city had both aged. There was still beauty and glamour on its steep hills and abrupt coastline, but the contrast between now and then made her think of a happy hooker who had turned into an almost respectable dowager. Despite the change, Judith still loved the place.

Although the official check-in time wasn't until three in the afternoon, Mr. Cruz had seen to it that the cousins could immediately settle into their suite, where a bucket of champagne and various other amenities awaited them. They were invited to attend the VIP cocktail party buffet aboard the *San Rafael* that evening at six o'clock. Another limo would pick them up at five-forty. Thirties wear was requested.

Judith couldn't help but be impressed. "Is all this due to Bub or did you make some of your own threats?"

"I let Bub handle it," Renie said, gazing out the window at the San Francisco skyline. "We can actually see the city. There's no fog this morning. Let's order lunch."

"It's only ten o'clock. How about breakfast?"

"Sure. Any meal will do." Renie picked up a room-service menu that was encased in a leatherette cover. "Pancakes with ham and eggs and fruit and juice—"

"Don't tell me, tell whoever takes food orders," Judith said. "I want cereal and a slice of fruit."

"Coz!" Renie was scowling. "How many times have I told you to stop trying to lose weight? I swear I could slip you into an envelope and mail you home. I'll bet you don't weigh ten pounds more than I do, and you're five inches taller."

"Less weight is easier on my artificial hip," Judith contended. "Unlike me, you've never had to worry about what you eat."

"Again, I'm a freak of nature," Renie said, still with a frown. "I'm going to order for you."

And she did, requesting waffles, pork sausages, eggs, fruit, juice, coffee—and extra butter. Judith cleaned her plate. "Maybe I *was* hungry," she admitted.

An afternoon of leisure lay before them. The cousins decided to play tourists. During the next four hours, they visited Fisherman's Wharf, Ghirardelli Square, the Old Cathedral of St. Mary, and finally Chinatown, where they enjoyed a late Dungeness-crab lunch at the R&G Lounge. There was a breeze, scattering the pigeons and swaying the palm trees in Union Square, but not enough to unfurl more than the smallest of whitecaps out in the busy bay.

Judith had balked at riding the cable car, insisting that the hurried starts and stops could imperil her hip and Renie's shoulder. Luckily, some kindly San Franciscans—or other tourists—helped them get on and get off. During the ride, they heard a barrage of languages, just as they had done when walking the streets or standing on corners. French, Japanese, Russian, German, Chinese—San Francisco was a far more cosmopolitan city than their hometown.

By the time they finished sightseeing, the cousins were both tired. Renie had a headache from drinking so much; Judith had a headache from dealing with Renie. It was a little after three. Back in their suite, they each took a nap.

When the alarm woke them at four-thirty, Judith noticed that a sleek black folder with gold lettering had been slipped under their door. The attached note bore Renie's name.

"Here," Judith said, kicking the folder toward Renie, who was sitting on the brocade sofa sorting her cosmetics. "It's probably the notification of our checkout tomorrow. The ship sails at ten, right?"

"Right," Renie replied, bending over to pick up the folder. "This isn't for checkout, though," she went on, looking inside. "It's the guest list for the party tonight."

"Oh." Judith sat down to Renie. "Anybody you know?"

"Not really, except for Magglio Cruz and his assistant, Paul Tanaka. I've never met Mrs. Cruz." Renie handed the list to her cousin.

Judith scanned the names:

Magglio and Consuela Cruz
Paul Tanaka
Captain Randolph J. Swafford
May Belle Beales
Émile Grenier
Erma Giddon
Anemone Giddon
James Brooks
Ambrose Everhart
Horace Pankhurst
Carole Cecile Orr
Richard and Rhoda St. George
Serena Jones
Judith Flynn

Judith looked up from the folder. "Are we supposed to be impressed?"

Renie shrugged. "I'm guessing that only a select few from the passenger manifest have been invited to this function. It sounds like some of the ship's crew, a couple of people from the cruise line, and maybe two or three investors. We certainly wouldn't be on it if it weren't for Bub. Almost two thousand people are taking this maiden voyage."

"Then I *am* impressed," Judith said. "We're not just getting first-class treatment, presumably we're VIPs."

Retrieving the folder, Renie looked askance. "Not really. San Francisco high society is as snobbish as New York's. I figure the two Giddon women are mother and daughter or sisters. Captain Swafford is probably our skipper. And May Belle Beales—I know the name . . . Ah! She's better known as Dixie and is a cruise director for the line. But other than that, I'm guessing."

"St. George," Judith murmured. "That name sounds familiar, but I can't think why. What about you?"

Renie shook her head. "Nothing comes to mind." She stood up. "We'd better get ready. We're time-traveling back to the thirties."

The old clothes Judith had found in the basement were long on practicality if short on glamour. But Gertrude's wedding dress was perfect. She had been tall and relatively slim in those days. The simplicity of the white satin lines suited her daughter.

Renie looked up from her own toilette. "Does your mother know you're wearing that?" she asked.

"Are you kidding?" Judith responded. "She'd kill me."

"It's held up pretty well," Renie remarked, moving closer.

"I found Aunt Ellen's black turban with the rhinestone brooch," Judith said, holding the item up for her cousin's viewing. "We played dress-up with this stuff. You always made me wear the ugly outfits."

"That's because I was older and had better taste," Renie said, slipping into a black crepe evening gown. "How about this?"

"Elegant," Judith declared.

Renie unzipped a garment bag. "And this?" she asked, putting on a short silver-fox fur jacket. "It belonged to my other grandmother, the one who was nuts about clothes."

"Wow." Judith suddenly felt underdressed.

Renie grinned at her. "Granny had more than one evening coat." She reached into the garment bag again. "Here," she said, handing Judith an evening wrap that was two shades of red with black fur trim. "It really goes with your new hair color."

Judith was thrilled. After the drudgery of the past few months and the nerve-racking start to the trip, she was suddenly feeling giddy with excitement. "Oh, coz—I can't believe we're doing this!"

"We are," Renie affirmed. "Let's go find our chariot."

The limo was waiting outside. In the twilight, the cousins gawked a bit as they headed for Pier 35. They gawked even more when they caught their first sight of the *San Rafael*. The ship seemed huge, more like a building than a seagoing vessel.

From her work on the original brochure, Renie had memorized the basic facts. "Ninety-one thousand tons, nine hundred and sixty-five feet long, occupancy of seventeen hundred and fifty, cruising speed of twenty-four knots."

"I won't remember," Judith said as the chauffeur opened the limo's door.

"You don't need to," Renie replied. "What I really want to know is, how's the food?"

Judith noticed that the lettering on the ship's stern indicated Mexican registration. Liveried footmen stood at the bottom and top of the flower-festooned gangway. Old ballads from the thirties crooned over the speaker system.

As the cousins reached midship on what Judith calculated was the second deck from the top, two more men awaited them. The lean, handsome man with the dark mustache and sideburns was wearing a single-breasted tuxedo with black piping on the trousers and black patent leather shoes. He would, Judith thought, have been perfectly cast as a lounge lizard in a Depression-era melodrama. His bearded, heavyset companion wore a captain's formal dress uniform with enough gold braid to decorate Lord Nelson.

"Serena!" the man in the tuxedo exclaimed, kissing Renie on each cheek. "You look ravishing. *Muy bonita.*" He turned to Judith. "And this must be your charming cousin Señora Flynn."

"Thank you for letting me join Serena, Mr. Cruz," Judith said.

Magglio put a finger to his lips. "No, no. You must call me Mags. All of my friends do. And tonight we are all great friends, awaiting the cruise of a lifetime."

Judith allowed him to kiss her hand. "Please call me Judith. As a matter of fact, I've never been on a cruise of any kind."

Magglio smiled genially; so did Captain Randolph J. Swafford, who stepped forward to greet the newcomers. The cousins also smiled.

"Believe me, ladies," the captain said with an English accent, "this will be an unforgettable event in your lives."

The cousins both froze. How often had they heard similar words, only to discover that they'd much prefer to forget than to remember.

Chapter Four

Art Deco ruled the ship's design, from furniture to paneling to floors. Teak and mahogany flowed in clean curves and sleek symmetry. Glass was everywhere—tabletops, doors, wall inserts, and around the saloon where the party was being held.

"Remember," Renie said as they hesitated in the doorway, "we should get into a thirties mood. Snappy patter, wisecracks, screwball antics."

"For us, that sounds contemporary," Judith murmured as an elegant woman in a Grecian gown of flowing white pleats and three-inch gold sandals approached the cousins. Consuela Cruz definitely evoked the gilded edge of the Depression era. She was as lean as her husband, with jet-black hair combed away from a heart-shaped face.

"We're so glad you're here," she said to Renie. "There must have been a misunderstanding regarding your consulting fees.

Mags would never dream of cutting you loose so abruptly." Consuela pointed at a young man at the bar. "You know Paul Tanaka, of course?"

Renie nodded. "He often sat in for Mags at our design meetings." She nudged Judith's arm. "My cousin hasn't met him, though."

"We'll attend to that at once," Consuela said. "He's standing by the bar with Mrs. Giddon and Mr. Brooks. And do call me Connie."

Connie Cruz made a graceful gesture with her right hand. "I'll take you both around the room. Almost everyone is here, I think, except the St. Georges and Émile. Of course, Émile is the ship's purser, and may have business to take care of."

The tall, stout woman with the steel-gray hair swept up on top of her head was indeed imposing, Judith thought. It wasn't just her Amazonian size, but her piercing blue eyes and tight red lips.

"Serena Jones, Judith Flynn," Connie said, "meet Mrs. George Elwood Giddon."

Mrs. Giddon studied the cousins through a jewel-studded lorgnette. She was wearing a long, straight gown of black lace over white taffeta. A parure of diamonds and emeralds adorned her ears, neck, and wrists. The grande dame's imposing presence practically overwhelmed Judith. "A pleasure, I'm sure," Mrs. Giddon proclaimed in a lofty voice. "Who are you?"

"Who—or what?" Renie shot back with a deceptive smile. "The way you're looking through that lorgnette makes me feel like a microbe."

"I said *who*—not *what*," Erma Giddon snapped. "Are you anybody I should know?"

Renie gave a languid shrug. "My forebears came over on the *Mayflower*—first class. They were fleeing their bridge debts. Judith's ancestors were the first white settlers in our city, arriving circa 1850. Before that, they founded Philadelphia."

Mrs. Giddon didn't seem amused. Connie swiftly intervened. "For many years, Serena has been doing the graphic-design work for Mags. Mrs. Flynn is her cousin. Unfortunately, Mr. Jones couldn't get away from his work."

If Mrs. Giddon gave a damn, she didn't say so. Instead, she turned her back on the cousins and asked a server to fetch her evening wrap.

"It's chilly in here," Erma declared. "The captain must adjust the temperature before we sail. You know I'm inclined to chest colds, Consuela."

"Those cold germs must be really tough to get around her chest," Renie said, lowering her voice a mere notch.

"*Coz,*" Judith said in a warning tone.

But Erma had moved her chest and the rest of her away, commanding the youthful blond bartender to mix her a Manhattan.

"Make that Bud in a bottle for me," Renie called out from behind Mrs. Giddon. "Or mead, if you've got it. My family *really* goes way back."

Judith winced. She had a feeling that Renie was going to be difficult, at least as far as Mrs. Giddon was concerned.

"Please don't mind Erma," Connie begged from behind her hand. "She adheres to a very strict social code. Her own family dates back to one of the original San Francisco railroad magnates."

"Which one?" Renie shot back. "The guy who threw the fusies from the back of the crummy?"

Connie looked pained. "No, a Stanford or a Crocker or a Hopkins or a Huntington. You know—the Big Four."

"I thought they met at Yalta, not Nob Hill," Renie muttered. "Or was that just the Big Three?"

Connie's smile was feeble. "Here's Paul Tanaka. I must find Dixie Beales. She's providing a brief entertainment later on."

Paul greeted Renie with a hug. He was a squarely built young man, part Japanese and part African-American. The handshake he offered Judith was firm and the big smile seemed genuine. "You're Bill's stand-in, I hear," he said. Like the other men, except for the captain, he was wearing a tuxedo with thirties styling. And like several of the other guests, he was smoking. "What happened to him?"

Renie explained, stopping when the other young man who'd been at the bar came forward with a bottle of Budweiser. "I'm Jim Brooks," he said by way of introduction. "I'm attending medical school at Stanford."

"Congratulations," Judith said, releasing Jim's clammy hand. "I gather it's difficult to get accepted there."

Jim flushed slightly. "Yes . . . but sometimes knowing the right people helps." He gave Judith a sheepish look and nodded at a lithe, blonde who was talking to Captain Swafford. "I'm engaged to Anemone Giddon. Isn't she beautiful?"

Even from a distance, Judith could see that Mrs. Giddon's daughter was a winsome, lovely creature. In a lavender floral gown made of organza, she looked like a breath of spring.

"Is her father still living?" Judith inquired.

Jim shook his head. "He passed away from a heart attack almost ten years ago."

"Then," Judith asked, "who's the older bald man that just joined Mrs. Giddon?"

Jim Brooks snickered, a reaction befitting his boyish manner. "The great Horace Pankhurst," he replied. "Like Mrs. Giddon, he owns shares in the cruise line. He's also Erma's financial and legal adviser. Excuse me, I must see how Anemone's doing. The bartender asked me to deliver the beer to you, Mrs. Jones."

"Thanks," Renie said without enthusiasm.

Another member of the party had entered, surveying the gathering over a tall vase filled with calla lilies. He was small and spare, with a goatee and a slight limp.

"Émile Grenier," Paul informed the cousins as he followed their gaze to the newcomer. "He's the purser, and he's French. Ergo, he's the biggest snob of all."

"Quite a mixed background for these people," Judith remarked as Renie drifted toward the buffet, with its ice sculpture of a pheasant with a gold ring around its neck and a spray of frozen tail feathers. "Was Mr. Cruz born in Mexico?"

Paul nodded. "But his parents moved—or should I say swam—to the United States when he was a baby."

"A self-made man," Judith observed. "I have the greatest admiration for that type of person. Bloodlines don't impress me."

Paul smirked. "It also helps to marry the granddaughter of a wealthy ranchero from Argentina."

Judith's gaze shifted to the direction that Connie Cruz had taken upon leaving the little group. But their hostess was nowhere in sight. At that moment, the double doors opened to frame a striking couple with a large white dog. The trio stood very still for just a moment or two, giving the impression that they were striking a pose.

Judith gaped. "The St. Georges?"

Paul nodded. He, too, was looking at the handsome pair. Indeed, everyone was staring with the exception of Erma Giddon, who was fidgeting with an earring. Richard St. George wore a double-breasted midnight-blue tuxedo with silk piping and a gardenia in the left lapel. Slowly, deliberately, he removed his homburg hat, which matched his suit. His manner was casual, his mustache impeccable, and his expression was one of perpetual amusement.

By contrast, Rhoda St. George seemed indifferent to the stares. She was the epitome of thirties chic in a theater suit featuring a black velvet jacket lavishly embroidered with gold thread and the occasional small ruby, topaz, and seed pearl. The long skirt was dark green, gathered around the hips. But it was the hat that drew all eyes: black satin fitted to the head like a skullcap with two long, wide matching streamers, black veiling from hairline to neckline, and a golden rose nestled on top. Rhoda looked wonderfully self-confident. Judith couldn't blame her—any woman who could carry off such an ensemble deserved a medal that matched the gold and jewels on her jacket.

Yet in the end, it was the dog that evoked Renie's comment. "Sugliesmutievasa," she declared, returning from the buffet with her mouth full of shrimp.

Judith had grown accustomed to translating Renie's food-marred speech. "He's certainly an unusual dog, though not necessarily ugly. I don't think I've seen that breed before."

"It's not a breed," Renie asserted after swallowing the shrimp, "it's a conglomeration. It's got dreadlocks and no feet. It's a dog on wheels."

"The feet must be under all that curling fur," Judith said as the dog glided across the floor.

The St. Georges proceeded into the saloon, where they were effusively greeted by Émile Grenier, Paul Tanaka, Horace Pankhurst, and a platinum-haired beauty in a silver satin evening gown that clung to her curvaceous body like melted cheese on hot toast.

Renie leaned closer to Judith. "Where'd *she* come from?"

Judith shrugged. "The powder room, maybe. She's certainly a Jean Harlow look-alike. I'm beginning to feel like somebody's dowdy maid in Mother's old wedding dress."

"You look fine," Renie assured her. "Come on, get something to eat. You need to put on some pounds."

The cousins made their way to the buffet. Judith paused to admire the pheasant ice sculpture, which was holding up remarkably well.

"The caviar's great," Renie said, swiftly refilling her plate. "So are the wontons with crab and the oysters and the gravlax and—"

"I get the picture," Judith broke in. "It's a good thing you're wearing black. Your spillage doesn't show up very much."

"Huh?" Renie stared down at her bosom. "Oh. Right—it blends."

Connie Cruz had returned, looking a trifle worried. "Everyone, please enjoy the food and make sure you visit the bar in the next few minutes. Our cruise director, Dixie Beales, is going to play some of the great old songs from the thirties in the next room at seven o'clock."

"I never did get a cocktail," Judith noted, carefully choosing a selection of vegetables cut into exotic shapes. "Where's your beer?"

"In that potted palm by the model of the ship," Renie replied. "You know I hate beer. I just wanted to be annoying. Oh, for heaven's sake!" she cried, looking at her cousin's plate. "You're grazing, not eating. Here, have some smoked sockeye salmon *en croûte* and crab dumplings and anything else that might be considered real food. Get the servers to slice off a piece of rare Kobe beef from Japan. I intend to fatten you up."

"Well . . ." Watching a bearded young man wield a gleaming carving knife through a juicy roast tempted Judith. Somehow, she resisted. The cousins had, after all, eaten a late lunch. "Okay, I'll try a couple of dumplings," she said, allowing a waiter with a shaved head and a graying goatee to serve her. "Then we'd better get our drinks before the piano recital starts."

"I'm drinking Pepsi," Renie declared. "I can't bear the thought of alcohol after this morning."

"I don't blame you," Judith said drily. "Uh-oh," she whispered, "here come the St. Georges with Fido."

Richard St. George nodded at the cousins; Rhoda had lifted her veil and was smoking a cigarette through a silver holder. He ordered two double martinis; so did she. The big white dog with the long curls of fur stopped by the cousins and wheezed at Renie's hem.

"Nice doggie," Renie murmured, trying to disguise her antipathy for canines.

But the large animal moved closer, shedding white fur on Renie's black gown. "Beat it," Renie muttered, holding her hors d'oeuvres plate out of reach.

Wheezing and panting, the dog sat down on Renie's feet. "Excuse me," she said to Rhoda St. George, "would you please make your dog move? I'm immobilized by his very large—yet unusual—body."

Rhoda had just accepted two martini glasses. "Oh, don't mind Asthma," she said with a little laugh. "He's absolutely harmless. In fact, he has respiratory problems. I think he likes you. Or else he's collapsed." His mistress didn't seem particularly distressed by the idea.

Richard St. George, who also had both hands full of martinis, nudged Rhoda with his elbow. "Who's the blond dame with Pankhurst?"

"His latest trollop, darling," his wife replied. "Carole or Cecile or maybe both. I believe she's called CeeCee. Judging from her bust, DeeDee would be more . . . fitting." Rhoda turned back to the cousins. "I'm sorry, we haven't met. I'm Rhoda St. George and this is my slightly inebriated husband, Rick."

Rick had almost finished his first martini. "Swell," he said sarcastically. "You're giving me a poor send-off."

"Don't worry, darling," Rhoda replied. "These ladies have eyes."

"And feet," Renie put in. "I'm Serena Jones and I'd like to move mine. Feet, that is."

"Oh." Rhoda looked down at Asthma, who appeared to have fallen asleep, though it was hard to tell with all the long curls covering not only his body but his face. "Do move him, Ricky," she implored. "Otherwise, Ms. Jones is going to charge him rent."

Setting his now-empty glass on the bar, Rick searched through the fur around the dog's neck, presumably for a collar. "He's a Komondor," Rick said, "a guardian breed, and sometimes considered a working dog. Except I'm afraid he doesn't work very well anymore, poor fellow. Come on, Asthma, strut what's left of your stuff."

"He's . . . big," Renie said. "He must weigh over a hundred pounds."

Rick St. George finally managed to get the dog to move off of Renie's feet. "Yes," he agreed. "Asthma weighs in at a hundred and twenty, or, according to my darling wife, ten pounds more than she does. Good boy!" he said, patting the animal.

Feeling left out, Judith introduced herself. "I'm Serena's cousin."

Both St. Georges expressed their delight, and sounded almost sincere. They were immediately pounced upon by Captain Swafford.

Finally able to put in her drink request, Judith ordered a scotch rocks from Ray the bartender, whose smile was that of a young man eager to please. "Will Glenfiddich do?"

"Definitely," Judith responded.

But there was no Pepsi for Renie, Ray informed her in an apologetic tone. Would a Coke be acceptable? It would, Renie said, between mouthfuls of marinated chicken.

A gong sounded and a sliding door opened at the far end of the room. A golden-haired middle-aged woman wearing a black and red gown that evoked the Orient, held out both arms.

Renie spoke softly in Judith's ear. "May Belle Beales, cruise director—better known as Dixie," Renie said to Judith. "I recognize her from the brochure photos."

"Good evenin', honored guests," Dixie said in a soft Southern drawl. "It's mah pleasure to welcome y'all to an interlude of piano music from that long-ago era of the 1930s. Durin' the cruise itself, we'll have a big band—a verra big band—to play for your listenin' and dancin' enjoyment. Tonight is just a li'l ol' sample, courtesy of mah meager talents. Please join me in the other half of the saloon." With a gracious gesture, Dixie signaled for everyone to join her.

The cousins fell in behind Jim Brooks and Anemone Giddon. The ethereal-looking young woman glanced over her shoulder. "Hi," she said in a breathy voice. "I'm Anemone. Jim says you're the Cousins."

Renie grimaced. "You make us sound like a rock band."

Anemone giggled. "It's how I remember people. I can't ever recall anybody's name, so I give them a description." She pointed up ahead to the St. Georges. "They're the Dipsos, the captain is the Captain, Émile Whoozits is the Purser, my mother's lawyer is—"

"We get it," Renie broke in. "The Cousins get it."

The other half of the saloon was lighted only by mica-shaded wall sconces. Comfortable armchairs had been placed at small round tables. As her eyes adjusted to the demilight, Judith could make out a black grand piano on a cabaret-type stage.

"Sorry about this," Renie whispered in apology. "I didn't know there'd be entertainment that we'll have to pretend to enjoy even if we'd rather be hung from the yardarm."

"That's okay," Judith said, scanning the short program that had been left at each table. "She's going to play just six pieces. Piano arrangements inspired by Duke Ellington, Tommy Dorsey, Glenn Miller, Benny Goodman, and Artie Shaw."

Dixie Beales had arranged herself on the bench. She gazed at the sheet music, flexed her fingers, and scowled. Getting up, she moved to the edge of the stage and spoke to Émile Grenier. He stood up and limped to the rear of the piano.

"A moment only," Dixie announced. "The piano lid hasn't been fully raised."

Anemone and Jim were sitting at the table next to Judith and Renie. "The Fun Lady," Anemone remarked from behind her hand. "I bet she's wearing a wig."

Judith smiled politely. Renie remained immobile.

Dixie had moved to assist Émile. Their efforts were obscured from the audience by the piano itself.

"The lid must be stuck," Jim Brooks said. "Maybe I should help. Émile doesn't look like the strongest guy in the world."

"The purser's small but wiry," Anemone asserted, looking pleased with herself for making the observation. "Though he has a bad leg."

"I'd like to hear some Cole Porter," said Horace Pankhurst at the table adjoining the engaged couple. The big man used a cock-tail napkin to pat at perspiration on his thick neck.

"Cold what?" his blond companion asked. "You mean Cold-play? They're a great band. They're Brits, you know."

Horace looked as if he didn't know. "Oh? Well, whatever the music, it's taking long enough to get that piano open. Somebody ought to take a crowbar to it."

"You wouldn't want to use a crowbar on an expensive piano," Renie noted. "My good friend Melissa Bargroom, who just happens to be our newspaper's music critic, says that an instrument like that costs—"

A loud, piercing shriek from Dixie Beales cut through Renie's words. Both cousins stared at the stage. Dixie had disappeared, apparently having fallen to the floor. Émile suddenly went out of sight, too, presumably coming to the cruise director's aid.

Captain Swafford was on his feet. So was Rick St. George. A sense of apprehension engulfed the saloon.

"Stay put, everybody," Rick said in a loud if somewhat slurred voice. "I'll see what's going on."

The other guests seemed to defer to Rick, who bounded onstage, martini glass still in hand. Rick also disappeared behind the piano, but almost immediately resurfaced along with Émile Grenier.

"Is there a doctor in the house?" Rick asked, his speech no longer slurred.

Rhoda St. George burst into derisive laughter. "Oh, Ricky, can't you find a better line than that old cliché?"

But her husband looked serious and ignored the remark, casting his eyes around the room.

Jim stiffened in his chair before looking every which way. "Ah . . ." he began, awkwardly shifting his lanky frame into a standing position. "Um . . . I'm a medical student at Stanford."

"Then you'd better get up here, kiddo," Rick said. "Dixie Beales has passed out." He paused while Jim came forward. "Unfortunately, there's nothing you can do for the corpse in the piano."

Chapter Five

Damned funny, St. George!" Horace Pankhurst shouted, slapping his thick thigh. "I should've brought my harmonica as a backup!"

Judith, however, didn't believe that Rick St. George was trying to be funny. He certainly didn't look it, judging from the worried creases in his forehead.

Apparently Consuela Cruz didn't see any humor in the situation, either. She was on her feet, slim body trembling. Captain Swafford tried to calm her, but she broke free of his restraining hands and staggered toward the stage.

"Is it Mags?" she cried. "Is it Mags?"

Judith and Renie held back as the others—except for Erma Giddon—stampeded up to the piano. Captain Swafford, who was hurrying to join Rick, intervened. "Hold on!" he shouted. "Stand back! Please!"

Renie glared at Judith. "I don't believe this. Maybe it's really an act."

Erma Giddon was fanning herself with a lace-edged handkerchief. "Trouble follows Rick and Rhoda St. George just like their loathsome dog," she said, without making eye contact with the cousins. "They're like characters out of a 1930s detective movie. Why everyone makes such a fuss over that pair, I'll never know."

"I like them," Renie declared, at her most contrary.

Still not looking at the cousins, Erma sniffed. "They're frivolous, shallow dilettantes."

Renie pulled Judith out of Erma's hearing range. "Aren't you curious? Don't you want to find out what's going on?"

Judith shook her head. "The less I know, the better. In fact, I think we ought to get off this ship. *Now.*"

"I can't." Renie's expression was bleak.

Angrily, Judith grabbed her cousin's arm. "What do you mean, you can't? We've got to leave while everyone is distracted."

"I mean," Renie said grimly, "that I have to know who's in that piano. It could affect my livelihood."

Judith noted that a half-dozen white-coated waiters had surrounded the piano to keep the guests at bay. The cabaret was cloudy with cigarette and cigar smoke, as if the city's famous fog had crept inside the ship. Rick St. George was holding a hysterical Connie Cruz in his arms. "I'm afraid," Rick said, "that Maglio Cruz is dead."

Gasps went up from the other guests. Judith started for the cloakroom. "That's it. We're out of here."

Renie, looking grim, didn't budge. "I knew it. There goes my retainer."

"Coz!" Judith exclaimed. "Don't say things like that!"

Renie shrugged. "We need the money. We have children, remember?"

"Fine," Judith snapped. "You stay. I go." She kept moving.

Captain Swafford's voice boomed out: "No one leaves the premises! No one leaves the ship! I'm posting a senior officer at the gangplank in case anyone tries to disembark. This is a serious matter."

Incredulous voices broke out in the saloon. One of them was Judith's. "Damn!" She grabbed Renie by the arm. "It's your fault! If you'd come with me a few minutes ago, we could've escaped!"

"If Bill had come with me, you wouldn't be here acting like a twit!" Renie shot back. "Bill knows the importance of making a buck!"

Judith forced herself to simmer down. Briefly, she glanced toward the stage. Connie had collapsed in Rick's arms and was being carried to a divan at the far side of the room. Dixie was on her feet, walking to the same divan with the aid of Jim Brooks. Captain Swafford, Rick, and Émile were conferring near the piano.

"Okay," Judith said in a reasonably calm voice, "your father was a seagoing man. Is there a way to get off of a ship other than via the main gangplank?"

"Sure," Renie retorted. "Jump and swim. Or would you prefer lowering a lifeboat?"

Judith's expression turned sour. "You can't swim."

"So? I'm not leaving."

Frustrated, Judith gazed around the cabaret. Anemone clung to her mother; Horace Pankhurst was sweating more profusely; Paul Tanaka looked utterly stunned. Between sips of her martini, Rhoda St. George offered words of encouragement—or condolence. CeeCee Orr had lighted two cigarettes at once and was drinking out of a fifth of vodka. Maybe, Judith thought unkindly, she'd pass out, too.

Renie was moving slowly toward the stage. Reluctantly, Judith followed.

"Look, Skipper," Rick was saying, "I know one of the big wheels at police headquarters. Biff McDougal is tops when it comes to discreet investigations. With his help we can avoid damaging publicity."

Horace Pankhurst spoke up from the stage's edge. "As an attorney, I must advise you, Captain, to take all precautions against lawsuits that might arise from this unfortunate accident. It *is* an accident, isn't it?"

An accident, Judith thought. *That would be good.* Except, she realized, not for Magglio Cruz.

"We've called in the ship's doctor," Swafford replied. "We'll wait for him to announce the cause of Mr. Cruz's death."

"That's why we're leaving him in the piano," Rick said as he looked down at his wife, who was scratching Asthma's curly head. "Rhoda, be an angel and call Biff McDougal. He's probably at home." He winked.

"Right, darling," Rhoda replied, winking back as she opened her bejeweled evening bag to get her cell phone.

"Just a moment, Mr. St. George," Erma Giddon said in her loud contralto, "who, may I ask, is in charge here?"

With an ingenuous expression, Rick gazed around the room. "Who else but Captain Swafford? I'm merely an innocent bystander." His hazel eyes shifted to the sliding doors, which were still closed. Rick, mouthing what appeared to be the word *booze,* looked questioningly at the captain. Swafford nodded consent. "Ray," Rick said to the bartender, "would you mind opening the bar? I believe Mrs. Cruz and Ms. Beales could use some brandy. And I could certainly do with another martini."

Some of the guests, including the Giddon women, Horace, and a wobbly CeeCee Orr hurried out of the cabaret section. Others lingered: Jim Brooks was still tending to Connie and Dixie on the divan. Émile Grenier hovered over the trio. Rhoda hauled Asthma to an upright position. Captain Swafford stood erect by the stage, as if he were willing to go down with his ship.

"Who is this St. George anyway?" Renie demanded of Paul.

Paul looked sheepish. "He's what you might call a man-about-town. Rich beautiful wife, social entrées everywhere, amusing company even when he—and she—are somewhat blotto. He also considers himself something of a sleuth."

Judith snapped her fingers. "That's where I've heard the name! Isn't he known as the Gin Man?"

Paul nodded. "For obvious reasons. How did you come across him?"

"I saw his name on a Web site for amateur sleuths," Judith started to explain. "I'd cross-referenced my . . . ah . . ."

Judith was rescued from explaining her own Internet status as "FATSO" by a shout from Émile Grenier. "We need help with *les dames* here," he said in his French-accented voice. "Madame Cruz wishes to lie down in her stateroom, and Madame Beales refuses to remain with the . . . piano any longer."

"When's the doctor coming?" Paul inquired, going to the divan. "That is, the . . . real doctor."

Jim flushed. "Hey, I'll be a real doctor in three years."

"They probably can't wait that long," Renie put in. "The commencement ceremony would take too much out of them."

"Dr. Selig is on his way?" Connie bit her lower lip. "I forgot about him. He should have been invited tonight." She put both hands to her head. "Oh, what am I saying? How can I be concerned with social gaffes when my poor husband is dead?"

Judith figured that as long as she and Renie were stuck aboard the ship, they might as well make themselves useful. "Can we help?" she asked, moving closer to the divan.

Connie and Dixie both stared at Judith as if they'd never seen her before. Indeed, Judith realized that Dixie Beales hadn't met her or Renie. "I'm Judith Flynn," she said quietly. "This is my cousin Serena. We can help you get settled in your staterooms if you'd like."

Recognition dawned on Connie. "Would you?"

Émile, however, intervened, drawing himself up to his full height, but not tall enough to meet Judith eye to eye. "*I* shall take care of Madame Cruz," he declared. "You may tend to Madame Beales."

"Okay," Judith said, noting the apologetic expression on Connie's face. "We'll do that."

Émile and Paul helped the distraught women to their feet. "What can I do to be of help?" Paul inquired of the purser.

"Nothing," Émile replied, putting a supporting arm around Connie's slim waist. "I'm a crew member, reporting to *le capitaine*. You, Monsieur Tanaka, are support staff."

Paul's dark skin turned even darker. "Is that so? You seem to forget that I'm Magglio Cruz's second in command. Unless the board of directors say otherwise, I'm in charge of this whole operation."

"We shall see," Émile retorted. "The board members— including Madame Giddon and Monsieur Pankhurst—may have other ideas."

"For God's sake!" Connie cried. "Shut the hell up and get me out of here!"

"*Bien sûr,* madame!" Emile said, snapping the fingers of his free hand. "*Eh bien,* to your stateroom!"

Judith offered Dixie her arm. "Just tell us where to go," she murmured.

"Mah evenin' bag," Dixie gasped. "Please, would y'all get it? Ah left it on the piano bench."

Judith nodded, heading back toward the raised platform. Captain Swafford stopped her as soon as she approached the piano. "Please, madam. You can't come any further."

Judith glanced around the captain's imposing form. There was nothing on the bench. "Dixie left her evening bag up here. Do you see it?"

The captain scowled at Judith, but looked around the immediate area. "Perhaps it fell under the piano," he said impatiently. "We can find it later."

Judith had moved a few paces. She could see the piano from the side. To her dismay, she could also see part of Magglio Cruz's body. The black tuxedo seemed to shine like onyx.

But she spotted something else: A beaded evening bag lay a few feet from the piano. "Captain," she called. "I see it. Come over here."

With a heavy sigh, Swafford trudged to the place where Judith was pointing. His sturdy form wobbled slightly as he bent down to pick up the mislaid bag and tossed it at Judith. "Here," he said gruffly. "Now please move away."

Judith caught the bag, but it slipped out of her fingers. Gingerly, she bent down to collect the blue-beaded purse. She wanted to linger, but a crew member motioned for her to leave. Reluctantly, Judith rejoined Renie and Dixie.

"Oh, thank you!" Dixie exclaimed. "Mah best lipstick and powder are inside. Oops!" She, too, dropped the bag.

"Allow me," Renie said, snatching the elusive purse off the floor. "This thing's kind of slippery. It feels like it's got some kind of goop on it."

"Ah'll worry about that later," Dixie said wearily. "Right now, Ah just want to col-*lapse*."

Dixie, in fact, could barely walk, forcing the cousins to half carry her out of the saloon and down the companionway.

"Two decks down, aft," Dixie finally said as they found an elevator toward the stern.

None of the women spoke again until they reached the small

but well-appointed stateroom. Dixie lay down on the bed and kicked off her shoes. "Ah have aspirin in mah cosmetic case. It should be in the lavatory. There's bottled water in the itsy-bitsy fridge."

Renie went to fetch the pills and a glass for the bottled water. Judith asked if she could do anything to make Dixie more comfortable.

"Ah'd like to take off this evenin' dress," she replied in a fretful voice. "Ah feel all damp and clammy, like the very grave itself. There's a kimono in the wardrobe."

After a brief search, Judith found the brightly colored kimono. Dixie had removed her gown and tossed it over a chair. She let Judith help her put the kimono on and then fell back on the bed. Renie returned with aspirin and water.

"Thank you," Dixie said in a feeble voice. "Heavens to Betsy, Ah can't believe what's happenin'. It feels like a big ol' nightmare. How in the world did poor Mags end up in that piano?"

"How he ended up *dead* in the piano is more to the point," Judith said grimly. She couldn't resist asking a question. "Did you see any blood?"

Dixie, who was very pale, shuddered. "Ah don't think so. But all it took was one look, and Ah was . . . gone. Though," she added after a brief pause, "he did look wet."

Judith frowned. "Wet? As if water had been poured over him?"

"No, not like that," Dixie replied. "His clothes. At least what Ah could see of them."

Judith told herself she had to squelch her natural curiosity. She wasn't getting mixed up in whatever had happened to Magglio Cruz. Furthermore, her hip was bothering her. She dragged a chair over to the bed and sat down. But she couldn't resist one last query. "You fainted before you could take his pulse, right?"

Dixie frowned. "Ah must have."

The wind, which could turn a San Francisco spring day into an arctic chill, had risen off the bay. Judith felt the ship move ever so slightly in its moorings. She glanced at Renie, who had sat down in an armchair near a large horizontal porthole. *She can take over,* Judith thought. *It's her wallet that's involved.*

As if on cue, Renie spoke. "So who actually discovered Mr. Cruz was dead? Émile? Rick St. George?"

Dixie shook her head. "Ah don't recall."

"Rick, I'll bet," Renie said. "Émile seemed to be helping you. Is that right?"

Dixie shook her head again, this time with more emphasis. "Ah don't know. Ah was out cold."

Renie made a face. "This is hopeless. We can't figure anything out until we know what killed Magglio Cruz."

"His heart?" Dixie suggested. "People who have heart attacks sweat a whole lot. Maybe that's why his clothes were wet."

Renie looked skeptical. "And in the midst of the heart attack, he jumped into the piano?"

Judith frowned. "It beats the alternative."

The cousins exchanged meaningful glances. "Yes," Renie said slowly, "it does."

Dixie raised her head off the pillow. "What do you mean?"

Neither Judith nor Renie replied.

In the moments that followed, all three women remained silent. Judith could hear the slight groan of the ship, as if it were flexing its muscles in the wind. Maybe the *San Rafael* was anxious to get under way. Maybe the luxury liner was trying to tell them something.

Eventually, Dixie fell asleep. The cousins tiptoed out of the stateroom, but once they were in the passageway, they weren't sure what to do next.

"The saloon?" Renie finally said.

"I suppose. We've done all we can for Dixie. The doctor should be calling on her after he sees Mrs. Cruz."

The saloon, which had seemed so glamorous little more than an hour earlier, was now virtually deserted. Dirty dishes and glasses were piled everywhere, the sumptuous buffet had deteriorated, and the pheasant ice sculpture had begun to melt. The only people left were a couple of white-jacketed waiters, Rick St. George, and a burly man in a rumpled raincoat and a battered hat whom the cousins didn't recognize.

Rick spotted Judith and Renie right away. "Everyone's in the Sequoia Bar," he informed them. "Same deck, turn left on your way out."

Renie, however, wasn't so easily dismissed. "Biff McDougal?" she said, moving toward the man in the raincoat, who was chewing on a toothpick. "My husband has told me so much about you."

The toothpick remained in place as Biff's small brown eyes peered at Renie. "Your husband? Who's he?" the detective demanded, speaking around the toothpick.

"Bill Jones—better known to you as William Jones, PhD and criminal psychologist," Renie replied, putting out her hand. "Didn't the two of you work together on that serial arsenic-poisoning case in the Embarcadero a few years back?"

Biff moved his hat and scratched his balding head. "The Embarcadero? Arsenic? Oh!" He slapped his forehead. "You mean the Mission district. It was cyanide, as I recall. Was that Dr. Jones? I thought his name was Smith."

"Smith, Jones, Brown—a common mistake with such a common name," Renie said, smiling brightly. "If he'd known I was going to run into you, he would've sent his best. Bill always told me you knew the best watering holes in San Francisco."

"Har har." Biff chuckled. "You're darned tootin'. Some of those places are gone now, all this upscale stuff taking over, but in the old days . . ." He chomped away at the toothpick, apparently yearning for the seedy spots of yore.

Rick put a firm hand on Biff's wide shoulder. "Nostalgia has its charms," he said, "but we've got business to do here, remember? And we mustn't keep Mrs. Jones and her cousin from joining the others. I'm sure their nerves are as shattered as everyone else's."

Rick St. George couldn't possibly guess that the cousins were too experienced in sudden death to feel only a slight fraying around the edges. "Yes," Renie seemingly agreed, "we must leave you to your investigation. I don't suppose you've had time to figure out how poor Mr. Cruz died?"

Biff's smile was crooked, half affable, half sneering, though the toothpick stayed put. "Couldn't tell you if we knew," he said. "This is all hush-hush stuff."

But Renie looked disturbed. "We're terribly upset," she said. "We feel compelled—as ship passengers—to know if Mr. Cruz died of natural causes. And if he did, was it from one of those odd viruses that runs amok on cruises? Of course, there's always another possibility." She paused to let her meaning sink in. "What's our status? Does the *San Rafael* sail tomorrow? What did Dr. Selig say?"

"The sawbones is in," Biff replied, looking uncomfortable. "In Mrs. Cruz's stateroom, that is. He checked out Mr. Cruz. Let's just say that even as we speak, the stiff's going ashore for an autopsy."

Rick chuckled. "Oh, come on, Biff, these two aren't your nickel-and-dime dames. Nobody's getting off this ship tonight—

except for the late Mr. Cruz, of course. Thus, these ladies can figure out for themselves that there must be a suspicion of foul play."

Biff grimaced. "Yeah . . . well . . . the truth is, we can't be sure yet. Let's put it this way—we can't rule out accidental death or"—he sucked in his breath and tucked in his shirt—"homicide."

Renie nodded. "I understand."

So did Judith. All too well.

Chapter Six

I can't believe," Judith said to Renie as they sought out their stateroom, "that you tell even bigger whoppers than I do. Bill as a criminal psychologist? Bill advising the San Francisco Police Department? Bill delving into the mind of a serial poisoner? How did you know they ever had one down here?"

"I read about it in the newspaper," Renie replied. "It was years ago, not long after we had the product tampering in the suburbs at home. I just couldn't remember the details."

They had reached the stateroom suites toward the ship's bow. Judith noticed that each one bore the name of a famous movie star from the 1930s: Clark Gable, Ronald Colman, Claudette Colbert, Marlene Dietrich, Greta Garbo, Errol Flynn, Gary Cooper.

"You were playing detective," Judith accused Renie.

"Of course," Renie replied. "Somebody has to. I don't want to lose my link with Cruz Cruises, and thus my income."

Judith didn't respond.

Guilt was setting in. How many times had she coerced Renie into helping her solve a crime? Oh, her cousin might gripe and argue and be mulish, but basically Renie was a good sport. More than that—Renie had been willing to risk her neck for Judith's forays into detective work.

"If you want to try to solve this thing—whatever it may be," Judith amended, "I won't hinder you."

"Thanks," Renie said in a sour tone as they reached the door to their stateroom, which was named for Mae West. "Huh. I'm not sure I like being in a suite that's named for a lifejacket."

"I suppose," Judith went on as Renie fumbled with the key card, "you could use me as a sounding board."

Renie turned away from the door and looked straight into Judith's eyes. "Look. If I'd even thought for one second that we'd get mixed up in another mess, I wouldn't have asked you to come along. In fact, I wouldn't have come myself. Bill would have had a fit. You know how he dislikes having his routine disrupted."

"It's hardly your fault," Judith said as Renie reslid the key card through the slot in the door. "If anything," Judith went on, "I blame myself. I feel like a murder magnet."

"Don't be stupid," Renie responded. The red light still blinked after the third try. "Whatever happened to Magglio Cruz would have been the same whether you were here or eight hundred miles away at home."

"You're just trying to make me feel—" Judith stopped and snatched the key card from Renie, who had resorted to kicking at the door. "Let me do this. You are utterly inept at this sort of thing."

The green light flashed immediately. Judith offered her cousin a small smile; Renie growled in response.

But they both gaped in admiration when they turned up the torchère lamps to study their quarters in all its Art Deco elegance. The walls were paneled in golden mahogany; the sleek furniture was accented with gleaming chrome; the separate bedroom's dressing-table mirror was large and round, its beveled edge made of crystal.

"Nice," Renie murmured, going out onto the veranda after inspecting the rooms. "My God, look at the view!"

Judith joined her cousin. The ship seemed tucked in between the city's hills, surrounded by shimmering lights. Although the veranda was enclosed, they could hear the wind and the waves. Judith could smell the salt air, invigorating as nectar. It was easy to imagine that they were already at sea.

"This would be heaven," she said as they returned to the sitting room and collapsed on the navy-blue couch, "if Magglio Cruz hadn't died."

Renie studied Judith's worried face. "Hasn't it occurred to you that if foul play was involved, we'll be among the leading suspects?"

Judith grimaced. "I suppose that's true. Even counting the crew members, not that many people are on board tonight."

"When Joe finds out," Renie noted, "he'll pitch a five-star fit."

"We're only speculating about murder."

"No matter how discreet," Renie murmured, "this is bound to leak out to the media. Our mothers will be beside themselves."

"There was no shot, no blood that Dixie noticed, probably no obvious wound."

"Joe will never let you out of his sight again. You'll become a virtual prisoner at Hillside Manor."

"Was that piano always onstage? Or was it moved there just before we went into the cabaret? And why did Magglio Cruz disappear so quickly after we arrived?"

"I doubt that Joe will ever let you see me again. That's an unbearable thought."

Judith stared at Renie. "What did you say?"

"I said that Joe won't ever—"

Judith waved a hand. "I know, I know. But I was only half listening. Dammit, you've got me going. But *I'm not really getting involved.*"

Renie sighed. "I know."

"I mean it," Judith reiterated.

"I got it," Renie replied. "I already said I'd do it. It's my money."

"So you told me."

"Stop it!" Judith barked.

Renie looked at the two clocks on the wall, which displayed only chrome hands and numbers. "I see we're two hours ahead of the Cook Islands. It's eight-fifty here and six-fifty there."

"So what?"

"So it's too soon to go to bed, even if we did get up early," Renie explained, standing up and going to the minibar to check out the supplies. "Besides, I feel kind of wired. Ah, Pepsi. Good."

"I feel very tired," Judith replied. "I wouldn't mind some of that bottled water, though."

Renie removed the bottled water from the small fridge and handed it to Judith. "I think I'll wander around the ship. You know, check out the spa and the swimming pool and the gym. See you later."

"*The gym?*" Judith knew that Renie's idea of exercise was elbowing other women out of the way at a Nordquist's designer sale. "Hold it." Wearily, she rose from the sofa. "I know what you're up to, and you aren't going alone. You know darned well it could be dangerous."

Renie smiled. "How sweet of you, coz. Maybe we won't walk

very far. I wonder who these other suites are assigned to? I'll check the passenger list. There should be one on the table with the menus and other cruise information."

Sure enough, the passenger manifest was included with a ship diagram, safety regulations, navigational charts, and other helpful data.

"Erma and Anemone Giddon are in the W. C. Fields suite," Renie noted. "Jim Brooks and Horace Pankhurst are across the way in the Ronald Colman and the Marx Brothers suites. Let's start with the Giddons."

But the moment the cousins entered the passageway, they saw Rhoda St. George, urging her wheezing Komondor to keep moving.

"Is that dog okay?" Judith asked.

Despite all the commotion, Rhoda's stunning ensemble was impeccable, including the veiled hat, which remained firmly in place. "No, actually," she said, with a fond glance at Asthma. "He was born with a respiratory condition. That's why we could never show him—not that we really wanted to. It's such a bother. Unfortunately, this breed is prone to allergies. They also have hip problems."

"Who doesn't?" Judith murmured.

Rhoda looked curious. "You do?"

Judith nodded. "I've had a hip replacement."

"You move quite naturally," Rhoda said. "Asthma will have to get two hip replacements after we return from this cruise. Are you a dog owner?"

"No," Judith replied. "We have a cat."

"Cats are very lovable," Rhoda remarked. "And so affectionate. You must enjoy spending time relaxing with your pet curled up on your lap."

"Ah . . ." Judith winced. "Our cat's not exactly like that.

He's . . . independent." *As well as ornery, bad-tempered, and more self-centered than most of his breed.*

"Oh." Rhoda's amber eyes danced. "I understand." She turned to Renie. "And you?"

"We have a Holland dwarf lop named Clarence. He's adorable. And cuddly. Clarence has quite an extensive wardrobe. In fact, he has his own cruise wear, including a small Speedo."

"Really." Rhoda arched her perfect eyebrows. She actually seemed intrigued. "Does he enjoy wearing clothes?"

"In a way," Renie hedged. "Often, he prefers to eat them."

"Yes," Rhoda said thoughtfully. "But every animal has its own flaw—or fetish. Asthma, for instance, can be very impatient when we have to curl his fur. That cordlike effect is achieved by using soup cans. The poor darling only cooperates if we use beef noodle."

Renie nodded solemnly. "Clarence is opposed to any kind of grooming. He tends to hide behind the furnace on his little deck chair."

Rhoda leaned forward. "While wearing his Speedo?"

"No. Actually, the swimsuit was completely consumed last summer."

Judith felt like screaming. The growing bond between Renie and Rhoda was making her fractious. Usually, it was Judith who chatted amiably with possible suspects and witnesses while Renie kept to the background.

There was a pause before Rhoda spoke again. "I must get Asthma settled for the night. Why don't you come into our suite and have a drink? We're just a couple of doors down. Actually, we have two suites—one for us and one for Asthma." She continued walking, urging the dog along. "We're in the William Powell and Myrna Loy suites, just beyond yours."

"That figures," Renie whispered to Judith as they followed

Rhoda at a short distance. "They remind me of Nick and Nora Charles from the old *Thin Man* movies."

"Do they?" Judith was looking grim. "I never liked those films. Their solutions were too glib."

"That was because they were really screwball comedies," Renie replied.

"Whatever," said Judith.

The St. Georges' suite was similar in style and layout to Judith and Renie's. Rhoda urged the cousins to make themselves a drink—along with a martini for her.

"Maybe," Renie said as Judith revived her old skills from her bartending job at the Meat & Mingle, "I could bear a sip of Drambuie."

"They've got everything," Judith replied, studying the mirrored shelves above the teak bar. "Especially gin. I'll stick to scotch." Maybe a stiff drink would improve her disposition.

The St. Georges also had plenty of luggage, some of which was piled in a corner of the sitting room. Two large steamer trunks with shiny brass studs on hand-tooled leather boasted travel stickers from New York, Paris, London, Sydney, Hong Kong, Singapore, St. Petersburg, Buenos Aires, Capetown, and other foreign cities.

"It looks like they've been everywhere," Judith remarked, handing Renie a small snifter of Drambuie.

"And done everything, I should imagine," Renie replied.

"I wish we'd sent our bags ahead," Judith said, adding a dash of water to her scotch rocks. "We'll have to sleep in what we've got on."

"You're right." Renie tasted her Drambuie as Rhoda emerged from the adjoining suite.

"Asthma is tucked in," she informed the cousins, finally removing her hat and her bejeweled jacket. "Ah." She saw the martini glass on the bar. "Thank you. This has been a really tiring event. By the way, did I overhear you mention not having any essentials on board?"

"Unfortunately," Renie replied, "we don't. We didn't expect to spend the night here."

Rhoda picked up the ship's phone. "I can fix that. Will carry-ons do or would you prefer all of it?"

Judith had to admit to herself that Rhoda was not only friendly—if almost as goofy as Renie—but also helpful. "Yes, the carry-ons are fine. We both keep what we need most in case the airline loses the rest of our baggage."

Rhoda nodded. "The St. Francis?"

Judith confirmed that they were staying there.

Rhoda keyed in a number and made the request. "There you go. It shouldn't take long for the bags to arrive."

The three women seated themselves in a trio of dark red armless chairs placed in a semicircle around a glass and chrome coffee table.

"Did you know Mr. Cruz very well?" Renie inquired.

Rhoda slipped a cigarette into her silver holder. "Yes. I met him years ago in Los Angeles. He was just starting out with a small sightseeing line out of San Pedro. Actually," she went on, reaching for a cigarette lighter that matched the holder, "I met Connie first, before either of us was married. I'd come out from New York with my father to watch one of his horses run in the Santa Anita Handicap. Connie's father was a well-known owner and trainer. Two of his Thoroughbreds finished in the money at Belmont and several others were big winners in Europe, especially at Longchamps, outside of Paris. Connie had seen quite a bit of the world and was quite sophisticated. We found we had a great deal in common."

"So the two of you hit it off," Judith remarked, telling herself that she wasn't sleuthing, merely displaying her natural interest in other people.

Rhoda nodded. "By background, Connie was a California girl who knew all the best shops and restaurants. We kept in touch over the years, which wasn't that difficult, since she often accompanied her father to the East Coast and European tracks. I was a bridesmaid at her wedding to Mags. He began to expand his business, and had just moved up your way when Rick and I were married." Again, Rhoda paused. For a brief instant Judith thought she noticed the glimmer of tears in the other woman's eyes. But Rhoda blinked several times, pressed her lips together, and turned to Renie. "You're a graphic-design consultant to Cruz Cruises, correct?"

Maybe, Judith thought, *the rich really are different. They keep tight rein on both their money and their emotions.*

Renie was answering the query. "I've worked with them for almost four years."

"And still do?" Rhoda asked in an artless manner.

Renie spoke without expression. "I'm on retainer since the cruise line moved its operations to San Francisco. It's a bit different now."

"Ah." Rhoda's gaze was shrewd. "I see."

"I assume," Renie said lightly, "you and your husband can afford not to work."

Rhoda's smile was wry. "Oh, Ricky makes an occasional show of turning up in my father's bank headquarters. It pleases dear old Dad and temporarily keeps my darling spouse out of trouble. I understand the two of you are cousins."

"Yes, but more like sisters," Judith explained. "We were both only children who grew up two blocks from each other. We're our own best friends. We've seen each other through——" She stopped suddenly, annoyed with herself for babbling like a brook. Rhoda St. George seemed to have turned the tables on Judith. Worse yet, Renie had already done an about-face.

Rhoda seemed unruffled by the abrupt end of the sentence. "Yes?"

Judith stared. "Yes? Er . . . that's it. I came with Serena because her husband couldn't make the trip."

Rhoda sipped her martini and munched on the olive before speaking again. "But you didn't know any of these people personally?"

"No."

Rhoda polished off the olive before turning back to Renie. "And you?"

"I knew Mags and Paul Tanaka," Renie said, sounding slightly defensive. "What about your relationship with the rest of these people?"

Rhoda let out a little sigh. "Besides Mags and Connie, Rick and I are acquainted with the snooty Mrs. Giddon and her darling daughter, Anemone. We also know the pompous Pankhurst and Ambrose Everhart. I think we met Jim Brooks once, and Rick knew Captain Swafford from somewhere or other. Rick tends to know everyone."

Judith frowned. "Ambrose Everhart? Which one was he?"

"The no-show," Rhoda replied. "He's Mrs. Giddon's puppet-like private secretary."

"Why didn't he come tonight?" Renie inquired.

"It does seem odd," Rhoda said, putting her cigarette out in a lead-crystal ashtray. "Erma usually has him dancing attendance, in case she drops a canapé—or forgets to drop a name."

Renie swirled the Drambuie in her glass. "What about Pankhurst?"

"Erma's attorney and business adviser," Rhoda replied. "He, too, dances the dance. Though I suspect he's plying Erma for investment funds these days. Horace wants to build a museum in San Mateo."

"To himself?" Renie inquired.

Rhoda shook her head; the perfectly coiffed auburn hair didn't move. "It's to be a cork museum. Sponges, too, I think."

Judith gaped. "What for?"

"Oh—wine corks from all the world's finest labels—and the Napa Valley, naturally. Historic corks. Famous corks. Corked corks. Corks are beginning to lose favor, even with some of the finest vineyards. Thus, he figures they will become collector's items. Who cares? It's what's in the bottle that counts. As for the sponges . . ." Rhoda dismissed them with a shrug.

"What about the blond bombshell?" Renie queried. "CeeCee Something-or-other."

"Orr," Rhoda said. "Rhymes with . . . never mind."

"More or less than a gold digger?" Judith asked.

"Why," Renie put in, "does Mrs. Giddon allow her financial adviser to bring a cheap hussy on this cruise?"

"Who would you two think has the real leverage?" Rhoda queried.

"Who has the most money?" inquired Renie.

"What about influence?" Rhoda remarked.

"Influence or affluence?" said Judith.

The three women stared at one another and burst into laughter.

At that moment, the door opened and Rick St. George appeared, looking as dapper as ever. If he was startled to see the cousins, he didn't show it. "Ladies! Such a mirth-filled goddesslike trio! Given tonight's dire deeds, you should be somber, like the Fates. Which is Clotho, which is Lachesis, which is Atropos?"

"More like the Three Stooges," Renie retorted. "Two of them, at least. Why don't you tell Curly and Moe here how dire *are* the deeds?"

"Yes, darling," Rhoda put in, "I'm curious, too."

Rick sailed his hat across the room; it landed atop an abstract marble sculpture. "Dire enough," he replied, abandoning his urbane manner. "I'm afraid our host was stabbed to death."

"Really!" Rhoda sounded only vaguely surprised. "That's a shame. Do you know who did it?"

"Not yet," Rick responded, moving to the bar to fix himself yet another martini. "In fact, we aren't sure yet what weapon was used."

"It wasn't in the body?" Rhoda asked in a curious tone.

"No dagger, no shiv, no butcher knife, no quaint native spear. Removed by the killer, I presume." With a practiced hand, he wielded the martini shaker. "Might be that said weapon could be closely identified with the evildoer."

"Was there very much blood?" Rhoda inquired. "I don't care for blood, as you well know."

"Some blood, darling," Rick replied, putting one foot on a leather footstool. "We won't dwell on it. Whoever did the dirty deed knew exactly where to strike the lethal blow."

"And knew Mags well enough to get very close," Rhoda said.

"That," Rick declared, "doesn't rule out anyone at the party, including crew. But what's the motive? Come on, darling, let your intuition run amok."

"Stabbing is very personal," Rhoda mused. "I'm guessing the motive is about sex or love. That includes jealousy, of course."

"You can't rule out hatred," Rick said.

Rhoda patted her perfect curls. "But how many people carry an instrument that can be used to stab someone? Especially among this crowd."

"The fair sex," Rick replied, glancing at each of the women's feet. "Your high heels would be a perfect weapon."

"True," Rhoda agreed. "Maybe we're looking for a woman with four-inch stilettos who had been spurned by Mags. Or there's always the long metal nail file."

Judith's headache was growing to epic proportions. "Excuse me," she said in a piteous voice, "Serena and I must be getting back to our stateroom. All this conjecture makes my brain feel like it might explode."

Rick and Rhoda eyed Judith with interest. "Do you," Rick asked, "enjoy those mystery party games or perhaps a rousing round of Clue?"

"No! I mean . . . yes! Yes," Judith went on, lowering her voice. "I love to play mystery games. I even do the jigsaw-puzzle ones."

Renie sniggered. "But she's terrible at it. She wouldn't recognize a clue if it fell in her cornflakes."

Rick smiled benevolently. "It's not as tricky as you'd think, though I suppose it does require a certain knack. My adoring wife and I occasionally delve into the world of crime solving. Keeps us from getting bored." He took another sip of his drink and hiccuped. "Also keeps us from passing out."

Judith was on her feet; Renie followed her lead.

"We'll be passing out now," Judith said. "Out of your suite, that is. Thanks for the drinks and the conversation."

"Our pleasure," Rhoda asserted. "We like meeting new people."

"I do, too," Judith agreed as Rick let them out and closed the door. "But," she said to Renie as they moved toward their own suite, "are the St. Georges for real?"

"I'm not sure what you mean," Renie replied, watching Judith unlock the door.

"They claim to be amateur sleuths—or at least Rick does,"

Judith responded, sitting down on the sofa. "But their methods seem like guesswork."

"Yours don't?" Renie retorted.

"Sometimes I guess," Judith replied. "But my guesses are usually based on certain facts. You know how my logical mind works. Not to mention that I prefer merely talking to people. They tend to confide in me. They also let things slip out in casual conversation. That makes it easier to pick up on motivation as well as basic facts."

"Certainly you've had your successes," Renie remarked in a noncommittal voice as she poured two glasses of ice water. "Here," she said, handing Judith one of the glasses. "Take your meds. I noticed just now that you were walking as if your hip hurts."

With a grateful smile, Judith set the water down and reached for the pill case in her purse. "It does. So does my head. I was tired before this trip, and I still am. It's been a very long day."

Renie agreed. "It's not ten o'clock, but I could drop off right now."

"Mmm." Judith swallowed her tablets. "We have to wait for our carry-ons. Why don't you start getting ready for bed? I'll stay until the bags come."

Renie eyed her cousin curiously. "You're the one who's hurting. I'll wait. Besides, I'm not sure how well I'll sleep, being so worried about my financial future."

Judith didn't say anything for a few moments, and when she did, it was not of sleep that she spoke. "When is a weapon not a weapon?"

"Huh?"

"Rick had at least one good idea when he mentioned the heel of a woman's shoe," Judith explained. "Stiletto shoes are called that because they have a thin steel rod to support the foot. But I don't think he's right about the weapon disappearing because it could be identified with the killer. Why not just toss it overboard? And what would be at hand in these circumstances? Cutlery, an ice pick, even some part of the decor. It may or may not have been premeditated, so we have to figure out if the murderer was prepared or had to use whatever was at hand."

Renie's expression was sardonic. " 'We'?"

Judith looked away from her cousin. "Don't be a smartmouth. Was there ever any doubt?"

Renie grinned. "Of course not."

Judith didn't smile back. "But," she said grimly, "there *is* competition."

Chapter Seven

The cousins were still making conjectures about the weapon when they heard a knock on their door. Judith watched as Renie greeted a youngish man dressed in a dark suit and muted tie.

"Mrs. Flynn?" he said, holding out the carry-on bags for inspection.

"I'm Mrs. Jones," Renie said. "That's Mrs. Flynn on the sofa. Thanks very much. Wait. I must give you something for your trouble."

"No, no, no," the flustered young man replied. "I'm not a crew member. I'm Ambrose Everhart, Mrs. Giddon's secretary. I had to come aboard tonight to assist her in this time of travail."

"Oh." Renie smiled as Ambrose entered the stateroom and placed the bags next to the sofa. "You missed the party."

"Yes." Ambrose looked upset. He was of medium height with

thinning blond hair and glasses. "It's probably a good thing that I did. How very sad."

"You knew Mr. Cruz quite well?" Judith asked, getting up to shake the newcomer's hand.

Ambrose cleared his throat. "Well . . . no, not particularly. But I'd had dealings—professional, of course—with him upon occasion, such as arranging for Mrs. Giddon and her daughter to go on this cruise."

Renie moved to the bar. "Let us at least thank you with a glass of . . . whatever you like to put in a glass."

"I don't drink," Ambrose replied primly. "Really, I should be on my way. Mrs. Giddon requires my services."

"As a matter of fact," Judith said, "my cousin and I were just about to call on Mrs. Giddon. We wanted to make sure she was all right. Mrs. Cruz and Ms. Beales seemed to require all of Dr. Selig's attention. Why don't we go with you?"

Ambrose seemed taken aback. "Well . . . of course Jim Brooks fancies himself a doctor. But," he went on with a somber expression, "he isn't. Yet. Yes, why not join me? I must warn you, though—Mrs. Giddon's undoubtedly distraught."

"That's understandable," Judith said, though she remembered that Mrs. Giddon had seemed more annoyed than upset over Magglio Cruz's death.

The trio went down the passageway to the W. C. Fields suite. Ambrose Everhart knocked discreetly on the door. "I've always wondered," he murmured, "what the *W.C.* stood for?"

"Water closet," Renie retorted as Horace Pankhurst opened the door.

"Everhart," he growled. "It's about time."

"I had a very important meeting that I had to attend before we left town," Ambrose said stiffly.

Jim Brooks was sitting next to Anemone on a circular sofa. "The Cal alumni association?" He sneered.

"Oh, please don't start in on that, Jimmy," Anemone begged. She was wearing an emerald-green satin bathrobe and held an ice bag to her head. "I'm glad I went to Mills. We never had silly college rivalries like Cal-Berkeley and Stanford do."

Erma Giddon sat like an empress in a capacious purple arm-chair. She wore a robe that looked like gold damask and a pair of pearl earrings the size of quail eggs. Judith felt that the only thing missing was a tiara.

"This is no time for petty arguments," Erma asserted. "Really, Ambrose, you should have skipped your meeting. You missed a very nice party. That is, until Mr. Cruz died. It went downhill after that."

"I'm so sorry, Mrs. Giddon," Ambrose apologized, busily collecting dirty glassware, crumpled napkins, and other discards from various surfaces. "If you'd tell me where the proper recycling receptacles are . . . ?"

Jim pointed to the bar. "They're under there. For God's sake," he went on with a sarcastic expression, "don't make a mistake and put paper with aluminum."

Ambrose was affronted. "You know I'd never do such a thing."

Erma acted as if she'd just noticed Judith and Renie. "Excuse me, is there something we can do for you two?"

Judith's manner was sympathetic. "We thought we might be able to be of some assistance."

"Such as what?" Erma huffed. "My maid, Beulah, will be joining us when we sail. Naturally, she didn't come to the party, being a servant as well as colored."

"Colored what?" Renie said.

Erma looked at Renie as if she should have been put in the recycling bin along with the rest of the garbage. But Anemone spoke first, her voice high and jagged.

"I'm hungry. Do you think I could get something to eat? The stateroom fridge has only snack food."

Jim seemed offended. "Why didn't you say so, love biscuit? I could've done that."

"I can, too," Ambrose said eagerly. "Now that I'm here."

Horace Pankhurst, who had been pacing the room, stopped in his tracks. "Come, come. You should leave such things to me. I wield a great amount of influence with Captain Swafford and his crew."

"Don't be ridiculous, Horace," Erma put in. "I'm her mother, I can feed my own child."

Renie, however, had already picked up the phone. She turned to Anemone. "What appeals to you?"

"A taco salad," Anemone replied, her voice reverting to its usual softness. "With chicken."

Renie dialed the galley's number and placed the order. Apparently, there were obstacles. "Good grief," Renie barked, "can't somebody do takeout? I'm not asking for a six-course meal." She shut up as the response came back. "Good," she said, "and make it snappy."

With limpid blue eyes, Anemone expressed her thanks to Renie. Her mother, however, glowered.

"You might have asked if you could use our telephone," Erma grumbled.

"It's a pay phone?" Renie shot back. "There wasn't time. Your daughter was about to expire from starvation."

"Hardly," Erma retorted. "But as long as you two are here, and Beulah isn't, you could render a service. Please hang up our evening gowns. They're in the boudoir on one of the beds. Or perhaps the floor."

"Hey," Renie began, "we're guests, and—"

"We'd be delighted," Judith broke in. "That's why," she went on, flashing her cousin a warning glance, "we came here." With a shove at Renie's back, she headed through the open door on their left.

"You're forgetting the first rule of sleuthing," Judith said after she'd closed the door behind them. "Never overlook an opportunity to snoop."

"You're absolutely right," Renie said, picking up Anemone's lavender organza gown from the floor. "I'm not as experienced as you in such matters, but for the sake of my money, I'd search for secret panels and trapdoors." She nodded at the large studio portrait of W. C. Fields on the opposite wall. "The safe's probably behind that picture. Mae West is hiding it in our bedroom." Renie moved the picture a couple of inches. "Yep, there it is. I'm going to leave W. C. Fields tilted. If ever someone could drive a person to drink, it'd be Erma Giddon. What was that Fields quote when the doctor told him he'd have to quit drinking or he'd lose his hearing? Fields said he wouldn't quit because he liked what he drank a lot more than what he heard."

"Unfortunately, that can make perfect sense," Judith said, carefully placing Erma's capacious lace and taffeta dress on a satin-covered hanger.

"Wow—that's what I call a corset!" Renie exclaimed, holding up Erma's foundation garment. "This looks like it was engineered by NASA."

"Erma is a very large woman," Judith said. "It's a good thing Anemone doesn't seem to have inherited her genes. Mr. Giddon must have been slim. I'd describe their daughter as almost wispy."

"It looks as if they've brought most of their luggage," Renie remarked, surveying the various sizes of suitcases stacked in a

corner. "Of course it hasn't been unpacked," she added with obvious sarcasm, "since Beulah is colored and therefore not allowed
on board until the cruise gets under way."

"I wonder," Judith mused, "how Erma got on with the other
ethnic types at the party, including Magglio Cruz. Given her bigotry, I marvel that they're friends, or at least acquaintances."

"She probably considers him another servant, if of a higher
class," Renie said, tossing lingerie into a laundry hamper. "Not to
mention that money erases color lines."

"I suppose," Judith said in a detached voice. She was staring at
a black velvet case on the dressing table. "This looks like a jewel
box. The key is lying next to it." She couldn't resist taking a peek.
"Good Lord," she said softly, "have a look."

The parure of diamonds and emeralds lay on top, but underneath were ruby necklaces, pearl ropes, and more diamonds.

"There must be a fortune in here," Renie said in an awed
voice. "Why isn't this case in the safe? We don't have anything to
hide in ours unless you count chewing gum and breath mints."

"Because Erma's wearing those big pearl earrings?" Judith
guessed. "She hasn't finished flashing her gewgaws yet."

"Very impressive," Renie said as Judith closed the case and
locked it. "I'll bet she left a bunch more at home."

"Anemone doesn't seem to be into jewels," Judith remarked.
"She didn't wear any tonight except for her engagement ring. It's
a very simple, small diamond set in white gold. I'm not interested in Erma's gems or Anemone's lack thereof. I'm intrigued
by the personalities that make people behave as they do. For example, Erma has a large appetite—for food, for jewels, for
everything she can buy to fill up the emptiness inside. Anemone—
perhaps learning how *not* to live from her mother—has chosen a
simpler lifestyle. Is it because she knows her mother is wrong—

or because she somehow feels guilty about the old girl's excesses and is depriving herself to make amends?"

"Anemone didn't deprive herself of a taco salad," Renie noted.

"That's my point," Judith said, sliding the closet doors shut. "She wasn't going to gorge, she was only satisfying her hunger. Really, aside from you, I didn't notice anybody overloading their appetizer plates."

"Let's not talk about me," Renie said, attempting to look innocent. "In fact, did you notice the dresser set in here?"

"You mean the very long nail file with the crystal handle? Yes. We have one in our stateroom. There's also a long, sharp letter opener next to the stationery and postcards."

"Weapons galore," Renie murmured.

"But not the kind you'd take to a cocktail party," Judith noted. "We'd better get out of here. We've done everything that needs to be done. Erma will wonder what's keeping us."

Renie followed. "Maybe they'll let us swab the deck."

But the cousins' return went unnoticed. Erma was holding court, pounding her strong fists against the sides of her chair. "Really, Ambrose, you are so careless! You know I never go anywhere without Wilbur!"

"Please," the secretary beseeched his employer, "I arranged for Wilbur to be brought on board first thing tomorrow morning along with the rest of the baggage."

Erma began to shake with anger. "Do not ever refer to my husband as baggage! He was a very great man! If we weren't about to leave the city, I'd fire you on the spot!"

"Now, now," Horace began, but was cut short by an imperious wave of Erma's hand.

"Oh, Mumsy, do calm yourself," Anemone urged, visibly

upset. "Popsy will be with us. He always is," she added in a voice that was a trifle gloomy.

A knock sounded at the door. None of the Giddon entourage seemed inclined to respond, though Erma was regaining control of her emotions.

"The trouble with you, Ambrose," she said stiffly, "is that you aren't focused. You have outside interests, and they interfere with your job. You must decide what's more important—your so-called causes or your paycheck."

The knock sounded again. "Keep your shirt on! I'm coming!" Renie shouted, startling the others.

The waiter with the shaved head and goatee was holding a tray with a large and inviting taco salad. "Thanks," Renie said. "Say—could you find another one of those for me?"

The waiter shrugged.

"Anybody else?" Renie called over her shoulder.

No one answered, though Erma glared.

"Never mind," Renie told the waiter. "I'll chew on the furniture."

"I'll share," Anemone offered. "I can't eat all this. It's enormous."

"Thanks," Renie said. "I'll get another fork from the bar."

Horace was scowling. "You didn't tip the waiter," he said to Renie. "Now the gratuity will appear on Mrs. Giddon's cruise bill. It's an automatic eighteen percent, plus a courtesy tip."

"That sounds very civilized," Renie said, purposely making a loud clatter by dropping several forks. "Whoa! Just like pickup sticks!"

Judith wondered if it wouldn't be better if Renie took a portion of the salad back to their own stateroom. Her headache was abating, but her hip still hurt.

She was about to make the suggestion when Jim Brooks produced a stethoscope from a black leather case. "It might be a good idea if I checked everyone's vitals. Obviously, Dr. Selig doesn't have time to tend to everyone's needs."

Anemone looked up from her taco salad. "Oh, Sir Hugsalot, what a terrific idea! Me first!"

"Thanks," Judith said, motioning for Renie to follow her, "but all we need is some sleep. Good night, everyone."

Renie stuffed a large forkful of lettuce, avocado, and chicken in her mouth before reluctantly taking her leave. "You might have given me a couple more minutes," she groused on the way back to their suite. "I'd have had free rein on that salad while Anemone let Jim find out if she has a pulse."

Loud voices startled Judith as she was sliding the key card through its slot. "Where's that coming from?" she asked, turning in all directions.

"The Giddon menagerie?" Renie suggested.

Judith shook her head and withdrew the key card. "I don't think so. Listen."

The cousins stood quietly in the passageway. Judith distinguished two men, arguing. "There's nobody in sight. They can't be in the staterooms. I don't think their voices would carry out here."

"A stairway?" Renie offered.

"Could be. But where? We took the elevator."

"Amidships, at least. There must be more, though. How about toward the bow? That'd be closer."

Judith didn't argue. Renie, after all, was the daughter of a seafaring man, and knew more about ships than which side was port and which was starboard. The cousins trudged back the way they'd come from the Giddon suite. The voices grew closer.

"One of them is Biff McDougal," Judith whispered as they slowed their pace. "I don't recognize the other one."

Judith and Renie stopped just short of the stairway. The men were no longer shouting, but Biff still sounded angry. "Okay, okay," he said. "But one step out of line, and you're in the hoosegow for good, Blackie."

"I'm telling ya," the man called Blackie replied, "I've gone straight. Ask Mr. St. George."

"Yeah, right, sure," Biff replied, lowering his voice to a mutter as they continued up the companionway. "If you even look cross-eyed, I'm going to Captain Swafford and let him . . ."

The next words were inaudible. Judith and Renie stared at each other.

"Blackie?" Renie said.

"Blackie. By the way, you have sour cream on your chin."

Haphazardly, Renie rubbed at her chin. "Why the warning? McDougal makes Blackie sound like a crook. Isn't all this a bit unreal?"

Judith paused halfway to their suite and gave her cousin a hard look. "You're not suggesting that it's staged, are you? We've traveled that route before."

"No, no," Renie asserted. "That couldn't happen to us twice. It's the atmosphere, I guess. All this thirties stuff makes me feel as if I'm time-traveling or in an old movie."

"You're right," Judith said, opening the stateroom door. "We may not have been around during that era, but we've seen so much of it in movies and on TV that it's very familiar. Let's face it, Cruz Cruises has chosen an evocative theme for its new ship."

"True," Renie agreed, unzipping her carry-on bag. "They're not the only ones. I understand the new *Queen Mary* is bringing back the decor from the thirties. I frequently run across that concept these days in design work. It was such a period of contradictions. On the one hand, you had the nightmare of the Great

Depression. On the other hand, you had people knocking themselves out to have a good time. Prohibition ended, all of the arts were exploding with new ideas, technology was rapidly improving—and over it all loomed the prospect of war."

"Serena Jones, historian," Judith teased. "You still have sour cream on your chin."

"Hunh," Renie muttered, looking in the mirrored glass on the coffee table. "I might as well cleanse myself completely by taking a bath. I assume you'll use the shower in the morning."

"Yes," Judith said. She preferred showers since she'd had the hip replacement. Getting in and out of a tub was difficult—and dangerous.

Judith was sipping ice water and sorting through her carry-on bag when a knock sounded at the door. A glance at the chrome hands of the clock informed her it was exactly eleven. Wearily, she went to see who was calling at such a late hour.

A pretty, petite young black woman in a maid's costume looked as surprised to see Judith as Judith was to see her.

"Oooh-ah!" the young woman exclaimed. "Mah mistake. 'Scuse me, ma'am." She bobbed a curtsy.

Judith didn't know whether to smile or wince. "Are you—um—Beulah?"

The new arrival blinked twice before replying. "Yas'um. Ah's workin' fo' Miz Giddon."

Another source, Judith thought, putting out her hand and introducing herself. "Could you please come in for just a minute? I'd like you to meet my cousin. She'll be coming out of the bathroom any minute."

"Miz Giddon tol' me to hustle mah hustle on down," the maid replied. "But if Ah can help some way . . ." She shrugged. "Promise you won't tell on me, Miz Flynn."

"I promise," Judith assured the maid. "Your mistress is just a few steps away, in the W. C. Fields suite," she added, offering a chair.

"That's mighty kindly of you," Beulah said as she sat down and crossed shapely legs. "Ah guess Ah got Dubbyacee and Miz West all mixed up inside mah po' addled head."

"That's understandable," Judith replied, also sitting down. "They made films together many years ago."

"Befo' mah time, Ah expect," Beulah murmured, looking away in a deferential manner.

"Yes, even before my time," Judith replied, growing distressed by Beulah's subservient manner. She waited for a response, but apparently the maid spoke only when spoken to.

The awkward silence was broken by Renie, who entered the sitting room wearing a tiger-striped negligee and matching robe trimmed with marabou. Renie did a double take when she saw Beulah; Judith did a double take when she saw Renie.

"Did you escape from the zoo?" Judith asked. "You'll frighten our guest away."

Renie ignored the barb. Her eyes were fixed on the maid. "Chevy? What in the world are you doing here in *that* rig?"

"Whoa!" the woman known to Judith as Beulah exclaimed. "Don't freak out and blow my cover, Serena!"

Both women started to laugh while a mystified Judith stared at them. "What's going on here?" she demanded.

Renie and "Beulah" hugged. "This," Renie said, "is Chevy Barker-James. She was our product model at the KitchenSink exhibit booth I designed for the home-improvement show last summer."

Judith shook her head. "I should have guessed it was an act."

"But was it convincing?" Chevy asked eagerly. "I'm studying to be an actress."

"Very," Judith said. "How about a drink while you explain why you're Beulah? Not to mention Chevy. That's an unusual name."

"I'd better skip the liquor," Chevy replied, sitting down again. "My parents were saving up to buy a new Chevrolet. But my mother got pregnant with me and they had to forgo the new car. So they named me after it instead."

"And 'Beulah'?" Judith inquired.

Chevy sighed. "I have to pay bills between acting jobs. Mrs. Giddon had fired her French maid, the latest, I heard, in a long line of foreign servants. I applied, thinking it might be a hoot. Not to mention I could practice my acting by behaving like those caricature black maids in the old movies. So I called myself Beulah and the old bat—excuse me, *Miz Giddon*—bought it. I think she really believes a black maid should talk like that."

Judith laughed. "She's living in a time warp. How do you stand working for her?"

Chevy turned serious. "Good question. I'm also practicing patience. But the hours are good for auditions and even for taping commercials. Mrs. G. is gone a lot during the day—committee meetings, lunch out, playing bridge—all the stuff older rich women seem to do. I check her schedule—Ambrose Everhart is meticulous about times and places—and I plan my real career around it. I'd rather be Beulah than drive a cab or wait tables."

"I can't believe," Renie said with a grin, "that I ran into you again. We had such a good time at the home-improvement show."

Chevy gave the cousins her dazzling smile. "I can't believe it, either. I checked the guest list and saw your name, Serena. As I came on board tonight, I thought it might be wise to find out if you knew anything about poor Magglio Cruz's death. I was totally shocked when Ambrose told me about it and said he felt Mrs. G. needed me tonight."

"That's probably because my cousin and I failed to meet your high standards performing maid duties," Renie said.

Chevy had turned serious. "So was it really murder?"

As concisely as possible, Judith and Renie related what they'd seen and heard.

"Connie Cruz collapsed," Judith concluded. "And Dixie Beales wasn't in very good shape the last time we saw her."

"Poor Mrs. Cruz," Chevy said with a sad little sigh. "I only met her once, but she seemed like a nice woman—if highstrung. I don't know Dixie. With a name like that, do I have to like her?"

"It's really May Belle," Renie noted.

"That's not much better," Chevy murmured. "But you can imagine what a load it is being named Chevrolet." She stood up. "Thanks for the inside story. Mrs. G. wouldn't deign to tell me what happened, Anemone is a bit of an airhead, and Ambrose is too squeamish to give any gory details."

"Plus," Judith said as the cousins saw Chevy to the door, "Ambrose wasn't there."

Chevy gave the cousins a curious look. "But he was. He told me so himself. He saw everything."

Chapter Eight

"Why," Judith asked after Chevy Barker-James had left, "would Ambrose Everhart, who allegedly had an alibi, tell Chevy he was actually here at the time of the murder?"

"Beats me," Renie replied, yawning. "And I'm beat. Not sure I can think very well."

"I can't go to sleep with this question on my mind," Judith said. "Prop yourself up on this sofa and try to think. It's as important to you as it is to me."

"More so," Renie agreed, moving away from where she'd been leaning on the bedroom doorframe. "How's this?" she said, falling onto the sofa next to Judith. "Ambrose is lying."

"Why?"

"Mmm . . ." Renie's head slumped forward.

Judith poked her cousin in the arm. "Hey! Wake up!"

"Huh?" Renie shook herself. "Oh, sorry. Maybe Ambrose wants to impress Chevy. He might have a thing for her."

"That's possible," Judith murmured, "though I got the impression he was an admirer of Anemone Giddon. Did you notice how he was trying to curry favor with her?"

"Umm . . ."

"Coz!" Judith stabbed Renie a trifle harder. "Snap to it!"

"Right." Renie opened her eyes very wide and blinked several times. "Where were we?"

"Talking about why Ambrose told Chevy he was on board the ship when he supposedly wasn't."

"Ambrose? Who's Ambrose?"

Judith held her head. "You know perfectly well who Ambrose is. Could Chevy have misunderstood what he said?"

"Unlikely."

"Then there's the possibility that Chevy is lying," Judith pointed out. "She might have a grudge against Ambrose and wants to make him look bad."

"Chevy isn't a liar," Renie replied, yawning again.

"You don't know her that well," Judith declared. "Still, let's say she's telling the truth. Maybe Ambrose *was* on board at the time of the murder, but isn't the killer. He doesn't want to admit he could be a suspect. Perhaps he has a motive for killing Magglio Cruz."

"It's more likely he has a motive for killing Erma Giddon," Renie said between yawns. "If I had to work . . . for that . . . old . . . bag I'd . . ."

Judith didn't try to rouse her cousin again. Her own brain was drained. "Good night," she whispered, and retreated into the bedroom.

Five minutes later, Renie staggered in from the sitting room and collapsed on the other bed. Within seconds, Judith could hear her cousin snoring softly.

Rearranging the pillows, Judith was still wide awake. She felt as if she wasn't considering suspects in a homicide, but characters in a movie. Part of it, she realized, was the cruise theme. But the caricatures existed: the snobbish dowager; the ingenue daughter; the besotted suitor; the pompous family lawyer; the nervous private secretary; the blond gold digger; the able assistant; the Southern belle; the black maid; the doughty British captain; the snooty French purser; the lunch-bucket cop; and some guy named Blackie, who might or might not be a crook. Of course there were also the idle rich sophisticates with their dog that looked like a mop.

Yet taken one by one, they were not out of place on a luxury cruise ship. Judith rolled over and shut her eyes tight. She was bone tired, having been up for almost twenty straight hours. After what seemed like a long time, she finally slept.

But the strange dreams came back. James Cagney was tap-dancing with a machine gun in one hand and a grapefruit in the other. Bette Davis was a Southern belle carrying a wicker basket filled with daggers. Jean Harlow was wearing what looked like Erma Giddon's corset and playing a Duke Ellington tune on a solid-gold grand piano.

It was not a restful night.

Judith was startled awake shortly before nine by a voice that seemed to come from nowhere. It took her several moments to orient herself, realize that an announcement was being made over the ship's loudspeaker, and that it informed the passengers they were free to leave the *San Rafael* until further notice.

Getting out of bed, she went over to the still unconscious Renie. "Hey," Judith called, giving her cousin a slight shake, "wake up. There's news."

" 'S'alwaysis," Renie mumbled, pulling the covers over her head. "G'way."

"It's nine o'clock," Judith declared, trying to pull the blanket and sheet off of Renie. "You've slept over nine hours. At home, you stay up past midnight. Adjust, become alert before your usual ten A.M. awakening."

"Damn." Renie rolled over and exhaled deeply. "I'll get up if you order breakfast in bed for me."

"You're a brat," Judith accused. "They're telling us we can get off the ship. I doubt they're serving breakfast."

Renie tossed the covers aside and leaped up. "They damned well better serve breakfast! First, they try to take away my livelihood, now they want to starve me to death! That does it!" She grabbed the phone from the dressing table and dialed the galley.

Judith decided to seek sanctuary in the shower. The warm water brought her fully awake. Her mental processes shifted into gear as she scrubbed her body with a bar of rich oatmeal soap. *Sleeping till nine. No rush to feed guests breakfast. No lip from Gertrude. No coping with Phyliss. No ringing phones or demanding faxes. No Joe.*

That was the bad part. She already missed him. But she wasn't sorry that he hadn't been with her when Magglio Cruz was murdered. While getting dressed, Judith decided she'd call Joe when they got back to the hotel. He should be at home, since the trial didn't start until Monday. But if she phoned now, she'd have to fib about the previous evening's dire events.

Still in a quandary, she found Renie in the living room, attired in her wild tiger ensemble and watching the local news.

"Nothing so far," Renie said before Judith could ask the question. "It's all about pollution and city-hall politics and gay marriage. I'm thinking that if they broaden the description of what constitutes a marriage, and something—God forbid—ever happens to Bill, I'll marry Clarence."

"Your bunny?" Judith frowned. "Why not marry Oscar?"

"No," Renie replied. "I'd want a real change. Bill and Oscar have too many similar traits. Besides, I'd like to actually *use* the TV remote. Clarence doesn't care for television. By the way, breakfast is coming. I ordered waffles for both of us."

Judith was relieved, not just because Renie had ordered food, but because she had changed the subject. Sometimes the Joneses' ménage was hard to comprehend.

"I thought you were going to have breakfast in bed," Judith remarked. "Why are you out here?"

"*Breakfast in bed* is merely an expression," Renie explained. "Not that I don't actually do that sometimes, but it usually ends up kind of messy, bedclothes-wise."

"Yes," Judith murmured, "I suppose sleeping on a fried egg can be an unpleasant experience."

"Funny, coz," Renie muttered. As a knock sounded at the door, she jumped up. "Ah! That was quick."

But it wasn't breakfast that had arrived. It was CeeCee Orr, looking very nautical in a white sailor dress with navy-blue piping.

"Oh, hi there," she said in a breathy voice. "Have we met? I'm—"

"We know," Judith said with a smile, ushering the young woman inside. "I'm Judith Flynn and this is my cousin Serena Jones."

"A pleasure, I'm sure," CeeCee replied, showing perfect white teeth and a trace of a New York accent. "Could I borrow a whiff of Opium?"

Judith couldn't help but gape. "Uh . . . I'm afraid we don't have any. Maybe you could try Chinatown when you go back on shore."

Hands pressed against her deep cleavage, CeeCee laughed

merrily. "Oh, how stupid of me! I'm not talking about drugs, I mean *her, her, her.*" She pointed a finger at Renie. "Your *perfume,* Ms. Jones. You wear Yves Saint-Laurent's Opium. I smelled it last night at the party. It's my favorite, too, but I'm out, out, out."

"Oh—sure," Renie said. "I'll get it for you." She headed for the bedroom.

"I simply can't bear to start the day without my Opium," CeeCee declared, jiggling her Louis Vuitton handbag and various parts of her body. "It's so"—she paused, shut her eyes tight, and ran her hands over her voluptuous curves—"sensual."

"I'm a Red Door person," Judith replied. "I like a floral scent. For years, I wore White Shoulders."

"Red Door, huh?" CeeCee looked ingenuous. "Gosh, I've never used that. What's it like?"

"I'll let you try it," Judith said, going into the bedroom.

Renie was rummaging in her suitcase. "Where'd I put the damned stuff? I wore it last night. Oh—here it is, in the side pocket. What're you doing?"

"Being gracious," Judith replied, wrestling with the zipper of her cosmetic case. "This thing sticks. I've been meaning to buy a new one, but I didn't have time before we left on such short notice."

"Is CeeCee as ditzy as she acts?"

Judith shrugged. "I don't know. That act isn't easy to do." The zipper finally relented; the bottle of Red Door was extracted.

When the cousins returned to the sitting room, CeeCee was humming Cole Porter's "Begin the Beguine."

Judith sprayed a whiff of her own perfume on her wrist and let CeeCee sniff.

"Nice," she said. "Kind of floral. What's in it?"

"Several ingredients," Judith replied, handing over the bottle. "Too many to remember. Jasmine, wild orchid—see for yourself."

CeeCee squinted at the small print. "Gee, what a combo! Did you know that Connie Cruz makes her own perfume? She's allergic to most of the stuff they sell in stores. Connie always smells like lilies." She took another sniff of Red Door, and shook her head. "I still like Opium better." She returned the bottle to Judith. "Thanks, but no thanks."

"Here," Renie said, handing her own brand to CeeCee. "Squirt away."

"Mmm." CeeCee closed her eyes again, purring softly as she applied the scent to her cleavage, her throat, and her wrists. "Now," she said softly, "I can face the day."

Renie accepted the perfume bottle and set it on a side table. "Good. Frankly, I wear that stuff only in the evening. It's a bit overpowering for daytime use."

CeeCee's big brown eyes opened wide. "Really? Usually, I bathe in it. But I didn't bring all my fragrances with me yesterday."

"You're going ashore?" Judith asked in a casual voice.

CeeCee shrugged. "I guess. Racey says there's no telling when we'll sail."

Judith was puzzled. " 'Racey'?"

CeeCee laughed. "That's what I call Horace. Sometimes I call him 'Panky.' As in 'Hanky-Panky.' " She winked. "It all depends."

"Yes," Judith said in a noncommittal voice. "Do you live in San Francisco?"

Mischief still danced in CeeCee's eyes. "Most of the time."

Judith smiled in her friendliest manner. "I thought I heard a hint of the East Coast in your speech."

CeeCee laughed again. "Ain't it da troot?" she replied, exaggerating her accent. "I'm originally from Brooklyn. Brooklyn Heights, that is."

Judith wasn't skeptical about CeeCee's Brooklyn origins, but she was dubious about her claim to the fashionable—and expensive—Brooklyn Heights neighborhood.

The conversation was interrupted by yet another knock. In a swirl of tiger stripes, Renie got up to answer. Halfway to the door, she tripped over the hem of her robe and fell flat on her face.

"Coz!" Judith cried. "Are you okay?"

The response was a stream of profanity, befitting a seafaring man's daughter.

"I'll see who it is," CeeCee called out over the earthy din.

Judith did her best to haul Renie to her feet. "That tiger costume's too long for you. No wonder you tripped."

"Oh, shut up!" Renie collapsed back onto the sofa. "I got it on sale at Nordquist's and I'll be damned if I'll pay for alterations on a markdown. Besides, Bill hates it."

"No wonder," Judith remarked. "It looks like you're trying out for the cover of *National Geographic*."

CeeCee had admitted the waiter with the shaved head and goatee. She stepped aside as he wheeled the table in front of the sofa and began to uncover the various dishes.

"How do we pay?" Judith asked as Renie surveyed the food with an eagle eye.

"He said you don't," CeeCee replied. "Everything for you guys is free. Lucky stiffs!"

"Let's not talk about 'stiffs,' " Judith said. "Surely we can offer a gratuity."

But the waiter smiled slightly and shook his head. CeeCee walked him back to the door.

"Is he a mute?" Judith whispered, pulling a chair up to the other side of the table.

Renie was spreading soft butter on her waffle. "Huh? No, I think he's talking to CeeCee in the passageway."

Judith glanced up. The waiter was leaving; CeeCee remained on the threshold.

"Gotta run," she said. "Racey will think I've been kidnapped. He *worries, worries, worries.* Thanks for the perfume." CeeCee closed the door behind her.

"Hunh," Renie said after devouring half of a pork sausage, "she may be what we thought she was. What you see is what you get?"

"Perhaps," Judith responded.

"What do you mean by that?"

"You know. It takes some digging to find the real person underneath the facade. How many times have we been fooled by appearances?"

"True," Renie allowed, wiping syrup off of her chest. "Especially by seemingly ordinary people who turned out to be heartless killers. Which, I assume, is what we have among us."

Judith grimaced. "I'm afraid so. We've no idea what the motive may be and only a limited knowledge of the method. Thus, I suppose the first thing we should consider is the third factor in any homicide—opportunity. How many people can we rule out because they never left the saloon?"

Looking thoughtful, Renie sipped her tomato juice. "Let's see. We saw Magglio Cruz alive and well when we came on board the ship. Did we see him after that? Other than in the piano, of course."

"Yes," Judith replied. "He was at the bar. I don't remember seeing him after that. Later Connie went to look for him. Which means," Judith added with a frown, "we can't rule out Connie as a suspect."

"The spouse," Renie remarked. "Always the prime suspect."

Judith paused, eating, but not really tasting, her waffle. She was focused on re-creating the saloon party in her mind's eye. "The St. Georges arrived last," she finally said, "so we don't know

where they were before they made their grand entrance. Émile
Grenier showed up just before that. We didn't see Dixie Beales
until the cabaret section was opened."

"True," Renie agreed. "But most of the other guests seemed
to have stayed put. Erma, Anemone, Jim, Horace, CeeCee, Paul,
Captain Swafford. Admittedly, everyone was milling around."

"Then there's Ambrose, who claimed he wasn't on board but
told Chevy that he was," Judith reminded her cousin. "That's a
real puzzle."

"It could be a miscommunication," Renie pointed out, gathering up her tableware and placing it to one side of the portable
table. "You didn't eat your egg," she said, pointing to a small dish
that was still covered.

"Egg?" Judith frowned. "I didn't know you ordered one for
me."

Renie bit her lip. "I didn't, come to think of it. I got two, although I ordered only one for myself. Sorry, coz. I *am* a pig."

"That's okay," Judith said. "You know I'm watching my cholesterol." She narrowed her eyes at Renie. "I suppose you want
this one, too?"

"No, I do not," Renie replied in an indignant tone. "I'm a pig,
but I'm not a hog. You eat it. You need to put on weight."

"It's probably cold by now." Judith lifted the lid.

There was no egg—only a folded piece of paper on the white
plate.

"What the heck?" Judith muttered. "Maybe we got a bill after
all." She unfolded the paper. "It's not a bill," she said grimly, and
handed the note to Renie.

The rather small letters had been individually pasted on a
sheet from a *San Rafael* memo pad. They read *Butt Out*.

"Good Lord," Renie gasped. "Who knows you're FATSO?"
She referred to the corruption of her cousin's Internet

acronym, which actually stood for Female Amateur Sleuth Tracking Offenders.

"Do you think that's what it refers to?" Judith responded, looking worried.

"What else?" Renie studied the message for a few more seconds. "There's something odd about this. The individual letters haven't been cut from a newspaper or a magazine. In fact, the paper they're printed on is quality stuff, too heavy for an ordinary publication."

Judith took the note and fingered each separate letter. "You're right. I suppose we shouldn't be handling this thing, but I'm willing to bet that there aren't any prints."

"Rick and Rhoda might know who you are, just as you recognized him as the Gin Man from the amateur sleuth Web site," Renie suggested.

"That's true. They might want to get all the glory in case they figure out whodunit." But Judith was dubious. "There's something odd about that waiter. I remember seeing him at the party, and later he delivered Anemone's taco salad. Now he shows up with breakfast."

Renie's expression was droll. "Gosh, coz, that's what waiters do—they wait on people. Besides, the complete staff wasn't on board last night. They probably haven't come aboard this morning, since our sailing time may be delayed."

"That's so," Judith admitted, standing up and slipping the note into her purse's side pocket. "It could have been anyone in the kitchen—or even someone passing through. For all we know, it might have been the captain himself. Come on, you'd better get dressed. I'd like to get off of this ship."

Judith didn't add that she wanted get off *alive*.

It was overcast in San Francisco that Friday morning as the cousins took a taxi back to their hotel.

"I'd like to find out how many of the guests are staying at the St. Francis besides us," Judith said as they neared Union Square, where pigeons fought for space on the bronze victory column.

"None's my guess," Renie replied, watching through the window as the usual ragtag-and-bobtail crowd mingled with protesters and supporters of various causes. "Most of the party guests live here, right?"

"Do they?" Judith responded as the turbaned taxi driver double-parked in front of the hotel.

Renie already had her money out. "Keep the change," she told the driver, handing him two bills and all but shoving Judith out the door.

"Hey, lady!" the driver shouted just as Renie put one foot on the street. "You big cheat! You give me two dollar!"

Renie jerked around to stare at the driver. "What?"

"Two dollar!" he cried, waving a one in each hand. "Ride cost eleven dollar! I call cop, you go to prison! Much torture!"

"Hold on to your hat," Renie snapped. "I mean, turban." She dug into her overstuffed wallet. "I meant to give you a five and a ten. Sorry," she added, tossing the bills into the front of the cab.

"Ah." The driver smiled broadly. "Have nice day, lady."

"Nice day, my butt," Renie muttered, squeezing between two town cars to reach Judith on the sidewalk. "I should have put on my glasses."

"I don't know why," Judith said, hurrying her step to avoid a very aggressive panhandler who was hurling verbal abuse in their direction. "The lenses are always so smudged and spotted that you can barely see through them."

"Yeah, yeah, yeah," Renie grumbled. She pointed to the bar just off the lobby. "Let's have a drink before we go to the room."

"At eleven-thirty in the morning?" Judith retorted. "Isn't that a bit early?"

"Hey—yesterday I started at four A.M.," Renie reminded Judith. "Besides, I didn't say a cocktail. I'm considering lemonade. They serve lunch here in the Compass Rose lounge."

Judith gazed at the bar area, which was raised a few steps up from the lobby itself. Several tables were already occupied. The place looked comfortable and quiet.

"Sure, let's do it," Judith agreed. "We can leave our carry-ons with the bellman."

"We can take them with us," Renie said, already climbing the carpeted stairs. "They're *carry-ons,* remember?"

They had just gotten seated when they heard a piano playing softly behind them. Judith turned around to look. "I hope there's no corpse in that one," she said grimly.

The cousins both ordered lemonades. Renie fingered the lunch menu. "We can eat here, too," she said.

"We just did, barely more than an hour ago," Judith pointed out.

"So?"

Judith didn't argue. The server took their beverage order before she spoke again. "You're probably right about the other party attendees. I assume the Cruzes live here as well."

"They always did," Renie replied, "though they maintained a pied-à-terre, a condo downtown, not far from Heraldsgate Hill. Paul Tanaka never lived in the Bay Area. He was over in the Eastside suburbs. I don't know if he's moved down here or not."

"What about Captain Swafford and Émile Grenier?" Judith asked. "Oh, and Dixie Beales."

Renie paused as a trio of Japanese businessmen seated themselves at the next table. The bar was beginning to fill up. "Since they're all part of the crew," she said, "I assume they were based out of the headquarters at home. It's possible they've been put up at a hotel—not to mention Dr. Selig—though I doubt they're staying anywhere as lavish as the St. Francis."

The lemonades arrived. Renie informed the server that they'd be ordering food a bit later.

"I'd like to know," Judith said as four very chic matrons passed by, "what, if anything, Rick and Rhoda St. George have found out. We should compare notes. Do you think they'd be in the phone book?"

"Possibly," Renie replied, wincing. "Unfortunately, here comes someone who could tell us."

Judith looked around Renie to see Biff McDougal huffing up the short staircase. He looked as out of place in the Compass Rose as Saddam Hussein at a Baptist picnic.

"Hey, there," Biff called out, making several well-coiffed heads turn. "I gotta talk to you two."

Clumsily, Biff pulled up an empty chair from a nearby table and plopped himself down. He didn't remove his hat, which evoked disapproving stares from the elegant matrons and the Japanese businessmen.

"Shoulda questioned you while you were still on the boat," Biff said, talking around the ever-present toothpick. "Too many witnesses, couldn't catch up with 'em all."

"But you're making progress?" Judith asked innocently.

"Huh?" The toothpick dangled from Biff's lower lip. "Oh, well, sure, but it's only been . . . what? Twelve hours or so?"

Judith didn't correct him. "Roughly," she said, remembering Joe's adage that if progress wasn't made in the first twenty-four hours of a homicide case, the trail quickly turned cold.

The server was moving toward Biff, but the detective waved

him away. "Let's start with you, Mrs. Jones, seeing as how I worked with your hubby awhile back."

For an instant, Renie looked puzzled. "My . . . ? Oh!" she said with a little laugh, recalling the tall tale she'd given to Biff. "Yes, yes. I thought you said 'Bubby.' That's my brother-in-law."

"Yeah, right." Biff rearranged the rumpled folds of his raincoat. "So how well did you know the vic?"

"The . . . ?" Again, Renie seemed briefly befuddled. "You mean, the victim, Magglio Cruz?"

"Har har." Biff chuckled. "Who'dya think I mean, Barry Bonds?"

Renie's expression was arch. "No. I thought you meant his father, Bobby."

Biff looked surprised. "You a baseball fan?"

Renie nodded. "You want stats or do you want to catch a killer?"

"Yeah, right," Biff mumbled. "Where was I?"

"Back in Candlestick Park forty years ago," Renie said drily. "You asked how well I knew Magglio Cruz. The answer is fairly well, but in a working relationship. I was the graphic-design artist for most of the cruise line's publications."

"Oh, yeah?" Biff tried to look as if he knew what Renie was talking about. "I heard you had a row with Cruz when he moved the company down here. You made some threats, too."

"Of a legal nature," Renie replied, wearing the serious expression that Judith called her cousin's "boardroom face."

Biff rolled the toothpick around his mouth. "You patched things up?"

"Yes. We came to a satisfactory agreement."

"Like a bribe, with this free cruise and fancy digs?" He waved a hand, presumably taking in the entire hotel.

"It wasn't a bribe," Renie declared. "It was compensation for any misunderstanding between us. I'm still a consultant to the Cruz line."

"Oh?" Biff's small eyes got even smaller. "You sure? Now that Cruz is a goner, I mean."

"There's hardly been time to discuss business," Renie asserted in her haughtiest tone.

"Huh." Biff paused. "So Cruz getting whacked wasn't good news for you, right?"

"Of course not. Aside from the work connection, I liked him."

The detective went silent again before turning to Judith. "How about you, toots?"

"*Toots?*" Judith scowled at Biff. "Only my mother is permitted to call me toots. You may address me as Mrs. Flynn."

Biff shrugged. "Sure, why not? Okay, Mrs. Flynn, how well did you know the stiff?"

Fleetingly, Judith wondered if Joe had ever been so crass when dealing with a suspect. Maybe he had. The rough armor worn by cops was an occupational necessity.

"I'd never met him before in my life," she stated.

"So how come you're on this cruise?"

"Because my cousin, Mrs. Jones, invited me," Judith explained. "Her husband wasn't able to join her."

"Hunh." Biff studied both women as if he were trying to see behind what appeared to be innocent facades. "Let's get back to the murder," he finally said. "Notice anything suspicious?"

The question seemed to be directed at Renie. "You mean like a dead body?"

Before Biff could reply, Judith spoke up: "I only glimpsed the body when I went to find Dixie Beales's evening bag. My cousin never saw it at all. Captain Swafford and his crew kept everyone away from the piano. It was Émile Grenier who found Mr. Cruz."

"Yeah, yeah, I know that," Biff retorted as a cell phone rang.

"I've questioned most of the rest of that hoity-toity crowd." The cell kept ringing. It sounded very close to the cousins. "Did either of you see anybody acting strange?"

"They're all a little strange," Renie replied as the phone rang again. "Say, is that your cell?" she asked Biff.

"My . . . ?" Biff looked around, perhaps expecting to see a phone floating in the air. "Oh!" He reached inside his raincoat. "You're right." Fumbling with the cell's buttons, he shook his head. "Whatever happened to dials? I can't stand these newfangled . . . McDougal here," he said into the receiver.

Judith and Renie exchanged bemused glances.

"The note?" Judith mouthed, discreetly nodding at Biff.

"The one on the plate?" Renie whispered.

"Should I mention it?" Judith asked in a low voice as Biff jabbered into the phone.

"Your call," Renie said.

Judith grew thoughtful. Anonymous notes connected to a murder were sinister, even when they only said *Butt Out*. On the other hand, she didn't want to explain that the sender might know about her guise as FATSO. Biff, however, was clearly preoccupied.

"Holy cow!" he shouted, again drawing attention from the other customers. "Be right there!" He dropped the phone, groped under the table, shoved Judith's carry-on bag out of the way, and grabbed Renie's shoe.

"Hey!" Renie snapped. "Keep your hands to yourself!"

"Huh?" The detective looked up. "Oh—sorry." He ducked under the table again.

Judith felt the phone next to her own foot. Gently, she moved it out onto the carpet. "It's right there. See it?"

Biff spotted his prey and snatched it up. "Gotta run," he said, almost knocking over his chair. "Big jewel heist!"

"Hold it!" Renie had slid down in her seat and put out a leg to block Biff's progress. "Whose jewels?"

Red in the face and looking annoyed, Biff staggered around Renie's outstretched leg. "The old Giddon broad. How crazy can this case get?"

Judith wondered, too.

Chapter Nine

I t figures," Renie said as notes from the Compass Rose piano filtered through the hotel's civilized air. "Murder, jewel theft—when do we find out who's being blackmailed?"

"That's not impossible," Judith said. "As far as Magglio Cruz's death is concerned, we didn't learn one thing from Biff McDougal."

"Except that Biff's incompetent?"

"He *seems* to be," Judith allowed. "He reminds me of one of the cops who was involved in that case last spring. What was his name?"

"His nickname was Trash," Renie recalled. "It suited him. He spent more time eating than working."

"You're not one to complain about that," Judith said with a little smile. "Speaking of which, let's not. Eat, I mean. I'm honestly not hungry and we, too, have work to do."

Renie gazed at the menu as if she were bidding farewell to a long-lost love. "You're right. I'll sign the bill on our way out."

Back in their suite, Judith got out the phone book. "Ah. The St. Georges *are* listed. They live on Sacramento Street." She wrote the number and address down on a piece of hotel notepaper and showed it to Renie, who was more familiar with the city.

"That's a Nob Hill address," Renie said. "It figures—they're rich, and housing there is sky-high in more ways than one."

Dialing the number, Judith really didn't expect that the St. Georges would be home. But Rhoda answered on the second ring.

"Judith—how nice to hear from you," she said in that cultured yet nonchalant tone. "Did you make it back to the hotel without getting pistol-whipped?"

"Yes," Judith replied with a thumbs-up sign for Renie. "But as soon as we got here, Biff McDougal paid us a visit."

"Biff." Rhoda sounded amused. "Ricky likes him, probably because he's such a suggestible kind of policeman. And he *is* discreet when it comes to publicity because he despises the media. Years ago, one of the newspapers—I can't remember if it was the *Chronicle* or the *Examiner*—poked fun at him. They called him a 'relic from the past,' and implied that he was inept. But his closure rate is very good, especially with homicides."

Judith wondered if that was partly due to Rick St. George's help. Maybe Rick and Biff were a successful combination of brain and brawn. "Biff doesn't work with a partner?" Judith inquired.

"Usually," Rhoda answered, "but Willie—William Jackson—broke his leg skiing at Lake Tahoe last week. He won't be back on the job until the end of April. Willie's young, eager, and reasonably bright. I believe another rookie has been assigned as a temporary partner—Buzz Something-or-other—but he showed up late last night. By the way, how was Biff when you saw him?

Judith frowned. "How?"

Rhoda laughed. "I mean, was he in a hurry?"

"Let's say he left in a rush," Judith hedged.

There was a momentary silence on the other end of the line. "I see. Why don't you and your cousin come by for a drink? We're only a few blocks up from the St. Francis. You can take a taxi or ride the cable car. I'll give you directions."

Judith made notes on the pad. "When?" she asked.

"How about right now?" Rhoda replied, her voice dropping a notch. "I've almost finished putting Asthma's fur up in soup cans."

"Beef noodle?"

"Right. See you soon?"

"You bet," said Judith, and hung up.

The St. Georges lived only seven blocks from the hotel, but it was all uphill—even steeper than the Counterbalance at home. As the old-fashioned red, gold, and black cable car pulled around the corner by one of the numerous flower stands, the cousins could see that passengers were hanging from the side like sausages falling out of a wrapper. There were no friendly out-stretched hands to help them this time. Renie grabbed Judith's arm to haul her aboard. Clinging to a steel pole, they hung on for dear life as the venerable conveyance rattled and clanged its way to the top of the busy street.

They could hear the hum of the tracks after they got off at the crest of Powell Street. It was windy—even chilly—as Judith and Renie walked a block west, where they stopped to catch their collective breath by the hallowed and exclusive Pacific Union Club. They gazed around at the Mark Hopkins and Fairmont hotels, two other well-known San Francisco landmarks.

"You can smell money around here," Renie noted. "It's like Park Avenue in New York or Boston's Back Bay."

Judith pointed to the street sign. "This is Sacramento. The St. Georges must live in that condo across the street from the Mark Hopkins."

The doorman tipped his hat before asking the cousins' names and which resident they were visiting. A moment later, they entered the marble lobby with its lavish floral arrangement. Rick and Rhoda lived in the penthouse. A uniformed elevator operator gave them a smooth ride to the top floor. The doors slid open onto what Judith and Renie assumed was the St. Georges' foyer. If there was any doubt, the sound of clanking tin cans rang in their ears. Rhoda and Asthma came into view.

"Judith! Serena! How nice! Come, sit, stay, behave."

Judith gave a start. "What?"

Rhoda laughed. "I was talking to the dog. He seems to be trying to cuddle Serena."

Renie was trying not to grimace as Asthma rubbed his fur-covered soup cans against her thighs. Managing to sidestep the dog, she followed Judith and Rhoda into a large sitting room with an Asian theme and a spectacular view of the city.

"This is lovely," Judith gushed. "Are these furnishings antiques?"

"Some of them," Rhoda replied with a shrug. "The butterfly trunk and the matching chairs with the lotus pattern date back a couple of centuries. The rest of it looks old because of Asthma. He's a bit clumsy."

Judith and Renie sat on a sofa covered in a silk poppy print. Rhoda had gone to the full-service bar. Its dark wood was painted with white peonies. A Chinese vase filled with real peonies sat atop the counter. It struck Judith that Rhoda St. George wore her air of wealth and entitlement the way a river ran to the sea: It was unaffected, it was accepted, it was almost a force of nature.

"I'm having a martini," Rhoda said, her long fingernails pointing to a half-filled glass next to the vase. "What may I serve you?"

"Scotch rocks," Judith replied. "Water back, if you don't mind."

"Not at all," Rhoda replied.

"Any bourbon or Canadian as long as it's not Wild Turkey," Renie said.

Rhoda arched a perfectly etched eyebrow. "You don't care for Wild Turkey?"

"Only when I fly," Renie replied.

"Will Crown Royal do?" Rhoda inquired, unfazed by Renie's response.

"Just fine," Renie said, nodding. "Water and plenty of ice, please."

With practiced expertise, Rhoda mixed the two drinks and refreshed her own. "I understand," she said, seating herself in one of the matching antique chairs, "we may not get out of port until tomorrow." She glanced inquisitively at the cousins.

"Because of the murder—or the jewel theft?" Judith responded.

Rhoda smiled, arranging the folds of her orange chiffon hostess pajamas. "I was wondering if you knew. I guessed that Biff McDougal may have been interrogating you when the call came through to him. The theft took place aboard the ship, not at Erma Giddon's home."

"That we didn't know," Renie said, trying to relax despite the too-close presence of Asthma.

"Erma discovered that the jewels were missing when she was preparing to leave the *San Rafael* this morning," Rhoda explained. "Naturally, she's blaming Beulah, her maid."

"Why?" Renie asked. "Because Beulah is black?"

"Of course." Rhoda shook her head. "Erma is such a bigot. You can imagine the unpleasantness she swears she's had to suffer because San Francisco has become such a mecca for the gay population. And that's so ridiculous of her because . . . well, just because it is."

Judith sensed that Rhoda had been about to say something else but had changed her mind. "Do you know the value of the stolen jewels?" Judith inquired, savoring the scotch, which had to be at least forty years old and probably cost close to a hundred dollars a bottle.

Rhoda waved a hand. "I can only guess. Rick's estimate was in the low seven figures."

"And more like them at home," Renie murmured.

"Oh, definitely," Rhoda said blithely. "Those were only her cruise baubles. Erma has quite a collection, some family heirlooms, some of them dating back to the Romanovs and the Hanovers—and the Vikings, for all I know. She likes to brag."

Judith tried to coax Asthma in her direction. "Did the thief take the case or just the jewels?"

"Case and all," Rhoda replied.

Judith knew the answer, but asked the question anyway: "Did Erma always keep it locked?"

"I've no idea," Rhoda answered.

"She didn't," Renie blurted out, deigning to pat one of Asthma's soup cans. "We know. We had to sub for Beulah when we called on Erma and company."

"Really." Rhoda's eyes danced. "Tell me all."

Renie did, despite the increased nudging and wheezing from Asthma.

"That makes sense," Rhoda said when Renie had finished. "If Erma was still wearing some of her trinkets and her maid wasn't around, she wouldn't bother locking the case until bedtime. It's stupid, but then Erma is a rather stupid woman." She held up her almost empty glass. "Refills?"

The cousins declined. Neither of them had made it even halfway through their own cocktails.

"I'll wait, too," Rhoda said with a touch of regret. "I hope Ricky calls back soon. I suppose Biff is picking my darling husband's brains. Tell me," she went on, leaning forward in her chair, "you two must have seen or heard something—anything—unusual at the party before Mags was killed. You seem very observant as well as perceptive. We arrived a bit late, you see."

Now who's picking whose brains? Judith thought.

"To be honest," she said, "we didn't notice anything unusual. Has the weapon been found?"

"No," Rhoda answered with a frown. "The fatal wound was made by something pointed, slim, and round." She made a quarter-inch circle with her thumb and index finger. "It sounds like a tool, rather than a knife or dagger. Still, there are many kinds of exotic weapons that don't readily come to mind. Ricky guesses that the killer threw it overboard."

"That makes sense," Judith allowed.

"You know most of the suspects better than we do," Renie said as Asthma dozed off at her feet. "Can you fill us in? It might help to discover the motive."

Rhoda looked amused. "I don't know where to start. Though money is always a good place, especially when murder is involved. Mags and Connie were never able to have children. They considered adoption, but her family—at least her father—is one of those snobbish Argentinians of Spanish hidalgo descent. God forbid they might have gotten a child who had native Latin American blood. Consequently, everything goes to Connie, since California is a community-property state."

"And Connie is already rich," Judith remarked.

Rhoda shrugged. "Not rich in the sense of *rich*—if you understand what I mean. Her father was very successful as a horse trainer and owner, having started out in Dubai working for a couple of emirs. I would say there's no money motive on her part."

"They were happy?" Judith inquired.

"Yes, I think so," Rhoda said. "Of course one never knows for certain."

Renie edged away from the dog, who was not only wheezing, but also snoring and drooling. "What about the business arrangement? I assumed—not that I ever thought Mags would die young—that being second in command, Paul Tanaka would take over."

"The board of directors has to decide that," Rhoda replied. "There are five members, including Erma Giddon and Horace Pankhurst. Two others are from your part of the world—two of those computer kings, Bill Goetz and Paul Allum."

"Who's the fifth one?" Renie asked.

Rhoda smiled. "Me."

Judith smiled back. "The swing vote?"

Rhoda inclined her head to one side. "It could be. I seldom agree with Erma and Horace. We all have stock in the company. Your billionaire entrepreneurs are usually sensible people when it comes to voting on issues. Of course," she added with only a slight suggestion of disparagement, "they *do* represent 'new' money."

"But," Renie pointed out, "they both allowed the line to move its headquarters out of town. Or did they vote against it?"

"The vote was unanimous," Rhoda said without expression.

Judith was puzzled. It didn't seem right for Goetz or Allum to deflect tourism from their hometown. They were not only civic leaders, but boosters as well. Both were very smart. They must have had sound reasons to permit the move.

"So the board can agree on some things," Judith remarked.

"Yes," Rhoda said, "and of course Mags wanted the move. He lives here—sorry—he *lived* here most of the time, and Connie has always loved California. She's still a big Thoroughbred-racing fan, and some of the best tracks are in this state."

"Money," Judith murmured. "It's such a good motive for murder. But I don't see who benefits financially from Mags's death."

"Neither do I," Rhoda agreed. "Erma has all of her family and hangers-on covered. Horace is well off, though he's sinking a great deal of his own cash into the museum start-up. Jim Brooks's Stanford tuition is being paid by Erma."

"That leaves the crew," Renie said. "Were there union problems?"

"Not to my knowledge," Rhoda replied. "Several unions are represented among the cruise line's employees. Culinary workers, marine engineers, longshoremen—you name it. Thousands of people on land and sea are involved in the cruise line's business. You must remember that the *San Rafael* isn't the only Cruz cruiser."

Renie nodded. "Of course. There's the *San Miguel,* the *Santa Rita,* and the *San Luis Rey*. I worked on the launch brochure for the *Rey* five years ago. That was my first gig for the line. I understand the ship sails on the Panama Canal voyages."

"Yes," Rhoda said, taking a cigarette out of a carved wooden box on the chinoiserie table between the chairs. "In fact, she was due in Miami this morning."

"Love," Judith said, not particularly interested in Cruz Cruises' routes. "Jealousy. Those are other good motives."

Renie and Rhoda both turned toward her. With a vague look of apology for her cousin, Renie agreed. "True. Motives. Murder. Who loves whom? In this group, there seems to be more antipathy than love."

"I love Ricky," Rhoda said with a fond expression, placing the cigarette in an ivory holder. "He loves me. We're the only ones I can vouch for. Mags and Connie—yes, probably. Mags and anyone else?" She shrugged in her elegantly nonchalant manner. "Dubious. Connie and another man? Also doubtful, though you never know. Anemone and Jim? I assume they're in love or they wouldn't be engaged. Still, Jim is . . . well, you know the word. *Poor*. Not," she continued quickly, "poor in the way really poor people are poor, if you understand what I mean."

Renie kept a straight face. "Like all those homeless beggars out in the streets?"

"Like that." Rhoda finished her martini. "Certainly Jim couldn't afford Stanford without Erma's financial aid."

"They act like they're in love," Judith noted. "Unless it is an act, perhaps on Jim's part. He *seems* devoted."

"And," Rhoda put in, casting a glance at the bar, "she appears smitten. They're very young, of course. I don't think people should get engaged until they're thirty. Ricky and I didn't. We had too many things we wanted to do on our own."

"I got engaged fairly often," Renie said. "It got to be sort of a problem. Once, I was engaged to two different men at the same time, and they were both named Bob. It was very confusing."

"I should think so," Rhoda remarked with a wave of her cigarette holder. "Did you marry either of them?"

"No. I went to a psychologist to find out what my problem was," Renie replied. "He told me I was too independent and a control freak."

"Obviously," Rhoda surmised, "he cured you."

Renie nodded. "He certainly did. I married him."

"Very wise," Rhoda said, with another longing glance at the bar.

"We must be keeping you from your daily schedule," Judith said. *Or at least the drinking part of it,* she thought. "We should go."

"Please," Rhoda responded. "I have no fixed schedule. In fact, I was hoping Ricky would get back while you're here." She looked at her diamond-studded wristwatch. "It's after one. He may have stopped for lunch. I'll call him on his cell phone."

Before Rhoda could get up, Rick St. George strode into the room. "Well! My beautiful bride is entertaining! But then she always is, even when we're alone." He smiled wickedly before kissing his wife's cheek. "Could it be," he said to the cousins with mock severity, "that the inquisitive love of my life has been subjecting you to her clever interrogative skills?"

"We've been throwing around some ideas," Judith admitted.

"Ah." Rick poured a drink for his wife and one for himself. "Very sensible. Talent, like knowledge, should be pooled. Ladies?" He tapped the scotch and Canadian whisky bottles. "May I?"

"Just half," Judith replied, taking the almost empty glasses to the bar.

Rick's idea of "half" was half booze, half ice. Judith didn't quibble. The ice would melt.

"So," Rhoda said as she accepted her fresh cocktail, "what did you and Biff learn about the jewel heist?"

Rick sat down in the matching lotus chair and carefully checked the pleats of his well-tailored trousers. "The basics. According to our friend Erma, she had Beulah lock the case shortly after midnight. This morning, while the Giddon bunch was preparing to disembark, Erma asked Beulah for her jewels. That was circa eleven-fifteen. Beulah couldn't find the case. Erma had some kind of fit—she insists it was a heart attack, but Dr. Selig disagrees—and once she recovered, she accused Beulah of stealing it and handing the loot over to an accomplice. No doubt, Erma insisted, one of the many 'coloreds' who are crew members."

Rhoda sighed. "Naturally."

Judith leaned forward on the sofa. "Did Erma leave the bedroom before she asked for her jewels?"

"Of course." Rick chuckled. "Even Dame Erma has to make use of the facilities now and then. Anemone sleeps in the other bedroom. I suppose there's a separate smaller accommodation for Beulah. Even Erma wouldn't expect her maid to sleep on the floor."

Rhoda cast her husband a skeptical look. "Don't be too sure of that, darling."

"Who'd been in the suite that morning?" Judith inquired after a small sip of scotch.

Rick swirled the olive in his martini. "Jim Brooks. Ambrose Everhart. Horace Pankhurst and CeeCee Orr. A crew member who came to repair a leaky faucet in Anemone's bathroom. A waiter with coffee. Oh, and Émile Grenier, making sure that all was right in Giddon world."

"Which it wasn't," Rhoda put in.

"Which waiter?" Judith asked.

"I don't recall his name," Rick replied, "but we're checking him out." He sounded even more blasé than usual.

"And the plumber?" Renie put in as Asthma shook himself with a mighty clanking sound and made an attempt to get up.

"Ozzie Oakes," Rick said.

Renie tried to distance herself from Asthma as the dog collapsed again near her feet. "Is anyone a serious suspect?"

Rick was lighting an unfiltered cigarette. "Too soon to say," he replied a little too casually after exhaling a dark gray cloud of smoke. "Biff will be taking fingerprints."

"Shouldn't he have done that last night?" Judith asked.

"He did, in a way," Rick said with an ironic expression. "That is, he had his men take prints off of the cocktail glasses and some other surfaces."

"Wait a minute," Renie said, looking very serious. "Are you saying that the prints taken last night can be matched to the drinks each individual had?"

"The *San Rafael's* employees are very good," Rick explained. "Like any bartender or bar server, they remember who drank what."

"Of course," Judith murmured, recalling her working nights at the Meat & Mingle. "It's an integral part of the job."

Rick nodded. "You drank Glenfiddich, correct?"

"Yes," Judith replied, anxiety beginning to gnaw at the back of her brain.

He turned to Renie. "Bud Light?" Rick seemed put off by her prosaic choice.

"I didn't actually drink it," Renie said, "but I ordered a bottle."

Rick tapped his cigarette into a marble ashtray. "So both of your prints are on record, along with most of the other guests'. Biff will cover everybody else."

There was a long and—it seemed to Judith—awkward pause. The cousins didn't dare look at each other.

"You see the problem?" Rick finally said.

"Yes," Judith and Renie replied in unison.

Rick took a final puff from his cigarette and put it out in the ashtray. "I'm sure you can explain everything to Biff. But until you do, I'm afraid you're both at the top of the suspect list. Your prints were found all around the area where the jewel case was kept."

Renie was stuffing her face with dim sum. "Dawishis," she declared, and swallowed. "I wonder if they serve food like this in prison."

"The St. Georges aren't serious about us stealing Erma's jewels," Judith responded, setting down the ladle for her hot-and-sour soup.

"The St. Georges aren't serious about anything," Renie said.

"Except murder," Judith murmured. "And jewel heists."

"Maybe." Renie attacked more dim sum. The cousins had left the St. Georges' Nob Hill penthouse shortly after Asthma had suffered a respiratory attack and had to be taken to the vet. On the cousins' way out, Rhoda had suggested that they try Brandy Ho's Hunan restaurant on the edge of Chinatown.

"At least," Judith said, "I found out that the rest of the crew is staying at the Fitzroy Hotel on Post Street. I'd like to talk to Dixie Beales and Émile Grenier. After all, they discovered the body."

Renie concurred. "Good thinking. Is that our next stop?"

"Yes. I'm certainly not going to confront Erma Giddon just after her jewels have been swiped. Especially," Judith added, using chopsticks to pluck a strip of beef from her noodle dish, "if she has any suspicions about us being the thieves."

It was almost two-thirty when Judith and Renie got out of the cab that had taken them from Brandy Ho's. An older, typically narrow San Francisco building, the Fitzroy looked as if it had just been renovated.

Judith snapped her fingers. "I know this place! It's a brand new B&B, only on a much grander scale than Hillside Manor. I got a mailing about it from the California innkeepers association."

"Maybe you can get a job," Renie said, pushing Judith along to avoid another mouthy panhandler.

The lobby was small but attractive. A young woman of Asian descent stood behind the desk, eyeing the cousins with polite curiosity. Her name tag identified her as MIYA.

"We're booked through tonight and possibly the weekend," she said before either Judith or Renie could speak.

"We don't need a room," Judith said, wearing her friendliest smile. "We'd like to see one of your guests, Dixie—that is, May Belle—Beales."

Miya turned to look at the mailboxes. "Ms. Beales is out," she said. "Her key is here. Would you care to leave a message?"

Judith was considering the idea when a man wearing an exotic African cap rushed into the lobby. "My taxi! Lady very sick!" he shouted. "I call to 911! She guest here! Come quick!"

Judith and Renie immediately followed the cabdriver outside. His vehicle was double-parked in the narrow street, causing horns to honk and drivers to curse. Renie had to fend off the offensive panhandler a second time.

Judith waited for the driver to open the rear door. "See?" he said. "She pass out. She very sick."

Leaning into the cab, Judith gently moved a paisley headscarf away from the woman's face. Recognition struck instantly. Judith felt for a pulse.

Renie had joined Judith and the driver.

"It's Dixie Beales," Judith said in a stricken voice. "She isn't sick. She's dead."

Chapter Ten

The cousins could already hear sirens approaching.

"I move taxi," the driver said.

"No," Judith responded, closing the cab door. "Ignore the traffic. It's only going to get worse when the emergency vehicles arrive. Here comes an aid car now."

The driver, who looked Nigerian to Judith, was wringing his hands. "Not my fault! Not my fault! Lady good when she got in taxi!"

Judith cupped her right ear. She could barely hear the agitated man over the din of honking horns, screaming drivers, and shrieking sirens. A crowd was gathering. Even the panhandler seemed curious.

Moving closer to the driver, Judith spoke loudly: "Where did you pick her up?"

"What?"

Judith repeated the question as the aid car came to a stop.

"Neiman Marcus," he answered. "She have many packages."

Judith glanced inside the cab. A half-dozen shopping bags bearing the Neiman Marcus logo were stashed on the other side of Dixie's body.

Renie was looking over Judith's shoulder. "I guess she shopped until she dropped."

"What?" But when Judith turned around, she saw that her cousin's expression was sad. Apparently, the glib remark had just tumbled out.

The driver had taken off his native hat and was holding it out in his hands like a sacrifice. "You see? She dead. Not my fault."

Judith nodded. "Of course not."

Renie poked Judith. "I'm going inside to tell the desk clerk."

"Okay." Judith watched the EMTs hurry to the cab. At least, she thought, she didn't know this bunch by sight, as so often happened at home. They immediately went to work, though Judith knew there was nothing they could do. After a minute or two had passed, they began questioning the driver, whose first name was Joseph, and whose Nigerian surname Judith couldn't catch.

She did, however, know the drill. The firefighters, the ambulance, and a couple of police cars had just pulled into the crowded intersection. Joseph would be questioned closely and his cab would be impounded. The poor man would probably have to go with the police and wait a couple of days until the vehicle was thoroughly checked. Judith ought to know; it had happened to her. Experience—and her gut feeling—told her that Dixie Beales had not died of natural causes.

The body would be placed on a gurney, put in the ambulance, and driven off to the morgue. A tow truck would arrive for the taxi; the emergency personnel would exchange remarks; the crowd would disperse; the panhandler would resume badgering passersby. There was nothing Judith could accomplish by staying on the sidewalk.

Except, making eye contact with a young police officer, she could ask a question.

"Excuse me," she called out, "can you tell me something?"

He moved briskly toward her. The young officer had red hair and green eyes. His name tag identified him as F. X. O'MALLEY.

"Yes?" he said politely.

"Did anyone mention the cause of death?"

"No."

"A heart attack, perhaps?"

O'Malley shrugged.

"Natural causes, I assume?"

He shrugged again, then eyed Judith more closely. "Did you know the deceased?"

Judith started to say yes, but stopped. "Thank you."

She walked back into the lobby.

"Miya's throwing up in the bathroom," Renie announced as Judith approached her by the hotel desk.

"She's that upset?" Judith asked, recalling the first time that a guest had died at Hillside Manor.

"No," Renie replied. "She's pregnant."

A couple of good-looking young men got out of the elevator. They placed their key on the desk and left. No one else seemed to be in the small lobby. Judith went around to the other side of the desk, put the key in the proper slot, and checked the guest register.

"Captain Swafford's here," she noted. "He should be informed at once." But a glance at the key in the captain's mailbox told her that Swafford was out. "Drat," she muttered. "Where're Émile Grenier and Paul Tanaka? They should be staying here, too. Ah. Here they are, in Rooms Twenty-five and Thirty-one."

But their keys were also in their slots. Judith was about to surrender when Émile Grenier himself entered the lobby, looking as self-important as ever.

"You are not Mademoiselle Miya," he accused Judith. The purser scrutinized her more closely. "But I know you. You are perhaps the maid most incompetent?"

"No," Judith replied, taking advantage of Émile's faulty memory. "I'm filling in for Miya. She isn't feeling well. I also own a B&B."

Émile looked as if he didn't think Judith was qualified to run a washing machine. *"Eh bien."* He gestured in the direction of the street. "Why this commotion? Is there a fire?"

"No," Judith replied, noting that Renie had turned her back and seemed absorbed in studying a framed photograph of the original building. "One of the guests has expired. A Ms. Beales. Were you acquainted with the poor lady?"

"Mon Dieu!" Émile slapped a hand to his forehead and had to prop himself up against the desk. "Madame Beales! *Non, non! Quelle horreur!* What happened to *la pauvre femme?*"

"I've no idea," Judith answered. "Apparently she became ill in a taxi on her way back from shopping. Were you close to her?"

The query seemed to catch Émile off guard. "Close?" He hesitated while resuming his usual erect posture. "We worked together. This is terrible news. Excuse me, I must make a telephone call from my room. My key, *s'il vous plaît.*"

With professional aplomb, Judith reached for the key to Room Twenty-five. "My condolences," she murmured.

"Merci, merci," Émile responded before limping off to the elevator.

As soon as the purser had disappeared, Renie rejoined Judith. "I thought if he saw us together, he might remember who you really are," she said. "It's best when I let you lie on your own."

"I didn't exactly lie," Judith said. "I *do* own a B&B."

Renie leaned an elbow on the polished mahogany counter. "Was there blood?"

"Not that I could see," Judith replied, both cousins keeping their voices down in case someone entered the lobby. "I only got a glimpse. The most I could tell—besides recognizing Dixie— was that her face seemed discolored and she looked far from serene."

"As if death hadn't been pleasant," Renie mused. "But you don't suspect the driver?"

Judith shook her head. "If he could act that well, he'd have left Nigeria for Hollywood, not San Francisco. His shock seemed genuine." Abruptly, she turned to face the mailboxes. "Damn! We should use Dixie's key to check out her room. How long is Miya going to be gone?"

"Who knows?"

But Miya was already coming out of a door at the end of the lobby. "Thank you so much, Mrs. Jones," she said. "I feel much better. For now." She looked curiously at Judith. "You're Mrs. Flynn?"

"Yes." Judith felt a bit embarrassed. "Mr. Grenier needed his key." Briefly, she explained that she, too, ran a B&B. "It was second nature to help him," she added with a lame little laugh.

Miya and Judith exchanged places. "That's okay. I'm just upset—not only because the baby makes me throw up, but because I suppose the police will come around here asking a lot of questions. That isn't good for business."

"Um . . ." Judith grimaced. "Over the years, I've had a similar problem or two." Or three or four or five . . . Judith stopped counting the times that the police had come calling at Hillside Manor. "Don't worry about it. Would you mind if we took a look in Ms. Beales's room? Dixie would probably want us to do that for her."

Miya frowned. "Is that . . . I mean . . . maybe I'd better call the manager."

"You should," Judith agreed. "Is he or she on the premises?"

Miya looked pained. "He's my husband. He's at the gym. He should be back anytime."

"You take it easy," Judith insisted as a lanky middle-aged man in a short, weather-beaten raincoat entered the lobby. "We'll take a peek in Dixie's room and be on our way."

Miya also saw the man approaching. His gait was none too steady, and he wore a world-weary smile. "This isn't a guest," she murmured. "Could he be a policeman?"

"Doubtful," Judith said, casting a sidelong glance at the newcomer. "Press, maybe."

"Oh, dear." Miya moved away from the desk, apparently in an effort to forestall the newcomer.

Judith moved swiftly, nipping around to the mailboxes and taking Dixie's key. Motioning to Renie, she hurried toward the elevator.

"You'll get Miya into trouble," Renie warned Judith after the door slid closed and the small elevator creaked upward.

Judith shook her head. "If Biff's put on this case—and don't tell me that if Dixie was murdered, there's no connection with Magglio Cruz's death—then I'll tell him to blame me, not Miya. Honestly, this trip has turned into the worst nightmare ever!"

"Aren't you used to it?" Renie asked wryly as the car stopped at the fourth floor.

"I never get used to it," Judith asserted. "How can you get used to murder?"

Renie had nothing to say.

t first, Judith thought that Dixie's room had been ransacked. But upon closer inspection, she realized that the dead woman was simply untidy.

"What are we looking for?" Renie asked, her eyes scanning lingerie, shoes, and other belongings strewn about the floor and furniture.

"I don't know," Judith answered. "A note, maybe, to see if she was meeting anyone."

There was no note, nor was there a notepad. The only items on the bedside table were the telephone, a lamp, and a small pile of leftover invitations to the VIP party. "Coz," Renie said plaintively, "the cops could be along any minute. You aren't touching anything, are you? I don't want our fingerprints found here, too."

"I'm being careful," Judith insisted, peering into the bathroom and the closet. "We should be wearing gloves. I remember the first time we came to San Francisco with Cousin Sue, all the women wore gloves. We looked like country bumpkins."

"We still do," Renie said, "compared to the way they dress here. We are from the Land of Plod."

"Nothing," Judith said after moving some of the scattered items aside with her foot. She glanced at the party invitations on the bedside table. "I want a souvenir," she said, carefully picking up the top three from the pile and putting them in her purse. "I think I threw mine out. Nobody will miss these, and they're so elegant that I can file them for future special events at the B&B. Otherwise, we're done here. Unless . . ." She spotted an open phone book half hidden under the bed. "You bend. I shouldn't. I think it's the restaurant section."

After putting on her murky glasses, Renie got down on her hands and knees. "You're right. It's open to the Gs. There's something written in the margin." Without touching the directory with her fingers, she managed to shove it out from under the bed. "It says '1 P.M.—GH.' "

"Shall we assume Dixie made that notation?"

"Somebody did," Renie said, standing up and removing her glasses.

"There must be tons of restaurants in San Francisco that begin with *G*," Judith mused.

"There are," Renie said. "I looked. But maybe not *GH*. Unless it's the initials of a person instead of a place."

"We can check our own hotel directory," Judith said. "Let's go. Dixie must have taken her other personal effects with her."

As the elevator door opened onto the lobby, Judith espied not only the man who looked like a reporter, but Captain Swafford and a couple of uniformed police officers. Quickly, she pushed the button for the basement.

After a few more creaks of the cable, the elevator opened onto a small foyer with a large sign that read GUEST PARKING ONLY. Paul Tanaka stood in front of them, looking as surprised to see the cousins as they were to see him.

"Serena! What are you doing here?" he asked, remaining in place.

Judith and Renie emerged from the elevator just as the doors began to automatically close again.

"It's a long story," Renie said with a sigh. "Maybe we should talk."

"Ah . . ." Paul looked uncomfortable. "Shall we go up to my room? I just heard about Dixie. Isn't it terrible? Captain Swafford says it may have been food poisoning."

"Really?" Renie sounded unconvinced. "How does he know? It happened less than half an hour ago."

"It must be a preliminary diagnosis," Paul said as the elevator doors opened once more and the trio entered. "I believe he's been in contact with the hospital. He also sent Dr. Selig to where they took her . . . body. The ship's physician is required to attend to such matters involving crew."

On the third floor, Paul led the way. While the decor was similar to that of Dixie's lodgings, the room itself was much neater. File folders were stacked on the small desk next to a laptop, and no personal belongings had been carelessly left about.

"Have you been out?" Judith asked casually, remembering that Paul's key had been in his mailbox when she was in the lobby.

He nodded as he checked for messages. "I had lunch with some old college friends." Paul scowled as he listened to the recording. "Excuse me," he said. "Connie Cruz called an hour ago. I should ring her back."

Except for the bathroom, there was nowhere Paul could go for privacy. Judith and Renie discreetly turned away.

"Really," Judith whispered, "I should phone Joe. I can tell him now that a crew member had an accident and delayed our departure. You should let Bill know, too."

"Not to mention our mothers," Renie said without enthusiasm. "If a reporter is down in the lobby, I'll bet this whole damned story has broken."

"Not necessarily at home." Judith pointed to a folded copy of the *San Francisco Chronicle* that Paul had left on the desk. "Look. That headline is about pollution in the Bay Area."

"The bays here certainly are a different color," Renie allowed. "Both San Francisco and Oakland's bays look really dirty."

"We've got our own problems," Judith said. "In more ways than one."

A few words of Paul's soft-spoken conversation filtered through: ". . . Not to worry . . . Must rest . . . Arrangements are under way . . . Yes, I'll check her file . . ."

With a sad shake of his head, Paul rang off. "Poor Connie. She's had more than she can bear. She really should have complete rest, but that's not her nature. I'm doing my best to take whatever load I can off her shoulders, but she insists on taking part."

Judith hazarded a guess. "You mean about her husband's services?"

"Partly." Paul turned on his laptop. "I'm sorry, I should check my e-mail, too."

"There can't be a funeral until the autopsy is complete," Judith said. "That is, so I understand."

"True." Paul was still studying the computer screen. "My God, nothing but trouble. The passengers are getting impatient to sail. I don't blame them."

Renie had wandered over to the window, which looked out onto a now relatively calm Post Street. "Will you cancel the cruise?"

"That's not up to me," Paul replied, closing the laptop with an almost defiant click. "Captain Swafford and Connie and maybe even the board of directors will have to make that decision. They'd better act soon. This is a publicity nightmare. I already had to dodge some creep from one of the papers in the hotel lobby."

"Has the story been on TV?" Judith inquired.

Paul nodded. His taut face seemed to have acquired fine lines overnight. "It said Magglio Cruz died of unknown causes during a prelaunch party. There was no mention of foul play, but the language was full of innuendos. Viewers may think we were having an orgy."

"And now," Renie remarked, moving away from the window, "they'll have Dixie's death on the five o'clock news."

"Yes." Paul was silent for almost a minute, staring straight

ahead as if he'd forgotten that the cousins were in the room.
"Sorry." He offered a crooked little smile. "Someone told me you
actually saw Dixie in the cab."

Judith nodded. "I couldn't tell anything. About how she died,
I mean. There was no sign of violence. She'd been shopping, and
maybe out to lunch. Did you know of her plans?"

Paul shook his head. "She loved to shop. She loved to lunch.
She'd made a lot of friends in different ports of call over the
years. She could have been with anybody." His eyes narrowed.
"You aren't thinking of . . . ?" He couldn't finish the question.

"You have to allow for the possibility," Judith said.

Paul must have understood that Judith meant *murder*. He put
his hands over his face. "My God!"

Seeing his distress, Judith couldn't help but think herself callous. She'd witnessed so many other tragedies in recent years
that it was hard to imagine what it was like for the uninitiated to
confront evil.

"Are you talking about a homicidal maniac?" Paul asked, removing his hands and revealing his stricken face.

Renie put a hand on his arm. "Don't overreact," she cautioned
in a calm voice. "Maybe Dixie did die of natural causes. It just
seems strange so soon after Mags was killed. You're a levelheaded
business-as-usual kind of guy with a thorough knowledge of the
company. Can you think of any reason why somebody would
want to harm anyone connected with Cruz Cruises?"

Paul sat down in the chair by the desk. "Of course not." He
seemed to be gathering himself together. "I've been with Cruz
for almost ten years. I joined the company right out of graduate
school, when Mags had only one ship and a couple of sightseeing
boats. There were some rough times, especially when those viral
illnesses broke out on some of the other lines. But since then,
growth has been phenomenal. After 9/11, our business slowly

picked up. People seemed to feel safer on cruise ships than in air-planes or big cities. The demographics favored us, too. Retirees living longer, a more affluent younger crowd—the downswing in the economy only marginally affected us because cruises are always booked so far ahead."

It struck Judith that Paul was talking by rote, as if he'd mem-orized his speech for an investors' presentation. Maybe he had.

"Has the company gone public?" she asked.

Paul shook his head. "No. And we haven't any plans to do that. It's all private investments. We're hardly a megacorporation."

"And," Renie noted, "I always assumed that Mags wanted to stay small."

"Yes," Paul replied. "It's a cruise line, not a conglomerate. We're not looking to buy resorts or hotels or any other vacation property as a tie-in."

Paul's phone rang. He jumped in the chair, gave the cousins an apologetic little smile, and answered the call.

It was a short conversation. Paul repeated "yes" three times and hung up. "It's Captain Swafford," he said, getting to his feet. "He wants me to meet him and Émile in the lobby."

Judith and Renie had no choice but to follow Paul out of the room and down the elevator.

But the hotel seemed calm enough. Captain Swafford was waiting in a wingback chair next to a wall of built-in bookcases. Miya was behind the desk, conferring with an older woman Ju-dith didn't recognize. There was no sign of the police or the re-porter. It seemed as if nothing untoward had happened at the Fitzroy in the last hour.

Swafford looked up when Paul approached, but the captain didn't acknowledge the cousins. Maybe he didn't remember them, either. Judith discreetly dropped off Dixie's key at the desk and led the way out of the hotel.

"Now what?" Renie asked, keeping an eye out for the irksome panhandler or any of his numerous brethren.

Judith surveyed their surroundings. "We're only a couple of blocks from the St. Francis. Let's walk."

The wind chased them down Post Street. The skies had cleared, but it felt more like deep autumn than early spring. Discarded paper, plastic, and other bits of debris flew around their feet as they joined the busy pedestrian traffic. Judith and Renie were accustomed to March breezes at home, but in San Francisco, the wind seemed sharper, just as the city itself appeared more vital and more dangerous.

"Lack of familiarity," Judith murmured as they waited for a stoplight to change at the corner.

"What?"

"I was thinking of this city," Judith said, noticing that unlike at home, pedestrians seemed perfectly willing to risk walking against the warning lights instead of patiently taking their turns. "San Francisco has always been more exotic. Its past clings to it, just like the buildings hang on the hills. The Barbary Coast, Alcatraz, Chinatown, the fire and the earthquakes—along with romance, its history suggests drama and menace."

Renie glanced at her cousin. "Your imagination is running away with you."

"My deductive powers certainly aren't going anywhere," Judith grumbled as they reached the hotel entrance. Inside, she gazed across the spacious lobby to the registration desk. "Let's check for messages before we go to the room."

"They'll be on our voice-messaging system," Renie said. "Save yourself some steps."

Judith agreed. Their suite, which had been cleaned and freshened in their absence, was a welcome relief from the city's bustling noise and brisk winds. Judith collapsed on the couch while Renie checked phone calls, and immediately began making notations. She took so long that Judith sat up straight, anxiety mounting.

Finally clicking off, Renie began to read off of the notepad. "Joe wants to know why we haven't left port. Your mother asked him to ask you if her check got deposited. Arlene Rankers can't find the spot remover. Phyliss Rackley didn't show up today because she has a plantar wart. Rick and Rhoda St. George want us to meet them at Farallon for dinner at seven."

Up until the final message, Judith had felt inundated with relative trivialities. "Why the urgency on the St. Georges' part? We just saw them."

Renie shrugged. "I repeated Rhoda's message almost word for word, except for the part about Farallon being a nearby restaurant on top of the elks' swimming pool."

"What?"

Renie waved a hand. "Maybe it's the Elks Club building. We can look it up in the phone book. Are you going to call Joe?"

Judith sighed. "Yes. I'll do it now. Hand me the phone."

Arlene, not Joe, answered at Hillside Manor.

"Judith! Where are you? Halfway to Hawaii, no doubt. Is it rough? How's the food? Have you met any interesting people? Why doesn't the oven turn on?"

Judith was used to her neighbor's rapid change of topics and occasional self-contradictions. "We haven't left yet. I'll explain in a minute." She paused to think. The Flynns had renovated the kitchen after a fire two years earlier. The new double oven was much more sophisticated than the old one, with digital controls that required only a touch. Judith realized that Arlene might not have had occasion to use the high-tech model until now. After offering directions, she asked what the spot remover was needed for.

"A guest spilled bean dip on one of your new sofas," Arlene replied. "Unfortunately, it was after he ate it."

Judith flinched. "You mean he . . . got sick on the sofa?"

"Yes, but it's fine now. I cleaned it. He's fine, too. At least I haven't seen him since last night."

After all that had happened since leaving Hillside Manor, Judith couldn't remember who or how many guests had been registered at the B&B the previous night. It seemed as if Heraldsgate Hill was a world away. She'd have to back off and let Arlene handle any problems on the home front. That was, in fact, the reason she had gone with Renie. To rest. To relax. To regain her strength. *To find herself in yet another murderous mess.*

"Where's Joe?" Judith asked, forcing a normal tone.

"He's with Bill," Arlene replied. "They're in jail."

Judith shot Renie a startled look. "What do you mean, Joe and Bill *are in jail?*"

Renie had to catch herself from slipping off the arm of the sofa. "What the hell . . . ?" she muttered as she hurried into the bedroom to listen on the extension.

"It has something to do with one of Bill's patients," Arlene explained. "He's been arrested for reckless embarrassment. Or something like that," she added just as Judith heard Renie pick up the other receiver.

"I'm here, too, Arlene," Renie said.

"What?" Arlene sounded taken aback. "Where?"

"On the other line," Renie replied. "What are you talking about?"

"Someone named—" Arlene stopped. "I don't know the name. Bill wouldn't say. Your husband can be very secretive sometimes, Serena. It bothers me."

"I've explained that a hundred times," Renie said impatiently.

"It's doctor–patient confidentiality. Ethics prevent Bill from revealing names."

"Hmm." Arlene was silent for a moment. "Is it someone I know?"

"I doubt it," Renie retorted, though Arlene's circle of friends and acquaintances spanned the city and half the state.

"Is he between the ages of thirty and sixty?" Arlene inquired. "Is he average height, brown hair, blue eyes—"

"Do you have someone in mind?" Renie broke in.

"No," Arlene responded, sounding offended. "I was just trying to get an idea who he might be."

"Forget it," Renie snapped. "Just tell us what happened."

Arlene sighed loudly. "Apparently this man tried to jump off a building. Bill helped him, and the man was taken to the county hospital, and now he's under arrest for . . . whatever I said before."

"Reckless endangerment," Renie murmured.

"Yes, yes, something like that." It was Arlene's turn to be impatient. "So Bill went to see him in the prison hospital or wherever he is, and Joe went along to help with the ransom."

"The ransom?" Renie gasped.

"Yes," Arlene said, still huffy. "This lunatic is holding Oscar hostage. He wants a helicopter and sixty-five dollars in unmarked bills."

"Oscar does?"

"No, no," Arlene replied. "The lunatic." She hesitated. "Or maybe not. What would Oscar do with a helicopter?"

Judith was holding her head. Through the bedroom door she could see Renie, who seemed to be gnawing on the satin counterpane.

Apparently, Arlene interpreted Renie's silence for understanding. "Anyway, I must dash. Now that I know how to turn the oven on, I must prepare the guests' appetizers."

"Wait!" Judith cried. "How's Mother?"

Arlene laughed in her merry way. "She's just wonderful! It was nice today, so we had a little picnic lunch on the patio. Carl brought her some pickled pigs' feet. She says you never buy them even though they're a great favorite of hers. Tonight she's having tongue sandwiches and sweet pickles."

Judith controlled her gag reflex. "Good."

"I'll tell Joe you called," Arlene promised. "Don't worry about a thing. You're not seasick, are you?"

Judith felt like saying that her stomach had been in great shape until Arlene mentioned Gertrude's menu. Instead, she explained that their sailing had been delayed because of a crew member's illness.

"I thought Joe mentioned something about you not leaving on schedule," Arlene said vaguely. "I hope it's not one of those viruses that gets loose on cruises."

"It's not contagious," Judith asserted, nervously wondering if what had befallen Magglio Cruz and Dixie Beales might not yet have run its course. "Thanks, Arlene. Bye."

As soon as she hung up, Judith swore. "Damn! I forgot about Mother's check."

Renie was staggering out of the bedroom. "I should call Bill," she muttered, leaning on an Italianate credenza. "Later, I mean." She focused on Judith. "What check?"

"I told you about it," Judith said, searching her purse for aspirin. "From the movie people. I was supposed to put it in the bank for her, but I ran out of time before we left. I hope to God she hasn't mislaid it. Again."

"It'll turn up," Renie said, sinking into an armchair across from Judith. "Oscar's another matter. I hope Bill's been able to get him back from that nutty Lorenzo. It makes me sick to think what a maniac like that might do."

"Oscar? Bill? Lorenzo?"

Renie shot Judith a dirty look. "Don't be a wiseass. You know that Oscar is part of the family, and has been for almost thirty years. I'd just had the upholstery cleaner freshen him up last week. He was looking very spiffy."

Judith decided to keep her mouth shut. It was always pointless to argue about Oscar's place in the Jones household. Sometimes she wondered why Renie and Bill didn't legally adopt the stuffed animal and be done with it.

Besides, she had problems of her own. Ignoring Renie, who was still moping, Judith dialed Joe's cell phone. But all she got was a recorded message saying that the customer was unavailable and to try later. Either Joe didn't have his phone on or he was someplace where the call couldn't reach him. Like jail.

"The phone book," Judith said suddenly. "We were going to check the G restaurant listings and also find Farallon's address."

"Oh. Right." Renie didn't seem interested.

Judith got out the directory, which was in the drawer of the table where the telephone was sitting along with a fax machine. "We should call Rhoda back, to acknowledge their invitation."

Renie still evinced indifference.

"I found Farallon," Judith said. "It's also on Post Street, just a couple of blocks from the Fitzroy. Let me take a quick look at the G listings, especially anything with *GH*."

Renie was staring off into space.

"Ghirardelli Square?" Judith murmured. "No, that's not near Neiman Marcus . . ."

Renie's words were barely audible. "If only Bill didn't hate the telephone so much . . ."

Judith looked up from the Yellow Pages. "What?"

"I said," Renie repeated, "if only Bill didn't hate using the phone, he'd have his own cell. Then I could call him directly. Now all I can do is wait until I think he might be home. I'm sure he won't try to call me. He might not even realize we're still here, men being what they are."

Regarding her cousin with a less-than-sympathetic expression, Judith uttered an impatient sigh. "Come on, coz, stop fussing about that . . . Oscar. You're supposed to be helping solve a homicide."

Renie hadn't seemed to hear Judith. "Oscar was kidnapped once before, years ago. Bill and I were out of town, and our kids had a party. A couple of them made off with Oscar, and it took three days to get him back. Unharmed, thank God."

Judith kept a straight face. "How could you tell?"

"*Physically* unharmed," Renie said, equally serious. "Emotionally—well, it took time."

"We're not going to talk about this anymore, okay?" Judith said, keeping her voice calm. "You're making me as crazy as you are." She fixed her eyes on the restaurant listings. "Ah. Maybe I've found something—Grandviews Restaurant in the Grand Hyatt off Union Square. That's close to Neiman Marcus, right?"

Renie nodded in a despondent fashion.

"Let's go over to the hotel and see if we can find out if Dixie had lunch there," Judith said. "It's just across the square. But first," she added, "I'm going to take some aspirin."

Judith was in the bathroom when the phone rang. She heard Renie scrambling around in the sitting room, apparently diving for the receiver. By the time Judith joined her cousin, Renie was hanging up.

"Who was that?" Judith asked.

Renie looked disappointed. "I thought it might be Bill, but it wasn't. Rhoda called to make sure we could meet them for dinner."

"You told her yes?"

Renie nodded.

"Did she say why they wanted to see us tonight?"

Renie nodded again.

Judith felt like shaking her cousin. "Well? Why?"

Renie finally met Judith's gaze. "Rhoda and Rick have found out what weapon was used to kill Magglio Cruz."

Chapter Eleven

You didn't ask what kind of weapon?" Judith demanded.

"No." Renie looked contrite. "Sorry. I'm still in shock about Oscar."

"Get over it!" Judith had shouted so loud that she startled not only Renie but herself.

After jumping halfway off the sofa, Renie lost her temper. "Okay, okay! You don't have to yell! What if it was Sweetums? You practically had a nervous breakdown last year when that awful cat wandered off for a few days."

"That's because Sweetums isn't a stuffed . . ." Judith shut up. Again, it was pointless to argue. "Look," she said, lowering her voice and trying to keep on an even keel, "it's almost five o'clock. We've just got time to go over to the Hyatt and show the staff a picture of Dixie Beales. There's one in the cruise brochure, right?"

Renie nodded. "By the way, Rhoda told me they'd tell us what the weapon was when we saw them. I guess she didn't want to mention it over the phone."

"Did she say anything about Dixie?"

"No. Rhoda sounded like she was in a big hurry."

"Oh." Judith wondered if the St. Georges knew about the most recent death. Maybe not, she thought. Rhoda—and possibly Rick—had been involved with taking Asthma to the vet that afternoon. "Let's check the news before we go," Judith said, clicking on the big screen in the living room.

Renie had already put on her raincoat, but sat down again. "Do you want me to call Fitzroy's to see if they've heard anything about Dixie?"

"Go ahead," Judith said. "You phone, I'll watch."

Renie's call was fruitless. "I got a recording saying that all lines were busy and to leave a message or call back."

"They may be overwhelmed," Judith remarked, waiting out a series of hour-turn TV commercials. "The police, the cruise personnel, the press. Not to mention other guests, who must be asking all kinds of questions." She ought to know. She sympathized with the Fitzroy's staff.

The headlines had nothing to do with Cruz Cruises, unless, Judith noted, she counted the persistent stories about pollution in the bay. Certainly, she thought, a murder most foul ought to muddy the waters as well. But social issues and city politics were the main topics.

"We'd better go," she said at the first commercial break. "We have to be back here in time to get dressed for dinner. And for heaven sakes," she added, noting Renie's lingering expression of gloom, "stop dwelling on that damned ape! You're driving me crazy!"

Rain was slanting down across Union Square when the

cousins left for the Hyatt. It was only a long block away, but they kept their heads down and their faces shielded from the chilling drops.

"Why do people who've never been to the West Coast assume that California is all sun?" Renie muttered as they entered the sanctuary of the hotel lobby. "And wouldn't you know, we brought cruise clothes."

"San Francisco's weather is very different from anywhere else on the West Coast. It was about ninety when we came here that first time," Judith reminded her cousin. "Late September, too."

"We wore wool and smelled like sheep." Renie pointed to a sign that informed them of the hotel's features. "Grandviews is on the top floor."

San Franciscans dined late. The restaurant was open, but at five-thirty, it was virtually deserted except for the staff. Judith barely had time to take in the spectacular view of Coit Tower and the Oakland Bay Bridge before a chic and efficient-looking dark-haired woman approached them.

"I'm confused," Judith said, and looked it as she fumbled in her purse for the photo of Dixie that Renie had clipped from the cruise brochure. "We're supposed to meet someone, but . . ." She made a helpless gesture before showing the picture to the woman. "Could she have meant lunch, not dinner? Do you recognize her?"

The woman put on a pair of half-glasses and gazed at the color reproduction. "Is she from the South?"

"Yes," Judith replied eagerly. "She has quite an accent. In fact, her nickname is Dixie."

The woman didn't look as if she approved of nicknames. "It would be," she remarked drily. "No, I don't remember seeing her."

"But . . ." Judith stared as the woman removed her glasses. "I thought . . ."

"I *heard* her," the woman interrupted. "She had a very carrying voice, inappropriate for a dining room where guests enjoy quiet conversation. I asked the server to request that she speak more quietly."

"Is the server here?" Judith asked.

The woman shook her head. "Dominic is breakfast and lunch only. But he did ask her to keep her voice down. Apparently, she'd had too much to drink and was quarreling with her companion. Excuse me," she said abruptly as a distinguished-looking older couple entered from the elevator area. "I'm busy."

Renie snatched the cutout picture away from Judith and thrust it in front of the woman. "And *she's* dead. Is food poisoning the soup du jour?"

The woman froze. The couple approached.

"Good evening, Amalie," the silver-haired man said pleasantly. "We're early. As usual." He laughed softly. "Did I hear someone mention *poisson* soup for tonight?"

"Our usual savory seafood stew," Amalie replied, managing a ghostly smile. "Delighted to see you both. Would you mind waiting just a moment? Your favorite table isn't quite ready."

The couple nodded affably and withdrew a few paces. The woman called Amalie moved out of the newcomers' line of sight. "Is this extortion?" she demanded in a low, angry voice. "Explain yourselves, or I'm calling the police."

"They're already involved," Judith said quietly. "All we want to know is who Dixie—Ms. Beales—was with today."

Amalie looked Judith straight in the eye. "I don't know. Dominic mentioned it was a young—and attractive—man. They had a disagreement. They left. I'd appreciate it if you'd do the same."

A pair of waiters and a man in a dinner jacket had appeared behind Amalie. None of them, especially the formally clad man, looked friendly. Judith knew when she was about to get the bum's rush.

"Thanks," she said, and started out of the restaurant.

"Thanks?" Renie repeated, trailing behind Judith. "For what? Being almost no help?"

"This is a very nice establishment," Judith declared, pressing the elevator button. "We intruded."

"We usually do," Renie noted.

"This is different," Judith said, entering the elevator. "It's not only that this city is much more formal and less relaxed. We're not at home. We're not comfortable in this environment. People here have standards. Or something."

Renie sighed as the express car took them straight to the lobby. "I've rarely seen you give up so fast."

"I'm not giving up," Judith countered with a sly little smile. "Of course I want to know who lunched with Dixie Beales. And why they had a quarrel."

"So?"

The cousins had exited the hotel, once again facing the blustery wind and rain. "This isn't our town. This isn't our style." She leaned forward into the elements. "This is a job for Rick and Rhoda St. George."

The difference in style was evident when Judith and Renie met the St. Georges at Farallon: Judith had brought along a navy-blue shirtwaist dress for the cruise; Renie relied on sleeveless basic black. Rhoda swept into the restaurant wearing a green silk georgette evening gown with spaghetti straps and a swath of white fox fur draped over her arms. At first glimpse, Judith thought she was wearing the dog.

"This," said Rick, whose dark suit might have come from London's Savile Row, "is the next best thing to being at sea. How do you like the ocean theme? The restaurant's named for some islands just off the coast."

Judith had admired the blue glass sculptures and the mosaic tiles upon their arrival. They were now seated in the vaulted dining room, which was indeed above the Elks Club swimming pool. It wasn't hard to imagine that they were on a ship.

"It's lovely," she said, though the decor wasn't uppermost in her mind. "I hear you have news. So do we."

"All in good time," Rick said, summoning a waiter. "The usual for us, Marco. Ladies?"

After the cocktail orders had been taken, Rick offered advice about the menu. "Definitely the seafood," he asserted. "There's a touch of French in the edibles, but mainly this is a place to let your palate explore."

"Yes," Judith said tersely. "We'll do that." She offered Rhoda an encouraging look. "You told Serena you'd discovered what weapon was used to kill Magglio Cruz."

Rhoda cast a smile in her husband's direction. "That was Ricky's doing. Oh—here come the drinks. A toast, darling," she said. "You do the honors."

Ricky raised his double martini. "To new friends from the woodsy world of the great Northwest." The foursome clicked glasses. "To old friends who have sailed beyond the bar. Poor devils." They clicked again.

If there was supposed to be a moment of silence, Renie broke it: "Are you including Dixie Beales in that toast? Because she is— toast, I mean."

Rhoda looked a bit wistful. Rick inclined his head to one side. "Yes, I suppose I am," he said quietly. "Poor woman. There's no autopsy report as yet. I heard you were actually at the Fitzroy when she arrived."

"She'd already departed," Renie put in.

Rick chuckled. "Well put. Biff questioned the hotel staff late this afternoon. Dr. Selig will keep us informed as to cause of death as soon as he finds out."

Rhoda was shaking her head. "Such a waste."

Judith's expression was sad. "Yes. She must have been quite talented."

"What?" Rhoda seemed taken aback. "Oh—yes, I suppose. I mean to waste all those clothes she'd bought at Neiman Marcus. Of course, Dixie's taste was a bit florid."

"To get back to the weapon," Judith began, turning to Rick, "what was it?"

Marco returned, sliding up to the table as smoothly as olive oil on a baguette. "May I recommend the crab with cardoons?" he inquired.

"Cartoons?" Renie said. "Are they animated? How about Donald Duck or Porky Pig?"

Rick smiled in his urbane manner. "I recall advising the seafood."

"Cardoons are similar to artichokes," Marco explained, managing to look as if he didn't believe Renie was an out-of-town idiot.

Renie was undaunted. "Is the crab Dungeness?"

Marco didn't even blink. "Of course."

"Okay," Renie said. "Sounds good to me."

At Rhoda's urging, Judith selected sea urchin custard with caviar. The St. Georges settled on lobster-and-scallop stew—along with another round of martinis.

Judith was in a stew of her own. But as soon as Rick had his second drink in hand, he picked up his table knife. "Items such as this should be dismissed immediately as the weapon. Dr. Selig informs me that Mags was stabbed to death, but not with a knife of any kind. Rather, it was a puncture wound. Quite deep, and in a vital spot, which I won't detail because we're at dinner. Suffice to say that death came quickly." He paused to sip his fresh drink.

Judith had long ago stopped being squeamish. "Did he bleed out or was it internal?"

Rick raised an eyebrow. "My, my. That sounds like the voice of a hardened expert."

"My husband is a retired policeman," Judith said in a non-committal tone. "Homicide, in fact. I've heard stories."

"Ah." Rick smiled again. "The answer is internal bleeding."

"Gruesome," Rhoda murmured, though she seemed unfazed.

"But tidy," Rick remarked. "So we eliminate the usual type of weapon associated with stab wounds. We also must consider what was at hand."

"You mean as a weapon?" Judith put in.

Rick nodded. "Think back to the party. There were other means."

"Like part of the decor?" Renie offered.

Rick's expression was droll. "If you're referring to someone dismantling the ship, no. Nothing was found to be out of place, missing, or damaged. The solution is quite simple. Think beef."

"Darling," Rhoda said in a reproachful voice, "you're being obscure. You already ruled out knives."

"But, my dove," Rick inquired with a twinkle in his eye, "what do you use to make those knives work?"

Rhoda snapped her fingers. "A sharpener! Of course! They're long, pointed, and can be very dangerous."

"That's right," Judith agreed. "I often plunge the sharpener into a roast to remove it from the oven. Those things are extremely strong."

"Gack," said Renie.

"The carving sets were right in plain sight," Judith declared.

"I remember watching one of the servers slice the roast beef. I assume there was more than one set. Has the sharpener that killed Magglio Cruz been found?"

Rick shook his head. "Too easy to toss overboard. An inventory of the galley has been taken, but frankly, it's not exact. Carving sets, even standard ones such as they use on the cruise line, come in all kinds of assortments—carver, slicer, fork, sharpener, and variations thereof."

"But," Judith persisted, "the medical examiner is sure that was the weapon?"

"It has to be," Rick replied. "I figure Mags's murder wasn't premeditated. The killer used whatever was at hand—in this case, a knife sharpener. It would be easy to hide under clothing, and not missed right away as a knife would be."

Rhoda was applauding. "Fantastic, darling. You've done it again!"

Rick, however, didn't seem that pleased. "We know how, but we don't know why—and more importantly, we don't know who."

The appetizers arrived. Judith had never eaten sea urchin, and wasn't sure she wanted to now. But the custard presentation was invitingly nestled in an eggshell. To her delight, the taste was delicious.

"Is there anything new on Mrs. Giddon's jewel robbery?" Judith asked after savoring the first few bites.

"Not yet," Rick replied. "Erma would have insisted on arresting Beulah, but the old girl relies on her so much that she'd have to post immediate bail. Frankly, I have some other ideas about that."

"Such as?" Judith asked.

Rick chuckled. "Let's say we could round up the usual suspects." He stopped as Renie rose from the table. "Don't you like your crab and cardoons?"

"Yes," Renie replied, "but my appetite is off. I have to make a phone call. I'll finish when I come back."

Rhoda's eyes followed Renie out of the dining room. "She seems a bit upset. Is it because of the murders?"

"Ah . . . yes and no." Judith didn't feel up to explaining the Joneses' domestic situation. "There's a small crisis on the home front. I believe she went to call her husband."

Rick gazed at Judith over the rim of his martini glass. "The shrink?"

"Why, yes," she replied, surprised. "How did you know?"

"Biff told me," Rick said. "Apparently, Dr. Jones worked with him on a poisoning case years ago."

Judith had forgotten about Renie's tall tale. "Yes," she said, and quickly changed the subject. "Is there any word of when we sail?"

Rick shook his head. "The skipper's fit to be keel-hauled. All of the senior crew members are lodged at the Fitzroy. Naturally, they're agog. Or aghast. Some of them are getting a persecution complex. Maybe your cousin's other half could help them out. If he happened to be here."

Judith's eyes strayed around the restaurant as it began to fill with affluent customers of every nationality, some wearing their finest native garb. San Francisco had always been the gateway to the Orient, but in later years, the city on the hill had welcomed visitors from all over the world. Judith tried not to gawk even as she posed a question. "Are you saying that the crew believes they're being targeted by a killer?"

Rhoda nodded. "First Mags, then Dixie. Who's next? At least that's how Émile and Paul and the others feel, from the board room to the engine room."

"That might indicate a grudge against the company," Judith reasoned.

"Possibly," Rick allowed. "More remote—but still worthy of consideration—is an effort to put Cruz out of business."

"But who benefits?" Judith queried.

"Only rival cruise lines," Rick said. "But no reputable outfit would dream of such a thing. They'd offer a buyout first."

"Which," Rhoda noted, "no one has done."

"Not to mention," Judith said, "there must be ways of causing a business to fail that don't involve cold-blooded murder." She glanced from one St. George to the other. "You do think Dixie was murdered, don't you?"

Rick looked resigned. "Probably."

Judith took the opportunity to tell Rick and Rhoda about the frustrating visit to Grandviews. "Amalie and her colleagues thought we were a couple of snoopy rubes," she said in summing up. "Which, I guess, we are. But if you—"

She stopped as Marco approached with menus—and Ambrose Everhart.

"Excuse me, Mr. St. George," Marco said, bending to speak into Rick's ear, "but this young gentleman says he knows you. Is it all right?"

"Of course, of course," Rick said genially. "Ambrose, my lad, pull up a chair."

Marco was swift to comply. "Would the gentleman care for a beverage?" the waiter asked.

"Just water, please," Ambrose said, picking up Renie's napkin and wiping small beads of perspiration from his forehead. "I didn't mean to break in like this, but Mrs. Giddon insisted I find you. I've already been to five other restaurants around here."

"You've struck gold," Rick said. "Here we are, along with the charming Mrs. Flynn and her cousin—wherever she may be."

Ambrose didn't look as if he knew Judith or cared if her cousin was lying at the bottom of the Elks Club swimming pool.

Suddenly realizing that the napkin had been well used by Renie, he fastidiously placed it on the vacant chair. "Mrs. Giddon put in an insurance claim this afternoon, and she's going to sue the cruise line. She says her late husband would never forgive her for letting those jewels get stolen. Some of them had been handed down in his family for five generations. She's really beside herself."

"Quite a vision, that," Rick murmured.

But Ambrose wasn't finished. "Mrs. Giddon may sue the police department and the city as well," he added before suddenly noticing Judith. "Oh! I beg your pardon! Maybe I shouldn't be talking about this in front of . . . that is . . ." He ran a finger under his shirt collar.

Rick patted Ambrose's shoulder. "You're among friends, young Everhart. In other words, Mrs. Giddon is acting like Mrs. Giddon. Has it occurred to her that in suing the cruise line, she's suing herself?"

Marco brought the glass of water. Ambrose took a big gulp before he answered. "She resigned from the board this afternoon. Horace Pankhurst is furious."

Rhoda put both hands on her hips and stared at the private secretary. "No one told me. I should have been notified, since I'm on the board, too."

Ambrose hung his head. "Sorry," he mumbled. "Truly."

"It's not up to you," Rhoda said. "Erma should have personally informed me."

Rick leaned toward his wife. "Maybe one of them did call while we were out. I only checked the important messages." He winked.

Rhoda looked slightly appeased, but before she could speak, Renie staggered up to the table. "It's over!" she announced, causing heads to turn at the surrounding tables. "Oscar's been freed!"

"Oscar?" Rhoda repeated in a curious voice. "Who is Oscar?"

Judith made a frantic gesture at her cousin. "Never mind," she said airily. "It's a long story, and has nothing to do with what's going on here. Sit down, coz. Finish your appetizer."

Renie shot Judith a baleful look, but removed the napkin from her chair and sat. "Ambrose?" she said, noticing the newcomer. "Do you want to hear about Oscar?"

"What?" The young man drank another swig of water.

Judith kicked at Renie under the table, but missed and hit the chair leg instead. She winced before speaking up: "Erma Giddon resigned from the cruise-line board this afternoon."

"No kidding," Renie said, gobbling up the rest of her crab. "Say, Ambrose, do you like animals?"

Ambrose seemed startled by the question. "Yes, certainly, I'm involved with PETA. You know, People for the Ethical Treatment of Animals." He avoided looking at the fox pelts that were draped over the back of Rhoda's chair.

Rhoda, however, read his mind. "These little devils," she said, running her fingers through the luxurious fur, "were tried and convicted of killing four dozen helpless baby chicks—just before Easter. Which comes first, Ambrose—the chicken or the vixen?"

"Well . . . that's a good question, ma'am," Ambrose responded, scratching his head.

"So if you like animals," Renie said, "you'd enjoy spending time with—"

Judith aimed another kick at Renie. This time she connected. "You haven't decided on your entrée, *coz dear.*"

"Oh." Renie finally took the hint.

"Are you joining us?" Rhoda inquired of Ambrose.

"Oh—no, thank you. I must get back to Mrs. Giddon. Anemone is having quite a time keeping her mother calm. Jim

Brooks is there, but he worries more about his fiancée than about his future mother-in law."

"I should hope so," Rhoda remarked. "Run along now, Ambrose, and do your duty. By the way, where is Mr. Pankhurst?"

Ambrose looked pained. "He and Mrs. Giddon had an awful row. She even threatened to fire him as her financial adviser and attorney. I guess he went off with Miss Orr to lick his wounds."

"Or something like that," Rick murmured. "My, it sounds as if they had a high old time in the Giddon manse. Report back to us if there's any serious bloodshed."

But nobody—not even Rick—cracked a smile.

Chapter Twelve

Ambrose Everhart's departure seemed to signal a change in the atmosphere. Rick and Rhoda took eating as seriously as they did drinking, which, Judith calculated, seemed to be about the only things—other than murder—that the couple didn't dismiss with glib tongues and flippant attitudes. Certainly Farallon's food was worthy of attention.

"So we're still landlubbers awaiting anchors aweigh," Rick said as they finished their meal with fruit and a cheese tray. "Fortunately, we don't have schedules to keep. Do you?"

Judith explained that she had a B&B to run; Renie worried that if Cruz Cruises suffered a serious scandal, she'd have to get busy finding another client to fill the void.

"Not to mention," Judith added, "that our husbands wouldn't like to have us gone for too long. They miss us. I think." She omitted mentioning Gertrude, who was probably more anxious for her daughter's return than she'd ever admit.

Marco had glided up to the table once again. "There's another gentleman to see you, Mr. St. George," he said in his soft-spoken manner. "He won't come into the dining room. He's not dressed."

"At all?" Rick responded casually.

Marco cleared his throat. "I meant to say that he isn't wearing proper attire. He looks a bit . . . unkempt."

"Biff," Rick said, getting up from the table. "Excuse me, ladies. There may be news."

"Biff," Rhoda repeated after her husband had gone. "Such a shambles of a man. But he doesn't mind doing the dog work."

Judith glanced at her watch. It was after ten o'clock. She was anxious to call Joe, which she'd planned to do when they returned to the hotel. But if Biff McDougal really did have some new information, it might take a while to sort out. Excusing herself, she sought out Marco and asked where the telephones were located. She preferred not using her cell, since she hadn't taken time to recharge the battery before leaving town.

Marco pointed the way. The booths, which were shaped like seashells, also happened to be near the alcove that led to the restrooms. Rick and Biff could be heard—but not seen—talking in the open area between the men's and women's entrances. Judith couldn't resist listening in.

"It's gonna be all over the news tomorrow," Biff said in a disgusted voice. "That dopey Buzz Cochran let himself get conned by Flakey Smythe."

"Flakey's conned more than one cop out of a story, Biff," Rick said. "Don't beat yourself up over that. Buzz is a rookie. Give him some slack. He's not used to subterfuge from journalists. That's what makes Flakey a hotshot reporter. He's sharp, he's clever, he gets the scoops."

"Flakey's drunk half the time," Biff grumbled. "I ought to know—I run into him all the time at my own hangouts. You can bet he doesn't get anything out of me, even if he does offer to buy now and then."

Judith was sitting in the booth at the end of the row. She pretended to dial, just in case the men suddenly came out of the alcove.

"What about Blackie?" Rick asked.

"He's up to something, all right," Biff replied. "But he's not talking. Not yet. Don't worry, I've got my ways."

"Of course you do," Rick said agreeably.

"Anything new on Wilbur?" Biff inquired.

"He's still missing."

Biff cursed under his breath. "That Giddon woman's gonna drive me 'round the bend. C'mon, Rick—you know anything I don't?"

Judith heard Rick chuckle. "Do you think I'm holding back on you, old son?"

There was a pause. "Well—you do sometimes. I mean, you got all that stuff running around in your head like so many rats in a sewer—no offense, Rick—but you don't always open up until you're sure of a thing. You know what I'm saying?"

"Yes, I do, Biff. It's my way of solving cases. No point in tipping my hand too soon. I may have misread my cards or misjudged another player. Be patient. I'd better get back to the dining room now. Keep me posted from your end."

"Right." There was a brief silence. Judith pretended she was talking into the phone. But Biff spoke again. "I might as well use the facilities while I'm here. Will they throw me out because I'm not dressed like the rest of the swells?"

"Of course not," Rick said. "I'll go with you. Say, I hear there's a horse named Sweet Pea running down at . . ." His voice died away as the pair entered the men's room.

Judith moved to the far end of the phone booths. She misdialed twice before the phone finally rang at Hillside Manor. *Wilbur.* The name was distracting her. She'd heard it before, but couldn't recall where or when. The last twenty-four hours had been so full of new names and places and—

"Joe?" she said in a startled voice. "Is that you?"

"Of course it's me," he said, sounding hoarse. "I've got a cold. Where are you? Where're the cough drops?"

"I'm still in San Francisco," Judith replied. "The cough drops are in the medicine closet by the decongestants and the nose drops. How did you get a cold?"

"Standing out in the rain waiting for Bill's lunatic to drop that damned Oscar out of the hospital window," Joe said in an annoyed tone. "It took two hours and four firefighters from Bayview."

"Are you serious?"

"Of course I'm serious. Where's the decongestant?"

Judith could hear rummaging in the background. Joe must have taken the phone into the bathroom. "The middle shelf," she said. "There are two bottles. One's blue and the other one's green. Use the blue one. It's for nighttime symptoms. Is your throat sore?"

"Sore as hell."

"Gargle with warm salt water." Judith waited a moment. "Do you see the cough drops?"

"No. Yes, here they are. Ooof!"

There was a clatter followed by muffled swearwords. "I thought you were at the jail, not the hospital," she said after the cussing turned into a cough.

"That was later," Joe croaked. "The nut was at Bayview Hospital for evaluation. Then he got unruly. That's when he made a dive for Oscar." Joe sneezed a couple of times. "I still can't find the cough drops."

"I told you, they're by the decongestant."

Silence. Judith waited, visualizing Joe's search of the medicine closet. The red-and-gold box was probably right in front of him.

"I found them," he said, coughing again. "They were on the floor. I guess I knocked them off the shelf."

"You couldn't have gotten a cold this fast," Judith said. "It must have been coming on earlier. Or maybe it's allergies."

"Bunk. I don't have allergies. I know a cold when I get one. It started about two hours ago. We didn't get back from the jail until almost eight. The rain was coming down in buckets, not like the usual drizzle."

Judith didn't want to hear the details—although if Joe kept talking about his misadventures, she wouldn't have to reveal hers. "Bill must be glad he got Oscar back," she remarked.

"I had to lend Bill twenty bucks," Joe replied, his speech apparently further hampered by the cough drop he was sucking. "He only had forty and change on him."

"You mean for Oscar's ransom?"

"Right." Joe sneezed some more.

Judith held the receiver away from her ear an inch, as if the germs could travel along the phone line. "What about the helicopter?"

"We tricked Lorenzo on that one," Joe said. "One of the medevacs landed on the hospital pad and we told him it was his chopper. That's when he fell out the window."

"He was threatening to jump again?"

"No, he was trying to look up at the copter on the roof. He

leaned too far. Luckily, the firefighters were there and caught him."

Judith was confused. "Why were they called in if Lorenzo wasn't going to jump?"

"Because he was going to throw Oscar out the window after the copter got there." Joe sounded weary. "Hey, I really have to get some sleep. I can't be sick for the trial when it starts Monday. How come you haven't left yet?"

"Personnel problems," Judith said blithely. "Don't worry, Renie and I are fine. We just had a nice dinner with some new friends. Take care of yourself. I'll call again tomorrow."

"If I'm still alive," Joe said.

Judith liked his chances better than those of some other people she could name.

Dixie Beales had been poisoned. Dr. Selig had passed on the medical examiner's findings to Biff McDougal around nine o'clock that evening. The exact type of poison had not yet been determined.

"Did it happen at lunch?" Judith asked Rick as they sat in Farallon's bar having after-dinner drinks.

"Dixie didn't eat much," Rick said. "She had drinks instead. We'll know more details in the morning."

Rhoda placed a hand on her husband's arm. "We must go to Grandviews and find out who Dixie lunched with. 'An attractive young man' is a rather vague description. It needn't even be anyone we know."

Rick turned to Judith. "Dominic was the server?"

Judith nodded. "That's what Amalie told us."

Rick sighed. "Dominic is over seventy. He's an institution among San Francisco waiters. He's amazing, but has the temperament of a prima donna *assoluta*. I believe Dominic started out at the age of seventeen at either Ernie's or the Blue Fox. To him, 'young' might mean anybody under sixty."

Rhoda pressed Rick's arm more firmly. "You forgot to mention that he's half blind. Dominic is far too vain to wear glasses, and unable to use contact lenses."

"But his hearing is adequate," Rick pointed out. "We'll breakfast there tomorrow, my darling."

Judith regarded the St. Georges with awe. "Is there anyone in San Francisco you don't know?"

Rick and Rhoda exchanged bemused glances. "Probably not," Rhoda said. "At least not anyone we *ought* to know. My dear husband is particularly democratic. He knows all sorts of people." Her meaning was quite clear to Judith.

Renie failed to suppress a yawn. "I'm beat," she admitted. "We should settle the bill."

Rick smiled. "It was settled long ago."

The cousins thanked their hosts. But Judith didn't stir from her chair. "It does begin to sound like a vendetta, doesn't it?"

Rick maintained his customary urbane manner. But Rhoda frowned. "It does, I suppose." She again locked glances with her husband. "It's a bit unsettling, really. After all, darling, I'm on the board. I could be next."

The cousins woke up to sunshine Saturday morning. Standing by the window, Judith thought the bright day could be deceptive. The tall glass-and-steel buildings that shone so brightly didn't necessarily mean it was warm outside. There could be wind. There usually was in San Francisco, whipping off from the bay, swirling up and around and down the many hills.

Renie was in an uncharacteristically good mood, even though it was not quite nine o'clock.

"What's with you?" Judith asked as her cousin perused the room-service menu.

"I feel so much better since I talked to Bill last night and found out about Oscar," Renie explained.

Judith sat down on her own bed opposite Renie. "Look at me," she commanded.

Puzzled, Renie complied. "Do I look funny?"

"No funnier than you usually do in the morning." But Judith was serious as she studied her cousin's face. That was the problem—Renie was also serious. There was no indication that she was fantasizing. Oscar was a genuine part of the Jones family. Judith knew that Bill and Renie's three children—and now their spouses—all treated Oscar as if he were a real being. Indeed, Judith recalled to her dismay, at least once when visiting the Jones household, she'd almost sat on the stuffed ape—and—without thinking—had apologized to him for the near miss.

"Yes," Judith said grudgingly, "I'm glad Oscar's back in his usual place on the sofa. What did you tell Bill about our delay?"

"Nothing." Renie had gone back to reading the menu, a task she always concentrated on as if she were a scholarly monk studying an illuminated manuscript from the Middle Ages. "He didn't ask. But my mother did."

"You talked to Aunt Deb?" Judith said in surprise. "When was that?"

"After I talked to Bill," Renie replied, still scouring the breakfast selections. "As usual, the conversation with my husband was brief and to the point. But I knew that Mom would be worrying her head off because I hadn't called her yet. You know how she is—a day without at least one visit and three phone calls from me is tantamount to my demise. So I phoned her, and merely said that the crew was having some problems. That led to the usual cautions about not talking to strangers, not going anywhere without forming a human chain, avoiding lounge lizards, protecting myself against germs, and wearing warm clothing. By the time she finished, I had to get back to the table. But," Renie added, finally handing the menu to Judith, "the part about warm clothing was apt. We need to go shopping, or we're going to freeze."

"You're thinking Neiman Marcus?"

Renie made a face. "I'd rather go to Saks. It's right across the street. But if we're going to sleuth, then it's Neiman Marcus."

"Sorry if you have to suffer for the sake of truth," Judith said, always slightly awed by Renie's freewheeling ways when it came to buying clothes. Not that her cousin actually spent much on her regular wardrobe, which was basically a ragged collection of old jeans, tees, and sweatshirts. But for professional purposes, Renie splurged a couple of times a year, and had a closet filled with designer items.

"It's too bad," Renie said later as they walked past Union Square to the department store's location on Stockton Street, "that you didn't get a peek into any of Dixie's shopping bags. Then we'd know what departments to check out."

"Rhoda mentioned that Dixie's tastes were florid," Judith replied, noticing that the morning was as pleasant as it looked.

"That's a help," Renie said as they stopped to wait for the traffic light to change. "What do we expect to find out from the sales staff?"

"If Dixie was with anyone, if she mentioned meeting a specific person—you know, all the things that women chatter about when they're trying on clothes. She might even have—" Judith stopped as a headline in the news box next to the street lamp caught her eye. "Coz! Look!"

Renie looked.

MURDER COUNT UP TO TWO; CRUZ LINE SINKING FAST

Judith managed to find exact change in her purse and bought a paper. "The byline belongs to Flakefield Smythe," she said. "I overheard Rick and Biff talking about a reporter by that name last night. Apparently, he'd gotten some information out of Biff's rookie partner."

The light had changed and changed again. Judith waited impatiently until they were able to cross the street and enter Neiman Marcus. The atmosphere was quiet, almost stately, with customers moving at a leisurely pace. The place reeked of affluence and self-indulgence.

"Shoes," Judith said, gesturing straight ahead. "We can sit down and read the article."

"Whoa!" Renie cried as they passed the first display table. "Check out the Manolo Blahnik ruched pumps! And how about these patent Giuseppe Zanottis with the—"

Judith yanked Renie by the arm. "Sit down and shut up. We're here to read, not buy."

"But we have to pretend," Renie reasoned, allowing herself to be dumped into a chair next to a grouping of evening shoes. "Thus we must at least try on a pair or two."

"You try, I'll pry," Judith muttered, spreading the newspaper out in her lap. "Okay, here's what it says . . ."

But a sales associate was already standing in front of Renie, materializing as if from a genie's lamp. He was dressed almost as nattily as Rick St. George and his name tag identified him as REUBEN.

Judith did her best to disassociate herself from Renie and Reuben. Hiding behind the newspaper, she read Flakefield Smythe's semisensational coverage.

> Thursday night's brutal stabbing death of Magglio Cruz, owner and CEO of Cruz Cruises, and yesterday's fatal poisoning of May Belle (Dixie) Beales, the *San Rafael*'s entertainment director, could sink the well-known luxury line, according to observers.

Judith wondered if *observers* should be singular, and that the opinion was that of the writer.

". . . Seven medium," Renie was saying. "I have a narrow heel, but my . . ."

The next paragraph was mainly factual, dealing with the ship's proposed maiden voyage, the VIP party, and the ensuing events.

> Police sources stated that Cruz wasn't known to have any personal or professional enemies, but that the murder may have been an unpremeditated crime of passion.
>
> "Stuffing the body into a piano while a VIP party was going on seems like the work of a desperate killer," said an unidentified police source. "That took nerve and a lot of luck."

Judith frowned. Even Biff McDougal wouldn't be so crass— or indiscreet. The quote—if it was authentic—had to come from his partner. Judith searched her memory for the rookie's name. Bub . . . No, that was Bill's brother . . . Bud . . . That didn't sound right, either . . . *Buzz*. That was the name. Buzz Cochran. Judging from his loose tongue, Judith didn't think Buzz had a very bright future with the San Francisco Police Department.

"Real snakeskin?" Renie said to Reuben. "Goodness, at three seventy-five, that's quite a bargain."

The same source added that the poisoning death of Beales might be connected. "You can't have two people who work for the same company get murdered within twenty-four hours of each other and not be suspicious," the police-department employee said.

The next paragraph related how Beales had died in a taxi en route to her hotel from a shopping expedition. The rest of the article was devoted to a brief history of Magglio Cruz and the company he'd built.

Judith emerged from behind the paper just as Renie slipped her feet out of a pair of Kate Spade slides. "I'll take those, too," she informed Reuben. "I want them all shipped to my home address."

" 'All'?" Judith repeated.

"Just three pairs," Renie replied, digging out her Neiman Marcus credit card. "I couldn't resist."

Reuben, having gathered up the three shoe boxes, accepted the card and smiled invitingly at Judith. "Was there something I could show you, madam?"

"The door," Judith murmured.

"I beg your pardon?"

"The floor—the floor where they carry dresses," she said more loudly.

"Of course." Reuben managed to cover his disappointment. "Take the escalator . . ."

"How much?" Judith demanded as the cousins glided up to women's apparel.

"Don't ask. I won't tell."

"I already did. Ask, I mean."

"A little over a grand, okay?" Renie was defensive.

"Good grief!"

"I know." They reached the second floor. "Now I feel guilty. I'll have to start handing out twenty-dollar bills to homeless persons."

Judith, however, was ready to put Renie's extravagance aside. "Where do we start?" she asked, gazing around at the various sections.

Renie also studied the layout, then gave a start. "Why not over there where Anemone Giddon is pawing through the racks?"

Judith spotted the young woman instantly. "She's alone. This is a piece of luck."

"It's probably where she shops," Renie said as the cousins strolled in Anemone's direction. "Where else besides Neiman Marcus and Saks would old-line rich women go after I. Magnin went out of business? Erma has undoubtedly influenced her daughter's buying habits."

"Why, Anemone!" Judith said in mock surprise. "How are you?"

"Oh!" Anemone almost dropped the black silk shantung suit she was holding up by its hanger. "I know you! The Cousins!" She grasped the hanger more firmly and blinked several times. "Mrs. Flynn and Mrs. Jones?"

Judith nodded. "That's a very smart suit."

Anemone scowled at the garment. "I guess. I don't like black, but Mumsy told me I had to buy something for Mr. Cruz's funeral. It's going to be held Monday morning at the cathedral."

Judith tried to gauge the young woman's attitude, which seemed unfeeling despite her customary appearance of fragility. "So the *San Rafael* won't sail until after the services?"

Anemone shrugged. "I suppose. The cruise was Mumsy's idea. I hope the whole thing gets canceled, so we won't have to go."

"You don't like cruises?" Judith asked.

"Not particularly," Anemone replied, putting the suit back on the rack. Her big blue eyes glistened with tears. "I certainly don't want to take one without Jim. He could only join us during his spring break," she explained, regarding the rest of the dark-colored ensembles with something akin to revulsion. "The postponement means he'd have to take time off from classes. If he doesn't go, I don't want to, either." She burst into tears.

A sales associate, who had been drawing nigh, stepped back a few paces and began rearranging a mannequin's silk scarf. Judith watched Anemone try to find a handkerchief in her handbag without success.

"Here," Judith said, taking a packet of Kleenex out of her purse. "Wouldn't you like to sit? There are some chairs over by the dressing-room entrance."

Anemone accepted the Kleenex and wiped at her eyes. "I'm so embarrassed!" she murmured. "I don't even know you!"

"Actually," Judith said gently, "you do. We've met, we've shared a tragedy, we've got a sad sort of bond. Come, sit down. You're shaking like a leaf."

Anemone allowed Judith to lead her to the matching easy chairs, which Judith figured were for tired men waiting for their women to try on clothes. It wasn't until she sat down next to Anemone that Judith realized Renie had disappeared.

But her cousin's defection didn't divert her. "I'm surprised your mother still wants to go on the cruise, at least until her jewels are recovered."

The tears had been stanched, but Anemone was sniffling and snuffling, using tissue after tissue. "Once Mumsy's mind is made up, there's no changing it. Besides, she's not going to look for the jewels herself. If you see what I mean."

"I take it she wasn't that close to Mr. Cruz? I mean," Judith amended, "that his loss wouldn't ruin the voyage for her?"

Anemone shook her head. "She knew him, of course. And Connie—Mrs. Cruz. Mumsy's own circle is very small—and very tight."

And, Judith was certain, didn't include a mere employee such as Dixie Beales. "So your mother and you and Mr. Pankhurst and Mr. Everhart will be going on the cruise—if it's not canceled?"

"That's her plan." Anemone's expression was gloomy. "Except Mr. Pankhurst won't be going. He and Mumsy . . . well, it just wouldn't work out right now."

Judith thought before she spoke. "I understand they've had a difference of opinion."

"Yes." Anemone's small, perfect lips clamped shut. She got to her feet and went back to the racks. Judith had no choice but to follow.

"I'm puzzled," she said after a brief silence. "I mean, your mother resigned from the Cruz board of directors. Yet she still wants to sail on the *San Rafael*?"

Anemone had selected another black suit. "As I said, when Mumsy gets an idea in her head . . ." She shrugged. "This one won't make me look forty, will it?"

"I don't remember what being forty looks like," Judith admitted. "But it's got some pizzazz. The white touches at the collar and cuffs make it less severe."

"I'll try it on. It's nice seeing you again, Mrs. Flynn." Anemone made her way toward the dressing rooms.

It would be too obvious for Judith to traipse after her prey. Pressure would make Anemone really shut down—or dissolve into more tears. Instead, Judith went in search of Renie, expecting to find her in the midrange designer section, which carried some of her cousin's favorite brands. Only two other customers were browsing through the department. There was no sales associate in sight. Apparently Neiman Marcus let its clientele study the merchandise without interference. Judith paused by the sale rack where the previous winter's trend featured tassels, fringes, and short, short skirts. Not her style, and certainly not appropriate to her age. Judith passed on the markdowns, but a red ruffled cocktail dress hanging next to the customer-service counter caught her eye. It was Judith's favorite color. She couldn't resist inspecting it more closely.

She might have carried off the halter top and even the plunging neckline, but while the ruffles in back dropped to midcalf, in front they ended abruptly at high thigh. Furthermore, the dress was a size six and a memo attached was stamped SOLD. She moved on.

The more classic spring and summer designs looked as if they might appeal to Renie. Judith found the entrance to the dressing rooms. Aggravating as it might be, she guessed that her cousin had succumbed to another shopping impulse.

"Coz," Judith called softly, moving down the narrow hallway. "Coz?"

She was halfway to the end of the corridor when she heard her cousin's angry voice.

"Beat it, you pervert! Get the hell out of there or I'll set fire to your alligator shoes!"

"Coz?" Judith shouted, trying to determine the exact location. No one else seemed to be in the area. Except, Judith realized, Renie and the pervert.

The door on her right flew open. Judith saw her cousin wearing a purple halter with matching slacks and an irate expression.

"I've got a peeper," Renie announced, standing amid a pile of clothing. "He won't budge."

Judith's eyes followed her cousin's finger, which pointed at the shortened divider between the dressing rooms. At first she saw nothing except for an Ellen Tracy jacket and a pair of shoes.

But the shoes didn't belong to Renie. They were men's alligator shoes, and Judith realized that they were protruding just under the shortened divider that separated the dressing rooms.

Mouth agape, Judith stared at Renie. "He's peeping with his feet?"

"He must have lost his balance," Renie snarled. "Or maybe he passed out when he saw me in my underwear."

"You don't look *that* bad," Judith remarked, using her toe to nudge garments aside as she made her way into the dressing room.

"I don't look that good, either," Renie retorted.

Judith kicked gently at one of the alligator shoes. There was no response. "Maybe he did pass out," she said in a concerned voice. "We'd better get help."

Renie gestured at Judith. "Move it, coz. You can't get down on the floor to look under that panel, but I can. Not that I think I'll like what I'm going to see, perverts being what they are and doing what they do."

Judith frowned. "You sure?"

"Oh, yes." Renie moved more clothing out of the way and lay flat on her stomach. She suddenly tensed. "Holy Mother!"

"What?" Judith asked anxiously.

Renie turned a horrified face to Judith. "He's more than passed out. He looks dead. And," she added, reaching for Judith's outstretched hand to pull herself up, "he also happens to be the late Émile Grenier."

Chapter Thirteen

The impossible was not only possible, but for once, it was plausible as well. Judith went out into the corridor to open the adjacent door. Émile lay in an awkward position with his head and shoulders propped up by the dressing room's bench. His face was almost the same color as Renie's purple outfit and his eyes protruded. Judith winced as she saw the long gold rope with tassels at each end. It had been twisted around the purser's neck and pulled hard until the life drained out of his body. Even if she could have bent down, there was no need to seek a pulse. Judith was an old hand at death.

Renie was already putting her own clothes back on.

"Did you see anybody out on the floor?" Judith asked. "A salesperson, I mean?"

"Why? Did you find something you like?"

Judith tried not to let her exasperation show. She couldn't

really blame Renie for trying to make light of their situation. "I mean, an employee, a clerk, someone who works for the store."

"Yes," Renie replied. "Her name's Olga. She took an ecru blouse from me to remove a smudge I found. She should be right back."

"We need more than Olga, we need the manager," Judith said. "Not to mention the police, the emergency people, the——" She stopped as a dark-haired woman of forty poked her head into the open dressing room.

"How is everything?" she inquired in a voice that was heavy with what Judith guessed was a Russian accent.

"Not so good," Renie answered.

Olga glanced at Judith. "Excuse me?"

"I don't mean her," Renie explained. "She's my cousin. But I'm afraid we found a corpse. You'd better call the police."

Olga looked as if she thought Renie was joking—or crazy. "A corpse. I see. You mean you don't like the clothes? You think fashion is dead?"

At last, Olga spotted the shoes. She screamed. And screamed and screamed. Judith grasped the woman by shoulders. "Calm down! You have to help!"

But Olga had no intention of helping. She was almost as tall as Judith, and considerably stronger. Breaking away, she fled from the dressing-room area. She was still screaming.

"And she didn't even see the rest of the body," Renie said in disgust.

Judith leaned against the doorjamb. "Good God, this is the worst yet. Three bodies in three days, and all connected to Cruz Cruises. I'm about to announce that there's a maniac loose."

Renie was fully dressed. "So what do we do? Just stand here until somebody responsible shows up?"

"What else?" Judith glanced out into the corridor. No one was in sight. "Are you the only one trying on clothes?"

"I think so," Renie replied, "unless you count Émile."

"You didn't see anyone or hear anything?"

Renie shook her head. "They aren't that busy in this department. It's Saturday, it's nice out, people are probably doing other things."

"Maybe," Judith said in a worried voice, "we should be, too. As in pretending we're innocent bystanders."

"But we are."

Judith shot Renie a sour look. "You know what I mean. The first officers to arrive will be uniforms from this beat. For now, let's not tell them we know the victim. I don't want to spend the rest of the day at the jail. Our husbands have already done that this weekend."

The first to arrive wasn't a police officer, but store security. In fact, it was a young couple who could pass as husband-and-wife shoppers. They barely glanced at the cousins before going into the adjoining dressing room.

"Maybe we should've left while we had the chance," Renie whispered.

Judith shook her head. "That wouldn't be right." She could hear the security employees' shocked, yet low voices a few feet away. The man was on his cell phone at once, summoning the police. He began to check out the other dressing rooms. A moment later, the woman confronted Judith and Renie.

"Caroline Halloway, security," she said in a brusque voice. "Are you the ones who reported the accident?"

"Accident?" Renie echoed.

Anticipating hostilities, Judith moved between her cousin and the security woman. "Yes," she responded, giving her name and

Renie's, along with their home addresses and the hotel where they were staying.

"Visitors," the woman said, making rapid notes. "How long were you in here before you noticed the problem?"

"Problem?" Renie shot back.

"I wasn't here," Judith said, stepping aside. There was no choice but to let Renie talk, since she was the one who'd found Émile.

"At least five minutes," Renie said in a less hostile tone. "I was trying on clothes." She swept her hand over the items on the floor and hanging from the pegs. "I got involved. You know how that goes."

Caroline apparently did know. Judith figured she must be used to self-absorbed shoppers. "What brought the man's presence to your attention?"

"His shoes," Renie said. "I didn't notice them at first. I was carrying so many garments that I couldn't see over the top of the pile. Then I started trying on the Ellen Tracy separates, but I was looking in the mirror on the other wall. Finally I decided to pick up some of the items I'd let fall to the floor. That's when I realized that no man should be putting his shoes under my divider."

"What did you do then?"

"I figured he was some kind of pervert." Renie shot the security woman an arch look. "I'm sure you've heard about those weirdo types even in a place as high class as this one. I told him to take a hike, but he didn't react. Then my cousin showed up before I could do anything else. That all happened less than ten minutes ago. I peeked under the divider. My cousin went around to look in the dressing room. The man was definitely dead. That's it."

Caroline's plain features had remained unchanged, though her voice conveyed a hint of disbelief. "You didn't scream when you saw the shoes? You didn't run for help?"

Judith avoided looking at Renie. For once, it was her cousin's problem to talk her way out of a mess.

"There wasn't time," Renie replied.

"So," Caroline persisted, "you just waited in here for your cousin?" She shot Judith a swift, sidelong look.

"I told you, my cousin showed up almost immediately," Renie said.

Caroline's sharp blue eyes now fixed on Judith. "Is that right?"

"Yes. We're probably still in a state of shock." Judith could hardly admit that after all their misadventures, even "surprise" would have been too strong a word.

"Where had you been while your cousin was in here?"

"Looking for her." Judith waited a beat, but Caroline said nothing. "Before that, I was over in suits and dresses." She wasn't about to confess that she'd been with Anemone Giddon. Once Émile was officially identified, Caroline might pick up on the link with the dead man. And with Judith.

The male security employee returned, accompanied by a slightly older man who exuded quiet authority.

"I understand," the new arrival said in a sympathetic voice, "that you two ladies have made a very disagreeable discovery." He put out a hand. "I'm Daniel Goldfarb, the store manager. Would you please join me in my office? You'll be much more comfortable there and we can get you some water or whatever you'd like. I can't apologize enough for this unfortunate incident."

Judith was torn. Sitting around Daniel Goldfarb's office sipping Perrier was only a notch better than twiddling her thumbs at the police station. She needed answers, not comfort. But she knew there'd be official hoops to jump through. Renie would have to give the police her story.

Apparently Renie was thinking along the same lines. "What I'd like is to go back to our hotel and lie down," she declared, making herself tremble a bit. "I'm exhausted. I wouldn't want to collapse on your premises. You already have one dead body." She picked up her big purse and slung it over her shoulder. "You know where to reach us. Thanks for the offer, though."

Daniel looked perplexed. Caroline showed no emotion, but her male counterpart was scowling.

"You have to wait until the police arrive," he said. "I'm sorry, but we can't let you leave."

"Yes, you can," Renie asserted, reaching in her purse and taking out her wallet. "You have no legal grounds to keep us here. If you want to argue the point, here's my lawyer's name and number." She handed a business card to the security man and stomped out of the dressing room.

"She hasn't been well," Judith murmured, squeezing her way past the trio. "I must go take care of her."

Two uniformed officers were going up the escalator as Judith and Renie were going down. A squad car pulled up as the cousins exited the store. They kept moving without a backward glance.

"Do you think they'll actually call Bub?" Judith asked as they reached the main floor.

"Of course not," Renie said, briskly walking past handbags and leather goods. "I don't carry Bub's cards with me. The one I gave them was for Jerry, the window cleaner."

Judith realized that her cousin was leading them out of a different entrance from the one where they'd entered the store. "Where are we?" she asked, looking around at the immediate unfamiliar sights.

"We need a drink," Renie said after they'd walked half a block. "And lunch. Now we're back on Stockton."

"So why are we going uphill?"

Renie pointed straight ahead. "Do you want the cops following us back to the St. Francis right now? The Ritz-Carlton's close by. I'd like to get as far away from the scene of the latest crime as possible."

"You're in the wrong place for it," Judith said, puffing a bit and pointing to a street sign on their left. "See that?"

Renie grinned. "Oh, yes. I've seen that sign before. Dashiell Hammett lived in that building during the twenties. That part of Monroe Street's named in his honor. I guess he lived in a lot of other places, too, while he was writing *The Maltese Falcon* and *The Thin Man* and some of his other novels."

"Even famous people have to walk up these hills," Judith said, looking grim. "How far is the Ritz? My hip's hurting."

"Straight ahead. It's that neoclassical building that looks like a museum. I'll bet they can provide for our every need."

"What I need is information," Judith mumbled. "I'm not hungry."

"I have some information," Renie said as they approached the hotel steps. "It's a nice day. We can eat outside in the Terrace Restaurant."

"Do you refer to your endless knowledge of local food vendors," Judith inquired as they passed through the elegantly appointed lobby to the elevators, "or something more pertinent to the latest body count?"

"The latter," Renie said. "I'll tell you as soon as we're seated."

The rooftop restaurant was busy, but the cousins didn't have to wait for a table. Briefly, Judith paused to admire the garden setting, complete with large trees and a splendid view of the city. But her mind remained on murder.

"Okay, let's hear your information," Judith urged after they'd both ordered Rusty Nails from the bar.

Renie smirked. "And you thought all I was doing was shopping. Tsk, tsk."

"Coz . . ."

"Okay, okay. It was Olga. She'd waited on Dixie yesterday morning."

"Ah!" Judith made the exclamation just as their drinks arrived. The server apparently thought she was reacting to her cocktail.

"Thirsty, are we?" he said with a grin.

"Huh?" Judith blinked at the young man. "Oh—right. Thanks."

Renie didn't resume speaking until the server was out of earshot. "Olga was working in the department next to sportswear Friday. She's a floater. Naturally, she remembered Dixie because she not only bought a couple of grand's worth of clothes, but Olga had a hard time understanding her. Moving here from the Ukraine, Olga's not used to American Southern accents."

"Go on," Judith said as Renie was momentarily distracted by the dishes being served at the adjacent table.

"French onion soup," Renie murmured. "I can't resist." She turned back to Judith. "Where was I? Oh, Dixie was telling Olga that she needed a completely new wardrobe because she was moving back to South Carolina."

"What? You mean she was quitting her job?"

Renie shrugged. "That's what it sounded like. In fact, Olga thought she might be in love and planning to get married. Dixie mentioned something about meeting—let me get this right— her 'shugah.' Olga wasn't certain what a 'shugah' was, but I explained to her that it was Southern talk for sugar, meaning a sweetheart."

Judith rested her chin on her hands. "A mystery lover. Who?"

"Isn't that up to Rick and Rhoda to find out? They were having breakfast at the Hyatt this morning. It'll be interesting to hear if they learned anything."

"Yes." Judith fingered the menu. The aroma of fennel and curry and dill masked the exhaust fumes from the street below. "I suppose the St. Georges know about Émile Grenier. Or will, very soon. Biff would be quick to pass that along. How the heck did Émile get into the women's dressing-room area in the first place? Don't they have security cameras in those places?"

"I never saw anyone in that part of the store except Olga," Renie asserted. "There were a couple of other customers—both women—browsing. Unlike some places where the employees check to see what you're taking into a dressing room or stand guard to make sure you don't try to wear six outfits at once and leave without paying—there was none of that. Neiman Marcus has a higher class of clientele. They don't harass their customers."

"The chairs," Judith said suddenly. "Employees and customers are used to seeing men waiting in those chairs by the dressing rooms. Émile or any other guy might go unnoticed."

Renie was rubbernecking again. "Did you see that chilled lobster salad on the serving cart? Am I drooling?"

"No. Yes." Judith was thinking. "We have to assume Émile was killed in the dressing room. The cord-and-tassel thing that was used to strangle him looked similar to the ones on the sale rack items."

Renie's attention had turned back to the murder at hand. "So somebody—presumably a woman—lured him into the dressing room and killed him? Wouldn't she have to be strong as an ox?"

"Émile wasn't a very big man," Judith pointed out. "I doubt that he was much taller than you. If you know how to strangle someone, you can do it quickly and efficiently—especially if you catch the victim by surprise."

Renie feigned a shudder. "Sometimes you scare me. Maybe I should behave myself better when I'm with you."

"If," Judith said drily, "I haven't killed you by now, I probably won't. And stop ogling the poached halibut."

"Sorry." Renie was silent for a moment, eyes riveted on her cousin. "He must have been killed before I went into the dressing room."

Judith nodded. "His feet were already under the divider. You didn't notice because you're too short to see over a mound of clothes. I wonder . . . Did he go with someone else or did he plan to meet someone?"

"He certainly wasn't alone when he died," Renie pointed out.

Judith shifted uncomfortably in her chair. "No. The problem is, the only woman who we know was on-site is Anemone Giddon."

"But you were probably with her when Émile was killed," Renie reminded Judith.

Judith made a face. "Was I?" She thought back to how Anemone had dismissed her before taking the black suit to the other dressing room area. Judith had gone to designer sportswear, browsing for about five minutes. But Renie was already in the dressing-room next to the scene of the latest crime. The timing was wrong—unless Émile had been killed before Judith and Renie had run into the young woman. But Anemone was the most fragile of the suspects. Or so she seemed.

"Adrenaline," Renie said after Judith had put her thoughts into words. "If you're pumped enough, you can do anything."

"But why?" Judith's expression was bleak. "If all these murders are connected—and they must be—what would set Anemone off on a killing spree? There's no apparent motive, no sense to it, no *logic*."

"Because," Renie replied, beckoning at their server, "as my husband would put it in clinical terms, she's mad as a hatter?"

Judith glanced at the menu. She still wasn't hungry. "I'll have your classic Caesar salad, please."

"And after that?" the server prodded gently.

"That's it. Thank you."

He turned a hopeful face to Renie. She did not disappoint. "I'll have the artichoke-mushroom gratin, tomato tartare, caper red onion jus for my entrée. But first, I'd like some French onion soup."

"Excellent choices, madam." He smiled kindly at Renie and moved away.

"Pig," Judith murmured. "Do you even *know* what's in your entrée? It sounds pretty exotic to me."

"I'll find out," Renie retorted.

"It'd serve you right if you got a stomach—wait." Judith placed both hands on the table. "There *is* logic in these murders. Magglio Cruz gets killed at the cocktail party. But who were the first two people to find the body? Dixie and Émile. Did they see the killer? Did they see something that told them who the killer was? Or did they see something and not realize it, but the murderer thought they did—or that they'd would remember later?"

Renie sighed. "All possibilities. But if Dixie or Émile saw something or somebody, wouldn't they have told the police?"

Judith waited for Renie to exult over the thick crusty soup that had just been placed in front of her. "As I said, they might not have realized what they saw. Or," she added after the server had once again left them, "there's always blackmail."

Renie's eyes were closed. She was taking deep sniffs of the onions, Gruyère cheese, and toasted croutons, waving her soup spoon as if it were a weapon. "Ahhh." She opened her eyes. "Blackmail? Now there's a thought." The spoon engaged the soup.

"Certainly the list of suspects has some people with enough wealth to pay a blackmailer," Judith mused. "Almost everyone involved is rich."

"So's this soup. It's terrific." The battle was now underway; Renie had cheese on her chin, crouton crumbs on her bosom, and a puddle of broth next to the bowl. Her slurping noises sounded not unlike a combat zone. "Want a taste?"

"No thanks. After you've gotten hold of it, I don't know where it's been."

"Jim Brooks isn't rich," Renie pointed out, dusting off her chest. "Ambrose Everhart isn't. CeeCee Orr is rich only in the way that women like her are rich." She paused to slurp and chew. "You're right about the others, though. Unless you're counting crew members."

"We can't *not* count them," Judith declared. "If the original murder weapon was cutlery, one of the chefs or servers would have the easiest access."

"Surely the police are investigating everyone thoroughly," Renie contended. "Biff may seem a bit bumbling, but I'll bet that when he's in his own element—that is, not interviewing the rich and the really rich—he handles himself pretty well."

"You may be right," Judith said. "I wonder if Rick and Rhoda have tried to reach us at the hotel. If only we could talk to someone at police headquarters. It's well and good for Rick to have an in there, but we don't. I trust the St. Georges, but that doesn't mean they wouldn't leave out certain things. Especially Rick. Men don't listen the way women do."

"No ear for the ephemeral," Renie remarked.

"Exactly. But I don't want to step on Rick's toes by contacting Biff or—" Judith stopped as their server delivered her Caesar salad. To allow him more foot room, she moved her purse closer to the chair. "Thank you. It looks lovely."

Instead of picking up her fork, Judith reached into her purse. "I forgot about the newspaper article. You should read it."

Finishing the soup, Renie wiped cheese off of her chin. "Now?"

Judith nodded and handed the paper to her cousin. "Yes. Because we're going to talk to Flakey Smythe."

"To . . . ?" Renie frowned. "Oh. The reporter," she murmured, scanning the byline and the lead. "Why?"

The server had returned, this time to remove Renie's bowl and present her entrée. He started to describe the ingredients, but she waved him off. "Never mind. It looks great."

"Then may I sponge madam down?" he inquired, pointing to a damp towel on the serving stand.

Renie narrowed her eyes. "Only if you have a hose."

The server's smile was fixed. "Not at hand, madam. I apologize." He left.

"Read the story," Judith ordered Renie. "I'm going to check to see if we have any calls at the hotel."

There was only one, but it was from Rhoda St. George. "Breakfast at Grandviews was delightful," her recorded voice said, "as well as informative. Call me when you have the opportunity."

Judith dialed the St. Georges' number at once. Rhoda answered on the third ring. "You caught me just in time. The weather's so pleasant. I was about to take Asthma for a walk. He still hasn't dried out from his last shampoo."

"Have you heard about Émile Grenier?"

"Just. Rick has gone to see Biff. I wonder what Émile was trying on in that dressing room? He would have looked nice in puce."

"Actually, that was the color of his face," Judith said.

"I don't want to think about that part," Rhoda replied.

"Really, I'm not a ghoul. I must say, you and Serena have an absolute penchant for finding dead people."

"Unfortunately," Judith admitted, "that seems to be true. Can you tell me about Dixie and Grandviews?"

"I can tell you about the poison," Rhoda answered in her customary calm, cultured voice. "It was methanol."

Judith searched her memory. In their younger, more foolish years, one of Renie's fiancés had been a chemist. He'd frequently bring a form of alcohol home from work to use as a punch base. The cousins and their circle of friends had been lucky that they hadn't been punched out permanently.

"You mean lab alcohol?" Judith responded.

"The very thing," said Rhoda. "What moonshiners still use in the less civilized parts of this country."

"Not that difficult to obtain," Judith reflected aloud. "Virtually undetectable in a cocktail. How did Dixie ingest the poison?"

"You name it," Rhoda said. "Possibly in Harvey Wallbangers. In addition to the orange juice and the vodka, the Galliano sweetness would mask any unusual taste."

The next question was even more important to Judith. "So who did she lunch with?"

Rhoda laughed softly. "It wasn't easy getting Dominic to describe Dixie's male companion. He took umbrage when Ricky remarked that his eyesight wasn't all it could be if only he'd wear glasses. But Dominic's hearing is decent, and he's not above listening in on conversations. That is," Rhoda added quickly, "he doesn't eavesdrop, but while hovering and serving, he pays attention to what his customers are saying to each other."

Judith's patience was thinning. "Yes?"

"Sorry, dear Judith," Rhoda apologized. "I merely wanted to set the scene. Dominic's physical description of the young man was vague. But he did hear Dixie call him by name, and it was unmistakable as well as—I suppose—unforgettable. Her luncheon companion was Ambrose Everhart."

"Ambrose!" Judith gasped. "Well—why not? I mean, he's part of the mix. But it's hard to think of him as a mass murderer."

"Is it?" Rhoda sounded as if she were giving the statement due consideration. "It's not hard to think of anyone in that way if he or she has sufficient reason to kill people. But there is a problem."

"What is that?"

"Dixie was definitely drunk," Rhoda said. "But she only had two drinks at lunch. Methanol works slowly, according to what Dr. Selig told Ricky. Thus, Dixie must have been drinking before she got to Grandviews. In fact," she added in a voice that had suddenly grown tense, "she may have been poisoned the night before—possibly right after Magglio Cruz was murdered."

Chapter Fourteen

By the time Judith got back to the table at the Terrace, Renie had finished eating.

"I'm not sure what it was," Renie said, gesturing at her empty plate, "but it was certainly delicious." She saw her cousin's solemn expression and sat very still. "Okay, tell me all."

Judith did exactly that. She began to eat her salad only after she'd finished relaying Rhoda's information. "Maybe Dixie had a drinking problem, maybe she started early in the day. Dominic insisted that she was inebriated before she finished her first of the two cocktails at Grandviews. He didn't know her, so he couldn't be positive. But he told Rick that she acted quite drunk before the meal with Ambrose was over."

"Meal?" Renie looked quizzical. "I thought she didn't eat much."

"She ordered some food, but barely touched it," Judith said, recalling Rhoda's report from Rick. "Did you ever get sick when we used to drink lab alcohol?"

Renie grimaced. "Once. I threw up in Whazizname's car. That's when we became unengaged."

"I thought I remembered that the stuff could upset your stomach," Judith remarked.

"Not to mention make you go blind and also die." Renie shook her head. "I can't believe we were that stupid. And cheap. Of course none of us had much money in those days."

Briefly, the cousins pondered their youthful recklessness. "We thought we were immortal," Judith remarked.

"I never thought that," Renie said. "I was always sure that within twenty-four hours I'd be run over by a bus. Or something."

Judith smiled wistfully. "How many times have we come face-to-face with mortality in the last few years? Not just our own, but far too many others?"

"It's been gruesome," Renie allowed with a shake of her head. "Sometimes I feel like we're soldiers, growing accustomed to falling over dead people."

"I've never gotten accustomed to that," Judith asserted. "I've simply accepted that death is part of life. And somehow I've managed to get involved in more than my share of violent deaths. It sounds silly, but once in a while I wonder if my mission in life is to seek justice." She watched closely to see if her cousin's expression suggested cynicism. But Renie was looking equally somber. "Remember how I wanted to be a nurse when I was a kid?" Judith went on. "But I couldn't pass chemistry. That was when I decided to become a librarian instead. Books had answers. Writers search for truth. I couldn't heal bodies, but I could certainly find them. And then I realized that if I put my mind to it, I could—" She broke off, feeling foolish.

"Jeez," Renie murmured, "what's in that salad?"

Judith pressed her hands over her eyes. "I sound pretentious—or nuts. I guess this time there are too damned many bodies. I may have become unhinged."

"You've never been pretentious, and you don't sound like you're nuts," Renie assured her. "You're making perfect sense. I'm just a little overwhelmed. And guilty. If it hadn't been for me, you wouldn't be here. To think I thought I was doing you a favor!" Incredulous, she shook her head. "Instead of giving you a rest, I've managed to mire you in murder."

"That's not your fault," Judith insisted. "All of this would have happened if we were here or not. How would you and Bill have coped?"

Renie thought for a moment. "Bill would have said, 'We're outta here.' He'd have packed us up and come home. He doesn't like glitches when we travel."

"That's a sensible reaction, I suppose," Judith said as the server arrived to remove Renie's plate.

He glanced at Judith. At least two-thirds of the Caesar remained uneaten. "Is your salad satisfactory?"

Judith's smile was feeble as well as apologetic. "Yes, it's fine—I'm just not hungry. You can take my things, too."

A hint of disappointment appeared on his face, but he complied. "Could I tempt you ladies with dessert such as the chocolate profiteroles with vanilla ice cream and a luscious chocolate sauce?"

Both cousins declined. "Did Rhoda say what Dixie and Ambrose were quarreling about?" Renie asked as they waited for the bill. "Assuming that they were, that is."

"Dominic described it to Rhoda as a 'heated discussion,' " Judith replied. "He picked up only the occasional word, like *greedy, sycophant, liar,* and *sponger.* Unfortunately, those words could apply to any number of our suspects."

"Not helpful," Renie noted. "So how do we get hold of Flakey?"

"Through the newspaper office, I suppose." Judith paused; her face fell as she looked at the bill. "Do you realize you spent over fifty bucks on lunch?"

Renie shrugged. "It's San Francisco. Good food doesn't come cheap."

"And I thought prices at home were outrageous," Judith muttered.

"They are," Renie conceded. "It's the West Coast. All that money spent on shipping things around the Horn. Don't worry," she added, flipping her AmEx card onto the table. "I'm paying for this. I'll charge it to Cruz Cruises."

Judith glowered at Renie. "What if they go out of business? Who'll pick up the tab then? And don't tell me you're charging them for your new shoes!"

"I thought about it," Renie admitted. "I wouldn't have bought them if I hadn't come to San Francisco."

The cousins retreated to the lobby. Flakefield Smythe had a phone number as well as an e-mail address in the newspaper.

"We'll call first," Judith said. "He may be at work if he's covering this case."

Flakey's voice mail informed Judith that he was away from his desk, but that in cases of emergency he could be reached at another number.

"We'll try that one," Judith said to Renie, who was lolling against the wall next to the row of pay phones.

A live male voice answered on the second ring. "Lefty O'Doul's. How can I help you?"

Surprised, Judith hesitated. "Is Flakey around?" she finally asked.

"Sure," the man responded. "Can I tell him who's calling?"

"Never mind. We'll be there in person." Judith hung up and looked at Renie. "Isn't Lefty O'Doul's bar right by the St. Francis?"

"Yes, on Geary. We went there years ago."

"Then," Judith said, starting for the hotel exit, "we're going there again."

Lefty's hadn't changed much in over forty years. It was basic American bar & grill, befitting its founder, a former Major League Baseball player and longtime manager of the old Pacific Coast League's San Francisco Seals.

"Time warp," Judith said under her breath, scanning the long bar, the solid tables with their arrowback chairs, and the baseball memorabilia that covered the walls. She was so tired from walking the six blocks between the Ritz-Carlton and Lefty's that she had to lean against the door for a moment. But as her eyes grew accustomed to the dim lighting, she spotted her prey: The reporter she'd seen in the Fitzroy's lobby was sitting halfway down the bar. He was with another man whom Judith also recognized: Biff McDougal.

"This is trickier than I thought," she said to Renie.

"Yes," Renie agreed. "And only one space open on Flakey's other side. Now what?"

Judith was still staring. "I'd forgotten—all the barstool legs are made out of baseball bats."

Renie smiled. "So they are. Well?"

"We sit," Judith said, leading the way. "There's an open table not that far from where Flakey and Biff are having a quaff. Let's wait and see what happens."

"What happens," Renie grumbled, "is that we're going to have to order drinks. I'm afraid we'll pickle our livers before this trip is over."

"We can nurse the drinks," Judith said, breathing in the aroma from the nearby steam table where cooks prepared huge hot beef and turkey sandwiches. "Now I *am* getting hungry." But unlike Renie, Judith could ignore her hunger pangs. "How long has it been since we picked up guys in bars?"

Renie made a face. "I don't think I ever did. I was always too busy mopping myself up. Besides," she went on with a sideways glance at the bar, "one of our marks is leaving."

"Biff," Judith said under her breath. "I'll bet he got the call to meet Rick St. George. In fact, I wonder why Biff isn't at the scene of the crime already?"

"Maybe he's come and gone," Renie suggested. "We left the store well over an hour ago. It's going on two o'clock."

A waitress came to take the cousins' orders. Judith asked for a scotch rocks; Renie requested a Henry Weinhard root beer. "Make that a float, if you can," Renie added. "With hard ice cream."

Acting as if it were an afterthought, Judith held up a hand and smiled at the waitress. "Would you buy the man in the raincoat at the bar a drink on me? Thank you."

The waitress was young, but not naive. Still, she hesitated a split second, looking at Judith and then glancing toward the bar. "Sure," she said, and moved off.

Their own beverages arrived first. A moment later, Flakey Smythe shifted his lanky frame around on the bar stool. Judith didn't try to be discreet. The bartender had obviously fingered her as the "seductress." If Flakey was disappointed because she wasn't a nubile young love goddess, he didn't show it. His cynical demeanor indicated that he took his pleasures where he found them, and was damned grateful to get any at all.

Fresh drink in hand, Flakey removed his sweat-stained fedora hat and clumsily got off the stool. "Hi, ladies, new in town?"

Renie, who looked as if she wanted to crawl under the table and hide, clamped her lips shut.

"Just . . . visiting," Judith replied, surprised when her voice cracked between words. "Have a seat."

Flakey sat. His brown eyes were bloodshot, the lines in his long face were deep, and his nose had probably not always been so red or so bulbous. Still, there was something astute about his gaze, like the blurred lens of an old Speed-Graphic camera that could still record if not always keep focus. Flakey seemed to be taking Judith's measure, including her mental as well as her physical assets. She guessed he could be anywhere between forty and sixty-five.

"You look familiar," he said, holding his glass in a grip that indicated he was afraid somebody might take it away. "You sure you don't live around here?"

"Of course." Judith tried to remember how to smile coquettishly. She was also trying to figure out if it wouldn't be easier to level with Flakey. "You write for one of the papers, don't you?"

"Yeah." He squinted at Judith. "So?"

"I read your story today." Judith would've taken the newspaper out of her purse, but she couldn't reach it without imperiling her artificial hip. *Some siren,* she thought. *I don't need a drink, I need a Percocet and a nap.* "It must be thrilling to write about murder among the rich and famous."

Flakey shrugged. "It's a job."

"You must be very good at it. Tell me"—Judith simpered, forcing herself to lean closer while trying to ignore the noises Renie was making with the straw in the root-beer float—"do you ever try to figure out whodunit?"

The shrewd, if bloodshot, eyes regarded Judith with suspicion. "You were at the Fitzroy. You work for Cruz Cruises."

"No," Judith said quickly in her normal voice. "I mean, I don't work for them. Never. Not at all."

"But you were at the Fitzroy yesterday when the Beales broad showed up dead," Flakey persisted. "If you weren't staying there with the rest of the crew, who the hell are you?"

Renie held up a hand. "I work for Cruz Cruises."

The reporter stared at Renie as if seeing her for the first time. "What are you—the stooge?"

"Pretty much," Renie replied, after removing the straw that had gotten stuck to her palm.

Judith decided to give Flakey a partial explanation. He'd downed his bourbon by the time she finished. "So," he said, signaling for another shot, "you two ended up on this cruise and smack in the middle of a bunch of murders. What were you doing at the Fitzroy?"

"Visiting Dixie Beales," Judith fibbed. "She'd been so upset the night before—when Mags was killed."

"You knew her before this trip?"

"No," Judith admitted, "but we volunteered to sit with her after she got back to her cabin. We felt obligated to see how she was doing."

"She was doing pretty well if she went shopping and out to lunch," Flakey remarked drily.

"Women have amazing recuperative powers," Renie pointed out.

"Neither of you seem much the worse for wear," Flakey noted. "Tell me, how does it feel to be off on a carefree vacation and suddenly find yourselves menaced by murder?"

Judith could already see the headline:

CRUISE CURSED FOR
COWERING COUSINS

"Naturally," Judith said carefully, "the tragedies have altered our plans."

Flakey narrowed his eyes. "C'mon, you can do better than that. Were you there when they found Mags's body in the piano? Did you see the taxi arrive with the dead Dixie inside?"

Judith realized that Flakey hadn't mentioned Émile Grenier. Maybe he didn't know about the third death. Maybe Biff—despite the hobnobbing at the bar—had kept his mouth shut.

But that wasn't what bothered Judith most. Not only didn't she want to become a sensational human-interest story, but Flakey Smythe was interrogating *her,* rather than the other way around.

"You know," Judith said, suddenly looking vague, "our role in all this is strictly peripheral. What's much more interesting is your investigative prowess as a journalist."

"That's what I'm doing," Flakey said. "Investigating. How did you react when you found out Magglio Cruz had been murdered almost before your very eyes?"

Judith knew she was being sucked into a trap. She glanced quickly at Renie. No help there. Her cousin was scooping the rest of her ice cream out of the tall glass.

"No comment," Judith finally said.

Flakey looked at her in annoyed disbelief. "C'mon, sweetie, what's with the 'no comment' garbage? Who do you think you are—the freaking queen?"

Judith said nothing, staring past Flakey to the framed photos of major and minor leaguers from the past.

He turned to Renie, who was smacking her lips. "Okay, stooge. Will the ventriloquist here talk through you?"

"She wants to cut a deal," Renie said.

Flakey looked surprised, a reaction that struck Judith as unusual for him. "What kind of deal?"

"An exchange of information," Renie said, wearing her boardroom face. "You can write about two terrified tourists' reactions to the murders—if you don't use our names. In return, you can fill us in on some background that you haven't put in the newspaper."

Flakey looked from Renie to Judith and back again. "Why are you so interested?"

"I told you," Renie said. "I work for Cruz Cruises. I'm involved with their publications. I want to make sure that the company knows all the facts."

Flakey seemed skeptical. "You're a writer?"

Renie uttered a little laugh. "Isn't everybody? Deep down, I mean."

Flakey shrugged. "Whatever you say, babe. Let's hear it. What happened at the party when the music stopped?"

"It never started," Renie replied. "The piano music, I mean. Dixie couldn't play because the body was stuck inside. When we found out, Judith fainted. She didn't come to until one of the crew poured a bucket of water over her. I became hysterical and somebody slapped me over and over again. We all ended up in Dixie's cabin, having palpitations. I've never been so terrified in my life. Judith thought the killer was stalking us in the companionway. There were shadows and footsteps everywhere. It was a nightmare. We could actually feel the killer's cold, clammy hands on our throats and saw our graves open up before us." Renie paused. "How's that?"

"Not bad," Flakey said, only mildly impressed by Renie's tall tale. "You got a sex angle in there somewhere?"

"Not yet. I was just getting warmed up."

"I don't mind writing bull crap, but you gotta put some sex in it. Were you naked?"

"How about somebody savagely ripping off our clothes while we were in Dixie's cabin? Somebody who *leered*."

"That's better. 'Love nest' would help."

"Be my guest," Renie said.

"You're not taking notes," Judith observed.

"Don't need to. I've got a photographic memory. I'd better get going. I've got a deadline for Sunday's edition."

"Not so fast," Renie snapped. "We made a deal, remember? What have you got for us?"

"Huh?" Briefly, Flakey looked puzzled. "Oh, yeah, right." After a pause, he requested another drink. "What did you have in mind?"

"Background," Judith said, speaking for the first time in several minutes. "That is," she added with a faintly apologetic smile, "I'm very people-oriented. The relationship between Erma Giddon and Horace Pankhurst fascinates me. Are they somehow related?"

Flakey chuckled. "Only by money." He handed the waitress his second empty glass and glommed on to the refill. "Pankhurst's law firm was founded by his grandfather, way back before the big earthquake and fire. Giddon's grandfather was his contemporary, involved in real estate. They hooked up early on, and the families have been tight ever since. Old Erma wouldn't move a finger without Horace to guide her."

"Hmm," Judith mused. "We heard they quarreled."

"Oh, yeah?" Flakey's face actually seemed to come alive. "How's that?"

"I assume you knew Mrs. Giddon resigned from the Cruz Cruises board," Judith said.

"Right. Our business reporter flashed me that news this

morning." The reporter gripped his drink with both hands and frowned. "So that pissed off Pankhurst. Yeah, okay, that makes sense."

"It does?" Judith made no effort to hide her curiosity.

"Sure. It throws a spanner into the works as far as Pankhurst is concerned." Flakey smiled crookedly. "You see, he wanted Erma to take over the company."

Judith didn't try to conceal her surprise, either. "Before or after Thursday night?"

"Both," Flakey said. "You might even say that Erma would have killed to get hold of Cruz Cruises."

Chapter Fifteen

A moment later, the waitress came by to tell Flakey he was wanted on the phone. Oddly enough, the reporter didn't carry a cell phone. "I always lose 'em," he said, excusing himself to take the call at the bar.

"We've made a pact with the devil." Renie moaned. "Can you imagine what we're going to sound like in tomorrow's paper?"

"No worse than I did when I ended up on TV after finding the body in the old apartment house at the bottom of Heraldsgate Hill," Judith said. "And that time, they used my real name. That's how I ended up being FATSO on the Internet."

"Thank God," Renie said, "Flakey never asked us to identify ourselves."

Flakey loped back to the table, but didn't sit. He swallowed his latest drink in two gulps, announced "breaking news," belched, and left.

"Émile Grenier?" Judith said after the reporter had gone.

"Probably," Renie replied. "If Biff knew about the latest murder when he was drinking here, he didn't tell Flakey. It's Biff's partner who's the blabbermouth."

As they walked outside, Judith swore that if their hotel wasn't just across the street, they'd have to take a cab. "I'm absolutely exhausted," she declared. "I haven't walked this much in years."

"You're weak, too," Renie chided, entering the St. Francis. "You should have ordered one of those wonderful-looking sandwiches at Lefty's."

There was no argument from Judith. When they finally reached their room, she collapsed and slept until Renie woke her up shortly before six.

"You have to get dressed," Renie said. "We're going to a dinner party at Erma Giddon's."

Judith rubbed at her forehead and tried to focus. "Say that again."

"Anemone called while you were napping," Renie said, perching on the edge of Judith's bed. "She wanted to thank you for helping her choose a funeral outfit. She felt she'd been a bit rude."

"So they're throwing a party to celebrate mourning?" Judith asked, struggling to sit up. "Or is it a wake?"

"You're not awake," Renie retorted. "Go shower. We'll talk about it later."

But Judith insisted she *was* awake—her stomach was growling so loudly that she couldn't help being alert.

"Okay," Renie conceded, tucking her feet under her. "Anemone is repentant. She called to apologize. I said you'd get back to her. Meanwhile, Rhoda telephoned to say that the Giddons—Erma and Anemone—invited them to a small supper party with cocktails at seven. Anemone was feeling very glum and needed cheering up. The St. Georges must be famous for lifting people's spirits—as well as drinking them. Rhoda suggested that they ask us, too, which apparently led to Anemone thinking she could make it up to you with the invitation."

"Oh." Judith's expression was wry. "I certainly wouldn't expect Erma to ask us."

Renie agreed.

But Judith suddenly demurred. "I don't have anything to wear. Everything I packed, including the pantsuit I had on today, is cruise-oriented. I can't wear what I wore last night. I have no proper San Francisco clothing."

"Oh, yes, you do," Renie responded, hopping off the bed and going out into the sitting room. "Here," she said, hauling along a small caravan of boxes and bags bearing the Saks Fifth Avenue logo. "I was not idle while you slept. I went across the street to Saks and shopped my head off."

With as much enthusiasm as any huckster, Renie began removing the items from boxes and bags. "A couple of Tahari suits along with a jacket, camisole, and short skirt. A long skirt, slacks, and a sweater from Dana Buchman. They should fit, unless you're too damned skinny. May I suggest the pearl-gray pinstripe Tahari pantsuit for tonight?"

Judith stopped gaping and gasping. "How the hell am I going to pay for all this?" she demanded, now glaring at her cousin.

"Everything was on sale," Renie replied innocently. "Honest. I charged the stuff to my account. You can pay me when we get home." She indicated a couple of unopened boxes at the end of the bed. "I bought myself a few things, too. It's a good thing I didn't have to walk very far. I could hardly carry it all."

Judith was still glaring. "I could strangle you."

"Don't say that," Renie said. "Somebody may."

"You are absolutely impossible!" Judith fumed.

Renie shrugged. "When was the last time you bought anything for yourself? Other than the cruise wear, I mean. Frankly, you can probably return most of that. I doubt that we're going anywhere west of Sausalito."

The idea was small comfort to Judith. "This trip has been the worst I've ever taken," she grumbled even as she allowed herself to touch the fine fabric of the pinstripe suit. "On top of everything else, I'm going to be impoverished."

"But well clad," Renie said cheerfully, unzipping a garment bag. "I think I'll go with the hot pink Escada suit."

"I should go in a barrel," Judith muttered. But the more she stared at the pearl gray outfit, the more she wanted to try it on. "After all," she added, more to herself than to Renie, "it may not fit."

But it did. Judith tried to tell herself that she didn't look stunning. "I never buy gray clothes," she said, "but this doesn't wash me out."

"That's because your hair was so gray before you colored it. You blended."

In front of the full-length mirror, Judith turned every which way. "It doesn't seem to need any alterations," she admitted.

"Of course not. With your height, that type of outfit looks terrific. Besides," she added, "I have excellent taste. I *am* an artist, after all."

"This afternoon, you claimed to be a writer," Judith remarked drolly.

"So? Over the years, you've claimed to be everything from an astronaut to a zookeeper."

"But always in the search for truth and justice."

Renie's eyes twinkled. "Always," she said.

Judging from the age and style of the Giddon home in Pacific Heights, Grandfather Giddon had probably built the place back in the 1880s. In the Victorian Queen Anne style, it was three stories of jutting gables, patterned shingles, angles, curves, and a tower with windows that looked out over the bay. On a clear day, Judith wondered if the Giddons could see halfway to Rarotonga. It was the quintessential San Francisco house, though it sat on a corner lot and there was room for a well-tended garden.

"Four, five million on today's market for this place?" Renie said after they'd paid the taxi driver and were standing at the foot of the stone steps that led from the sidewalk.

"At least," Judith agreed. "I imagine it's been kept up extremely well, despite all the earthquakes."

Still, Judith felt there was something gloomy about the house. She almost expected to see gaslights and overdone Victorian furnishings inside.

"I never liked this style of architecture," Renie declared. "Too ornate, too complicated, too damned ugly."

"Be sure and tell Erma that," Judith said sarcastically. "That'll make her even happier to see the two of us."

The door was answered by Chevy Barker-James, in her guise as Beulah. She looked every inch the part with her black dress, white apron, and matching cap.

"I heard you were coming," she said under her breath. "Why in the world would you want to?" But Chevy didn't wait for a response, instead leading the cousins through the foyer and into the drawing room. "Miz Flynn and Miz Jones," she announced in a deferential tone.

Anemone, wearing a very short green-and-white cocktail dress, was the first to greet the cousins. "I'm so glad you could come. I can't thank you enough for helping me pick out that black suit. Even Mumsy approved of it."

"I didn't do that much," Judith objected as Anemone held her hand in a surprisingly tight grip.

"Oh, but you did," Anemone asserted, her usually soft voice rising as her mother and Jim Brooks approached. "You spent so much time with me looking at the racks and in the dressing room while I tried things on. I couldn't have done it without you."

Judith couldn't see any point in contradicting. She'd have to get Anemone alone to find out why the young woman was lying. At least Judith's hand had finally been set free.

Nor did she have a chance to respond: Erma Giddon was bearing down on her like a D-day landing craft on Omaha Beach.

"Such a sad time for all of us," she said with about as much emotion as she might lend to the loss of a dead houseplant.

"Scary, too," Jim Brooks put in. "I'm sure glad they never offered me a summer job on that cruise line."

"But they did," Erma said with a dark look at her future son-in-law. "Two years ago. I arranged it. Have you forgotten?"

Jim's boyish features looked pained. "You knew I couldn't take the job. I get seasick."

"Nonsense," Erma snapped. "You wanted to go on that field trip to Italy instead." Perhaps conscious of her duties as a hostess, she patted Jim's arm. "Never mind, that's all in the past. It's the future that counts, isn't it, dear boy?"

Jim flushed. "Yes, ma'am, yes, sure, it is."

Judith glanced around the room. The furniture was solid, expensive and unimaginative. Some of it could have come from the Victorian era, but several of the pieces looked like reproductions. The blue velvet drapes were pulled shut against the cold evening fog.

Except for Ambrose Everhart, fidgeting with some papers by a floor lamp with a beaded shade, no one seemed to be in attendance. Apparently, peace had not been made between Erma and

Horace. The St. Georges would probably make their usual slightly tardy entrance. But surely, Judith thought, the Giddons must have an intimate circle of friends that didn't include people connected to Cruz Cruises.

Chevy sidled up to the cousins. "What may Ah fetch y'all?"

"You're good," Renie said under her breath. "Too bad this isn't an audition."

"Yes, ma'am," Chevy replied with a bright smile. "It shore is."

The cousins both requested screwdrivers. "How about pliers and an ax?" Chevy murmured. "Or," she added, as Rhoda and Rick St. George entered in the company of Horace Pankhurst and CeeCee Orr, "a hatchet to bury?"

"My, yes," Renie said softly. "What now?"

Expecting fireworks, Judith tensed. But Horace lumbered over to Erma and kissed her cheek.

"In the face of these senseless tragedies," he stated, as much for everyone's benefit as for Erma's, "we must present a united front. Rhoda and Rick insisted that we come and bring you a peace offering."

Warily, Erma eyed Horace. "Such as what?"

Horace spread his hands. "Such as my unswerving loyalty. My years of devotion. My services, as always."

"Circling the wagons," Judith said to Renie.

Erma pursed her lips and shook her head. "Oh, Horace!" She leaned forward and let him kiss her other cheek. "What would I do without you, now that Wilbur is missing?"

"Aww . . ." CeeCee said with a big smile, "ain't that sweet? I could just bawl!"

"I'll bet she could," Renie muttered.

But Judith was staring at CeeCee's ruffled red dress. It was the same daring cocktail outfit she'd seen at Neiman Marcus.

Before Judith could say anything to Renie, Beulah showed in

Consuela Cruz and Paul Tanaka. The newly made widow was very pale and leaned on Paul's arm as if it were her only means of support.

"Consuela," Erma said in a low, incredulous voice.

"Erma," said Connie, her state of mourning emphasized by a black ribbed jersey dress. Docilely, she allowed Paul to lead her forward.

Rhoda stepped in between the two women. "Ricky and I couldn't bear to think of Connie being alone. We knew you wouldn't mind if we mentioned your generous hospitality to her. And Paul has been such a help."

"Not to mention," Rick said, removing his gold cigarette case from his suit jacket, "that it seems like a good idea to stick together. Our numbers seem to be dwindling, wouldn't you say?" He paused to light his cigarette. "Oh—the captain sends his regrets. I understand he was invited, too."

Erma shot Ambrose a sharp look. "Captain Swafford received an invitation?"

Ambrose had dithered his way toward the little gathering. "Why, yes—I thought—that is, it seemed—I mean . . ." His voice trailed off helplessly.

"Ambrose," Erma said, her jaw taut, "you're a nincompoop."

Ambrose reddened and stammered. But CeeCee intervened. "Well, I think he's cute." She slung an arm over the secretary's shoulder. "Honest, Mrs. Giddon, Ambrose is a real peach. You know he's always trying his best to please you." She glanced up at Horace from under her impossibly long eyelashes. "Just like Panky here. When did he ever do anything but what you asked him?"

"Excuse me," Paul Tanaka said, clearly impatient. "Could Mrs. Cruz sit down? She's feeling very shaky."

"I should never have come," Connie said in a faint voice. "I should be saving my strength for the funeral Monday."

Erma motioned at a beechwood sofa with toile cushions. "Yes, do sit. Beulah will serve you something." She snapped her fingers. "Beulah! Attend Mrs. Cruz."

"Yaz'um," Chevy replied, juggling the tray that held the cousins' drinks.

Judith moved quickly to relieve the ersatz maid. "Go ahead, we're fine."

"Damned straight," Chevy muttered, hurrying to the sofa where Paul was settling Connie against plush pillows embroidered with the elaborate initial *G*.

Judith managed to extricate herself from the little group dominated by Erma. Purposefully, she walked over to Connie.

"Serena and I feel remiss that we haven't been able to do anything for you these past two days," Judith said, gingerly sitting down on the sofa. "I know we've hardly met, but I was widowed at a young age, so I can certainly sympathize."

Connie's dark eyes were wary. "Was he murdered?"

Judith kept her aplomb. "It was more like suicide. He ate and drank himself to death."

Paul moved a few steps away, but remained within hearing range. Judith offered him a brief glance of acknowledgment while Connie hesitated before responding.

"Did your husband's death make you feel guilty?" she finally asked.

"Yes," Judith answered truthfully. "I always felt I'd enabled him. I worked when he wouldn't, I bought the Twinkies, the liquor, all the things he shouldn't have had if he wanted to be healthy."

Connie's gaze grew more intense. "How long ago has it been since he died?"

"Fifteen years."

"Have you forgiven yourself?" Connie asked softly, leaning closer.

"Not entirely," Judith replied. "Even though I know it wasn't my fault. He did it to himself. Ultimately, we're responsible for our own actions."

Connie nodded slowly, her thin body rocking back and forth on the toile cushions. "Yes . . . perhaps . . . yes."

Chevy appeared with brandy and a vodka martini. Paul took both glasses, then wordlessly handed the snifter to Connie. She nodded her thanks, but kept her gaze on Judith. "You must be very strong," she said.

Judith shrugged. "I had a son to raise. You do what you have to do."

"Mags and I had no children." Connie had looked away, her eyes staring blankly at the shifting scene across the room. Horace and CeeCee were talking to Jim Brooks; Erma appeared to be upbraiding Chevy despite Rhoda's wagging finger; Renie had been cornered by Ambrose; Rick was standing aloof, drinking gin and observing the others.

Judith never knew quite what to say to someone who had been married but remained childless. "I had an elderly mother to look out for," she finally said when Connie didn't elaborate. "My son and I moved home with her."

"She must have been a comfort," Connie remarked.

"Uh . . . yes," Judith replied. *If hearing "I told you so, you dumbbell" at least twice a day could be considered comfort,* she thought. But at least Gertrude had been there. And still was. "Are your parents living?"

Connie sipped her brandy before she answered. "My mother died when I was in my early teens. My father is still living, but in very poor health. He's sold his homes in New York and in Paris. He prefers his native Buenos Aires, and seldom goes out at all."

"My father died when I was a teenager," Judith said, making another honest effort to forge a bond.

"Oh, yes?" Connie's fine features softened almost imperceptibly. She leaned even closer and lowered her voice "Did that make you feel guilty, too?"

"No." Judith thought back to that unhappy time. "But of course I wished I'd been a better daughter. I had regrets, especially that I can't remember him as well I should. But that's because when you're young, you take time—and everything else—for granted."

"We do, don't we?" Connie had grown wistful. "We don't see our parents as people. We know them only as mother, father. That's the tragedy of being their children, isn't it?"

Judith didn't answer immediately. "I hadn't thought about it exactly in that way. But you're right. When we get older—while a parent is still living—we have more insight."

Connie's expression was ironic. "Do we?"

Paul touched Connie's shoulder, where white piping held the black froth of cap sleeve in place. "Can I get you something else?" he inquired. "I don't see any canapés, but you haven't eaten all day."

His words were like a tocsin. Erma had moved away from the others, pursing her tight red mouth. "Dinner is about to be served. Would you please follow me into the dining room?"

Paul moved to assist Connie to her feet. But Horace had thumped across the room.

"May I?" he said, offering a big hand to Connie. "Did you receive the flowers I sent? And the fruit basket?"

Connie allowed Horace to help her stand. "Yes. Thank you. They were very thoughtful."

Judith was left to fend for herself, no easy task since the sofa was low and the cushions were deep. She was the last to arrive, finding her place between Jim and Paul. Horace had kept Connie next to him, at the opposite end. A sidelong glance to her left told Judith that Paul was discomfited, perhaps even fuming. Erma had her rightful chair at the head of the table, but no one sat in the other place of honor, though there was a chair and a setting. Judith wondered if that was Horace's usual spot, but that he had been demoted because of the quarrel with Erma. Or perhaps, she considered, because he was so intent on being solicitous of the Widow Cruz.

Still, she felt obliged to inquire about the empty chair. "Who isn't here yet?" she asked Jim.

Jim looked puzzled, his gaze taking in the table. "We're all here," he said. "Even the ones who weren't asked. I mean—the ones Erma didn't expect. The kitchen help must have seen to it."

"But there's an empty place," Judith pointed out.

"Oh." Jim glanced at the vacant chair. "That's for Wilbur."

"You mean . . . ?"

Judith was interrupted by Erma, who was standing up and tapping a Waterford wineglass with a sterling-silver spoon. "Family and friends," she began, "we're gathered here this evening in mutual sorrow for the untimely passing of our dear friend Magglio Cruz. May I propose a toast to his memory?" She waited while her guests got their cocktail glasses in hand. "To a man of vision and charm who has crossed the bar. Thank you, Magglio, for everything."

A muffled response went around the table as glasses clinked.

Rick St. George was sitting across from Judith next to Renie. "At least," he murmured, "she didn't claim that he'd *passed* the bar. I certainly don't want someone saying that about me when I'm gone."

Judith couldn't help herself. She turned to Paul and lowered her voice. "What about Dixie and Émile? Shouldn't we toast their memories as well?"

Paul's usually pleasant features hardened. "They were employees. Peons," he added under his breath. "They don't count in Erma's world."

Judith winced. "I don't understand that attitude. It's so different from the one I know."

Paul shrugged. Two young men were presenting the soup course. It looked and smelled like lobster bisque. Judith stared into the bowl, recalling that she had, in fact, collided with this same world of wealth and privilege a few years earlier. Along with Renie, the cousins had been asked to watch over a wealthy woman who lived in a gated community north of the city. The house—a mansion, really—had been called Creepers because of the vines that grew up its stone walls. But the place had been more like a prison, and death had lurked in its corridors and corners. No one in that family had been happy. Their money and their status had brought only grief. Judith felt the same sense of misery in the Giddon house that she had experienced at Creepers. She was tempted to grab Renie and bolt.

Instead, she tasted her soup and discreetly surveyed the other diners. Thirteen place settings, but one was vacant. Wilbur. *Wilbur Giddon,* Judith suddenly realized. The *late* Wilbur Giddon. Judith shivered, despite the long sleeves of her new pearl-gray suit. For the first time, she looked at the damask-covered wall behind the empty chair. A large oil painting of a large—and possibly oily—man loomed over the gathering. She didn't understand how she could have missed seeing it upon entering the room, except that she had been focused on finding her place at the table. But the man in the portrait was bearded, balding, and wearing a Prince Albert frock coat with an ascot scarf. He evoked an era from the late nineteenth or early twentieth century, making it more likely that he was Wilbur's grandfather. Whoever he was, he looked formidable as well as arrogant.

Judith's gaze dropped down to Anemone, who was seated on

the other side of Paul. The young woman seemed so delicate and unprepossessing. It was difficult to believe that her bloodlines must carry some of the same genes as those of the man in the portrait.

Rick, who had been watching Judith, leaned across the table. "Elwood Edward Giddon," he said. "At one time he owned most of Pacific Heights. Imposing, I suppose."

"He looks like a big twerp to me," Renie said to Rick in a voice just loud enough for Judith to hear.

Rick laughed carelessly. "Aren't all robber barons twerps? Power corrupts and all that. It's such a relief not to have to work for a living. It'd ruin my disposition. I enjoy being a kept man."

Rhoda, who was seated between her husband and Horace, laughed. "Ricky, darling, has it ever occurred to you that it was often the kept women who've been the brains behind those powerful men? I would never have married you if you'd been stupid instead of merely dashingly handsome."

Ricky made a face. "Egad, my love, you're putting me in the same class as the Mesdames de Pompadour, du Barry, and Montespan."

Horace, who had been coaxing Connie to try the soup, turned to Rhoda. "Who? I've heard of de Pompadour and du Barry, but—"

"*Montespan*," Rhoda said loudly and clearly. "She was Louis XIV's . . ."

The explanation was lost in a clatter of spoon and crockery as Connie Cruz fell face forward into her lobster bisque.

Chapter Sixteen

Erma Giddon howled like a wounded hound, clutching at her bisque-spattered bosom. CeeCee and Anemone were screaming, too. Horace was bug-eyed, staring at his fallen companion's motionless figure. Ambrose, who was sitting directly across from Connie, picked up his bowl and poured the contents onto the Persian carpet.

"Poison!" he gasped, grabbing at his throat with a trembling hand.

"My Ferahan Sarouk!" Erma screeched. "You've ruined it, Ambrose! That rug cost more than you'll make in ten years!"

Rick had risen, moving quickly past Renie and Horace to reach Connie. Feeling for a pulse, he gave a single nod. "She's alive. I believe she merely fainted." Gently, he lifted her head and wiped her face with a napkin.

Next to Judith, Jim was making an awkward effort to get out of his chair. "Let me help. I'm almost a doctor."

"He needs the practice," Renie murmured from across the table.

On Judith's other side, Paul was doing his best to shush Anemone. CeeCee had stopped screaming when Ambrose pitched his soup on the floor. Rhoda was leaning her cheek on one hand and sipping the dregs of her martini.

"I wonder," she said musingly, "if there's a salad course?"

Ambrose's hand fell away from his throat. "You mean we're not all going to die?"

Briefly, Rick scowled at the secretary. "Hardly." He chafed Connie's hands as her eyelids began to flutter. "I suggest we move her onto the sofa."

"Yes," Jim agreed, now standing between Erma and Connie. "Yes, that would be my medical recommendation."

"Good thinking, old son," Rick said. "Would you mind helping me with the patient?"

"What? Oh! Sure, here let me . . ."

But Horace threw up his hands in protest. "Wait! Consider the liability involved! Should she be moved in her condition? Would it be better to let her lie there with her head on the table until she's fully conscious?"

"Good grief!" Renie exploded. "In that case, why not stick her face back in the soup bowl?"

Thoughtfully, Jim rubbed his chin. "She could drown that way, couldn't she?"

Horace shrugged. "You're the doctor."

"No, he's not," Rhoda declared. "This is ridiculous. Ricky, move the poor woman."

Rick, Jim, and Paul carefully eased Connie out of the chair. She was moaning softly and licking her lips.

Gesturing at Jim, Renie looked across the table to Judith. "Instead of the Mayo Brothers, we get one of the Marx Brothers. It figures."

"What's wrong with Mrs. Cruz?" CeeCee asked, her usually breathy voice shrill.

"Overwrought," Horace replied, dabbing at his forehead with a napkin. He'd begun to sweat and had grown very red in the face. "Nerves. Exhaustion. Grief." His eyes followed Rick, Jim, and Paul as they carried Connie out of the dining room. "Excuse me," he said, his chair bumping Renie's. "I must go to her."

"Why?" The word shot out of Erma's mouth like a bullet.

Horace stopped in his tracks behind Connie's empty place setting. A scant three feet away, Erma sat rigidly at the table's head, her fingers splayed like fat claws on the arms of the Hepplewhite chair.

"T-t-to see if I c-c-can do anything," Horace stammered.

"You can't," Erma snapped. "Sit down."

To Judith's surprise, Horace obeyed, again bumping into Renie, who was starting to look annoyed.

"Gosh, Panky," CeeCee said, her voice no longer shrill, "you don't look so hot. Maybe you'd better take your pills."

"Oh!" Horace felt around inside his suit jacket and withdrew a small bottle. With an unsteady hand, he removed a small pill and popped it in his mouth.

Renie was watching closely. She placed a fist over her heart. *Nitro,* she mouthed at Judith.

Heart trouble, Judith thought. Apoplexy would have been her own diagnosis.

Rick walked briskly back into the dining room to make the announcement that Connie had come around. "I've sent for Dr. Selig," he said. "Just in case. The poor woman is a wreck."

Anemone rose from her chair. "So am I. Excuse me, Mumsy, I'm going to go to my room and lie down."

Judith pushed her chair away from the table. "Let me go with you," she said. "You look a bit shaky."

"I am." Anemone's blue eyes fixed on Judith's face. There was nothing uncertain about her cool gaze. "Thank you, I'd appreciate it. You've been so kind to all of us, even though we hardly know you."

Erma snorted.

The staircase was steep and narrow, but it was carpeted and the handrail was solid. Judith took her time following Anemone to the second floor. The young woman didn't speak until she had locked the bedroom door behind them.

"You must think I'm a terrible person," Anemone said, indicating that Judith should sit on a chaise longue covered with a design of purple and yellow pansies. "I'm so glad you didn't give me away when I fibbed about you being with me at the store."

"It seemed prudent to keep my mouth shut," Judith said with a curious expression.

Anemone also sat, pulling a matching ottoman closer to the chaise longue. The boudoir was actually a small suite. Judith could see into a second room, where a bed was covered with— appropriately enough—a pattern of multicolored anemones.

"I didn't kill Émile," Anemone declared in a flat, quiet voice.

Judith waited. Anemone sat without moving a muscle, the blue eyes challenging her listener.

"Okay," Judith finally said. "So you must have another reason for lying about me being with you in the dressing room, right?"

Anemone finally blinked. "Yes."

"And that would be . . . ?" Judith coaxed.

The young woman shook her head. "I can't tell you that."

An awkward silence fell upon the room, as if the fog that crept along the city's steep streets and dark alleys had seeped through the walls to put distance between the two women. Through a lace-curtained bay window, Judith could see the ghostly glow of a street lamp in front of the house. She could imagine the same scene a century earlier, with the clip-clop of horse-drawn carriages moving in the night.

"Then I'm not sure why I should lie for you," Judith said at last. "I only stray from the truth when there's a very good reason."

Anemone leaned forward, her hands clenched together. "Please. This is very important to me. The reason, I mean. But I can't tell you. It's too . . . too humiliating."

"Humiliating?" Judith repeated. A romantic rendezvous between the winsome ingenue and the middle-aged purser seemed unlikely. "Were you meeting Émile?"

"No!" Anemone clapped both hands to her cheeks. "No, I never even saw him. I swear it."

As Judith recalled, the individual dressing room sections were divided according to the type and price range of clothing featured in the open display areas. Anemone had been shopping in the suit department; coats and outerwear were featured between that part of the store and the designer boutique where Renie had discovered Emile's body. If there was access between the separate dressing-room areas, Judith hadn't seen it.

"Have you been questioned by the police since Dixie and Émile were killed?" Judith asked.

Anemone looked offended. "No. Why should I be? I hardly knew either of them. They worked for Mr. Cruz."

"Did you know them before your mother arranged to go on the *San Rafael?*"

Anemone's eyes narrowed. "You sound like the police."

Judith waved an impatient hand. "You're asking me to give you an alibi. If I lie for you, I'm guilty of a crime. It's called impeding justice. My husband is a retired policeman. I refuse to do that, Anemone. I hardly know you."

"That's why I can't tell you my reason for . . ." Anemone's head drooped. "It's just too embarrassing. But it has nothing to do with Émile or anybody else getting killed."

"You may be wrong," Judith contended, "even if you didn't kill them yourself. You—and I—were in the store when Émile was murdered. You may have seen someone who was connected with his death." She paused, trying to determine if her words were having any effect. But Anemone continued to hang her head, refusing to look Judith in the eye. "Okay." Speaking sharply, Judith stood up. "As my Grandma Grover used to say, 'If you're not going to help, don't hinder.' You obviously went to Neiman Marcus to meet someone. Who was it? Émile Grenier? Or CeeCee Orr?"

Anemone's head snapped up. Her blue eyes were filled with tears. "I told you, I hardly knew Mr. Grenier! And I certainly didn't go there to meet a tart like CeeCee! Please, stop badgering me!" Seemingly on the verge of hysterics, Anemone suddenly seemed to get a hold on her emotions. "How did you know CeeCee was there?"

Judith decided to be cagey. "I know a lot of things. But I can't help you unless you tell the truth and get me off the hook with your phony alibi."

"It's not phony," Anemone asserted in a miserable voice. "Besides, I haven't talked to the police. But I can't tell you anything more. *Please.*"

Anemone wasn't worried about being interrogated by Biff McDougal. Judith realized this as she contemplated the young woman's obvious agony. That meant Anemone was afraid of someone other than the authorities.

That someone could only be her mother, Erma Giddon.

Dinner continued despite the disruptions. The salad course had followed, but by the time Judith left Anemone in her bedroom and arrived downstairs, only Erma, Horace, CeeCee, and Ambrose remained at the table. Presumably the others, including Renie, were in the living room with Connie Cruz.

Upon seeing Judith, Jim rushed up to her. "How's Anemone? Is she okay? Should I take her pulse?"

"She's upset, that's all." Judith glanced into the living room. A balding man with wire-rimmed spectacles was hovering over Connie, who was lying on the sofa. "Is that Dr. Selig?"

Jim nodded. "He's pretty good. Heck, he sure knows a lot of stuff about medicine."

"That's helpful," Judith said, keeping a straight face, "especially for a doctor."

"Maybe," Jim said, frowning, "I should go see Anemone."

Judith made no comment. Jim stood on one foot and then the other. Finally, he headed for the staircase.

Renie was nowhere to be seen. Rick and Rhoda had taken their salad plates to an Italianate credenza that stood within convenient reach of the glass-fronted liquor cabinet. Paul was standing guard by the sofa where Connie lay with her eyes half closed.

Dr. Selig stood up straight and removed his spectacles. "I'm prescribing a higher dosage of Valium," he said. "Your pharmacy will deliver it tonight. You must have complete rest until the funeral services Monday. Your nerves are completely shattered." He turned to Paul. "You will see that she follows my instructions, won't you, Mr. Tanaka?"

"To the letter," Paul said grimly.

"Well, then," Dr. Selig responded, closing his black case with the Cruz Cruise line logo embossed on the leather exterior, "take the lady home. She should never have ventured out this evening. I warned her about overdoing it the other night after the . . . tragedy aboard ship."

Connie opened her eyes. "I couldn't stand it, Doctor. I felt as if I were going crazy in that big condo without Mags."

"Understandable," Dr. Selig said, "but unwise. You need to recover your strength, physically and emotionally."

Judith had moved over to where the St. Georges were drinking martinis and nibbling on baby spinach leaves. "What set Connie off?" she whispered.

"Courtesans," Rhoda replied with a shrug. "What else? That's what we were talking about."

"Power," Rick said softly. "We were also talking about robber barons and kings and things."

Connie was being helped to her feet by Paul and Dr. Selig. Chevy had appeared from the foyer with coats and Connie's handbag. Renie was right behind her.

"Mags was a self-made man, but he wasn't exactly a robber baron," Rhoda said, still keeping her voice down.

Nodding farewell at Connie, Paul, and the doctor, Renie crossed the room to join Judith and the St. Georges.

"Mmm," she murmured, studying the salad plates, "any crab or shrimp in there?"

Rhoda shook her head. "Mainly greens. But the vinaigrette dressing is nice."

Renie seemed to lose interest. "I'll wait for the next course."

With long years of practice, Rick wielded the martini shaker. "May I refresh your cocktail?" he asked his wife.

"Of course, darling," Rhoda replied. "Thank you. We should

go back to the dining room, though it's really too, too grim. Why did we come?"

"To sleuth, my dove, to sleuth." Rick poured out fresh drinks for his wife and himself. "Ladies?" he said to Judith and Renie.

They declined.

"One thing," Renie said as the St. Georges picked up their salad plates. "CeeCee Orr was at Neiman Marcus yesterday when Émile was murdered."

Judith stared at her cousin. "I wondered. How can you be sure?"

"I decided to help . . . *Beulah* gather up Connie and Paul's belongings. We all left our purses in the foyer, right? I figured CeeCee for the red Kate Spade handbag because it matched her dress. A dress, by the way, I'd noticed at the store."

Judith nodded. "So did I. It's my favorite color," she added for the benefit of Rick and Rhoda.

"Mine, too," Renie said. "Anyway, I thought she might have kept the receipt in her purse. She had, and the time of purchase was listed. It was twenty minutes before I spotted Émile's body."

Rick whistled softly. "Bravo!"

Rhoda smiled her approval. "Very nice work."

Judith was tempted to reveal her frustrating conversation with Anemone, but held back. If the young woman hadn't killed Émile—and Judith doubted that she had—then there was no point in revealing the episode until the allegedly humiliating reason for Anemone's presence at the store was discovered.

The foursome resumed their places during Beulah's presentation of a crown rib roast of lamb. Erma nodded her regal approbation and allowed Horace the honor of carving the portions. Jim Brooks returned to the table a moment later.

"Anemone's going to take a nap," he announced.

"Very well," Erma said. "Tomorrow I shall consult a hypnotist."

"For Anemone?" Jim asked in surprise.

"No," Erma replied coldly. "For myself. I've been told that hypnosis is useful in solving crimes. Somewhere in my subconscious I may know who stole my jewels."

"How about that?" Rick remarked glibly. "I don't suppose your subconscious might reveal who killed Mags, Dixie, and Émile?"

Erma shrugged. "That's not my concern."

Chevy, moving in a diffident manner, entered the dining room and came up behind Rick's chair. She whispered something into his ear and shuffled away.

"Excuse me," Rick said, standing up. "I have an urgent phone call. I'll take it in the study, if I may."

Erma shrugged again. "As you will. While you're there, please don't breathe on my ananas."

"I wouldn't dream of it," Rick said with a charming smile.

CeeCee looked puzzled as she turned to look at Erma. "I thought you were sitting on it, Mrs. Giddon."

Erma glared at CeeCee. "An ananas is a houseplant, otherwise known as a pineapple plant. It requires a high amount of humidity."

"Oh." CeeCee beamed. "Ain't that something? Growing pineapples in your own house! Got any cantaloupes or kumquats around here?"

"Hardly." Erma looked as if she could barely endure conversing with CeeCee. "The particular type of pineapple plant I have doesn't produce fruit, only flowers."

CeeCee blinked a couple of times. "Well, gee, I think I'd rather have one with real pineapples." She looked across the table to Horace. "Why don't you buy me a banana tree, Panky? I'll bet I could grow one on your roof garden. Or," she went on, gathering steam, "how about this—you could put all kinds of fruit plants and stuff in the cork-and-sponge museum. Like . . . what do you call it where there's a glass roof?"

"A greenhouse?" Ambrose suggested.

"An atrium," Horace replied. The sour expression he'd been wearing disappeared. "That's not a bad idea, CeeCee."

"All those plants would perk up the sponges," CeeCee said. "I mean, sponges and corks are really swell and all that, but aren't they mostly brown? You need some green."

"I do at that," Horace said, and sighed heavily.

Rick reentered the dining room. "Nothing urgent," he asserted, sitting down at the table. "By the way, this lamb is delicious."

"It's from New Zealand," Erma said. "I had it flown in by New Zealand Airlines."

"You should've had duck," CeeCee said. "Then it could have flown in by itself." She let out a high-pitched giggle.

Judith didn't dare look at Renie. A surreptitious glance around the table caught Horace appearing as if he were on the verge of an anxiety attack; Erma in very high dudgeon; CeeCee apparently oblivious to everything except the mint jelly she was rolling around on her tongue; Ambrose with his head down in deep gloom; and even a silent Rick and Rhoda, who, for once, seemed to be at a loss for words.

But CeeCee certainly wasn't. Seated next to Ambrose, she poked his arm. "You aren't eating. What's up with that?"

"I'm a vegetarian," Ambrose replied, pulling away from his dinner companion. "I only eat fish and other seafood."

"Huh." CeeCee frowned at the secretary. "You don't feel sorry for the poor lobster who gave up his life for your soup? You didn't wince when you thought about him boiling away in a big old pot?"

"That's different," Ambrose mumbled.

Renie held up her fork from which dangled an asparagus spear. "How do you know that this little guy isn't screaming in pain? Or," she continued, pointing to Horace's wineglass, "those grapes weren't groaning in agony while they were being stomped?"

Ambrose shuddered. "I don't want to think about it. All living things are precious."

"Really?" Renie looked pugnacious. "Then why don't I see anybody lamenting over the corpses that are being stacked up like cordwood around here?"

Erma sucked in her breath. "Mrs. Jones! That's very crude!"

"It's very true," Renie shot back. "The only person who seems affected by the recent tragedies is Connie Cruz. You act as if human beings are as disposable as paper towels."

Although Judith agreed with Renie, she motioned for her cousin to shut up. But Erma had hauled herself to her feet and was wagging a pudgy finger.

"You are incredibly ill-mannered!" Erma bellowed. "You and that other person are no longer welcome in this house! Get out!"

"Gladly." Renie had also stood up. Whether by accident or by design, the damask tablecloth got caught on the big face of her wristwatch. Her own place setting, along with Horace's wineglass and Rhoda's silverware, crashed to the floor.

Erma let out a piercing yelp. Renie yanked the damask cloth away from her watch, tearing a small hole in the fine fabric. "Cheap crap," she said with a sneer. "I hope *that's* disposable."

Renie stomped out of the dining room, leaving Judith no choice but to follow. Erma shouted invective after both cousins, but didn't attempt to follow them.

"Coz," Judith said, aghast, "you shouldn't have done that! Erma will send you a bill for damages."

"Screw her," Renie snapped, picking up her handbag in the

foyer. "You knew from the moment we met her that I'd do something outrageous. She's exactly the kind of wretched, selfish person who drives me wild."

"Me, too," Judith agreed, "but I don't make scenes."

"Try it sometime," Renie said with a wicked grin. "It feels great. I'll use my cell phone to call us a taxi."

Renie was dialing when Chevy appeared in the foyer. "Can I give you a standing ovation?" she asked Renie.

"I wasn't acting," Renie replied. "I don't see how you can put up with that old bat for five minutes."

"Acting is all about discipline," Chevy explained, ignoring Erma's shouts for help.

"You deserve an Academy Award or a Tony or some damned thing," Renie declared. "Keep in touch. If Erma has a fit and falls in it, I want to be the first to know."

Judith and Renie waited outside for the taxi. Neither of their new suit jackets could ward off the fog's damp chill. Almost five minutes passed before they heard the front door close behind them. Through the thick gray vapors, Judith could barely make out the forms of Rick and Rhoda St. George.

"The party didn't seem quite as festive without you," Rick said. "May we share your cab?"

"If it ever comes," Renie said. "What happened after we left?"

"The maid came to restore order," Rhoda replied, keeping her champagne-colored Chanel coat wrapped closely over the matching cocktail dress. "Erma announced that dessert would be served in the parlor. That's when we decided to leave. Ricky and I spent a less stressful evening at Candlestick Park during the 'eighty-nine World Series earthquake."

"We became engaged there," Rick said, smiling at his wife. "I told her she made the earth move for me."

"He's so sweet," Rhoda remarked with an ironic expression.

"He'd never have proposed if they'd been able to play the game that night."

"Of course not," Rick agreed. "When the series resumed, the Giants ended up getting swept. I would have been glum for days, and not in a marrying mood."

A few yards down the street, Judith could make out two dim lights. "I think the taxi's finally here," she said.

"Ah." Rick nodded. "Before we get in, there's something you should know."

Renie looked alarmed. "The killer's driving the cab?"

Rick smiled and shook his head. "Doubtful. But the phone call I received during dinner was from Biff McDougal. He wanted to let me know that they've been checking the local bank accounts of everyone involved in the investigation. It seems that on the first of the last four months, Connie Cruz made cash withdrawals on a personal account in the amounts of twenty, forty, fifty, and seventy-five thousand dollars."

The headlights veered close to the curb. The taxi stopped.

"Were there any canceled checks in that amount?" Judith asked.

"No," Rick replied, moving toward the cab. "Suggestive, though, don't you think?"

"Yes," Judith said as Rick opened the rear door for the women.

One word had leaped into Judith's mind.

Blackmail.

Chapter Seventeen

Despite the fact that their cabdriver didn't seem conversant in English, the foursome spoke only of inconsequential matters during the ride back to the St. Francis.

"Maybe," Judith suggested as they drove past Union Square, "you should come up for a drink."

"What a splendid idea!" Rick exclaimed. "I could use a martini about now. It's been minutes since I've had one."

Upon arriving in the suite, Renie ordered a liter of Tanqueray No. 10, a fifth of Kina Lillet vermouth, and a jar of cocktail olives from room service. The small liquor bottles in the honor bar wouldn't go very far with their guests.

"It might not be blackmail," Rhoda said while they waited. "It could be gambling debts, or even purchases. You know, like clothes or jewelry that she didn't want Mags to know she was buying."

Rick looked dubious. "It's the increments and the regularity of dates that bother me. According to Biff, her other finances—as well as Mags's—are in order. So, apparently are those of the cruise line itself."

Rhoda didn't seem convinced. "Connie has led a blameless life. That is," she continued with a hint of cynicism in her expression, "as far as I know. I've always considered us confidantes—up to a point. There are some things women don't even tell their dearest friends."

"Such as a lover?" Judith put in.

Rhoda looked ambiguous. "Like that."

"Nominees?" said Renie.

"Oh, dear." Rhoda pressed a finger to her forehead. "Their circle includes some very charming men." She shot a glance at Rick. "Not you, darling. That is, you're relentlessly charming, but I'd know if you were straying. Our liquor bills would be lower."

Room service arrived. Rick insisted on doing the honors, including a hefty tip for the waiter. Judith and Renie, however, both insisted on drinking soda from the honor bar.

"I never could handle gin," Renie admitted. "Frankly, I hate the taste. It's like drinking a Christmas tree."

Rick's eyes twinkled. "And to think I thought you were a person of refined taste and habits."

"Don't get sidetracked, darling," Rhoda cautioned. "We were speaking of other sins before the gin bin arrived."

"Speaking as an outsider," Judith began as she scooped ice cubes out of a silver bucket, "I noticed how solicitous Émile Grenier was of Connie after Mags was killed."

"Proprietary," Renie added. "But Paul Tanaka behaved the same way this evening."

"That's the effect Connie has always had on men," Rhoda said, accepting a martini from her husband. "Perfect, darling," she murmured after a first sip. "Connie is the type of woman who appears as if she needs protecting. The male sex has always treated her with the utmost gallantry. When we were younger, I used to find it annoying."

Rick grinned at his wife. "That's because you look like you can take care of yourself ten times better than any man could."

"Except for you, darling," she responded with a semisweet smile.

Judith poured Diet 7UP into her glass. "I still have to wonder what caused Connie to faint at the dinner table. Until then, she seemed relatively composed."

"Was anyone else conversing at the other end of the table?" Renie inquired. "I was way down there sitting by the late Wilbur Giddon's empty chair."

"No," Rhoda stated firmly. "You and Rick and I were the only ones talking at that point, except for Horace, who asked about Madame de Montespan. He was on my left, then Connie, with Erma at the head of the table. Ambrose and CeeCee were across from them, and at that point, they were keeping their mouths shut."

"So was everybody else on my side of the table," Judith said. "It wasn't what you'd call a lively social gathering."

Rhoda removed her cigarette case and holder from her evening bag. "Do you mind?"

Both cousins shook their heads. Three lives in three days had been lost through violence; smoking seemed like a minor vice.

"It beats me," Rick said, gazing out into the foggy night. "If anyone should have passed out during a discussion of courtesans, it'd be CeeCee. But her skin is as thick as it is fair."

Renie, who was sitting in an armchair with her shoes off, set her Pepsi on a sidetable. "How long has CeeCee been Horace's girlfriend?"

Rick and Rhoda exchanged glances. "A year?" Rhoda offered.

Rick shrugged. "About that. Horace has never married. Over time, he's squired a number of beautiful blondes. As Horace gets older, the women keep getting younger. Some of them have had a bit more class than CeeCee. But not much."

"What does he do?" Renie asked. "Pay them off when they get tiresome?"

"It's more the other way 'round," Rhoda said, using a small porcelain dish as an ashtray. "The girls get tired of Horace. Of course they accumulate enough jewelry and cash or whatever before they pack up and leave. And in some cases, he's acted as a sort of marriage broker."

Judith frowned. "How do you mean?"

Rhoda laughed carelessly. "Think about it, my dear. In today's world, few women want to be kept by a rich sugar daddy. If Horace doesn't choose independent career girls—or should I say they don't choose him?—they at least want legal and financial security. It isn't difficult for him to find one of his cronies a second or third bride, particularly of the trophy-wife variety."

"In fact," Rick put in, "Horace has made a couple of matches for younger men who have—old-fashioned as it may sound— fallen in love with the ladies in question—or, if you will, questionable ladies."

"Why," Renie murmured, "do I feel as if I'm out of this league?"

"Because you are," Rhoda said kindly. "And I think it's terribly refreshing."

Judith felt equally at sea. "Is Horace recompensed for making these marital arrangements?"

Rick turned away from the window and winked. "In his own way. Financial advice, shall we say."

"You mean stock tips?" Judith responded. "Inside-trader kind of information?"

"Whatever the market will stand," Rick answered blandly. "Horace is generous with his ladies, but he's not rich in the way of really rich people. If you know what I mean."

"We don't," Renie replied.

"We *really* don't," Judith emphasized.

"It's like . . ." Rhoda looked at Rick. "You explain, darling."

Rick blew a couple of smoke rings. "A rich person might decide to take off tomorrow for the islands—Hawaii, Tahiti, the Bahamas. A really rich person might fly to an island, too—but he or she would probably own it."

"Oh," Renie said. "But," she went on, "Horace is rich enough to sink his money into corks and sponges."

Rick's expression didn't change. "Perhaps."

"I find this all really creepy," Renie declared. "Or maybe I should say sordid. How does a seemingly gentle soul like Anemone Giddon float through these polluted waters?"

"Erma's very protective," Rhoda replied. "Anemone has gone to private schools, would-be suitors are thoroughly investigated, and she rarely goes anywhere without her mother. You can imagine what Jim Brooks has endured."

Judith poured more soda into her glass. "I gather that Jim isn't from a wealthy family. How did he make the cut?"

"A good question," Rhoda said. "Jim's family used to be moderately well off. Unfortunately, they made some foolish investments in Silicon Valley-dot.com stocks that collapsed about four years ago. His father died not long after that, and his mother is a victim of early Alzheimer's disease. She's in a home near Walnut Creek. Jim had always wanted to be a doctor, but the money simply wasn't there. About that time he met Anemone at the wedding of mutual friends. They began seeing each other and eventually became engaged."

"But, I assume," Judith interjected, "only after Erma had thoroughly investigated him."

"That's right," Rhoda affirmed. "Erma didn't like the idea that Jim's family had become poor because of bad judgment, but she tried not to hold the sins of the father against the son. She agreed to pay Jim's way through Stanford, but only on the understanding that the couple wouldn't marry until he finished medical school."

"An offer Jim couldn't refuse," Rick remarked.

Judith nodded. "I assume that Jim and Anemone are deeply in love?"

Rhoda was quick to catch the skepticism in Judith's voice. "You think not?"

But Judith merely shrugged. "These people seem more motivated by money than emotion."

Rick chuckled. "I was motivated by both. I certainly wouldn't have married Rhoda if she'd been—excuse the expression—*poor*."

Judith glanced at Rhoda to see if she'd taken offense. But she hadn't.

"Of course not, darling," she said. "If I'd been poor, I'd have been a completely different person. Not to mention that I wouldn't have looked half so enticing. Money may not buy beauty, but it certainly can enhance one's natural endowments."

Again, Judith considered telling the St. Georges about Anemone's strange request for an alibi. And again she decided not to say anything until she knew the reason for the young woman's behavior. Instead, she asked about Ambrose Everhart's background.

Rhoda responded, but only after allowing Rick to refresh her cocktail. "As you can imagine, Erma has had problems keeping hired help. She pays fairly well, but she's so hard to please. Ambrose has been her secretary for about a year. Previously, he'd been working for some environmental agency. I understand he wasn't keen on leaving that job because he's very conscientious about the environment, but such organizations have to keep a lid on salaries. The money tempted him, and because of Erma's social and civic obligations, Ambrose has sufficient spare time to still take part in issue-oriented concerns."

"Does he have a social life?" Renie asked.

"Not much time for that," Rick said, between puffs on his cigarette. He blew a few more smoke rings. Rhoda waited a moment, and then did the same. Her smaller rings drifted through Rick's larger ones. It was obviously a trick they had taught themselves by long practice. It occurred to Judith that there was something romantic—if unhealthful—about the stunt. The St. Georges seemed to be perfectly attuned to each other.

For a moment, Judith reflected on a different domestic situation, the more dysfunctional relationships inside the Pacific Heights mansion. "Propinquity," she finally murmured. "Is it possible that Ambrose might have fallen in love with Anemone? Or vice versa?"

Rick cocked his head to one side. "I don't doubt Anemone's feelings for Jim. But I would say that Ambrose may have his eye on someone else in the Giddon household."

"Beulah?" Renie blurted in surprise.

Rick shook his head. "No. He may have fallen for Jim. You see, Ambrose is gay."

After the St. Georges had left, Judith kicked herself. "I should have guessed. It's not as if we don't have a sizable gay community at home."

"Your gaydar must have gotten lost in the fog," Renie suggested.

"Until now," Judith said as the cousins began to get ready for bed, "I thought maybe Anemone was meeting Ambrose at Neiman Marcus and that's why she was so embarrassed. *Humiliated* was the word she used. Obviously, I was on the wrong track."

"We're assuming Jim is straight?"

Judith threw up her hands. "Who knows? The only thing I can believe about him is that he fell into a sweet deal when he hooked up with Anemone. Of course he seems to be someone Erma can control. Having his way paid through Stanford medical school isn't exactly a token bribe."

"If he makes it," Renie noted. "Jim doesn't strike me as the sharpest blade in the butcher block."

"True enough," Judith allowed, carefully hanging up her new suit. "On the other hand, he may be one of those people whose brains are science-oriented, but don't cope well with everyday matters."

"He may also be Anemone's first love," Renie pointed out. "They're both very young. She's led a sheltered life. And the wedding isn't supposed to take place until after he's out of med school. That'll take years. A lot can happen between now and then."

Wrapping the plush terry-cloth hotel robe around her tired body, Judith sat down on the bed. "We're not looking at any of this in the right way. Let's go back to the beginning."

"You mean to Magglio Cruz's murder?" Renie asked, sitting down opposite Judith.

"Right. What's the one thing about all these deaths that's the same and yet different?"

Renie thought for a moment. "The manner thereof. Mags was stabbed, Dixie was poisoned, and Émile was strangled."

"Exactly." Judith smiled her approval. "The weapon used to kill Mags was something at hand, and possibly not premeditated. That suggests an argument, a sudden burst of violence. It could also indicate that the killer panicked."

Renie frowned. "Not enough to keep him or her from getting rid of the weapon. Or, for that matter, to let that panic show after the crime was committed."

"Which indicates the killer has a certain amount of self-control or is used to working under pressure," Judith pointed out.

"I'm not sure that description lets us eliminate anybody involved," Renie said after a brief pause. "Every one of the suspects we know is either obnoxiously up-front—like Erma—or may have a hidden agenda—like CeeCee. Furthermore, they all live in a pressure-cooker kind of world. Not to mention that someone of this ilk who has just committed murder—especially under volatile circumstances—usually has strong survival instincts. Even a frail flower like Anemone would hardly walk out into the middle of the ship's saloon and announce, 'I done it.' "

Judith nodded. "But I'm also referring to the kind of panic that doesn't show but stays inside and eats away at the person who did do it. Given that Dixie and Émile were the first to discover Mags's body, why then did they become the next victims? I still think they saw something or someone that would've given the killer away. If they didn't name names, then it had to be a *thing,* not a *person.*"

Again, Renie paused before responding. "Did Mags fall or was he pushed into the piano?"

Judith shook her head. "It could have happened either way, though pushed—or should I say stuffed?—seems more likely. He was a slender man, but it strikes me as peculiar that he would have landed in such a way."

"On the other hand," Renie pointed out, "you never saw enough of his body to tell what might have happened."

"That's true," Judith admitted. "Biff McDougal must know. So should Rick and Rhoda. Unless Biff's withholding some of the facts even from them."

"That doesn't seem likely—" Renie stopped as the phone rang on the bedside table. "Now what?" she muttered, picking up the receiver.

Judith watched her cousin's expression became perplexed. "It's kind of late. Can't it wait until tomorrow?" Renie said. "No? Okay, come on up."

"Who was that?" Judith asked as Renie replaced the receiver.

"Captain Swafford. He says he has to see us immediately," Renie replied. "Jeez, it's going on eleven o'clock. He called from the lobby. We're going to have to hold court in our bathrobes. What could be so important?"

"Any number of things," Judith murmured, "but not anything serious that involves us. I mean, if the cruise has been canceled, why not say so over the phone?"

"Because I work for the line as a consultant?" Renie suggested in a dubious tone.

The cousins returned to the sitting room. Judith attempted to open a window to air out the cigarette smoke, but the casements were sealed shut. Unable to sit still, she put the half-empty liter of gin and the bottle of vermouth away in the armoire that held the TV set.

"I was going to watch the news," Judith said, shutting the armoire's doors. "I guess I won't now. I assume Émile's murder will be one of the big stories."

"Nobody can keep a lid on a triple murder when they all seem to be connected," Renie pointed out.

A knock sounded on their door. Both cousins turned at the same time and bumped into each other.

"Sorry," Judith murmured.

"I'm okay if you're okay," Renie said, reaching the door first.

Wearing his regulation uniform instead of his much-decorated formal attire, Captain Swafford still managed to look imposing. Indeed, he looked severe. Judith resisted an impulse to salute.

"Come in," Renie said, though by the time she got the words out, the captain was halfway across the sitting room. He didn't speak right away, but clasped his hands behind his back and gazed first at Renie and then at Judith.

"I have significant news, Mrs. Jones, Mrs. Flynn," he announced in his deep British-accented voice. "Perhaps you should sit down."

The cousins both sat on the sofa. Swafford remained standing. He cleared his throat before speaking again. "First—and least important—is that the *San Rafael*'s maiden voyage has been postponed until an unspecified date in April. The reason we are giving is that certain minor technical adjustments need to be made."

Like removing the crime scene tape, Judith thought to herself. But she was too cowed to say anything out loud. The captain was only of average height, but he was broad and bearded, a looming authoritative figure who somehow evoked Holbein's portraits of Henry VIII.

"The other matter," Swafford continued, "is much more grave. A complete search has been made of the ship during the past two days. Mrs. Giddon's stolen jewels were found this evening."

"So?" Renie said, her manner indifferent.

The captain glowered at her. "So indeed, as far as you're concerned, madam. They were discovered aboard ship in the safe of your Mae West suite. Biff McDougal should be here any moment to arrest you both."

Chapter Eighteen

Hold it!" Renie cried. "Are you crazy? We didn't steal the old bat's jewels!"

"I'm afraid," Captain Swafford said solemnly, "that your fingerprints were all over the case as well as on some of the individual pieces. Can you deny that you handled Mrs. Giddon's stolen property?"

Before Renie or Judith could answer, they heard a heavy pounding on the door. Captain Swafford moved briskly to let in Biff McDougal. He was accompanied by a pale young man with a crew cut so blond that it was almost white. Judith assumed that the newcomer must be Buzz Cochran, Biff's temporary partner.

"I see you beat us to the punch, Skipper," Biff said to the captain before gesturing at Judith and Renie. "Any trouble with these two?"

"They deny having stolen the jewels, of course," Captain Swafford replied.

"Open-and-shut case," Biff declared, rolling the ever-present toothpick around his mouth. "Let's go, ladies."

"Let's not," Renie retorted, folding her arms across her chest and planting her bare feet firmly on the floor. "This is stupid. Furthermore, I don't go anywhere in a hotel bathrobe. And I'm not responsible for our daughter Anne shopping at Falstaff's Market in her jammies. We didn't raise her that way."

"Huh?" Biff looked puzzled.

"My cousin's right," Judith said, although she got to her feet. "If you're serious about going to headquarters, you'll have to let us change clothes. If you merely want to question us, please sit down so we can have a conversation." She looked Biff right in the eye. "My husband's a retired policeman. I know the drill, and I doubt that you have any real evidence other than some fingerprints, which we can easily explain."

"So start by explaining how the jewels got in your safe?" Biff demanded.

"Obviously," Judith said, keeping her voice calm, "we can't." She had gone over to the honor bar next to the armoire. "Shall we behave in a civilized manner and have a drink?"

Captain Swafford's expression was stolid. "Certainly not."

"Not what?" Renie shot back. "Have a drink or behave in a— oh, never mind!" She waved her hands in disgust.

Biff, however, was watching Judith remove the expensive liter of gin from the armoire. "Well . . . I don't usually drink on duty, but it's kinda late, and I could use a little pick-me-up. How about you, Buzzy?"

Buzz Cochran, who looked as if he'd be more comfortable in the frosh section of a Cal–Stanford football game, shook his head. "You know I don't drink. *Sir,*" he added in a deferential tone.

"That's because you're probably not of legal age yet," Biff muttered. "You got a lot to learn, kid."

Biff looked not at Judith but at the gin bottle. "On the rocks," he said.

The captain let out a heavy sigh. "I daresay I could use a jot of brandy, if you have it."

"A Coke, please?" Buzz said in a small voice.

"Sure," Judith responded, opening the honor bar. "Coz?"

"There's Drambuie in there," Renie said. "Let's split it."

Judith didn't argue.

"I thought you were gonna change your clothes," Biff said as Judith poured the drinks into every available clean glass.

"You mean," Judith said, handing Biff his gin rocks, "we still have to go to the station?"

"It's only three minutes away," Biff replied, sniffing at his glass. "Hey, this is really good stuff. Go ahead, put on your duds. We won't use the cuffs, but we gotta follow procedure." He turned to Buzz. "Take a note, kid. This is how a real cop works."

"You mean," Buzz said, aghast, "I *have* to drink gin?"

"Nah," Biff responded with an avuncular expression, "but it sure helps."

"Good grief," Judith muttered, warily checking Renie's reaction.

Renie, however, stood up. "Why not? What would a trip to San Francisco be like without getting arrested? In *my* day, it was a badge of honor." She downed the Drambuie in one swig and sashayed into the bedroom. Judith followed with a less flamboyant gait.

As soon the bedroom door was closed, Renie began to choke. "My God, that stuff's strong!" she gasped, clutching her throat. "I'd forgotten why you're supposed to sip it!"

"Show-off," Judith chided. "Honestly, this is ridiculous!"

"Of course it is," Renie responded. "That's why we're not wearing our new clothes. We'll wear the comfortable yet tasteful outfits we wore on the plane—sweats and slacks. Can you imagine what the central police station is like on a Saturday night?"

"Good Lord," Judith groaned. "I can. But I don't want to dwell on it."

Five minutes later, Judith and Renie presented themselves to Biff, Buzz, and the captain. Swafford announced that his responsibilities were done for the time being, but he'd keep in touch with the police. Meanwhile, he had to pay a call on Erma Giddon. Doffing his braided cap, he left the hotel suite.

"Jail," Renie murmured as they walked to the elevator, "or Erma? Which is worse?"

Judith merely shook her head. "At least we're not in handcuffs," she said.

Buzz drove the unmarked police car as carefully as if he were pushing a baby buggy. They practically crawled through the Stockton Street Tunnel, even though traffic was comparatively light so close to midnight. The cousins, sitting in the backseat, didn't speak until after they'd reached the station on Vallejo Street. The only sounds inside the vehicle were the frequent belches of Biff McDougal and a couple of fruitless pleas for Buzz to drive faster.

But if the ride had been slow, central booking was a frenzy. Every race, religion, and lifestyle seemed represented in the crowded station. A cacophony of languages assaulted their ears, along with a number of obscenities the cousins understood all too well. The air reeked of booze, marijuana, sweat, and more putrid odors that Judith didn't want to define.

"The best-dressed people here are the transvestites," Renie

noted. "I wonder where the . . . *person* by the desk got that emerald-green ball gown?"

"Don't ask, don't tell," Judith murmured. "And watch out for that guy with the dreadlocks and the oversize baseball cap. He's coming right for you."

"Yo!" cried the young man, who was built like a bull and covered in tattoos, "who you think you are, struttin' aroun' in that damn Sea Auk sweatshirt? This is *Raider* country, mama. Yo' football team sucks soup cans!"

"Yo' mama sucks everything!" Renie shot back. "That's 'cause she got no damn teeth! Like these!" She bared her formidable prominent front fangs. "Yo' don't be givin' me no sass! Are you the homey who boosted my do-rag? Why, yo' mama's so fat that—"

"Hey!" Biff grabbed Renie's arm and hauled her out of the way before the startled young man could react. "Watch it. You can get hurt around here."

"Raider thug," Renie muttered.

Buzz coughed slightly as the cousins were whisked down a busy hallway. "Actually," he said, "that Oakland Raider fan is one of ours. He's an undercover policeman."

"He's still a Raider fan," Renie snarled. "Just like Cleo, our foulmouthed doll."

Judith was relieved when Buzz made no comment. She didn't need any more of Renie's fantasies. Reality was grim enough.

Years ago, when Joe was still working, he'd given Judith a tour of police headquarters. He had shown her the interrogation areas, which looked more spartan than some of the sets she'd seen in movies and on TV. The room into which the cousins were ushered simply looked bleak: a Formica-topped table, straight-backed chairs, a clock, and a window with one-way glass.

"You could do something with this place," Renie said to Biff. "Some Erté Art Deco posters, an oval rug, maybe a couple of candlesticks. A window that looked outside would be nice."

Biff grunted. "Funny lady. Take a seat. Buzz, you listen up. See how the big boys do this."

"You mean like scratching myself in strange places the way you're doing now?" Buzz inquired in a puzzled voice.

Biff scowled and put his hands behind his back. "Don't get smart with me, sonny. I mean, like professional police interrogators."

"When are they coming?" Renie asked.

"Hey!" Biff glared at Renie. "You've got a big mouth, sister. I'm beginning to think you made up that story about your old man helping me out on that serial-poisoning case."

Renie glared right back. "Did you check your case files?"

Biff yanked off his hat and slammed it down on the table. "Hell, no! When do you think I have time to do stuff like that? Now sit down and shut up, both of you."

"Yes," Buzz said in a small voice. "Please."

Judith and Renie sat. The chair was hard, a sure sign that Judith's back and hip would begin to ache momentarily. Buzz remained standing, looking distinctly ill at ease.

"Okay," Biff said, dropping his voice while keeping the toothpick in place. The chair creaked under him as he rocked back and forth. "How'd your fingerprints get on Mrs. Giddon's jewelry and the case?"

Judith began to speak before Renie could say anything that might further exacerbate the situation. "It happened after Mr. Cruz's murder when we went to see how the Giddons were doing," she said. In a few brief sentences, she recounted how Erma had put them to work, and in the process, the cousins had seen the jewelry and taken a peek.

"That's it," she concluded. "As to how the stolen goods ended up in our suite's safe, I've no idea. We never used it."

Biff didn't look convinced. He glanced at Buzz. "You hear that? What do you make of it?"

"Um . . ." Buzz fidgeted with the ballpoint pen he'd been holding. "I guess I don't see why they'd hide the jewels in their own safe. I mean, there must be all sorts of other places they could've put them. That is, if they knew they had to leave the ship, why would . . . er . . . ah . . ." He grimaced and dropped the pen.

"Because," Biff barked, "that's what they want us to think! Holy moley, it's a trick!"

"Some trick," Renie said. "Why didn't we just wear them and parade around Union Square like the rest of the nuts?"

"Hey!" Biff shouted. "Lay off the locals! Aren't you the creeps who got all the serial killers?"

"Not quite all," Judith said. "With three murders in three days, you seem to have one of your own."

"Yeah, well, maybe," Biff mumbled. "How do we know you two didn't do those jobs yourself?"

Renie held up a finger. "Motive, anyone?"

"Not to mention," Judith put in, "why would we steal Mrs. Giddon's jewelry? I assume you've checked to see if either of us has a rap sheet."

"Don't mean a thing," Biff declared. "You could have stolen somebody else's identity. Happens all the time these days. You're the perfect types for a jewel heist—muddleheaded middle-aged dames who may *seem* harmless, but are really a pair of smart crooks, fooling your victims with the old housewife-and-mother act. Besides, you don't fit in with the rest of the snooty crowd who were at the boat party. I figure you finagled your way into that bunch to get at the jewels." Biff pointed his stubby thumb at

Renie. "The original invite was for a Mr. and Mrs. William Jones. If that's not a phony name, I know don't what is." He swung his thumb in Judith's direction. "And you don't look like *Mister* Jones to me. Though," he added, more to himself than to the cousins, "around this place, sometimes it's hard to tell."

Renie sighed. "We've been through this before. My husband couldn't come on the cruise. My cousin came instead. And I work—worked—for Mr. Cruz. Mrs. Cruz and Paul Tanaka can vouch for me."

"Sez you." A tap on the window caused Biff to give a start. "Buzzy, see who that is."

Buzz went to the door, immediately admitting Rick St. George.

"Good Lord," Rick said to Biff, "can I ever leave you alone for five minutes? What are you doing here with poor Mrs. Jones and Mrs. Flynn?"

Biff struggled to his feet. "The loot was in their safe on the ship. Their fingerprints were all over the—"

"Calm down, old son," Rick urged. "I think you jumped the gun. I can assure you, these ladies are above reproach." He turned just enough to smile reassuringly at Judith and Renie.

Biff's face was getting very red. "Yeah, well, maybe, but evidence is evidence. And if they didn't stash the jewels in the safe, who did?"

"An excellent question," Rick responded, "and one, I might add, that perhaps I can answer for you quite soon." He chuckled and tapped his temple. "I have a hunch who really stole Mrs. Giddon's glittering glory."

"No kidding!" Biff exclaimed. "Who?"

"Not yet, not yet," Rick replied with a wink. "We'll get together for a drink in a day or so. For now, let me escort Mrs. Jones and Mrs. Flynn back to their hotel. They must be very tired. First, though, I'm sure you want to apologize to them for the inconvenience."

"Uh . . ." Warily, Biff peered at the cousins, who were already on their feet. "Sorry. Anybody can make a mistake. In fact," he continued, raising his voice and looking over to the place where Buzz had been standing, "this goes to show that good police work requires you to eliminate suspects before—hey! Where's Buzz?"

Judith had noticed that Buzz had left as soon as Rick entered.

"I believe," Rick said in his casual manner, "your partner departed."

"Oh." Biff shrugged, obviously relieved that the junior officer hadn't witnessed the recent turn of events. "Just as well."

"Shall we?" Rick said to Judith and Renie.

"We shall," Judith said. "Good night, Detective."

Biff didn't respond.

"We'll go out the back way and miss the riffraff," Rick said after they'd entered the corridor. "It's a good thing I called Captain Swafford to see how the search for the jewels was going. I was able to reach him while he was on his way to the Giddon residence. He told me that Biff had brought you in."

"We should sue," Renie muttered as they reached a rear exit.

"Don't even think about it," Judith retorted. "Your legal threats are what got us into this in the first place."

"Don't you start in on that again," Renie said as they walked out into the cool, damp night.

Judith let the subject drop. The air might be chilly, but it smelled fresh after the dank odors of the police station. The fog had lifted a bit, and Judith could see several yards down to the far end of the alley.

But she didn't like what she saw.

Two men stood at the corner of the building. A streetlight

shined down on them, making recognition easy. They were in deep conversation, paying no attention to the trio about to head in the opposite direction.

The men were Buzz Cochran and Flakey Smythe.

I don't speak French," Judith insisted the next morning when Renie finished consulting the Mass schedules at nearby Catholic churches. "Why do we have to go to a service in French?"

"You don't speak Latin, either," Renie pointed out, "and for the first twenty-odd years of your life, that was the language of the liturgy. Besides, you can doze off during the sermon. If we hurry, we can just make the ten-thirty at Notre Dame des Victoires. It's a beautiful church just a few blocks away, originally built to serve the large French-speaking community."

"Fine." Judith reached into her purse to get out her lipstick. It wasn't in the side pocket, so she felt for it at the bottom of the bag.

"Come on," Renie urged, standing at the door. "It's ten-twenty."

"I'm coming!" Judith snapped as she began to toss items out of her purse. Among them were the three VIP party invitations she'd filched from Dixie's hotel room. "I don't know why I kept those damned things anyway. I'm hardly going to forget—"

She stopped and stared at the elegant invitations, which lay scattered on the carpet. One of them had small holes cut in it.

"Hold on," she said, picking up the damaged invitation. "Let me check something." She reached into her purse again, this time pulling out the note that had appeared under the covered dish aboard ship. "I thought so!" she breathed. "Dixie must be the person who told us to butt out!"

Renie, who'd been looking annoyed, stepped back from the door. "What do you mean?"

"Look." Judith pointed to the carefully clipped holes. "The capital *B* is missing from *Beales,* the lower case *u*'s are cut from *Pankhurst* and *Cruz,* the *o* is gone from *Magglio,* and the two *t*'s are from *Everhart* and *Pankhurst.* Taken together, they spell this." She held the note out to Renie.

"You're right." Renie grimaced. "I should have realized that. I knew the note's type font looked familiar. But why would Dixie threaten us? We hardly knew her."

Judith put the invitations and the note into a hotel envelope. "Now we do have something to hide in a safe. I'm locking these up." She opened the armoire and found the key inserted in the lock. "We can only assume it was Dixie who sent the note. But you're right—I can't imagine why."

"You can mull during the French sermon," Renie said. "I'll be trying to translate it. Or some of it. Maybe."

The eighty-year-old church with its twin towers and stained-glass windows was indeed beautiful. Judith had no trouble following the familiar liturgy, though her mind did wander during the readings and the homily. And in every direction that her thoughts traveled, they arrived at Dixie Beales.

Had Dixie killed Magglio Cruz? Had she been poisoned in revenge? What would have motivated her to send a warning note to the cousins? Or had someone else on board the ship sent the note and somehow the invitations had ended up in Dixie's hotel room?

The Mass ended; the priest and the acolytes processed back down the aisle. Judith hastily crossed herself and said a very quick Act of Contrition. She felt that for the past hour the world had been too much with her.

As they made their way out of the church, Renie was shaking

her head. "The priest was a visiting missionary who spent twenty years in Africa. He thinks he's still there."

"He looked sort of old," Judith said.

"He *is* sort of old, like eighty-*cinq*. Or eighty-*sept,* I forget. I'm not good at numbers in any language," Renie admitted. "In fact, I couldn't catch all of the words, but he seemed to be warning us to stay in *le patolin*—the village—and not go off to find temptation in Bafoussam."

"Maybe it's just as well I missed it," Judith remarked. "I don't know where Bafoussam is."

"In Cameroon, Africa," Renie replied as they stepped outside into an overcast day. "Okay, what's your game plan?"

"I'm not sure," Judith admitted. "Research, maybe. I'd like to know what—if anything—has appeared recently in the newspapers about Cruz Cruises. We have a computer setup in our suite. I can go online and check."

"Are you thinking about the blackmail possibility?" Renie asked as they started walking along Bush Street.

"I don't know what I'm thinking of," Judith admitted. "We don't have access to very many facts. If Connie was withdrawing increasingly large amounts from her personal account, where did the money go? Is Biff a complete bungler or is he holding back? And if it's the latter, why? Because pressure is being put on him?"

"By Erma or Horace?"

"They pop to mind first," Judith said as they started down Powell Street's steep incline. "In fact, why don't you arrange to meet with your old pal Paul Tanaka?"

"You mean," Renie responded, "if he can take time off from his care and feeding of the Widow Cruz?"

"Yes." Judith was feeling more purposeful. "Call him. He might be staying at the Cruz residence instead of the Fitzroy, at least until after the funeral tomorrow. Do you know where Connie lives?"

"Not exactly," Renie said as they waited for a cable car to rattle by before crossing the street. "I know it's an expensive condo near the bay, maybe in the Marina district."

"Okay," Judith said, moving more briskly despite her weary hip, "you contact Paul while I finagle a computer out of the front desk. I don't want to have to use one of the public PCs."

"Got it," Renie replied as they neared the hotel entrance. "What about checking out Flakey Smythe in the newspaper archives?"

"Good thinking," Judith said, smiling at the welcoming doorman. "Whatever he got out of Buzz Cochran wouldn't be in the paper yet, though."

"Let's hope Buzz's information didn't include our near arrest," Renie said, moving toward the elevators. "I'll try to run down Paul and also make nice with Connie Cruz."

Nodding, Judith went to the front desk. A handsome young man of Middle Eastern descent greeted her with a dazzling white smile. Judith went straight for the bald-faced lie.

"My laptop PC broke," she declared. "Is there some way I can borrow one to use in *our suite?*"

The implication didn't overtly affect the young man, but he said he'd find out and disappeared through a door behind the front desk. Judith eyed the clocks on the wall, which showed the time in various parts of the world: Sunday, March 23—noon in San Francisco; 3 P.M. in New York; 5 P.M. in Buenos Aires; 8 P.M. in London; 9 A.M. Monday in Tokyo. It had turned from winter to spring since the cousins had left home. Judith hadn't noticed. So much had happened in the past few days that it seemed to her as if weeks, not days, had gone by. She should call Joe again. And her mother.

The young man returned with a laptop computer in hand. "Do you mind signing for it?" he asked in a diffident voice.

"Not at all," Judith said. "I should be done with it this afternoon."

She found Renie talking on the phone, presumably to Connie Cruz. "It couldn't hurt to visit your father in Argentina," Renie was saying. "The change of scenery might do you good. I'm sure he'd like to see you." Noting Judith's arrival, she made a thumbs-up sign. "We can talk about that when we see you this afternoon. Are you sure it's all right? Okay, two o'clock, then. Bye." She turned to Judith. "We're on. Paul's still there."

"Good," Judith said, putting the laptop down on the mahogany desk. "We're two for two. And I've got plenty of time to do my research."

Renie glanced at the phone. "I'll call Bill. He won't answer, but I'll leave a message telling him we're still alive. Then," she continued, grimacing, "I'll call my mother."

Judith nodded. She was already absorbed in getting on the Internet and finding a good search engine.

Renie spoke into the receiver: "Cruz dead, cruise canceled. We'll be home after the funeral. Love you."

Judith looked up from the screen, where a story about pollution in local waters was downloading. "That's terse. Won't Bill be puzzled?"

"No," Renie replied, dialing again. "After all these years, it's the kind of information he'd expect to get when I'm with you."

Judith was still perplexed. "But Bill never uses the phone unless he absolutely has to. Does he know how to retrieve a message?"

"No."

"Oh." It was pointless to ask Renie any further questions. After so many years, she'd given up trying to figure out how her cousin and her husband ran their household. Stuffed apes, small dolls, a rabbit wearing a tutu—it was beyond even Judith's superior powers of deduction.

She looked back at the screen. She'd started her search for *Cruz Cruises* from January 1, but drew a blank until February, when rumors surfaced about the company's move to San Francisco. The change of headquarters was confirmed in early March, with two subsequent articles giving details. But the story that held her attention ran ten days later, on March 11.

The California Environmental Protection Agency (Cal/EPA) is planning to launch an investigation of Cruz Cruises to learn if the line is in violation of wastewater dumping in San Francisco Bay.

Judith started to read aloud, but her cousin was already talking on the phone, presumably to Aunt Deb. "Not exactly a problem . . . I'm not sure when we'll get home. We have to check with the airlines . . . Of course it's windy . . . No, I absolutely refuse to put weights on my feet to prevent getting blown away . . ."

Current regulations require a limit on the amount of waste dumped by ships with as many as 5,000 passengers and crew.

" . . . Not a contagious disease . . . Mr. Cruz had what you might call a shipboard accident . . . We won't be going back on the ship, Mom. How can I fall overboard if I'm on dry land? . . . Hey, do I wear a miner's lamp on my head in the fog at home?"

Cruise-line owner Magglio Cruz, who recently moved his company headquarters to San Francisco, denies that his ships, including the new *San Rafael*, qualify as "behemoth ocean liners. Even the largest," Cruz said yesterday, "including our new flagship, will carry fewer than 3,000 people."

" . . . Not a tremor . . . Yes, I know, stand in a doorway or get under a sturdy man . . . What? No, I didn't say 'man.' At least I didn't mean to say that. I meant *table*." Renie seemed rattled.

Environmentalists claim that the numbers for passengers and crew are not only much higher, but that Cruz has been in violation of wastewater regulations in Alaskan waters. A demonstration is planned at Cruz headquarters tomorrow at 10 A.M. Several hundred protesters are expected to be on hand.

Judith finished the article and turned to watch Renie more closely. Her cousin suddenly looked alarmed. "What? You did? How high on the Richter scale? . . . That's high enough. Are you okay? . . . Oh, that's too bad, but I'm sure Mrs. Parker will find him . . . Hey, I've got to go. Judith needs me . . . No, she's not sick . . . yes, she's being careful of her hip . . . No, we haven't lost our mittens. I'll see you soon, Mom . . . Yes, *very* soon . . . As soon as we can get there . . . *Soon*."

Renie hung up. "They had a five-point-six earthquake at home this morning. Mrs. Parker's wretched poodle is missing. No serious damage except for the usual broken crockery and stuff falling off of shelves."

Judith couldn't help but feel some concern. "I must call home. I've got my heirloom items on the plate rail in the living room, not to mention Grandma Grover's breakfront with the family china."

"You've never lost much of it yet," Renie said with a shrug. "If you live in earthquake country like we do on the West Coast, you expect to get a few things trashed now and then."

"I know," Judith agreed, "but I'm still going to call Joe as soon as I finish this search." She moved on to the next story covering the protest at Cruz headquarters, which, judging from the Ferry Terminal Building in the background of the accompanying photo, seemed to be near the bay.

"Cruz had—or has—a problem with dumping wastewater," Judith explained. "Cal/EPA was starting an investigation about two weeks ago." She scanned the protest article. Almost three hundred protesters had turned out, but there had been no violence. There were a couple of quotes from both sides, including a brief statement from Paul Tanaka, asserting that the cruise line was in compliance with state regulations.

"I didn't realize there was an environmental problem," Renie said. "Of course, I probably wouldn't have been informed unless they needed a design for a friendly-looking Mr. Garbage. Maybe that's why Paul Allum and Bill Goetz didn't protest the headquarters move. They're both concerned about our own environment."

Judith was studying the photo of the protesters. "These people may not be physically violent, but they sure don't look very friendly. Some of those signs are downright vicious. I'm glad they didn't show up for the VIP prelaunch . . . Hey!" She pointed to a face in the crowd. "Look, coz. Isn't that Ambrose Everhart?"

Renie stared at the four-column picture. "Egad! You're right. And look at that sign he's holding up."

"I know," Judith said with a worried expression.

Ambrose's sign read, SHIPS STINK! SINK CRUZ! KILL CRUISES!

The cousins exchanged hard stares.

"Is that a motive for murder?" Renie asked.

Judith again considered the passion on Ambrose's face. He certainly looked like a man on a mission. "It's probably not," she said, before adding in a forlorn voice, "at least not for a sane person."

And the more she examined the photo, the more Ambrose Everhart looked unbalanced.

Chapter Nineteen

Y ou didn't hear the latest?" Connie asked in an excited voice as Judith and Renie sat down in the spacious living room of the two-story condo overlooking San Francisco Bay.

"We've spent a quiet Sunday," Judith said, not untruthfully. "Exactly what happened?"

Connie and Paul were seated on a dark brown leather double sofa that looked out over the view in one direction and into the middle of the room on the other. Judith thought Connie seemed much improved since the debacle of the previous evening. She even apologized for the disarray of the household.

"The housekeeper was supposed to come in after we sailed," she said with a rueful expression. "I haven't had a chance to reschedule. There's dust everywhere and even a couple of cobwebs on the ceiling. Don't you just hate it when you have live in the midst of filth?"

Recalling the squalid rental that she and Dan had lived in on Thurlow Street in the city's south end, Judith could only nod. *Filth* was hardly a word she'd use to describe the Cruz condo. And Judith was certain that Connie—unlike the McMonigles— hadn't heard rats doing the mambo inside their bedroom walls.

"Rhoda called less than an hour ago," Connie explained before interrupting herself to ask Paul to pour some wine for the guests. "You do drink wine, don't you?" she asked the cousins. "Mags always kept a really decent cellar. What would you like?"

Neither Judith nor Renie were wine drinkers, but they wanted to be polite. "You choose," Judith said.

"Have you got one that tastes like Pepsi?" Renie asked.

Connie laughed. "You *are* a tease, Serena." She put a hand on Paul's arm. "Let's open that Beringer 1997 private reserve cabernet sauvignon. We can't serve our guests anything but a California label, can we?"

Paul merely smiled and left the room.

"What was I saying?" Connie asked with a frown. Despite the obvious improvement in her manner, she retained her quick, nervous gestures. "Oh. About Rhoda telephoning. She told me how the two of you had actually been taken to police headquarters and questioned about Erma's jewel theft. I couldn't believe it!" She laughed rather unnaturally. "Anyway, it turns out that the jewelry found in your suite was fake!"

"Fake?" Judith echoed. "As in . . . imitation?"

Connie nodded vigorously. "That's right. Which means, according to Rick, that the robbery had been planned for some time. You can't create imitations of the real thing without having them copied first."

Renie grinned. "How's Erma taking it?"

"She had a fit," Connie replied, not without a certain amount of glee. "Of course Erma is always having a fit about something, but this time I suppose you can't blame her."

Paul had returned with two wine bottles and four glasses. "Shall I act as sommelier?" he inquired.

Connie nodded again. "Of course. You know what you're doing."

Paul did. He scrutinized the label, expertly opened the bottle, sniffed the cork, gave the wine a moment to breathe, poured an eighth of an inch into one of the glasses, and took a sip. "Excellent," he declared. "The cork test is usually a mere formality in restaurants. It's done quickly, because the customers want to start drinking and eating. But a serious connoisseur will take time to make sure the cork has no musty odor. If it does, the wine may be musty, too."

Connie smiled fondly at Paul. "You see? I told you he knows what he's doing. Paul's so capable. That's why I intend to let him take over the cruise line. I trust him completely."

"That's probably a wise decision," Renie said.

"A very generous one," Paul murmured as he carefully poured from the bottle.

"But deserved," Connie insisted. "The board of directors will have to approve, of course. But I have the majority of shares in the line. Besides, with Erma's departure, there shouldn't be so many obstacles. I'm afraid Erma likes to create problems where none actually exist."

"So her jewels are still missing," Judith said, accepting a glass of wine from Paul.

"Yes." Connie smiled again at Paul as he sat down beside her. "I wonder if they were real to begin with."

Judith couldn't keep her eyes from wandering around the room. Not only was the view spectacular, but the walls were covered with paintings. Except for a couple of country scenes, the rest featured horses: horses racing around the track; horses in the paddock, horses in their stalls; horses in the field; horses posing with jockeys. Quickly, she counted fourteen such pictures.

There were also a number of photographs displayed on the gleaming cherrywood table next to her chair. More horses, with not only jockeys, but presumably owners and trainers. In one photo, a very young Connie stood next to a black filly in the doorway of a barn. A slightly older Connie—early teens, Judith figured—sat astride a piebald colt while a distinguished-looking older man held the reins. Maybe it was Connie's father. Another picture showed the same man standing next to a jockey at a racecourse. The jockey was small, lean, and mud-spattered. He reminded Judith of so many of the riders she'd seen over the years at the local track. They were always small and lean, of course. But there was something familiar about this particular jockey. Judith wondered if she'd actually seen him ride in the days when she went with Dan so that he could blow the grocery money on a long shot. It was possible. Jockeys moved from city to city, following the best mounts they could find.

"Do you mean," Renie was asking, "Erma never had the real thing or that she'd sold the pieces and replaced them with paste?"

"Oh," Connie replied, "originally she had the authentic goods. Some were heirlooms, handed down through several generations. Mags told me . . ." Connie paused, her face sobering. "Damn. I still can't believe . . ." She raised her head, closed her eyes for a moment, and cleared her throat. "Anyway—Mags thought Erma had been hard hit by the post–9/11 recession. She'd always had her money invested in thoroughly stable companies and bonds and such, but someone—Horace, no doubt—had urged her to buy Silicon Valley stock and make some very speculative investments. Between the dot-com fiasco and 9/11,

Mags figured she lost a bundle." Connie turned to Paul. "Isn't that right?"

He nodded. "Mags told me the same thing. Erma also loaned Horace—assuming it was a loan and not a gift—a big chunk of money for his cork-and-sponge museum. Unfortunately, she seems to have relied on him for all her financial advice since Wilbur died."

"It seems to me," Judith put in, "that to Erma, Wilbur *hasn't* died. She behaves as if he's still alive."

"A quirk," Connie said.

"A delusion," Renie asserted. "Not a good sign about Erma's mental state. What did she mean aboard ship about Wilbur being . . . what was it? Missing?"

"His urn," Paul replied. "She takes his ashes everywhere."

"Did he ever turn up?" Renie asked.

Connie shrugged. "I've no idea."

Judith had made the mistake of sitting in a zebra-stripe chair with a deceptively hard seat and back. Maybe zebras were more thin-skinned than they looked. She was forced to stand up and relieve the discomfort in her hip.

"Sorry," she apologized. "I have an artificial hip. I think I've done too much walking since we came to San Francisco, especially with all these hills. They're much steeper—and there seem to be more of them—than at home."

"You're right," Connie agreed. "I've noticed the difference myself. Is there something I can do to make you more comfortable?"

"No, thank you," Judith said with a grateful smile. "I'll see if I can loosen up a bit."

She strolled around the room, admiring the view and then the paintings. Renie, Connie, and Paul were talking about the future of the cruise line. A replacement for Erma on the board of directors sounded like the top priority. Several names were mentioned, but they meant nothing to Judith.

Four of the oil paintings seemed to have been done by the same artist. Small brass plates attached to the frames were etched with the horses' names. A handsome chestnut standing proudly in his stall was called Tierra del Fuego. A powerful bay named Belgrano charged across the finish line. Beau Noire, an imperious black stallion, stood in the winner's circle wearing a mantle of red roses. Lastly, grazing in an emerald green field, was a beautiful milk-white mare. Judith stared at the name on the brass plate: MONTESPAN.

She peered at the painting's background, where she could see an old windmill and, beyond that, the spires of a Romanesque church. The scene had a European feel to it. The picture had been signed— they all had—but Judith couldn't read the artist's signature.

Momentarily stumped, she suddenly had a wild idea. "Excuse me, Connie," she said, moving closer to the sofa, "would you mind if I went into the bathroom to take some pain medication?"

Connie gestured with her forefinger. "The guest bathroom is right off the foyer."

"Actually," Judith said with a little grimace, "I need to lie down for just a couple of minutes. Is there a bathroom near the bedroom?"

"Of course," Connie answered graciously. "My bathroom and dressing room adjoin the bedroom. They're downstairs. Can you manage? Please, take your time. I'm so sorry you're in pain."

"All the walking," she mumbled, noticing that Paul seemed to tense up while Connie was speaking. "But I can do the stairs," Judith added quickly.

That, however, was no easy task. Although the steps were carpeted, the staircase was a spiral. Judith had to hang on for dear life, lest she misjudge her footing and take a header.

Double doors opened onto the master suite. The room was divided into three parts—boudoir, dressing room, and a small office. It was the latter that interested Judith most. Judging from the feminine decor, this was not where Magglio Cruz worked when he was home. No doubt his own study or den or office was elsewhere in the spacious condo. Judith had noticed that Connie's sleek red Cartier shoulder bag was on a table in the living room. No doubt her checkbook was inside. But if Connie had been making withdrawals for the past few months, her less recent bank records might be in the office.

Connie was organized.

Judith was thankful for that. She remembered an occasion when Renie and Bill had been out of town. Renie had forgotten one of her credit cards and needed it to make a purchase. She'd told Judith where to find the spare key to let herself in, but wasn't sure exactly where she'd put the card. "Try the pencil caddy on the dinette table or the drawer by the wine rack or the one by the spice rack," Renie had said. "If it's not there, it could be in my spare cosmetic bag on top of the file cabinet by the kitchen table or under the electric can opener on the counter by the microwave." It had been in none of those places. Judith had never found it. Renie later discovered it had been stuck between the C-major and D-flat keys of her piano.

Connie had a well-ordered filing cabinet. Judith easily found the bank statements. There were three accounts in her name— checking, savings, and a money market. Judging from the canceled checks that had been filed, Connie could write on all three. Judith hurriedly flipped through the ones that went back to the first of the year. There weren't that many. Apparently, all the household bills were paid from a joint account that Mags had probably kept in his own records.

Indeed, there were no checks made out to anyone whose

name Judith recognized. There was a jeweler, an alterations shop, a furrier, a personal trainer, a masseuse, a hairdresser, and various other service and sales persons. The most recent check was dated March 17. It had been made out to CITES in the amount of one thousand dollars. The initials meant nothing to Judith.

She paused, listening for any suspicious sounds. She heard nothing. Opening another drawer, she spotted two bankbooks. The first one she picked up was for Connie's regular savings account. Since early November, there had been seven withdrawals. Two were in November, in the amounts of thirteen hundred and twenty-one hundred dollars. Gump's was printed next to the dates. Christmas presents, perhaps, Judith thought. Gump's was a very expensive store off Union Square. Maybe Connie had bought gifts for Mags.

There were also two withdrawals in December: Fifteen hundred dollars for *NM*. Judith thought through the suspect list. No one had those initials. Maybe the letters stood for Neiman Marcus. But the next and final four withdrawals occurred in December, January, February, and March. They were in the amounts of twenty, forty, fifty, and seventy-five thousand dollars—exactly what Connie was reported to have taken out of her account during that time period.

The initials next to those big sums were *MBB*.

Judith frowned. She couldn't think who that might be.

Then it dawned on her. Judith might have known her as Dixie, but her real name was May Belle Beales.

Had Dixie been blackmailing Connie? It was possible, Judith thought, doing her best to put everything back in order. That might explain why Dixie had sent the note telling the cousins to butt out. But what did Dixie know that was worth so much money that Connie had to buy her silence?

A sound from out in the hallway caught Judith's attention. Swiftly, she shut the desk drawer, hurried out of the office, and fell upon the king-size bed.

Paul Tanaka called from outside the closed double doors. "Is everything okay?"

"Yes," Judith answered. "Come in."

Paul entered the boudoir with a puzzled look on his face. "How did you get into the bathroom?"

"The bathroom?" Judith thought quickly. If Paul had to ask the question, there must be a problem. "I didn't. Not yet. I thought I'd lie down first. I don't like to take my pain pills unless I have to. The doctors are so stingy about prescribing very many at one time."

"Oh." Paul couldn't quite hide his relief. "Connie forgot to mention that the door is tricky to open. It sticks. The last earthquake apparently damaged the alignment."

"I understand," Judith said, overemphasizing the difficulty of sitting up. "In fact, we had a small quake at home this morning. Like San Francisco, all of our houses are uneven."

"Are you rejoining us?" Paul inquired.

"I think so," Judith said. "I'll walk around just a bit before I attempt the stairs."

"I'll wait." Paul's smile was slightly sheepish. "So I can help you," he added.

"Thanks," Judith said, dutifully walking to and fro around the boudoir. "By the way, I couldn't help but admire those wonderful horse and racing pictures upstairs. Are the oil paintings of horses that Connie's father trained?"

"Trained *and* owned," Paul replied. "After many years, he was able to buy some Thoroughbreds of his own."

"I understood Connie's grandfather was wealthy," Judith remarked, still walking.

"He was." Paul, who was usually unflappable, seemed edgy.

He centered a tissue box on the nightstand and moved the bed-side lamp an inch to the right. "Over the years, Argentina has had so many political shifts. Connie's grandfather lost his estancia—ranch, I should say—during one of the coups."

"So Connie's father managed to—excuse the expression—recoup his losses?"

"He managed to cut them," Paul explained, "because Guillermo de Fuentes—Connie's dad—was so successful training racehorses. His first Thoroughbred was a gift from a grateful emir in Dubai."

"Is that one of the horses in the paintings?" Judith asked, beginning to get tired of her promenade.

"No. The gift horse was put out to stud. He sired Belgrano, Guillermo's first champion." Paul paused. "Are you better now?"

"Yes," Judith said. "Going upstairs isn't as scary as coming down."

Paul stayed directly behind Judith so that he could catch her if she made a misstep. Moments later they'd rejoined Renie and Connie in the living room.

"I thought you'd fallen asleep," Connie said with a little laugh. "Is your hip less painful?"

"Yes," Judith replied. "It's just something I've learned to live with. Speaking of ailments, how is your father, Connie? Paul and I were just talking about him."

"You were?" She shot Paul a sharp look. "My father is not well. He hasn't been for some time. I was telling Serena that I may visit him in Argentina next month. Easter would be a good time to be in Buenos Aires."

"Is he confined to his home?" Judith inquired, wearing a sympathetic expression.

"Yes," Connie replied, indicating to Paul that he should open the second wine bottle. "It's very sad."

"He must miss the racetrack," Judith said, pretending she didn't notice the sudden frozen expression on Connie's face. "Our Uncle Al is a serious horseplayer. During the season, he goes to the races almost every day. He loves to hang out around the barns and the paddock. Of course he knows everybody."

"He insists he gets great tips from his old pals," Renie put in, picking up on Judith's train of thought. "He certainly seems to win pretty often."

Paul offered the cousins a refill. Renie declined, but Judith accepted just enough to be sociable. "How long has he been retired?" she asked.

"A few years," Connie said, her tone distant. She tasted the wine Paul had poured for her. "Do you think this is as good as the first bottle? It seems a little off."

Paul took a sip. "No, I believe they're comparable."

Connie shrugged. "It must be me. Goodness knows," she went on, speaking more rapidly, "I find the Beringer label generally very good. Have you considered taking a vineyard tour while you're in the area?"

"I did that many years ago," Renie said, "when I was in the city for a graphic-design conference. Everybody ended up drunk as skunks with grape leaves in their hair."

"I understand that some of the vintages from your own state have gained in reputation," Paul put in. "I believe Mags recently purchased some very nice whites from up your way."

It occurred to Judith that like the cousins, Paul and Connie seemed able to keep on the same wavelength. Apparently, the Thoroughbred-racing discussion had come to an abrupt halt, like a horse going lame in the backstretch.

Judith finally guided the conversation back to the matters that were uppermost in her mind. "Some of our wineries are popular places for young couples to get married. I don't suppose that

Anemone and Jim have made any concrete plans since their date is so far off in the future."

"Very far," Connie said drily, with a quick glance at Paul.

Paul smirked, but didn't respond.

"You sound skeptical," Renie said bluntly. "What do you figure? Jim will do what so many doctors do, and let wife number one—or in this case, fiancée number one—put him through medical school and then say, 'Take two suitcases and *don't* call me in the morning'?"

"Serena," Connie said with mock severity, "you ask the most embarrassing questions!"

Paul smiled ruefully. "She does that at business meetings, too."

Renie shrugged. "Well? My cousin and I sense trouble in paradise."

"Really?" Connie frowned. "I didn't think it showed that much."

"Show and tell," Renie said.

"Really?" Connie leaned forward on the sofa. "Such as what?"

Renie looked at Judith, urging her to take up the tale. But Judith refused to betray Anemone's confidence. "Let's merely say that we suspect there's Someone Else."

Paul tipped his head to one side. "Ah."

Connie took a deep sip of wine. "You're right. There is."

"That's not surprising," Judith said. "Anemone and Jim are very young. She's been so sheltered. It's only natural that her first real love wouldn't turn out to be the man she marries."

Connie stared at Judith. "Are you suggesting that Anemone isn't in love with Jim?"

Judith was taken aback. All along she'd assumed that Anemone was meeting another man at Neiman Marcus, even if it hadn't turned out to be Ambrose Everhart. "Well . . . I mean, if she hasn't dated much—" She stopped, realizing that she was mistaken and unwilling to say more.

Connie laughed shrilly. "No, no! It's Jim who isn't in love with his betrothed. He's fallen head over heels for CeeCee Orr. Anemone suspects the truth, and if Erma finds out she'll kill him." Wide-eyed, she put a hand over her mouth. "Oh, my God! What am I saying?"

Not another corpse was what Connie meant—but Judith wasn't going to say that out loud, either.

Chapter Twenty

"Jim's an idiot," Renie declared as the cousins rode home in a taxi from the Marina district. "Not only is he risking his expensive education, but can you imagine CeeCee at an AMA convention? The only socializing she could manage would be *playing* doctor, not behaving like the wife of a real one."

"I don't know about that," Judith said, "but it makes sense. Not the falling-for-CeeCee part, but what Anemone was doing skulking around Neiman Marcus. We know CeeCee was there that day because she bought the red dress I saw in the salon. I'll bet CeeCee may have gone there with Jim, or else planned to meet him after she finished shopping. No wonder Anemone was too embarrassed to tell me."

"So which one of them killed Émile Grenier?" Renie asked, keeping her voice down, just in case the uncommunicative Turkish cabdriver could understand them. "Anemone? CeeCee? Jim? Or somebody else?"

The taxi rocketed along Lombard and zoomed down Van Ness as if the driver had a date with destiny. He wove in and out of traffic, honking the horn and making the occasional obscene gesture. The cousins stopped talking, certain that they were going to meet their own kismet. There was construction on California Street, and although no one was working on a Sunday, there were several traffic barriers. The cab ran them like an obstacle course before starting the steep—and swift—descent on Powell. Pedestrians scattered; a double-parked limo was missed by less than an inch; a U-Haul truck barely escaped collision. By the time the driver screeched to a halt in front of the St. Francis, Judith had turned white and Renie had dug her fingernails into her hands so hard that she broke the skin.

"Thanks," Judith gasped, not bothering to look at the meter. She yanked a bill out of her wallet and dropped it onto the front seat.

"That was a fifty," Renie said as they reeled into the hotel. "Are you nuts?"

"A fifty?" Judith grimaced. "Oh, well. At least we arrived alive."

"Good point," Renie agreed. "What's our next move?"

Judith poked the elevator button. "Rest. Think. And call Joe. Maybe that's first."

Upon arriving in their suite, Judith noticed that the message light was blinking on their phone. There were three calls: Rhoda St. George, Flakey Smythe—and Joe, whose message had been recorded at two fifty-six.

"You haven't checked out," he said in an irritated tone, "and the yahoo at the desk told me the cruise was canceled. When the hell are you coming home? My cold's worse. The trial starts tomorrow, so I can't pick you up at the airport if you're flying during the day. By the way, we had an earthquake. Sweetums is still hiding under the dining-room table and your mother's card table collapsed. Unfortunately, she wasn't under it. Call me."

"Joe's mad," Judith said, dialing the number of Hillside Manor. "I don't know what to tell him."

"How about the truth?" Renie suggested, removing a Pepsi from the honor bar. "Or part of it, like having to attend the funeral for Mags tomorrow. Blame it on me, I worked with him."

Joe didn't answer. Instead, she heard her own voice on the answering machine. Judith winced and collected her wits. "Hi, Joe," she began in something less than her normal manner. "One of the reasons the cruise was canceled was due to Magglio's ill health." She winced again. "That is, he . . . died. Renie feels we should go to the funeral tomorrow. In fact," she went on, sounding more like herself, "we just came from visiting his widow, Connie." She paused, seeing her cousin drawing dollar signs in the air and pointing to her purse. "Renie wants to stay an extra day or so to see if she can help. We should be back Wednesday, if we can get a decently priced flight. Of course I'm not sure what to do about the original return tickets. I'll keep you posted. I love you."

She clicked off, but kept hold of the receiver. "I'd better call Mother. I hope the card table isn't broken. That's her primary source of life."

As usual, Gertrude didn't pick up the phone until the tenth ring. "Why are you calling me?" she rasped. "Are you seasick? It'd serve you right. All this highfalutin gadabout showing off! The only boat trip I ever took was in a canoe with your uncle Cliff, and it sank."

"We never . . ." Judith interrupted.

But Gertrude wasn't in a listening mood. "You ought to see

the mess I was in this morning. Deb told me she'd heard from *her* idiot daughter, so you know about the earthquake. In fact, Deb's called about six times." The old lady stopped. "Come to think of it, she said you two nitwits were still in Frisco. How come?"

"The cruise was canceled," Judith said. "We'll be home in a couple of days. Where were you when the card table collapsed?"

"In bed," Gertrude replied. "It happened around six. I was awake, though. That crummy bed you bought me shimmied all over the place. What's it made of—twigs?"

"It's quite solid," Judith insisted. "Will you have to get a new card table?"

"No," Gertrude retorted. "Arlene fixed it. The legs just went out from under it, that's all. By the way, since you were too addled to do it before you ran off to Frisco, I had her cash that movie check for me."

"Oh! Good!" Judith exclaimed. "I was worried about leaving it around the toolshed for so long. I'm glad it's safe in the bank. Twenty grand is a large check to leave sitting around. Now you can earn interest on it."

"It's not in the bank," Gertrude replied. "I said I had her *cash* it, not put it in the bank."

"What do you mean?" Judith asked, startled.

"I mean I wanted the money, dummy," Gertrude snapped.

"For what?" Judith asked, starting to worry anew.

"None of your beeswax. I'm hanging up now. Arlene and Carl are coming to play gin rummy with me." Gertrude banged down the phone.

Renie eyed Judith with sympathy. "What did she do, cash the check and send the money out to the track with Uncle Al?"

"She cashed it all right," Judith said angrily. "But she won't tell me what she's doing with it."

"Humor her," Renie soothed. "Maybe she just wants to count

it. You know how people of her generation are. They still have that Depression-era mentality. Some of them don't trust banks because so many failed back then and their customers lost all their money."

"Mother's not that nutty," Judith replied. "She's got something up the sleeve of her housecoat. Damn, I hope she isn't being victimized by some scam artist."

"*Your* mother?" Renie laughed. "Neither of our mothers are sucker bait. Maybe she wants to buy some things. Like a new card table."

"Maybe." Judith gave herself a good shake. "There's nothing I can do about it from here. I'd better check those other messages."

Flakey Smythe informed the cousins that the interview he'd done with them wouldn't run for a day or so, probably not until after Magglio Cruz's funeral. He also wanted to do a follow-up— a sidebar, he called it—about their interview with the police.

"Double damn!" Judith swore. "I was afraid of that! We won't talk to him again. Maybe he'll forget about the whole thing if we stall."

"Don't count on it," Renie said. "Would you rather he made up something?"

Judith didn't respond. Instead, she listened to Rhoda's message. "We must compare notes. Dinner? I'm feeling Italian. Ricky's feeling—stop that, darling!" A giggle interrupted the message. "Ricky has a yen for Japanese, excuse the pun. Call us."

Judith dialed the St. Georges' number. Once again, it was Rhoda who answered. "Oh, Judith," she said in a forlorn voice, "we can't do dinner after all. Rick is sleuthing in a most serious way. Methanol and all that scientific mumbo jumbo I don't pretend to understand. I'm even surprised that he knows about more than one kind of alcohol."

"You mean the poison that was used to kill Dixie?" Judith asked.

"Yes," Rhoda replied. "Lab alcohol. It sounds so crude. Whatever happened to classics like arsenic and cyanide?"

"I assume," Judith said, "that they're harder to obtain. Can't you buy methanol without raising suspicion?"

"That's what Ricky tells me," Rhoda said. "He's with Biff right now, checking recent sales from local chemical companies. Honestly, I can't remember when Biff worked on a weekend. In fact, I can barely remember Biff working." She laughed. "Oh, I shouldn't say that. He *does* work, in his own peculiar fashion. It's just that Ricky has to prod him. Do you know anything we don't?"

Judith recapitulated the visit with Connie and Paul. "They seem very comfortable together," she added. "I mean, it's nice that she has someone she can rely on now that Mags is dead."

"Lie and re-lie on?" Rhoda remarked in a provocative tone.

"I wondered," Judith said.

"So have we," Rhoda responded. "The fact is, I don't think they're lovers. Connie was crazy about Mags, and vice versa. But Paul has always been the faithful puppy type. I think he adores her. But he was very loyal to Mags in every way."

From embarrassment, Judith held back about going through Connie's bank accounts. But she no longer felt obligated to keep Anemone's secret, since Jim's obsession with CeeCee was known at least to some of the others involved.

Rhoda, however, professed mild surprise. "I've noticed that Jimmy has trouble keeping his eyes off of CeeCee, but most men do. Maybe it's not as serious as it seems. Poor Anemone. She's definitely the jealous type."

"So I gathered," Judith said, hearing Asthma bark in the background. "What do you make of Anemone, CeeCee, and perhaps Jim being at Neiman Marcus when Émile was strangled?"

"A quartet became a trio," Rhoda murmured. "It's even possible that they weren't the only ones. Horace may have accompanied CeeCee. Erma might have been lurking in Large Sizes. Ambrose may be stalking Jim. You see how my devious mind works?"

"Yes," Judith said. "Mine works the same way."

I'm glad I didn't return that laptop when we left to see Connie," Judith said, booting up the PC. "I'm going to research horse racing."

"Starting with Montespan?" Renie inquired, leaning over Judith's shoulder.

"Exactly." The first screen of listings all referred to the famous courtesan, Françoise-Athénaïs de Montespan, Louis XIV's brilliant and beautiful mistress. On the second and third screens, there were more references. On the fourth try, portraits of the lady commingled with china, flowers, and even furniture named for her. But no horses.

"I'll try Thoroughbreds," Judith said.

"Or try another search engine," Renie suggested, stretching out on the sofa.

"I'll do both." Judith stared in confusion as the first results came up. There were too many sites from too many sources. Trusting to luck—which was usually the way she bet the ponies—she typed in *Montespan* again.

Three references came up—all in French. "You'd better take a look at this, coz. I think there are mentions of Montespan in some newspaper articles, but they're from *Le Monde* and Agence France-Presse."

Renie took Judith's place at the computer. "Too bad we don't have a printer," she said. "I hope I can translate this accurately, but

I'm not making any promises. My Spanish is better than my French." She clicked on the first article, dated some twenty years earlier. "Ah! You can read this headline as well as I can."

Judith peered over her cousin's shoulder. *"Scandale,"* she said. "Coupled with Montespan. What do you make of it?"

For several moments, Renie didn't speak. Slowly, she scrolled through the article, occasionally shaking her head. "It's about a big-stakes race for fillies and mares that Montespan was in. She won the race, but there was an inquiry. I think her jockey was accused of bumping another horse. Apparently, this wasn't the first time that a Guillermo de Fuentes horse—Connie's dad—had been involved in that kind of incident. But the inquiry was disallowed." She kept reading. Suddenly she gasped. "Good grief! The jockey was Émile Grenier!"

"Émile!" Judith practically fell on top of Renie as she saw his name at the bottom of the screen. "It makes sense, though. He was built like a jockey. In fact," she added in a rush, "he was in one of those photographs at Connie's place. I thought he looked familiar just because . . . well . . ."

"All jockeys look alike?" Renie nodded. "They do from a distance unless you know them really well. They have to stay so lean, and their caps hide their faces."

"So how did Émile go from jockey to purser?" Judith mused.

"Maybe we can find out," Renie said, moving on to the next story.

Judith noted the date, which was a week later than the first article. There was nothing in the headline about a scandal. "What does it say?" she asked her cousin, who was scratching her head and grimacing.

"I'm kind of rusty," Renie confessed. "Montespan was in the race at Longchamps but didn't finish because—" She shut up and concentrated. "There was an accident on the rail," Renie finally said. "Montespan threw her rider—Émile—who was badly injured. Montespan was disqualified, and there was another objection, this time from de Fuentes—I think—but that was overruled, too. The winning horse was owned by the same person who'd been edged out in the stakes race. The owner was somebody named Liam Ford Mackey, with a horse called Green Colleen. The trainer was L. C. O'Leary."

"A grudge match?" Judith suggested.

"Could be," Renie said. "Mackey may have thought he'd been screwed in the previous race, which was for some big bucks. Let's look at that last story."

This time, Renie translated with relative ease. "Émile got really banged up in that fall. This is two weeks later, and he's out of the hospital, but has to retire."

"He did have a limp," Judith pointed out. "Maybe the purser job was a consolation prize."

"Émile earned it," Renie said. "He broke his leg, his collarbone, and his ankle. Ah! De Fuentes also retired from racing, citing . . . I can't quite get this quote, but it's something to the effect that he didn't want to endanger his horses and riders any further."

"That sounds very noble," Judith said.

"Maybe not." Renie paused, still translating. "The article states that people in the know believe that de Fuentes may have been involved in—bribes, I guess—with the stewards and other officials. It sounds as if he left the sport under a cloud."

"Hunh." Judith leaned against the desk. "Is that blackmail-worthy?"

"Could be," Renie responded. "It certainly wouldn't be good publicity for Cruz Cruises if it got out that Mrs. Cruz's father is a crook."

"It's no big secret," Judith objected. "I mean, here we are, reading all about it on the Internet."

"True," Renie agreed. "But how many people have done that?"

"At least one," Judith said. "Dixie. Is that why she was killed?"

Renie considered. "It'd make sense if Dixie and Émile had been the only victims. They may have been in cahoots. But why murder Mags? There's no mention of his name in these articles, and I'm not even sure if he and Connie were married back then. What's more, I never heard him talk about horses or gambling—except, of course, for the casinos he had on his ships."

"That's odd," Judith said in a distant voice.

"What do you mean?"

"Mags's wife had a living room full of horse pictures, yet he never mentioned anything about it?"

Renie shrugged. "I was always at business meetings with him, except for the occasional lunch or cocktail party. The subject probably never came up."

"Maybe." Judith sounded vague.

"Well?"

"Nothing," Judith said, shaking her head. "Nothing important, anyway. Let's get back to basics. Like weapons."

"I thought we knew what the weapons were," Renie said, signing out from the Internet. "Knife sharpener, methanol, decorative cord."

"Two out of three are right." Judith was pacing, arms folded across her chest. "Either Rick is holding out on us—or Biff's not telling Rick everything he knows. I don't like it."

"So which of the three weapons is wrong?" Renie inquired, but held up a hand before her cousin could answer. "The knife sharpener. There can't be any doubt about the poison because of the lab results, and we saw the cord for ourselves. But whatever killed Mags wasn't found."

Judith nodded. "That's why I think there's something the cops know—and maybe Rick does, too—that we don't." She sat down on the sofa. "Think back to the cabaret, the cocktail party, everything that led up to Mags's murder. You have a visual memory, what do you see?"

One elbow resting on the desk, Renie closed her eyes. "Food."

"Naturally." Judith's tone was dry.

"Beverages, the bar, the buffet, the cigarette and cigar smoke." She stood up and went to the honor bar. "Which reminds me, I need another Pepsi." Opening the door of the small fridge, Renie swore. "We're out. They must have forgotten to restock today. I'm going down the hall to the pop machine."

Judith sighed. "I thought we were sleuthing."

"Not without Pepsi," Renie replied, heading out the door.

Judith drummed her nails on the sofa arm. Just when she felt they were getting somewhere, the train of thought had been broken by her cousin's Pepsi addiction. But Renie was back in two minutes, carrying a can of Pepsi and a plastic bucket.

"Ice," she said. "I have to have ice for my Pepsi."

"Of course," Judith said with a tinge of sarcasm. "Okay, where were we?"

Renie, however, had gone back to the honor bar. "Hold on. Let me pour the Pepsi and some ice in a glass like a real person. Then I'm putting the ice in the fridge so it won't melt. I'll have to take out some of these snack foods to make room. Want some pretzels?"

"No, thanks," Judith snapped. "You're driving me—" She stopped, leaning forward on the sofa and staring at Renie. "That's it! Coz, you're a genius!"

"Huh?" Renie, who was on her knees tossing small bags of chips, nuts, and other snacks onto the floor, looked over her shoulder. "What are you talking about?"

"Ice," Judith said, standing up. "The pheasant ice sculpture with long sharply pointed tail feathers."

"Oh, come on!" Renie cried, closing the honor bar door and also getting to her feet. "Explain yourself."

"I will," Judith said reasonably. "It's been done before, with icicles. The weapon melts and disappears. No fingerprints. That's why the floor around the piano was slippery, why Dixie's bag fell off the bench and skidded. The ship was rocking a bit, remember? The deck couldn't have been even."

Renie was looking very dubious. "So nobody notices the killer breaking a piece off the ice sculpture?"

"It could be managed," Judith asserted. "When you're at a buffet, what are you looking at?"

"The food," Renie admitted. "You're right—nobody has eyes for anything else. But there were servers there."

"Servers serving very demanding people," Judith pointed out. "I realize whoever did it had to act fast before the ice melted. But think about it. It's possible."

"It had to be fast," Renie allowed, "no matter what the weapon. There must have been people backstage getting ready for Dixie's recital."

"That's true," Judith agreed. "Not to mention that you'd have to act fast before the ice began to melt. Now who in that gathering suddenly realized that Mags had to die? And why?" She glanced out the window, noting that the fog was rolling in once more. "My brain's fogged," she said. "Besides basic information, there's something we're missing."

"Like Erma's jewels," Renie said. "I wonder where they are."

Judith stopped in the middle of the room. "Coz! We've been idiots!"

"What? A minute ago, I was a genius."

"That was then, this is now," Judith said in a disgusted voice. "Do you realize that if our fingerprints were on the stuff they found in our safe aboard ship . . ."

"The ones we looked at in her suite were fake," Renie finished for her. "Erma never had the jewels in the first place when she was on the *San Rafael.*"

"And we didn't know the difference because we aren't used to diamonds and emeralds and rubies and such." Judith came to rest on the sofa's arm. "The others might have noticed, but we wouldn't, not even up close."

"And everybody else was so used to seeing Erma all decked out in her gem-laden glory that they wouldn't pay much attention." Renie got up from the chair and returned to the honor bar. "I'm hungry. Shall I nibble or should we consider dinner?"

"Only you could think of food at a time like this." Judith glanced at her watch. "It's not even five-thirty."

"It's always time to think of food," Renie grumbled. "I'm going to eat those pretzels."

"Do that," Judith said as the phone rang. "Joe?" She moved to the desk and picked up the receiver.

"You must come by for a drink," Rhoda said in less than her usual nonchalant manner. "Ricky is so brilliant I can hardly stand it. He has news."

"What is it?" Judith asked.

"I can't tell you over the phone," Rhoda said. "We'll send a car. You must be absolutely worn out from all those reckless cab-drivers in this town."

"That's really not necessary," Judith replied. "It's only a short ride to your place."

"But it's all uphill," Rhoda asserted. "I must insist. Is fifteen minutes enough time?"

"Well . . . yes," Judith said, glancing at Renie, who was slurping Pepsi and stuffing her face with pretzels. "We'll be out front at"—she checked her watch—"six forty-five."

"Perfect. See you soon." Rhoda hung up.

"Do you suppose they'll have hors d'oeuvres?" Renie asked wistfully.

"We can eat dinner afterward," Judith replied, with an anxious gaze at the phone. "I wish Joe would call back before we leave. I should have told him to reach me on my cell."

"You never have it on," Renie said, dropping the empty pretzel bag into the wastebasket. "I never turn mine on either, unless there's an emergency. It took me three years to memorize my own number."

"You never were good at numbers," Judith said absently. Her mind was elsewhere, going over her theory about the weapon that had killed Mags. Surely the forensics experts had figured it out. Maybe that was Rick's big news.

The cousins headed out, arriving at the curb a couple of minutes before the appointed time. Judith, wearing her new gray suit, felt the damp chill through the jacket.

"Don't they ever have spring around here?" Renie demanded. "I was here in June once when it was so foggy I got lost in Maiden Lane, and it's only two blocks long."

A Lincoln Town Car glided out of the fog and was forced to double-park in front of the busy hotel. Judith could see the driver inside and motioned for him to stay put. The cousins hurried to get inside.

"Hi," Judith said, noting the chauffeur's cap on the man at the wheel. "I assume you're the St. Georges' driver."

The man nodded.

"I knew they had a maid," Renie noted. "Rhoda mentioned that they'd sent her on vacation because they expected to be gone on the cruise."

"Like Connie's housekeeper," Judith remarked as they climbed up Nob Hill. She was thankful that the ride was much smoother than their nerve-jarring trip from the Marina district.

The chauffeur pulled the Town Car into the garage of the St. Georges' building and parked in a reserved space. The cousins got out before he could assist them. Wordlessly, he led them to an elevator.

"I'm anxious to hear what Rick has to say," Judith said as they waited. "He and Biff must have come up with something."

The elevator doors slid open; the cousins stepped inside. The driver followed, backing in and pushing the button for the penthouse. He was still turned away from Judith and Renie. Suddenly curious, Judith moved forward just enough to see the man's profile. Under the cap, all she could glimpse was a sharp nose and a graying goatee. But as the elevator moved directly to the top floor, she realized that he looked familiar.

"Have you worked very long for the St. Georges?" Judith asked.

The man nodded.

"How long?" Judith inquired as the car slid slowly to a stop.

"Two years," the man replied.

Judith knew that voice. She'd heard it somewhere, but couldn't place it. She was concentrating so hard on trying to remember that she almost tripped getting out of the elevator.

Rhoda wasn't in the foyer to greet them. But as soon as the cousins and their driver walked into the living room, they saw their hostess sitting in a chair that looked as if it had been occupied by a Chinese emperor. Judith didn't remember the elaborate piece of furniture, which was in front of the closed draperies.

"My dears!" Rhoda exclaimed, still not sounding like her usual self. She wasn't acting like the Rhoda they'd come to know, either: There was no martini at hand. "Come in," she urged, "sit down."

Judith and Renie obliged. The chauffeur remained in the doorway between the foyer and the living room.

"Where's Rick?" Judith asked.

"Rick's not here at the moment," Rhoda replied. "Unfortunately."

"For you," the chauffeur said loudly, startling Judith.

The voice. Judith knew it, but still couldn't place it with a face. At that moment, the man came into the middle of the living room and took off his chauffeur's cap, tossing it across the room, where it landed on a Chinese marble horse head.

His head was shaved. Judith recognized him at once. So did Renie.

"Hey!" Renie cried. "You're the waiter dink who wouldn't bring me a taco salad! What's going on?"

"We want what you've got," the man said, jabbing a finger at the cousins. "Old Lady Giddon's jewels."

Judith stared at the man. She hadn't put face and voice together because she'd never heard him speak—not when she could see him. But she had listened to him talk aboard ship. It was the conversation she'd overheard from the gangway between Biff McDougal and a man called Blackie.

In shock, Judith looked beyond him to Rhoda. "I don't understand. Rhoda, you know we didn't steal the jewels! How could you let this happen?"

Rhoda sighed. "It wasn't easy. But I can always be persuaded at gunpoint."

Judith gaped as the draperies rustled behind Rhoda's chair and CeeCee Orr slipped out from behind them holding a very shiny revolver.

Chapter Twenty-one

I *tried* to tell them you didn't steal the jewels," Rhoda said in a plaintive voice, "but they wouldn't listen. I'm so sorry I had to lure you up here, but I didn't have much choice. I think they really would have shot me, and the idea of being dead isn't terribly appealing. It's even worse than the prospect of inedible hospital food."

"You talk too much," CeeCee said, her features hardening as she moved farther into the room and kept the gun aimed at Rhoda. "Keep your trap shut and let these other two dames tell us how they switched the loot and where the real stuff is now."

"You mean," Judith blurted, "you two stole Erma's jewels?"

"Sure," CeeCee replied. "It was a cinch. The old broad was so damned careless. Blackie and I had it all set up beforehand. After he delivered Anemone's salad, he told me to go get Horace out of the Giddon suite. You two were gone by then, so I made an excuse to use Erma's powder room and swiped the case. The next morning, I hid the jewels in your safe while you two were in the bedroom getting perfume. I left just after Blackie brought your food, and told him it was done. I knew you'd never look in your safe—you didn't seem like the type who'd own anything worth stealing. You never even bothered to open the thing. The key was still in the lock."

"We never did touch that safe," Judith said hotly. "The one place the police *didn't* find our fingerprints was there." Biff had never told them so, but it was true. "We never knew the jewels were in there. The items you stole were fake from the get-go."

"That's crap," Blackie retorted. "You think we wouldn't know what was fake and what was the real deal?"

"I think *you* would," Judith said. "I'm not sure about CeeCee."

CeeCee shot Blackie a sharp look. "What's she talking about?"

"Damned if I know," Blackie growled.

"We both know real goods," CeeCee asserted. "We've done this before, back in the Big Apple. We can't be conned."

"Yes, you can," Judith insisted. "You're too vain to wear glasses, and maybe you can't use contact lenses. I'm positive you couldn't read the ingredients on my bottle of Red Door perfume. And I'm certain that you couldn't tell glass from my . . . from diamonds," she amended.

"I'm telling you," CeeCee began angrily, "Blackie here knows—"

"Yes, he does," Judith broke in. She smiled in a pitying manner. "Let's end this farce. Blackie, tell CeeCee to put the gun down. I know you're an undercover cop."

"That's bull!" CeeCee cried. The gun wavered in her hand. Blackie dove for her, but she fired twice. One bullet hit him in the shoulder. The other went right between the cousins into the sofa.

Blackie reeled in front of CeeCee. She was panting and staring at his writhing body. Rhoda leaped out of the chair from behind, grabbed the martini shaker from the bar, and smacked the heavy silver jug against CeeCee's blond head. The gun dropped to the floor. CeeCee fell on top of Blackie.

"Good Lord," Rhoda said under her breath. "We must call for help."

Judith was already picking up the receiver from the end table by the sofa. Renie had gone to assist Rhoda, who was trying to pull the unconscious CeeCee off of Blackie. The wounded man was holding his shoulder as blood spread over his gray jacket.

"Do be careful of the carpet," Rhoda cautioned as she and Renie succeeded in rolling CeeCee away. "It cost the earth, and bloodstains are so difficult to remove." She put an arm around Blackie to help him sit up straight. "Serena, could you please get some sheets—not the Egyptian cotton, but the cheaper ones— from the linen closet in the hall?"

Judith finished her call, having given the 911 operator the necessary information. She used a cocktail napkin to pick up the revolver and place it in her purse.

Despite his obvious pain, Blackie was cursing a blue streak. "Women's intuition!" he finally gasped, looking at Judith. "You got me shot!"

"It was hardly intuition, womanly or otherwise." Judith made a self-deprecating gesture. "We didn't steal the jewels, so we realized later that they must have been fake when we saw them in Erma's stateroom. If you were a real jewel thief, you'd have known that, too. CeeCee wouldn't because her eyesight isn't very good, especially up close. But you did know, didn't you? I wondered about you—except that I only knew the name, not the face. I overheard you talking to Biff on the ship and then I happened to catch part of a conversation between Biff and Rick

St. George. I wasn't sure if you were a good or a bad guy, but it dawned on me tonight that you must be working with the police." She saw Blackie nod. "So what were you doing? Trying to figure out what happened to Erma's real jewels?"

Renie returned with the sheets. A staggering, wheezing Asthma was right behind her. "He was locked in the linen closet," Renie said.

Rhoda rushed to the dog. "Baby! I've been so worried! I wondered what CeeCee had done with you!" Rhoda buried her face in the animal's ropelike fur. "Komondors are so loyal. CeeCee must have known he'd defend me to the death. If he didn't collapse first, of course."

CeeCee was moaning, her eyes still closed, but turning her head and attempting to grope her skull. "Where am I? What happened?" she gasped.

"Where've I heard that before?" Renie muttered. She went to CeeCee and put a foot on the dazed woman's stomach. "Be thankful I'm not wearing spike heels," she said.

CeeCee slowly opened her eyes. She looked up at Renie and began calling her a colorful variety of obscene names.

"Hey!" Renie shouted, applying more pressure with her foot. "I can outcuss you any day! My father was a seafaring man."

CeeCee shut up. Judith could hear sirens, but that didn't mean they were headed for the St. Georges' address. Sirens in San Francisco seemed almost routine.

She watched Rhoda deftly minister to Blackie, despite Asthma's licking of his mistress's face. "It's not too bad," Rhoda declared. "You'll definitely live. By the way, did you used to be a crook?"

"Yeah," Blackie replied, his voice a bit stronger. "That dame's right," he said, nodding weakly at CeeCee. "We worked together eight, nine years ago. Not long after a job we pulled on Central

Park West, I got caught going solo. I tried to cut a deal with the cops while I was in prison. When I came up for parole, I offered them my services. They laughed their heads off, so I moved out here. I met a guy in a bar who worked as a consultant for the local boys in blue. I told him my idea. He liked it, and I got hired on a year ago."

"Really. How nice for you." Rhoda finished her task, giving Blackie a gentle pat on his good shoulder. "And who might that consultant be?"

Blackie laughed, though it obviously hurt. "You ought to know. It was your old man, Rick St. George."

Ricky," Rhoda said in a severe tone, "doesn't always tell me everything." She'd poured herself a martini and asked the cousins to help themselves. "So why the farce?"

"It was CeeCee's idea," Blackie said. "She was sure those two"—he pointed at Judith and Renie—"really had the jewels. I had to play along or blow my cover."

CeeCee was still on the floor, though Renie no longer held her down. "If they didn't do it, then that old bat Erma must have hocked them!" CeeCee railed. "Nasty old bitch! Why doesn't somebody bump *her* off?"

"Why would she pawn her precious jewels?" Judith inquired, now hearing sirens very close by.

"Because Racey—" CeeCee stopped and made a disgusted face. "That jerk of a Horace has blown all his money on his stupid cork-and-sponge museum, that's why. He's in debt to his eyeballs. If you ask me, he's bringing Erma down with him. Serves her right for hanging out with that old creep. If he'd set me up the way I wanted, I wouldn't have had to steal anything. But the SOB can't afford me." She waved a finger at Blackie.

"And you! I'm not sorry I shot you, you double-crosser! All you guys are a bunch of lying, cheating, cheap bastards! I hate men!" CeeCee burst into blubbering tears just as Rick arrived with the cops.

An hour later everyone, including the EMTs and the firefighters, had left except for the cousins and the St. Georges. Seemingly unruffled, Rick and Rhoda were sipping martinis. Calming their own nerves, Judith cradled a stiff scotch while Renie sipped Canadian whiskey and tried to ward off Asthma's nuzzling advances.

"Really, darling," Rhoda said, pretending to pout, "you might have told me about Blackie. This entire charade could have been avoided."

Rick shrugged. "Sorry, sugar. But I'd promised Biff—and Blackie—to keep mum. It was a police matter. I can't violate their trust."

Rhoda blew Rick a kiss. "I forgive you. But next time, consider the possible consequences of leaving me in the dark."

"Ah," Rick said in a seductive tone, "but that's where I like to find you."

Rhoda seemed appeased. Judith, however, had a different kind of question for Rick. "Do you really think Erma pawned her jewelry?"

"I think she sold it in some underhanded manner," Rick said. "We've been getting reports of a couple of pieces showing up in some very odd places, including Hong Kong and Bangkok. I suspect Horace has been acting as her go-between."

"So," Rhoda remarked, "Erma intended to cash in on the insurance money?"

Rick nodded. "Horace knew more than he let on about

CeeCee's background. He chose her, not the other way around. Horace knew that sooner or later, temptation would get the best of CeeCee."

"How," Judith inquired, "did Horace get the jewelry out of the country?"

Rick smiled in his devilish manner. "I believe Wilbur was his unwitting accomplice."

Judith gaped. "You mean . . . ?"

Rick nodded. "The urn. Horace probably dumped poor old Wilbur into the landfill somewhere and shipped the urn off for burial abroad. There'd be records. Biff's checking on that."

Rhoda raised her glass. "To my adorable, clever Ricky."

The cousins joined the toast. Asthma barfed on the carpet.

"Oh, no!" Rhoda jumped from her chair. "Poor doggie, he must still be upset. Excuse me while I clean up after him. Come, Asthma, follow Mommy." The dog stumbled and wheezed after his mistress.

"At least he missed my shoes," Renie noted.

Judith, however, was still considering crime. "But CeeCee didn't kill Mags or Dixie or Émile, right?"

Rick was busy with the cocktail shaker. "No. It's a wonder she didn't kill Horace, though. And a damned good thing she didn't shoot either of you or my darling wife," he added, almost as an afterthought.

"Yes," Renie said drily, "I hate it when my new Chetta B outfit from Saks gets riddled with bullets."

"Speaking of weapons," Judith put in, her mind far from fashion, "are you and Biff still certain that a knife sharpener was used to kill Mags?"

For just a brief moment, Rick's hand froze on the cocktail shaker. "Why, yes." He undid the stopper and began to refill his glass. "You ask because . . . ?"

"Because . . . I just wondered." Judith's smile wasn't quite convincing, and she knew it. "That is, it seems like an odd weapon if the killer was a woman. It would be hard to hide, given the simplicity of those thirties evening gowns."

"But not impossible," Rhoda said, returning with rags, a pail, and a spray bottle of carpet cleaner. "For example, I could have hidden it under my jacket. There was so much padding at the shoulders."

"But you didn't, did you, darling?" Rick asked.

Rhoda, who was wearing something elegant in green and pink that might have come from Versace, was scrubbing the rug on her hands and knees. Judith thought it was a little like watching Marie Antoinette clean house at the Petit Trianon.

"Ricky," Rhoda said without looking up, "why on earth would I want to kill poor Mags? Frankly, I can't think why anyone would."

"Stop worrying your beautiful head about that," Rick said, sitting down again. "After the funeral tomorrow, I intend to reveal all."

Rhoda glanced at Rick; Judith gazed at him with curiosity; Renie was staring in the direction of the kitchen, apparently wondering if appetizers were available.

"Is that why we offered to hold the funeral reception here?" Rhoda asked.

"Of course." Rick twirled his glass. "You can wait that long, can't you? Certain facts need to be verified."

"Facts?" Rhoda tossed the rags into the bucket and stood up. "Since when did you rely on facts, darling? It's your hunches that usually pinpoint the killer."

"True enough," Rick conceded. "Yet it's wondrously strange how bringing people together and discussing the crime can force the guilty party to spill the beans."

Renie looked puzzled. "Does it really work that way?"

"It can," Rick replied. "It has. It might."

Judith's expression was noncommittal. "Let's hope so." She savored the expensive scotch before posing the question she'd wanted to ask ever since relative peace had broken out. "Did Biff track down that methanol sale?"

"Yes, finally," Rick replied. "Only chemical companies sell it, and there are several in the Bay Area. *Denatured alcohol* is another term for it, with all kinds of purposes other than poisoning people. It's perfectly legal."

"And?" Judith prodded.

Rick lighted a cigarette in a leisurely manner. "The methanol receipt was signed by Ambrose Everhart."

"Ambrose!" Judith exclaimed. "Why?"

Rick shrugged. "Good question. He's at a Save City Hall Plaza rally, so we can't talk to him until the demonstration breaks up. But the other thing we learned was that the methanol—I'm not saying Ambrose did it—was put in Dixie's bottled water, possibly on the ship. It seems Dixie liked freebies—she took all the bar and snack items with her when she went ashore."

"I understand," Judith said, "that it takes a while for methanol to do its damage. No wonder Dixie seemed drunk when she showed up at Grandviews to meet Ambrose. Instead of liquor, she must have been drinking bottled water all morning. The symptoms of methanol poisoning are the same as those of any kind of excessive alcohol intake—headache, dizziness, upset stomach, the works. Dixie may have attributed her condition to whatever she'd drunk the previous night, coupled with the shock of Mags's murder."

"Very logical," Rick remarked with a touch of irony. "You have a logical mind, Judith."

"She's had it for quite a while," Renie remarked.

"The question is," Rhoda said, waving the plastic pick that held the olive from her martini, "why *did* she meet Ambrose for lunch?"

"It was right after Mags was killed," Judith said. "What's the connection between them?"

Rick shrugged. "Other than casual acquaintances, I don't know."

Rhoda leaned back in her chair, gazing up as if she could read answers off of the ceiling. "Ambrose is her illegitimate son by Horace Pankhurst. Ambrose is her half brother, abandoned at birth by their hard-drinking Southern belle mama. Ambrose is soliciting money for one of his worthy environmental causes. Ambrose," she added on a darker note, "is the one who bought the methanol to poison Dixie and thought he'd avoid suspicion by being the last one to see her alive."

"All possibilities," Rick remarked airily. "But not terribly plausible, my darling. Except, perhaps, for the last of your bright ideas."

"Oh, Ricky." Rhoda sighed. "Do you always have to put a damper on my brainstorms?"

Sitting next to Renie on the sofa, Judith could hear her cousin's stomach growling. It was clear that the St. Georges planned to drink their dinner. Maybe they considered the cocktail olives as a meal. The happily soused couple did, however, recommend several restaurants, including Ozumo in the Embarcadero district. The cousins took a cab.

"We don't have a chauffeur," Rhoda had said as she showed them to the elevator. "I sometimes wonder why we have a car in this city. Parking costs a fortune and is impossible to find when you go anywhere."

Arriving at the restaurant without a reservation, Judith and Renie had to wait over half an hour in the bar, but nibbled on sushi and sipped just enough warm saki to make them feel a little giddy.

"How many times have we almost been killed?" Renie inquired idly.

"Offhand, I don't know," Judith replied. "I'd have to count. It wouldn't come out even, though. I've had more close calls than you."

"Braggart," Renie said. "I've got more kids than you. Ha ha."

"I've got more grandchildren. Double ha ha."

"We've got Oscar and Clarence. You only have Sweetums."

"He makes up for any number of animals, real or imaginary."

"Oscar's real."

"Is not."

"Is, too."

The conversation deteriorated until they were escorted to their table. With a magnificent view of the bay, a Zen-inspired setting, and a tempting menu, Judith and Renie grew more serious.

"You didn't mention the blackmail aspect to Rick and Rhoda," Renie pointed out after she'd ordered a charcoal-broiled fillet of beef with shiitake mushroom Madeira sauce.

"They know," said Judith, who had requested the big-eye tuna marinated in a sweet soy herb dressing. "I'll bet the police have discovered that Dixie's bank account—or wherever she put her money—increased dramatically the past few months. The problem is, I'm not entirely convinced that a twenty-year-old racing scandal in France would be worth that much money or that a mention of the horse's name would send Connie into a swoon."

"It'd make more sense if that other owner—the one with the Irish horse—had been someone involved in this case," Renie noted.

"But he wasn't." Judith paused, gazing out onto the bay,

where the fog had lifted just enough to see the lights from ships that had dropped anchor for the night. "The cruise might have been fun," she said wistfully. "A vacation would have been nice."

"Yes," Renie agreed. "Instead, we're going to a funeral tomorrow."

"Why," Judith asked on a note of resignation, "am I not surprised?"

Renie didn't bother to answer. Judith could only hope that their next close call wouldn't come too soon.

But, she grimly reminded herself, the killer was still out there.

Chapter Twenty-two

The Cathedral of St. Mary of the Assumption was startlingly modern and unconventional in design, an ode not only to God, but to geometry. It reminded Renie of a spaceship. "If this thing took off, would we go straight to heaven?" she asked after the impressive service had finished.

"Doubtful," Judith said, walking across the broad plaza along with the several hundred other mourners who'd attended the funeral Mass.

Connie had rejected the suggestion to hold a reception at the cathedral. She simply wasn't up to it, according to Rhoda. Since Mags was being cremated, there would be no cortege to the cemetery. Connie couldn't deal with that, either.

Judith felt a tap on her shoulder. It was Rhoda, asking if they'd like a ride to the private reception at the St. Georges' Nob Hill home.

"I promise it won't be like the last ride I offered," Rhoda said, making a face. "I must warn you, though, Ricky is a terrible driver."

Rhoda wasn't exaggerating. Rick St. George seemed oblivious to other vehicles, driving their Bentley Arnage as if he were competing in a NASCAR race. Judith barely had an opportunity to savor the car's quilted leather upholstery or the aura of luxury. Admittedly, it was a smooth, if harrowing, ride as Rick ran through at least three red lights, took an illegal left-hand turn, and circumvented a double-parked van by driving on the sidewalk. Yet fifteen minutes later, they arrived unscathed atop Nob Hill.

"Survival of the fastest," Rhoda murmured as they got out of the car in the parking garage where Blackie and CeeCee had taken the cousins the previous day.

"We had to get here before our guests arrive," Rick said breezily. "Let's hope the caterers have everything prepared."

They did. In fact, Biff McDougal was already sampling the lavish spread that had been set out on a temporary table in the living room. The white linen cloth was covered with every kind of salad, from greens to pasta; *fruits de mer* included oysters, crab, prawns, salmon, lobster, clams, and mussels; the cheeses were too numerous to count, let alone identify by sight; and delectable desserts swam in a sea of calories, with several topped by clotted or Bavarian cream. Judith was overwhelmed; Renie's eyes were enormous.

"Ha!" Biff cried as the cousins and the St. Georges came into the living room. "I beatcha here! I put on the siren."

"You also left early," Rick said. "You and Buzz were at the back of the church. We saw you when we came in."

Buzz was standing away from the table, looking deferential as usual. Renie couldn't keep from ogling the buffet, but Judith put a hand on her arm.

"Hold it," she whispered to Renie. "Try to control yourself for once. Even Biff can't eat it all at once."

"He's hogging the lobster," Renie declared, sounding almost in admiration of his audacity. "Look at him, slathering it in drawn butter."

Rick had gone behind the bar. "Drinks, anyone?"

Biff mentioned that he was on duty—sort of. With an unconvincing show of reluctance, he accepted a shot of whiskey. Judith and Renie both asked for shooting sherry. It seemed like a proper choice for a postfuneral gathering.

"Good," Judith said to her cousin. "You're behaving in a civilized manner. Just don't spill. You may keep your consulting fee yet."

"I'd damned well better," Renie muttered. "Oh, no—here comes Erma and her crew. You'd better lock me in the linen closet."

Erma Giddon was draped in a black coat and matching dress. Her only jewelry was a short double strand of pearls, which Judith thought might—or might not—be real. Anemone was wearing one of the black suits Judith had seen at Neiman Marcus. Horace, Jim, and Ambrose were all clad in conservative black suits. To Judith's surprise, Chevy followed them at a discreet distance, attired in her maid's outfit.

"How sweet of you to let us borrow Beulah!" Rhoda exclaimed. "I hated to ask, but my maid is still in Cancún."

Erma grunted. "Not that Beulah will be much help. These coloreds are so lazy." She snapped her pudgy fingers. "Come, girl. Get busy. Help serve the buffet." Her piercing eyes ran the length of the table. "And save me three of those cream puffs," she added under her breath.

"Yaz'um," Chevy said, bobbing a little curtsy. "I be workin'."

"You'd better be," Erma snapped.

Judith noticed that Horace seemed very subdued. Even if he had set CeeCee up for a fall, he might be suffering from disappointment at her defection. Or loneliness. Indeed, he was eyeing Chevy with a lecherous gaze.

The next to arrive were Captain Swafford and Dr. Selig. Both men looked worried—and weary. Renie, however, barged between the two men, head down and arms folded across her chest as if she were going for the goal line. "Coming through!" she cried, and all but bounced off Biff, who was still barring the way to the buffet. "Move it, flatfoot," she said. "I know people in high places. Like God."

Biff moved.

Judith sidled up to Anemone, who was waiting for Jim to bring her a drink.

"That suit is very becoming," Judith declared. "It's a shame you had to buy it for such an unhappy occasion."

"At least," Anemone said in an unusually waspish tone, "I won't have to go to Dixie and Émile's services. They're being buried back wherever they came from, like maybe in the South and someplace in France. I hate funerals. They're too sad."

"Yes," Judith agreed. "That's a good way to describe them."

"I don't want to be sad anymore," Anemone asserted. "I want to be happy. I want to get married and have a home and raise babies."

The fervor in Anemone's voice took Judith by surprise. "I thought you and Jim planned to wait until he finished his schooling."

"I don't want to wait," Anemone said flatly.

"How does Jim feel about that?"

Anemone pursed her lips in a manner reminiscent of her mother. "He'll do what I want," she said. "Now."

"I wouldn't rush into anything," Judith cautioned. "You're both very young. Remember, there are worse things than *not* being married." *I ought to know,* she thought, recalling the bleak years with Dan.

But Anemone didn't seem to hear Judith. The young woman's attention had been diverted by Jim's arrival with two glasses of white wine. Meanwhile, Rick had moved to the fireplace, martini in hand.

He raised his voice to quiet the murmurs among the gathering. "Friends, fellow mourners," he said in his usual debonair manner. He stopped, his gaze traveling to the entryway between the foyer and the living room. "And the press. Flakey, what are you doing here? This is a private reception."

"Not anymore," Flakey replied, a cigarette dangling from his lower lip. "This is news." He paused. "Isn't it?"

"Why, yes, dear boy," Rick responded. "You could call it that."

"Swell," Flakey said, removing the cigarette and tapping ash into a vase filled with yellow iris. "I'll stick around, then."

Connie, who was looking pale and tired, sat up straight on the sofa. "Really!" she gasped. "Weren't there enough reporters and such outside of the cathedral? I had to leave the back way."

"Never too much of a good thing," Flakey retorted.

Paul, who had been sitting next to Connie, was on his feet. "Do you want me to get rid of him?" he asked her.

Rick interrupted before Connie could reply. "No need for that," he asserted. "Flakey knows the score. He might as well stay. Have a drink, old boy. And try the Norwegian sardines. We had them flown in this morning."

Flakey meandered over to the bar. The others watched him for a moment until Biff waved his arms and called for silence. "Rick here has something to say. Everybody gather 'round." He indicated the seating arrangement that Rhoda had set up earlier in the day. Connie and Paul remained on the sofa with Dr. Selig hovering nearby; Erma headed for the carved emperor's chair as if she felt a place of honor was her due; Horace positioned himself behind her; Anemone and Jim sat in matching side chairs; Ambrose commandeered a footstool; Rhoda leaned against the bar; Captain Swafford remained standing as if at attention by the chinoiserie wall plaques; Biff and Buzz flanked each side of the fireplace; Flakey lingered at the buffet, where Chevy stood ready to help; Judith and Renie stood near the table, too, next to one of the tall windows that looked out over the fog-draped city.

After everyone had assembled with expressions of curiosity, Biff spoke again. "Rick is going to tell us who killed Mags, Dixie, and Émile. Go ahead, Rick. It's all yours."

"Nonsense!" Erma exclaimed.

"Piffle," said Horace.

"Is this a joke?" Ambrose inquired.

Rick shook his head. "It's no joke. Murder isn't a laughing matter. The problem with this case," he began, "is that it seemed so complicated. It was not just one murder, but three, each with a different method. There was a jewel robbery. There was blackmail."

Rick didn't seem to notice Connie's shudder, but Judith did. She also saw that Erma was looking indignant. Biff was staring at Connie as if he were about to pounce.

"Easy, Biff," Rick murmured before taking another sip of his martini. "I've just started. We know now that Erma's real jewels were never stolen, only the imitations."

"How dare you?" Erma shouted, struggling to rise from her regal chair.

Biff jabbed a thumb at the angry woman and looked inquiringly at Rick, who shook his head.

"Calm down, Erma," Rick said with a droll expression. "You remain a victim, in a way. I'm not suggesting that you stole your own jewels. You sold them, perhaps not illegally. The insurance claim is a fraud, of course. But you were coerced—and fleeced—by Horace."

Judith noticed that Horace had gotten very red in the face. She was certain that he was apoplectic. It was, she thought, a good thing that a doctor was in attendance. Once again, Biff looked questioningly at Rick; once again, Rick shook his head—and polished off his drink.

"Liar!" shouted Horace. "Why, you—"

"Please," Rick said calmly as Rhoda brought her husband another martini. "Let me finish. You were in a bind, Horace. The post–9/11 era hasn't treated you kindly. It's adversely affected Erma, too. You were both strapped for ready cash. That was especially unfortunate for you, Horace, because you had deadlines to meet for the construction of your sponge-and-cork museum. Contractors and subcontractors like to get paid. You had to come up with some money fast. They can be tough customers, and at least one of them made some nasty threats."

"I can handle them," Horace growled.

"I could handle some more liver pâté," Renie whispered, edging Flakey out of the way.

"I doubt you could handle a couple of those contractors' goons, old boy," Rick said. "But the jewel heist had nothing in and of itself to do with the murders. The blackmail, however, is another matter." He cast a glance at Connie, who was cowering next to Paul. "My dear, I know you were victimized by a pair of ruthless crooks. Dixie Beales and Émile Grenier intended to soak you for a big wad of dough. You're rich, but not rich in the way that really . . ." He feigned embarrassment and downed more gin. "Well, you all know what I mean. Mags was very successful, but the *San Rafael* cost a bundle to build. The cruise business has also suffered since 9/11, though it's been improving. But other problems persist, including a fight with the state and city over dumping in the bay, the need for a new pier in at least two ports of call, additional security, and general updating of the already existing fleet. Mags gave you a hefty allowance, but that was your only personal source of income. Money from your father dried up years ago."

"That's not true!" Connie wailed. "Paul," she cried, starting to sob, "tell them it's not true! Papa's rich! Like really rich people are——" She broke off, overcome by convulsive weeping.

Paul remained silent, his dark features a mask of pain. He could do nothing except take Connie in his arms and try to comfort her. Rhoda went to the bar, poured out some brandy, and glided across the room.

"Drink this, my dear," she urged. "It can't hurt and it may help. Though," she added in an aside to Paul, "I doubt it."

"So far," Judith said under her breath, "Rick's on the mark."

"And the sauce," said Renie, devouring liver pâté and crackers.

"It's sad," Rick remarked, motioning at Rhoda to bring him yet another martini, "but Guillermo de Fuentes lost his fortune years ago, only a short time after you married Mags. Your husband got no help from the de Fuentes family fortune. By then it had evaporated. Your father not only used dirty tricks to win races, but he bribed judges and stewards. These matters were well publicized at the time. One incident crippled Émile Grenier, who was de Fuentes's jockey."

Still holding Connie, Paul finally spoke up. "Mags gave Émile a good job. Señor de Fuentes saw to it that Émile could study accounting and other courses to prepare him for his career as a ship's steward."

Rick nodded. "Very kind. Yet it wasn't the accident that spurred—excuse the expression—Émile and Dixie to blackmail poor Connie. Somehow, her father wiggled out of that jam. But he wasn't content to use time-honored—if disreputable—methods to win races. In Dubai, he had the electronic starting gate rigged to shock his own horse—a notoriously slow starter named Nieves—into a quick sprint at the beginning of the race. There was a tragic miscalculation, however. All the horses were electrocuted, and several of the riders were badly injured. That sort of thing might not make the hometown gazette, but it certainly offended the local emirs and other horse-loving poohbahs. De Fuentes was forced to pay damages, and it ruined him financially and emotionally. His wife, Elena, committed suicide." Rick paused to glance at Connie, whose slim figure lay convulsed in Paul's arms. "I'm sorry, my dear," Rick said softly. "The scandal destroyed her, too. And your father isn't living the high life in Buenos Aires. He's confined to a nursing home in Lodi, California."

"Lodi!" Anemone squealed. "That's like . . . nowhere!"

"It's somewhere, all right," Ambrose said in a sour voice. "They have terrible groundwater problems, despite their best efforts to clean it up."

"Oh, damn your environmental concerns!" Horace shouted. "Your kind would have stopped progress in 1602!"

Ambrose shook his fist. "And your stupid museum would add pollution in the bay! You plan to build it on the water!"

"Boys!" Rick raised his voice, even though his stance was growing slightly unsteady. "Let's all get along, shall we?" He looked again at Connie, whose sobs had subsided while she received attention from Dr. Selig. "I'm sorry, Connie, to have brought up painful memories. Believe me, it's better in the long run to get this all out in the open. You weren't to blame for what your father did years ago. But you shouldn't have kept it a secret from Mags."

Connie looked over the doctor's shoulder. "But I didn't," she protested. "Mags knew about . . . the racing accidents."

"But he didn't know the details about how your father lost his money or that your mother killed herself," Rick said, allowing Rhoda to fill his glass to the top. "No one did until Flakey did some solid investigative reporting in the past few days."

"Ah." Judith's voice was barely audible.

"Flakey's smarter than he looks," Renie whispered.

"Now," Rick said, growing solemn though certainly not sober, "we come to the murders. The terrible part is that there was no real motive for the first murder—it was, in fact, an accident. The killer's intended victims were Dixie and Émile, not Magglio Cruz. The entire evening was staged—not just to suit the ship's theme and decor, but also for murder. The killer knew the plans for the event, including the pheasant ice sculpture that adorned the buffet table."

"Do we have to listen to this?" Jim Brooks asked in a cranky voice. "I should be helping Dr. Selig. I could take everybody's blood pressure. It seems to be running kind of high."

"Captain Swafford," Rick said, "you had been given detailed instructions about the event, correct?"

Biff gestured at Swafford, but Rick waved him off.

The captain, however, took umbrage. "Of course. The *San Rafael* is my ship."

"Yes." Rick smiled benignly. "You were given command despite your dumping violations in Alaskan waters. Mags was a loyal employer."

"I'm a bloody good mariner," the captain averred. "I've been sailing ships for almost forty years. How's an old sea dog like me supposed to keep up with all these damnable new rules and regulations?"

"It's your job, you twit!" Ambrose shouted.

The captain turned on Ambrose, who was standing only a few feet away. "Why, you little . . ."

"Enough." Rick's voice remained calm, but the authority in it made Swafford hesitate.

"The murders," Judith whispered to Renie. "Can't we get back to the murders?"

"Your favorite," Renie retorted, moving on to the smoked salmon.

"In any event," Rick continued, "the stage was set—literally and figuratively. Now I must amend the original statement about the weapon." His gaze moved quickly around the room, though Judith thought it lingered just a second longer on her.

"Initially, there was some confusion," Rick said, "because a stabbing death suggests a knife or similar sharp instrument." He paused to hiccup twice. " 'Scuse me." His smile was decidedly off center. "But I—that is, our gallant police—knew the weapon was no ordinary item. I—that is, they—felt it best to mislead everyone, 'specially the killer."

He paused to sip more of his martini. "Dixie had gone backstage to get ready for her piano performance. The killer waited for that moment, leisurely went behind the buffet, broke off a very sharp tail feather, and followed Dixie. But the first person to show up behind the saloon was Mags. Naturally, he wanted to know why this person was clutching a lethal-looking piece of ice. The killer made a joke. Mags apparently believed it was a harmless prank and turned his back. Panicking, the killer struck—and Mags fell into the piano. There was nothing the killer could do about Dixie now. She would have to be disposed of later. The methanol was originally intended for Émile, but the plan was altered, to be used for Dixie instead. And," Rick said, lowering his voice slightly, "we know that Ambrose purchased a quantity of methanol earlier in the week. The police have the receipt."

"Darn tootin'," Biff said, making a move toward Ambrose. "Should I . . . ?"

"No!" Ambrose had turned ashen. "I didn't . . . I mean, I did . . . but I bought it for——" He fell facedown on the carpet at Biff's feet.

"I can handle this one!" Jim cried, rushing to the fallen man's side.

"Never mind," grumbled Dr. Selig. "I'll do it."

"Brandy," Rhoda murmured, going back to the bar.

Ambrose was already coming around. "Relax, my young friend," Rick said, motioning for Biff to back off. "I know you didn't buy it for yourself. You got it for Connie so she could make her own perfume. She's always done that because of her allergy to commercial scents. Isn't that so, Dr. Selig?"

"Certainly," the doctor replied, forcing Ambrose to look him straight in the eye. "You'll be fine. Have some brandy."

"Maybe," Jim said in a sullen voice, "I should forget Stanford and just go to bartending school."

Anemone threw her arms around him. "Oh, do that, Jimmy! Then we can get married much sooner! You'll get lots of tips working in a bar."

"I didn't," Judith muttered. "Dan's regular bartender was skimming. His girlfriend even stole my wallet."

Rick had resumed speaking. "Yes, the methanol was purchased by Ambrose for Connie. She asked him to do the favor because he'd been lobbying her for a donation to one of his causes. She agreed to help save the black-footed ferrets or the Big Bear Valley sandwort or whatever is currently endangered. Naturally, he was happy to oblige her."

Judith leaned toward Renie. "I'll bet that was Connie's check for a grand she wrote to something called CITES. I should have twigged to that. I saw the entry in her regular checking account."

"Oh—right. It stands for something-or-other about endangered flora and fauna."

"So," Rick went on, "Ambrose acted innocently in buying the methanol. He couldn't have known its fatal consequences."

Paul leaped from his seat. "All right! I did it! I killed Mags! I poisoned Dixie! I strangled Émile! I confess everything!" Swiftly, he moved over to where a befuddled Biff was standing. "Arrest me. Take me away."

Puzzled, Judith poked Renie. "What's going on? This doesn't make sense."

"Sure doesn't," Renie replied. "Try the clam dip."

"Hold on, Biff," Rick called to the policeman. "Paul, please sit down. I know you didn't kill anyone. You're covering for the person you think may have done it. Please let me continue." As Paul reluctantly took a couple of steps backward, Rick grew rather unsteady. "I go by my hunches in solving a case," he asserted, holding on to the mantelpiece for support. "All along . . . I've had one about the killer . . ." He hiccuped again and dropped his empty glass, which bounced harmlessly into the kindling box on the hearth. "The killer is—" Rick gasped, hiccuped, and reeled into Rhoda's arms.

"I think he's passed out!" she exclaimed, staggering under her husband's weight.

Captain Swafford and Dr. Selig hurried to help her. They eased Rick onto the floor.

"S'all right," Rick mumbled as the guests began to stir uneasily. He cocked his head and half opened his eyes. "You f'nish, Mish Flynn."

Startled, Judith began to protest, but Renie gave her a shove. "You're on, coz. Go."

"I'm embarrassed," she announced while the others began to grow quiet and give her their anxious attention. "I'm not in the same league as Rick."

Asthma had crept out from under the buffet table and was

licking his master's face. "But you're not drunk as a skunk," Rhoda said pleasantly, kneeling at Rick's side. "Please enlighten us, dear Judith."

Judith grimaced. "I must give you my reasons for coming to certain conclusions. I realize that Connie never wanted to bring shame to Mags because of her father's misdeeds. I'm aware that she didn't display Señor de Fuentes's racing-career photos until after Mags had died." Judith turned a pained face toward Connie. "I suppose that after the blackmail threat ended with Dixie and Émile's deaths, it was a show of bravado on your part, to keep up the pretense that your father wasn't a ruined man and hadn't destroyed your family."

"My God!" Connie exclaimed. "How do you know that?"

"Because you—like Rhoda—had sent the domestic help away. Yet the table where you placed the racing photographs was not only dust-free but gleamed as if it had just been polished."

"Oh!" Connie raised a limp hand. "Those old photos were a comfort, especially after having just lost Mags. They reminded me of happier times. You were clever to figure that out."

"Just logical," Judith said modestly. "I also knew that Ambrose had been on board the *San Rafael* the night of Mags's murder. He had confided as much in . . . Beulah, the Giddons' maid." She shot Chevy a quick glance. Chevy didn't even blink. For once, Ambrose kept quiet.

"Ambrose had received a call from the ship to bring the methanol," Judith explained. "He hadn't yet delivered it to Connie because of all the precruise preparations. But he was told that she had to have it right away. It wasn't Connie who called him, which is what made him suspicious, especially after he found out that Mags had been murdered. That's why he told Beulah he'd been on the ship." Again, she looked at Chevy. "He also told you when he went to the *San Rafael,* didn't he?"

"Yes, he made a point of mentioning that—" Chevy began. "I mean—yaz'um. He sho' did. Ten o'clock."

Judith nodded. "Everyone remembers the decor," she continued, "but I also recall the temperature. It was smoky, but very cool in the saloon. Yet one person was sweating—or so I thought. Later I realized it wasn't perspiration. The person was *wet,* just as Mags's tuxedo jacket and the floor were wet. The ice that had been used to stab Mags had melted just enough to dampen the killer as well."

Judith paused, not daring to look at the person she suspected of being a triple murderer. "Mags's death wasn't premeditated, but his presence ruined the original plan to kill Dixie. After she'd been disposed of, the killer arranged a meeting with Émile while CeeCee Orr was buying a dress in the designer boutique. The women's dressing rooms may be off-limits, but men often sit by the entrance to wait for their wives and girlfriends. A male presence wouldn't rouse suspicion."

Judith stopped to catch her breath, but still avoided eye contact with her audience. "I believe that Connie wasn't the only blackmail victim. The blackmailers had something on another person, and they were greedy. They knew about their other prey's involvement in many illegal dealings, including embezzlement. They also realized that their new victim was obsessed with creating an image, with becoming an immortal San Francisco icon like Stanford and Crocker and the rest of the great ones. Dixie and Ambrose touched on this matter at lunch the day she died. Dominic, the waiter, overheard them talking about greed, liars, sycophants—and spongers." Judith took a deep breath. "I think Dominic mistook that last word—it was *sponges,* not q A museum often bears the name of its founder, thus lending an aura of great civic accomplishment. And," she added, running out of steam, "only one person here paid CeeCee's dress bills.

You'll find his signature on the Neiman Marcus receipt. That's why I'm certain that the killer is Horace Pankhurst."

A s Judith spoke his name, Horace made a dash for the elevator and pushed the button. The car, which must have been resting on the top floor, obligingly opened its doors. Biff and Buzz gave chase. Asthma left his post at Rick's side and loped toward the fleeing man. The dog put his bulk in front of Horace, tripping him. He fell a few inches away from the elevator. Asthma put his forepaws on the fallen man's back and barked twice.

"You can't pin this on me!" Horace yelled, writhing under the big dog. "I'm innocent, I tell you!"

Rhoda called Asthma off. "Good doggie," she said. "Have some salmon."

Biff and Buzz managed to haul their furious suspect to his feet and deposit him on the foyer floor.

"Cuff him," Biff ordered his subordinate.

"Great stuff!" Flakey Smythe declared, taking pictures. "I should get a Pulitzer for this one!"

"Wretch!" Erma screamed, now on her feet and waving a fist at Horace. "My poor jewels! You might as well have stolen them! No wonder I seem to be . . ." Her tight little mouth formed the word *poor,* but she couldn't say it aloud.

"Good," Anemone said, linking arms with Jim. "If Mumsy doesn't have any money, we can elope."

As soon as Horace had been handcuffed, Biff turned to Rick, who had gotten to his feet. "Hey—wait a minute, Rick," he said, motioning at Judith. "Is this dame right?"

Rick, who didn't seem quite so drunk anymore, nodded. "Of course." He turned around and looked at Judith, who was still standing in the middle of the room. "Nice work," he remarked, strolling to her side. "I wondered if you'd figured it out."

"What?" Judith stared at Rick.

"Mmm." Rick paused to accept a fresh martini from Rhoda. "Incidentally, Mrs. Flynn," he said with a disarming smile, "you don't look at all like someone who'd ever be known as FATSO. In fact, you could use some weight. Shall we eat, drink, and be merry?"

When Judith and Renie arrived at the airport Tuesday, Bill met them in the baggage area.

"Joe's in court," Bill explained. "He's been so tied up with his testimony that I've hardly talked to him. What happened to Magglio Cruz? There wasn't much in the local paper except that he died."

Renie did a double take. Judith was glad that Bill was watching the baggage conveyer belt rather than his wife.

"No details about him dying?" Judith inquired in a casual tone.

"I don't think so." Bill's attention was still riveted on the procession of suitcases, golf bags, ski equipment, and satchels passing by. "You know our media—they got mad when Cruz moved the headquarters out of town. When that happens around here, the person and the company cease to exist."

"Yes," Judith said softly. "That's true. Oh—there's one of my bags, with the yellow sticker on it."

"Good," Bill said. "Grab it."

"Huh?"

Bill gave her a helpless look. "I can't. I threw my back out after I got here."

Judith had no time to hesitate. The suitcase was going around the curve, starting back up the belt. She stumbled and would have fallen if a bearded young man hadn't caught her. He also snagged the suitcase.

"Thanks," Judith said, slightly rattled. She turned to Bill, who was watching Renie collect one of her luggage pieces. "What happened to you?"

"I was fine until I had to unload the steamer trunk."

"What steamer trunk?" Judith asked as Renie hauled her big green suitcase away from the conveyer belt.

"Your mother's," Bill replied.

Judith stared. "My mother's?"

"Oh." Bill's blue eyes were again fixed on the moving baggage. "I guess you wouldn't know. By coincidence, I had to bring your mothers out here today for a flight to Miami. They're going on a cruise."

"What?" Renie shouted, her ears still plugged from the plane's final descent.

Bill nodded. "Aunt Gertrude decided to take that money she got from the movie people and go on a cruise. She talked Deb into going along. It was spur-of-the-moment, I guess. Hey, there's another one of your bags," he said to his wife. "And the last one. Be quick. I've got to go to the chiropractor."

Renie picked up the bags and lugged them away. "That's it," she said in an overly loud voice.

"Okay," Bill said, turning toward the escalator that led to the parking garage. "Let's go, let's hit it, let's get boppin'!"

Judith would have preferred bopping Bill.

Judith was not in a good mood upon arriving home shortly after three o'clock. She found Joe lying on the living-room sofa, reading Sports Illustrated.

"Welcome back," he said, not getting up. "Feeling rested?"

"No." Judith dumped the luggage in the middle of the entry hall. "What are you doing home? Aren't you going to help me?"

"Oh. Sure." He got up, slowly walked across the room, and kissed Judith. "We had an early recess. I've been sitting for two days in that damned courtroom. I'm stiff as a board and my cold's still bad. Funny, I've been so busy that it hardly seems like you've been gone at all. What was it four, five days?"

Judith scowled at her husband. "It seems like a month."

Joe looked down at her luggage. "I'll take that up later," he said, going back into the living room and resuming his place on the sofa. "None of the guests are here yet. It's really peaceful, especially with your mother gone. Hey, sorry you missed the cruise, but a few days in San Francisco can't be all bad. Did you have a good time?"

"I . . ." Judith flopped down on the matching sofa. "No. It was like a screwball movie from the thirties, with three people murdered, a man named Blackie, a blond bombshell, a snobbish old bat, and a bumbling cop. We would have been shot if it hadn't been for Rick St. George, an amateur sleuth, and his rich wife, Rhoda—who, by the way, own a dog named Asthma."

Joe chuckled. "That's cute." He picked up the newspaper from the coffee table and flipped to the TV listings. "That reminds me, let's kick back tonight. There's an old *Thin Man* movie on."

Judith stared at Joe. She started to rant, but changed her mind.

"Sounds good," she said. "I like fantasy."